One More for
Christmas

SARAH MORGAN

HQN

Recycling programs
for this product may
not exist in your area.

ISBN-13: 978-1-335-21300-6

One More for Christmas

Copyright © 2020 by Sarah Morgan

One Night with the Laird

Copyright © 2013 by Nicola Cornick, excerpt used with permission from Nicola Cornick

This edition published by arrangement with Harlequin Books S.A.

For questions and comments about the quality of this book, please contact us at
CustomerService@Harlequin.com.

HQN
22 Adelaide St. West, 40th Floor
Toronto, Ontario M5H 4E3, Canada
www.Harlequin.com

Printed in U.S.A.

Praise for the novels of Sarah Morgan

Family for Beginners

"A perfect read for someone who feels lost when it comes to family [or] looking for a second chance at love."

—*Fresh Fiction*

"Sarah Morgan's writing always hits me right in the feels."

—*Harlequin Junkie*

A Wedding in December

"Morgan's gently humorous aesthetic will leave readers feeling optimistic and satisfied."

—*Publishers Weekly*

"Set around the Christmas holiday, it will make you cry, make you laugh, and it's an unforgettable read."

—*Romance Reviews Today*

One Summer in Paris

"A cheerful and heartwarming look at friendship, family, love, and new beginnings."

—*Kirkus Reviews*

"Packed full of love, loss, heartbreak, and hope, this may just be Morgan's best book yet."

—*Booklist*

The Christmas Sisters

"The perfect gift for readers who relish heartwarming tales of sisters and love."

—*Booklist*

"The Scottish Highland setting adds special moments in this tender family drama."

—*Library Journal*

How to Keep a Secret

"Fans of Karen White and Susan Wiggs will savor Morgan's pairing of a second-chance romance with an intense family drama."

—*Booklist*, starred review

"Her lovingly created characters come to life, the dialog rings true, and readers will fly through the pages and then wish for more."

—*Library Journal*, starred review

For Ele and Si, with love

One More for
Christmas

"I will honour Christmas in my heart, and try to keep it all the year."

—CHARLES DICKENS, *A CHRISTMAS CAROL*

Gayle

When Gayle Mitchell agreed to a live interview in her office, she hadn't expected her life to fall apart in such a spectacular fashion in front of an audience of millions. She was used to giving interviews and had no reason to think that this one might end in disaster, so she sat relaxed, even a little bored, as the crew set up the room.

As usual, the lights were blinding and kicked out enough heat to roast a haunch of beef. Despite the frigid air-conditioning, the fabric of Gayle's fitted black dress stuck to her thighs.

Beyond the soaring glass walls of her office lay what she truly believed to be the most exciting city on earth. Also one of the most expensive—but these days Gayle didn't have to worry too much about that.

Once, the place had almost killed her, but that had been a long time ago. That memory contributed to the degree of satisfaction she felt in being up here, on top of the world, gazing down from her domain on the fiftieth floor. Like planting a stiletto on the body of an adversary, it was symbolic of victory. *I won*. She was far removed from those people scurrying along the freezing, canyon-like streets of Manhattan, struggling to survive in a city that devoured the weak and the vulnerable. From her vantage point in her corner office she could see the Empire State Building, the Rockefeller Center and, in the distance, the broad splash of green that was Central Park.

Gayle shifted in her chair as someone touched up her hair and makeup. The director was talking to the cameraman, discussing angles and light, while seated in the chair across from her the most junior female reporter on the morning show studied her notes with feverish attention.

Rochelle Barnard. She was young. Early twenties? A few years older than Gayle had been when she'd hit the lowest point of her life.

Nothing excited Gayle more than raw potential, and she saw plenty of it in Rochelle. You had to know what you were looking for, of course—and Gayle knew. It was there in the eyes, in the body language, in the attitude. And this woman had something else that Gayle always looked for. *Hunger.*

Hunger was the biggest motivator of all, and no one knew that better than her.

She hadn't just been hungry—she'd been starving. Also desperate. But usually she managed to forget that part. She was a different woman now, and able to extend a hand to another woman who might need a boost.

"Ten minutes, Miss Mitchell."

Gayle watched as the lighting guy adjusted the reflector. In a way, didn't she do much the same thing? She shone a light on people who would otherwise have remained in the dark. She changed lives, and she was about to change this woman's life.

"Put the notes down," she said. "You don't need them."

Rochelle glanced up. "These are the questions they want me to ask. They only handed them to me five minutes ago."

Because they want you to stumble and fall, Gayle thought.

"Are they the questions *you* would have chosen to ask?"

The woman rustled through the papers and pulled a face. "Honestly? No. But this is what they want covered in the interview."

Gayle leaned forward. "Do you always do what other people tell you?"

Rochelle shook her head. "Not always."

"Good to know. Because if you did, then you wouldn't be the woman I thought you were when I saw you present that short segment from Central Park last week."

"You saw that?"

"Yes. Your questions were excellent, and you refused to let that weasel of a man wriggle out of answering."

"That interview was the reason you asked for me today? I've been wondering."

"You struck me as a young woman with untapped potential."

"I'm grateful for the opportunity." Rochelle sat straighter and smoothed her skirt. "I can't believe I'm here. Howard usually does all the high-profile interviews."

Why were people so accepting of adverse circumstances? So slow to realize their own power? But power came with risk, of course, and most people were averse to risk.

"Things are always the way they are until we change them," Gayle said. "Be bold. Decide what you want and go after it. If that means upsetting a few people along the way, then do it." She closed her eyes as someone stroked a strand of her hair into place and sprayed it. "This is your chance to ask me the questions Howard Banks wouldn't think to ask."

Which shouldn't be too hard, she thought, *because the man had the imagination and appeal of stale bread.*

Howard had interviewed her a decade earlier and he'd been patronizing and paternalistic. It gave Gayle pleasure to know that by insisting on being interviewed by this junior reporter she'd annoyed him. With any luck he'd burst a blood vessel in the most valuable part of his anatomy—which, for him, was probably his ego.

"If I don't give them what they're expecting, I could lose my job."

Gayle opened one eye. "Not if you give them something *better* than they're expecting. They're not going to fire you if the ratings go up. What's on their list? Let me guess… My work–life balance and how I handle being a woman in a man's world?"

Boring, boring.

The woman laughed. "You're obviously a pro at this."

"Think of the people watching. Ask the questions *they'd* ask if they were in the room with me. If you were a woman eager to make a change in your life, what would *you* want to hear? If you were struggling to get ahead in the workplace—" *which you are* "—constantly blocked by those around you, what would you want to know?"

Rochelle picked up the papers from her lap and folded them in a deliberate gesture. "I'd want to know your secrets—how you handle it all. How you handled it at the beginning, before you had everything you have now. You started with nothing. Put yourself through college while working three jobs. And you've become one of the most successful women in business. You've transformed companies and individuals. I'd want to know whether any of your experiences might be of use to me. Whether you could transform *me*. I'd want to come away feeling so inspired I'd call the show and thank them."

"And you think they'd fire you for that?"

The woman stared at her. "No, I don't." She slapped the papers down on the desk. "What is *wrong* with me? I've read all your books several times, and yet I was about to ask the questions I'd been handed. One of my favorite sections in your last book was that bit about other people's expectations being like reins, holding you back. You were our role model in college."

She pressed her palm to her chest. "Meeting you is the best Christmas gift."

"Christmas?"

"It's only a few weeks away. I love the holidays, don't you?"

Gayle did not love the holidays. She didn't like the way everything closed down. She didn't like the crowds on the streets or the tacky decorations. She didn't like the uncomfortable memories that stuck to her like bits of parcel tape.

"Aren't you a little old to be excited about Christmas?" she asked.

"Never!" Rochelle laughed. "I love a big family gathering. Massive tree. Gifts in front of the fire. You know the type of thing..."

Gayle turned her attention to the makeup artist, who was brandishing lipstick. "Not that horrible brown. Red."

"But—"

"Red. And not an insipid washed-out red. I want a *look at me* red. I have the perfect one in my purse."

There was much scrambling and an appropriate lipstick was produced.

Gayle sat still while the makeup artist finished her work. "This is your opportunity, Rochelle. Take it and ride it all the way home. If you make an impression on the public, your bosses won't be able to hold you back."

There.

Done.

Gayle had the power to give her a boost and she'd used it. She liked to give people the kind of chance she'd never been given. The rest was up to them.

"Five minutes, Ms. Mitchell." The director scanned her shelves. "When we've finished the interview we might take a few stills for promotional purposes."

"Whatever you need." If her story inspired people, then she

was happy. She wanted women to understand their own strength and power.

Rochelle leaned forward. "In case I don't have a chance to thank you properly after, I just want to say how grateful I am for your support. Do you have any idea how inspiring it is to know that you live the life you talk about in your books? You're the real deal. You're right at the top of your game, but still you take the time to reach out and give others a helping hand."

Her eyes glistened and Gayle felt a flash of alarm.

The helping hand didn't come with tissues. Emotion had no place in designing a life. It clouded decision-making and influenced those around you. Gayle's staff knew better than to bring emotion to a conversation.

Give me facts, give me solutions—don't give me sobbing.

Rochelle didn't know that. "At college we had a mantra—what would GM do?" She blushed. "I hope you don't mind that we called you that."

Some said that GM stood for Great Mind, others Guru of Management. A few of her own staff thought it stood for Genetically Modified, but no one had the courage to tell her that.

Rochelle's admiration continued to flow across the desk. "You're afraid of nothing and no one. You've been an inspiration to so many of us. The way you've shaped your career, your life. You never apologize for the choices you make."

Why should she apologize? Who would she apologize *to*?

"Use this opportunity, Rochelle. Did my assistant give you a copy of my next book?"

"Yes. Signed." Rochelle appeared to have reined in her inner fangirl. "And I think it's *so* cool that you have a male assistant."

"I employ the best person for the job. In this case it's Cole."

Out of the corner of her eye she checked the desks of her top executives. She and Bill Keen were the only members of the company to have their own offices. The others worked in the bright open space that stretched the width of the building. Occasionally Gayle would survey her domain from the protection of her glass-fronted oasis and think, *I built this myself, with nothing more than guts and a grim determination to survive.*

The shiny globe of Simon Belton's bald head was just visible above the top of his cubicle. He'd arrived before her that morning, which had boosted her mood. He was a hard worker, if a little lacking in truly innovative ideas. Next to him sat Marion Lake. Gayle had hired her the year before as head of marketing, but she was starting to think the appointment might have been a mistake. Just that morning Gayle had noticed her jacket slung casually over the back of her chair, its presence indicating that Marion was somewhere in the building.

Gayle's mouth thinned. When she gave people a chance, she expected them to take it.

Even now, after all these years, people constantly underestimated her. Did they really think she'd see a jacket draped over the back of a chair and assume the owner was somewhere in the office? There had been no coffee on the desk, and Gayle knew that Marion couldn't operate without coffee. And the place had the atmosphere of a cemetery. Marion had a loud voice and an irritating compulsion to use it frequently—a flaw possibly related to the volume of coffee she drank. If she had been anywhere in the vicinity, Gayle would have heard her.

She often thought she would have made an excellent detective.

"Going live in three minutes," one of the film crew told her, and Gayle settled herself more comfortably, composing her features.

She'd done hundreds of interviews, both live and recorded. They held no fear for her. There wouldn't be a single question she hadn't already been asked a hundred times. And if she didn't like a question, she simply answered a different one. Like everything else, it was a matter of choice. They weren't in control—*she* was.

In her head she hummed a few bars of the Puccini opera she'd

seen the week before. Glorious. Dramatic and tragic, of course...
But that was life, wasn't it?

Rochelle smoothed her hair and cleared her throat.

"Live in five, four, three..."

The man held up two fingers, then one, and Gayle looked at
the young reporter, hoping her questions would be good. She
didn't want to have misjudged her.

Rochelle spoke directly to the camera, her voice clear and
confident. "Hi, I'm Rochelle Barnard and I'm here at the offices of Mitchell and Associates in downtown Manhattan to
interview Gayle Mitchell—more commonly known as GM to
her staff and her legions of fans—one of the most powerful and
celebrated women in business. Her last book, *Choice Not Chance*,
spent twelve months at the top of the bestseller lists and her latest
book, *Brave New You*, is out next week. She's one of the leading
authorities on organizational change, and is also known for her
philanthropic work. Most of all she's celebrated as a supporter
of women, and just this week was presented with the coveted
Star Award for most inspirational woman in business at a glitzy
event right here in Manhattan. Congratulations, Ms. Mitchell.
How does it feel to have your contribution recognized?"

Gayle angled her head, offering her best side to the camera.
"I'm honored, of course, but the real honor comes from helping
other women realize their potential. We're so often told that we
can't compete, Rochelle, and as a leader my role is to encourage
other women to challenge that view."

She smiled, careful to portray herself as approachable and ac-
cessible.

"You're known to be a fierce advocate for women in the
workplace. What drives that?"

Gayle answered, the words flowing easily and naturally.

Rochelle threw a few more questions her way, and she handled those with the same ease.

"People either love you or hate you. There seems to be no

middle ground. Does it worry you that some people consider you to be ruthless?"

"I'm tough, and I make no apologies for that," Gayle said. "There are people who will always be threatened by the success of another, and people who shy away from change. I embrace change. Change is progress, and we need progress. Change is what keeps us moving forward."

"In your company you run an internship program with one of the most generous packages of any industry. You also offer scholarships. Why have you chosen to invest in this area?"

Because once, a long time ago, when she'd been alone and desperate, she'd vowed that if she was ever in a position to help someone like herself, then she'd do it.

But she didn't share that. Such an admission might easily be seen as weakness. And how could they possibly understand? This girl sitting opposite her had never experienced the hard grip of fear. Gayle knew how deeply those claws could bite. She understood that fear could make you a prisoner, holding you inactive. Breaking free of that wasn't easy. She was willing to hand a key to a few worthy individuals.

"I see it as an investment…" She talked a little more about the role she'd played fighting for the underprivileged and saw Rochelle's eyes mist with admiration.

"Some people think you've been lucky. How would you answer that?"

Not politely.

Luck had played no part in Gayle's life. She'd made careful choices, driven by thought and not emotion. Nothing had happened by chance. She'd *designed* her life, and now it was looking exactly the way she wanted it to look.

"It's easier to dismiss someone as 'lucky' than it is to admit that the power for change lies within the individual. By calling someone 'lucky' you diminish their achievement, and the need to do that often comes from a place of insecurity. Believing in luck absolves you of personal responsibility. Whatever you do in life, whatever your goals, it's important to make active choices."

She looked into the camera.

"If you're feeling dissatisfied with your life, find a piece of paper right now and write down all the things you wish were different. You don't like your life? Do something about it! You envy someone? What do they have that you don't? How do you want your life to look? Deciding that is the first step to redesigning it."

Rochelle was nodding. "Your last book, *Choice Not Chance*, changed my life—and I know I'm not alone in that."

"If you have a personal story we'd all love to hear it…"

Gayle drew in the audience, as she would if she were speaking to them live. She knew that right now, in living rooms and kitchens across the nation, women would be glued to the screen, hoping for a magic bullet that would fix their lives. Phones would go unanswered, babies would go unfed and unchanged, doorbells would be ignored. Hope would bloom, and a brief vision of a different future would blast away fatigue and disillusionment.

Gayle knew that once the interview ended, most would just sink back into their own lives, but right now they were with her. They wanted to be inspired.

"Hearing people's personal experiences can be motivational and uplifting for everyone. My approach to life is relevant whether you run a household or a corporation."

"I ended a relationship." Rochelle gave a nervous laugh, as if surprised that she'd actually admitted that on prime-time TV. "After I read the chapter 'Obstacles to Ambition,' I wrote down everything that might stop me achieving my goals, and the guy I was seeing was top of the list. And that chapter on auditing friendships…? Decluttering your contacts…? Brilliant! Asking yourself, *How does this relationship bring me closer to my goals?* And I wanted to ask *you*, GM, is this something you've done yourself?"

"Of course. My books are basically a blueprint of the way I've lived my life—but it can apply to anyone's life. The main take-away from *Choice Not Chance* is to challenge yourself. *Brave New You* focuses on confronting our innate fear of change."

There. She'd slotted in a mention of the book, and because it was live it wouldn't be cut. Her publisher would be pleased.

"I want all women—from the barista who serves me my coffee every morning to the woman who manages my investments—to feel in control of their destiny." She gave the camera an intense look. "You have more power than you know."

Rochelle leaned forward. "You're famous for saying that no one can have it all. Have you made sacrifices for your career?"

"I've made choices, not sacrifices. *Choices.* Know what you want. Go for it. No apologies."

"And you've never had any regrets?"

Regrets?

Gayle's world wobbled a little. How well had this woman done her research?

She sat up a little straighter and looked at the camera. "No regrets."

And just like that, the interview was over.

Rochelle unclipped her microphone. "Thank you."

"You're welcome." Gayle stood up. "How did you get your start in TV?"

"I applied for a ton of things after college but had no luck with anything." Rochelle was relaxed and chatty now the inter-view was over. "Then I was offered an internship at the studio. I shadowed a reporter, and they let me present a little because they thought I looked good on camera. So I suppose you could say I fell into it."

Gayle winced. You fell into snowdrifts—not jobs.

"Today is a crossroads for you. Doors will open. I hope you walk through them."

"Thanks, GM. I'm never going to forget what you've done

for me." Rochelle glanced at the crew and then back at Gayle. "We need photos so we can promote the interview on our site and social media."

"Of course." Gayle walked to her bookshelves and posed in what she knew was the most flattering position, careful that both her books were in the shot, face out.

Did they know that today was her birthday? No, why would they? Her digital team had scrubbed all mention of her birth date from the internet, so her age was shrouded in mystery. Birthdays slid past like the seasons—unmarked and frankly unwanted. She preferred to keep the focus on her achievements.

The photographer glanced around him. "Could we have a photograph with the award?"

The award?

Gayle glanced upward. The award had been placed on the top shelf of the bookcase that lined the only solid wall of her office. Had it been attractive she might have displayed it somewhere more prominent, but it was an ugly monstrosity, the brainchild of someone apparently devoid of both inspiration and artistic skill. The golden star itself was inoffensive, but it had been attached to a particularly ugly base. The first thing she'd thought on being presented with it the night before was that it reminded her of a gravestone.

Her opinion of it hadn't mellowed overnight.

She looked at the award again, loathing it as much as she had when she'd received it—although of course at the time she'd smiled and looked delighted. What message would it send for her to be photographed with something so lacking in aesthetic charm? That she was ready for the grave and had the headstone to prove it?

She glanced outside to where Cole, her assistant, was supposed to be sitting during the interviews in case he was needed. Where *was* he? He should have anticipated this and had the statue ready.

She could either wait for his return—which would mean the

TV crew lingering in her office—or she could get the damn thing herself.

Irritated, she slid off her shoes and pulled her office chair over to the bookcase.

The photographer cleared his throat. "I should get that for you, Ms. Mitchell. I'm taller than you, and—"

"Chairs were invented so that women could stand on them when necessary."

Still, she was about to curse Cole for putting it on the highest shelf when she remembered she was, in fact, the one who had instructed him to do that.

Stepping onto the chair, she reached out.

Why had he put it so far back? Presumably Cole found it as loathsome as she did.

She rose on tiptoe and felt the chair wobble slightly.

She closed her right hand around the base of the award, remembering too late that it had required two hands to hold it steady when she'd been handed it the night before. As she swung it down from the shelf, the chair wobbled again, sending her body off-balance.

By the time she realized she was going to fall, it was too late to recover.

She groped for the bookcase with her free hand, but instead of providing solid support it tilted toward her. She had time to make a mental note to fire the clueless individual who had forgotten to secure the bookshelves to the wall, and then she was falling, falling, falling… One of the points of the heavy golden star smashed into her head and she crashed onto the hard office floor.

She was conscious for long enough to wish the decorator had given her deep-pile carpet. And then everything went black.

She missed the sound of Rochelle screaming and the sight of the camera rolling.

For a brief period of time she was blissfully oblivious to the chaos erupting around her.

Her return to consciousness was slow and confusing. She heard a low humming sound, a whirring in her head. Was she dead? Surely not. She could hear things.

She could hear people panicking around her, even though panic was an emotion specifically banned from her office.

"Oh my *God*, is she dead? *Is she dead?*"

"Not dead. She's definitely breathing."

Gayle was relieved to have that confirmed by an outside source.

"But she's unconscious. I called 911. They're on their way."

"Is that an actual *hole* in her head? I feel a little faint."

"Pull yourself together." A rough, male voice. "Did you get the shot, Greg?"

"Yeah, the whole thing is on camera. It'll be a happy day for the headline writers. My money is on STARSTRUCK!"

"Could you be just a little sensitive here?" Rochelle's voice, sounding traumatized. "She's badly injured and you're writing headlines!"

Didn't they *know* she could hear them? Why were people so clueless? She had no idea how long she'd been knocked out. A minute? An hour? A day? No, if it had been a day she'd be lying in a hospital bed now, surrounded by a chorus of beeping machines.

Her chest hurt. Why did her chest hurt?

She remembered the bookshelves falling with her.

Someone must have caught them, or lifted them off her. As for the fate of the award—she had no idea. If the pain was anything to go by, there was a possibility it was still embedded in her head.

There was a crashing sound and the doors to her office burst open.

Gayle tried to open her eyes and give someone her scariest stare, but her eyelids felt too heavy.

She heard more voices, this time firm and confident—presumably the EMTs.

"What's her name?"

Why was he asking her name? Didn't he recognize her? *Everyone* knew who she was. She was a legend. She'd just won an award for being inspirational, and if they couldn't see the actual award then surely they could see the award-sized dent in her skull.

She was going to write to the organizers and suggest a brooch for the next winner.

"Gayle, can you hear me? I'm Dan."

Why was he calling her Gayle when they'd never met? She was either Ms. Mitchell or GM. Young people today had no respect. This was why she insisted on formality in the office.

This "Dan" barked out some instructions to his partner and proceeded to assess her injuries.

Gayle felt herself being poked and prodded.

"Has someone contacted her family? Loved ones?"

"Her...what?" That was Cole, sounding stressed and confused.

"Loved ones. Nearest and dearest." The EMT was pressing something to her head.

"I don't think—" Cole cleared his throat. "She doesn't have loved ones."

"She must have *someone*." Dan eased Gayle's eyes open and used a flashlight.

"That's probably the first time anyone has looked into her eyes in a long time."

Funny, Gayle thought. Until that moment she hadn't even realized Cole had a sense of humor. It was a shame it was at her expense.

"Partner?" Dan again, doing something that apparently was meant to support her neck.

"No. Just work. She loves her work."

"Are you telling me she has no one in her life?"

"Well, there's Puccini…"

"Great. So give this Puccini guy a call and tell him what's happened. He can meet us at the hospital."

Gayle wanted to roll her eyes, but her head hurt too badly. She hoped this EMT knew more about head injuries than he did about culture.

"Puccini was a composer. Opera. GM loves opera. People? Not so much. She isn't a family type of person. GM is married to her work."

Dan clipped something to Gayle's finger. "Oh man, that's sad."

Sad? *Sad?*

She ran one of the most successful boutique consulting firms in Manhattan. She was in demand as a speaker. She'd written a bestseller—soon to be two bestsellers if preorders were anything to go by. What was sad about that? Her life was the subject of envy, not pity.

"Makes her a bitch to work for, actually," Cole muttered. "I couldn't go to my grandmother's funeral because she had a ten o'clock and I needed to be here."

Cole thought she was a *bitch*?

No—*no*! She wasn't a bitch. She was an *inspiration*! That journalist had said so. Yes, she worked hard, but there was a perfectly good reason for that. And if she hadn't worked hard and turned the company into the success it was now, her team wouldn't have their nice comfortable secure jobs. Why couldn't they see that? Maybe she should use that award to knock some sense into her staff on a daily basis.

It was time she showed them she was awake—before she discovered more about herself she didn't want to know.

"I don't get it," the EMT said, slapping the back of Gayle's hand to find a vein. "I guess if you don't have family, then you work. It's that simple."

He slid a needle into Gayle's vein, and if she'd been capable of speech or movement, she would have punched him—both for the pain and his words.

It wasn't that simple *at all*. They were implying she worked because she was lonely, but that wasn't the case. Her work wasn't her backup plan—it was her *choice*.

She'd chosen every single thing about her life. She'd *designed* her life. Written a book about it, dammit. Her life was perfect for her. Custom-made. A haute couture life. Everything she'd ever wanted.

"I guess her life must be pretty empty."

Empty? Had they looked around at *all*? Seen the view from her corner office? True, she didn't often look at it herself, because she was too busy to turn around, but she'd been told it was magnificent. Hadn't they seen the photographs of her with industry leaders?

She led a *full life*.

"Yeah, poor thing…"

She wasn't a poor thing. She was a powerhouse.

All they saw was the businesswoman. They knew nothing else about her. They didn't know how hard she'd had to work to arrive at this place in her life. They didn't know *why* she was this way. They didn't know she had a past. A history. They didn't know all the things that had happened to her.

They didn't know her at all. They thought she had an empty life. They thought she was a lonely, sad figure. They were wrong.

They were—

Were they wrong?

She felt a sudden wash of cold air and saw a blinding light.

That question Rochelle had asked her, echoed in her head: *And you've never had any regrets?*

The faint wobble inside her became something bigger. It spread from the inside outward until her whole body was shaking.

She didn't have regrets. She did *not* have regrets.

Regret was a wasted emotion—first cousin to guilt. Gayle had no room for either in her life.

But the shaking wouldn't stop.

"We'll get her to the ER."

As well as the shaking, now there was a terrifying pressure in her chest. Had they forgotten to lift the bookcase from her mangled body? No. No, it wasn't that. The pressure was coming from the inside, not the outside. Heart? No. It wasn't physical. It was emotional.

"Her pulse rate is increasing."

Of *course* it was increasing! Emotion did that to you. It messed you up. It was the reason she tried never to let it into her life. She had no idea who had allowed it in now—because it certainly hadn't been her. It must have crept in through the hole in her head.

"She might be bleeding from somewhere. Let's move. If there's no one at home to care for her, they'll probably admit her."

She was going to be admitted to the hospital because all she had in her life was work and Puccini. Neither of those was going to bring her a glass of water or check she was alive in the night.

She lay there, trapped inside her bruised, broken body, forcing herself to do what she urged others to do. Acknowledge the truth of her life.

She ran a successful company. She had an apartment full of art and antiques on the Upper East Side and enough money that she never had to worry about it. But she had no one who would rush to her side when she was in trouble.

Cole was here because he was paid to be here, so that didn't count.

She wasn't loved. There was no one who cared about her. Not one person who would hear about the accident and think, *Oh no! Poor Gayle!* No one would be calling a florist and ordering flowers. No one would be delivering a casserole to her door or asking if there was anything she needed.

She was alone in this life she'd designed for herself.

Completely, totally and utterly alone.

She realized why most people were reluctant to examine the truth of their lives. It was an uncomfortable experience.

What had she done?

She'd chosen her life, designed her life, and now she didn't like the way it was looking.

In that moment Gayle had an epiphany—and not a good one.

What if she'd chosen the wrong design? What if all the choices she'd made had been wrong? What if all these techniques she'd recommended to people through her books were wrong, too?

She needed to stop publication.

She needed to tell her publisher she wanted to rethink the book. How could she promote *Brave New You* when she was lying on the floor shivering like a wounded animal?

She opened her mouth and tried to croak out some words.

"She's moving. She's conscious! Gayle— Gayle, can you hear me?"

Yes, she could hear him. She was unloved—not deaf.

She forced her eyes open and saw a uniformed EMT and behind him Cole, looking worried. There was the cameraman, and also Rochelle, scribbling frantically. Making the most of an opportunity, Gayle thought. Taking the advice she'd been given and redesigning her life.

And that was when she had her second epiphany. Who said you could only design your life once? People remodeled houses all the time, didn't they? Just because you'd lived with white walls for decades didn't mean you couldn't suddenly paint them green.

If she didn't like the way her life looked, then it was up to her to fix it.

And, although she didn't regret her actions, exactly, she did regret the outcome of those actions.

Maybe she could have done more.

Maybe it wasn't too late to rebuild what had been knocked down. But she had to be the one to make the first move.

"My daughter." Her lips formed the words. "Call...my daughter."

She saw Cole's face pale. "She's conscious, but she has a serious head injury. She's confused. She has amnesia."

The EMT frowned. "Why would you say that?"

"Because GM doesn't *have* a daughter."

Gayle thought about the baby they'd put into her arms. The way it had felt to be entirely responsible for the well-being of a tiny, helpless infant, knowing what lay ahead. How hard life could be. If it hadn't been for the child, she might have given up, but motherhood had driven her on. How could she give up when she had her daughter to protect? She'd wanted to swaddle her in steel and surround her with an electric fence to keep the bad at bay.

"Gayle, do you know what day it is?"

Yes, she knew what day it was. It was the day she'd started questioning everything she'd believed was right. The day she'd realized that regret could hurt more than a bruised head and crushed ribs. How could she have got everything so wrong?

She tried again. "Call my eldest daughter."

What if she died before she had a chance to fix things?

"Eldest...?" Cole looked nervous. "She doesn't have one daughter, let alone more. Ms. Mitchell—Gayle—how many fingers am I holding up? Can you tell me?"

Right at that moment she wanted to hold up her own finger. Her middle one.

"Call my daughter."

"She isn't confused. Gayle Mitchell has two daughters," Rochelle said. "I did a deep dive into her background before the interview. My research suggests they're estranged."

Estranged? No, that wasn't right. True, they hadn't seen each other for a while. Maybe a few years. All right, perhaps it was nearly five years… Gayle couldn't remember. But she did remember their last encounter. When she thought about it—which she tried not to—she felt affronted and hurt.

None of it had been her fault. She'd been doing her best for them—which was all she'd ever done. She'd worked hard at being the best mother possible. She'd made sure she'd equipped her children to deal with the real world and experienced a mother's frustration when her girls had made bad choices. She'd discovered the anguish of having all of the anxiety but none of the control. She'd done her best. It wasn't her fault that they preferred the fairy tale to the reality. It wasn't her fault that they were unable to appreciate how well she'd prepared them for adulthood.

Yes, relations between them were tense, but they weren't *estranged*. That was a truly horrible word. A word with razor-sharp edges.

Cole appeared to be suffering from shock.

"She has *kids*? But that means that she—I mean she must have had—"

The fact that he was struggling to picture her having sex wasn't flattering. He clearly thought his boss was a robot.

"All right. If you're sure, then we should call the daughters." His voice was strangled. "Is there a phone number, Ms. Mitchell?"

Would Samantha have changed her number?

She hadn't called, so Gayle had no way of knowing. She'd been waiting for both of them to call her and apologize. Days had melted into weeks and then months. Shame flooded through her. What did it say about a mother when her own children didn't want to make contact?

If she admitted the truth, would her judgmental staff and the medical team decide she wasn't worth saving?

Instead of answering, she moaned.

That caused more consternation among the people gathered around her.

"She's struggling to speak—can we find out her daughter's number?"

"I'm searching…" Rochelle tapped away on her phone. "One of her daughters is called Samantha."

Gayle gasped as the EMT and his assistant transferred her to a gurney.

Cole was searching, too. "There's a Samantha Mitchell in New Jersey. Comedian. No *way*."

Was he implying that she didn't have a sense of humor? That laughter didn't figure in her DNA?

"There's a Samantha Mitchell in Chicago…a Samantha Mitchell, dog walker, in Ohio. Samantha Mitchell, CEO of a bespoke travel company in Boston…" He looked up as Gayle made a sound. "That's her? She runs a travel company?"

Boston? Samantha had moved cities? It wasn't enough not to speak to her mother—she clearly didn't want to risk running into her on the street.

Gayle tried to ignore the pain. She was willing to be the bigger person. Kids disappointed you. It was a fact of life. She would forgive and move on. She wanted to do that. She wanted them in her life. Their relationship never should have reached this point.

And CEO!

Through the ashes of her misery, Gayle discovered a glowing ember of pride. *You go, girl.*

Whether Samantha admitted it or not, there was plenty of her mother in her.

As they wheeled her through the office to the elevator, she caught a glimpse of the shocked faces of her staff, who had never once seen GM vulnerable in all the time they'd worked at Mitchell and Associates.

But she felt vulnerable now. Not because of the head injury, and not even because of the photos that the wretched photographer had taken of her unfortunate accident, nor the prospect of headlines as painful as the injury itself.

No, she felt vulnerable because someone was about to contact Samantha.

And there was every possibility that her daughter wouldn't even take the call.

Samantha

"I suggest a European tour, focusing on the Christmas markets. Not only will you be steeped in holiday spirit, which is what you want, but you can buy all your gifts at the same time. It will be perfect."

Shoes off, hair caught in a messy bun, Samantha scrolled through the itinerary her team had prepared.

"Start in Prague. You will never forget Wenceslas Square. At Christmas it's filled with pretty wooden huts selling handcrafted goods and delicious treats—you *have* to try the warm gingerbread—and they always have an incredible tree. You'll sip mulled wine while you watch the ice-skaters, and there will probably be choirs singing in the background. It's gloriously festive!"

Skillfully she painted a picture. She talked about the smell of baked apples in the famous markets of Cologne, the scent of Christmas spices in Vienna and the beautiful medieval streets of Tallinn, Estonia.

"That horse-and-cart ride you dreamed about? We can definitely make that happen. You'll never want to come home.

I'm emailing a plan across to you now. Take a look and let me know what you think. You might prefer to reduce the number of markets and spend a little longer in each place. We can tailor it in any way that works for you."

She glanced up as her assistant opened her office door, her baby on her hip.

Samantha gave a brief shake of her head. Her staff knew better than to interrupt when she was on a call—especially when that call was to a client as important as Annabelle Wexford. Whoever it was could wait.

She waggled her fingers at the baby and carried on talking.

"It will be fabulous, Annabelle. In Prague, we've reserved you a suite with a view of the Charles Bridge. After you've enjoyed the markets, you'll be able to relax and drink in the same view…"

She gave her the full benefit of her research and experience—which was extensive. No one knew more about making the best of the holiday season than she did. She'd been designing bespoke winter vacations for people since she'd graduated. First for a big travel company who offered tailor-made holidays to anywhere and everywhere, and then for herself.

When she'd announced that she was setting up on her own, focusing exclusively on festive vacations, her competitors had predicted she'd last six months. She'd proved them wrong. There were people willing to pay a great deal of money to enjoy a magical holiday experience if it delivered what they wanted. And Samantha delivered every time.

Her company, RFH—Really Festive Holidays—was booming.

There was a card on her desk from a delighted client addressed to her as *The Queen of Christmas*. Another calling her *Mrs. Santa*.

Was there anything better than making someone's dreams of a magical festive season come true?

"We've sent over a couple of hotel options in Vienna—take a look and let us know your preference."

It was five minutes before she was able to end the call and follow up with her assistant.

She hit a button on the phone on her desk. "Charlotte? I'm done."

Charlotte appeared in the doorway, a tablet in her hand. A large damp patch spread across her midnight blue shirt, which clung to her breast.

"Sorry, I forgot you were on the phone to Annabelle—and sorry about this." She tugged at her shirt. "Amy started yelling, and my boobs took it as a hint to go into milk mode. Nature is an amazing but inconvenient thing. Fortunately there are no clients in the office at the moment. My mom is back tomorrow, so she won't be in the office again."

"Where is she?"

"My mom? Visiting my Gran in—"

"The baby." Samantha was patient. "Amy."

"Oh. She fell asleep after I fed her, so I popped her under my desk in her seat and I'm going to make the most of it and get everything done. Truly sorry about this."

"It's perfectly fine. This is an important time for both of you. Parent-child bonding is crucial—particularly in these early months. Family is everything. You need to spend as much time together as possible. Use my office to feed any time you need to."

"You're the best boss on the planet, and I might cry." Charlotte sniffed. "Yes, I'm going to cry. It's your fault for being kind. I'm so emotional right now. Even the news makes me sob."

"The news makes *me* sob, too, and I'm not hormonal." Samantha pushed tissues across her desk. "Here. You're doing great, Charlotte."

"I'm not as sharp as I used to be. My brain feels soggy. I cut Mr. Davidson off instead of putting him through."

"And you immediately called him back, and he was completely understanding—so don't worry. He's not likely to forget that you were the one who arranged to fly him home when he had a heart attack in India *and* that you visited him in the hospital."

"He's a dear man." Charlotte took a handful of tissues, stuffed a few into her bra and blew her nose with the others. "I'm worried I'll lose you a client."

"That's not going to happen." Samantha stood up and walked round her desk. "Are you doing okay? Are you just tired, or is it something more? Because if you need time off—"

"No. Honestly, I'm fine. It's an adjustment, that's all. I love my job, and I want to be here, but I want to be with Amy, too. I feel like a terrible employee *and* a terrible mother."

"You're wonderful at both—just very hard on yourself. You'll get back into it. Don't worry."

"That's what my mom says…but I'm worried you'll want me to leave."

"Charlotte!" Samantha was horrified. "You were the first person I employed. We've been in this together from the beginning."

Charlotte gave a watery smile. "Christmas every day, right?"

"Exactly! You are brilliant at your job. I am *never* letting you leave! For a start, you know every single thing about every single client, which is a big part of the reason we're doing so well. And there is no crisis you can't handle. You masterminded the search for Mrs. Davidson's precious cat while she was in the Arctic, for goodness' sake."

Charlotte's smile turned to a laugh. "That cat was vicious. I'm sure the neighbors let it out on purpose."

"Maybe, but she loved that animal and you fixed it. It's what you do. You're just having a difficult time, that's all. But you'll get through it. *We'll* get through it. You have a job as long as you want one, and I hope that's a very long time."

"Thank you." Charlotte blew her nose hard and picked up

one of the photos on Samantha's desk. "New photo? I haven't seen this one."

"Ella sent it last week. Apparently Tab is going through a princess phase."

"And, knowing you, you've already sent her four sparkling princess costumes."

"Two…" Had she gone over-the-top? "I just happened to see a couple on my way home. I wasn't sure which one she'd prefer."

"The doting aunt." Charlotte put the photo back. "Your niece is gorgeous. I can't imagine Amy being four and a half. Tab must be so excited about the holidays."

"She is. I'm going there this weekend, and we're going to make decorations for the tree."

"I can't wait until Amy is old enough to do that. This will be her first Christmas, and we've already bought way too much, considering she isn't going to remember any of it."

"Did you have messages for me?" Sam prompted gently, and Charlotte produced her tablet from under her arm.

"Yes." She tapped the tablet. "Eight messages. The Wilsons called to give the go-ahead for Lapland. They want the whole package—reindeer, elves, Santa—but they're not sure about the husky sled ride."

"They'd love it," Samantha murmured. "Providing they dress for the weather they'll have a blast. I'll give them a call and talk it through. Next?"

She sat down at her desk, dealing with each message in turn, scribbling a few notes to herself. Some she asked Charlotte to deal with; some she chose to deal with personally.

"The Mortons are an adventurous family—they'd love Iceland. We'll book them on a tour to see the Northern Lights, and they can do that snowmobile safari on a glacier that was such a hit with that family from Ohio."

"The Dawsons."

"Right. Also the ice caves. Anything else?"

ONE MORE FOR CHRISTMAS

"Brodie McIntyre called."

Samantha didn't recognize the name. "New client?"

"He owns that estate in the Scottish Highlands."

"Kinleven?"

Charlotte checked her notes. "That's the one. Amazing lodge, complete with fairy-tale turrets. You read about it in that magazine and then asked me to contact him after we had that inquiry from the family in Seattle. We talked about it last month and I called him."

"Of course. House parties in a remote Scottish glen... Don't they have an actual reindeer herd?" Samantha leaned back in her chair. "I know it's not something we've offered before, but I feel in my gut it would work. Everyone is wild about Scotland—particularly for the holidays—and the place is by a loch, on the edge of a forest. Guests could cut their own Christmas tree. A fresh one that actually smells of the forest, and not of chemicals. The possibilities are endless. Whiskey in front of a roaring log fire... Maybe we could add a couple of nights in Edinburgh for Hogmanay." She saw Charlotte's expression. "New Year's Eve."

"Ooh." Charlotte smiled. "I want to book that vacation myself. It sounds dreamy."

"And that's what we do. We give people their dream winter vacation. The Christmas they'll never forget." Samantha tapped her pen on the desk. "What did he say? Did you tell him that the demand for properties in the Scottish Highlands is going through the roof?"

"Yes. Also that you speak to all your clients personally, and that you're wicked good at what you do, so he can expect to be busy."

"And...?"

"He said that he's interested in principle, but he'd want to discuss it further. Because the lodge is a family home, and before he accepts guests, he'll need to know he's entrusted the task of renting it out to the right person."

"Get him on the phone and I'll convince him I'm the right person."

"He wants to meet you."

"Why?" Samantha tried not to think of her packed schedule. "Never mind. Whatever it takes. When is he in Boston?"

"He's not. He wants you to fly to Scotland."

Samantha shot up in her chair. "Scotland? You mean Scotland, Connecticut?"

"No." Charlotte frowned. "*Is* there a Scotland in Connecticut?"

"Yes. It's a town. There are others."

"I mean the *actual* Scotland. The country. Land of hill and heather. And those cute cows with horns."

"Highland cattle. Are you serious? He wants me to fly to *Scotland*?"

Charlotte held up her hands in surrender. "I'm just the messenger. But is it so hard to understand? He's emotionally attached to the place. It's his home. He was born there. Imagine being born in a Scottish glen instead of a sterile white hospital room…"

"He told you all this?"

"Yes. We chatted for a while. He says it won't suit everyone and that you'll need to know what you're selling."

"He's right, of course. And I usually do visit before we start recommending. But I'm snowed under."

Samantha loosened another button on her shirt and paced to the window. The view always calmed her. From her office in Back Bay she could see Boston Harbor, the water glittering pale under the winter sun. It was barely December, but the first flurries of snow had fallen the week before—a reminder that winter had arrived.

Samantha was one of those few people who loved snow. No amount of cold weather could damage her love affair with this city. There were no memories here. No ghosts haunted the brick sidewalks and historic architecture. Moving from Manhattan was the best thing she'd ever done. Boston was *her* city. She loved everything about it—from the art galleries and up-market boutiques of Newbury Street to Beacon Street with its vintage gas lamps. Even at this time of year, with a bitter wind blowing off the Charles River, she loved it.

"Boss?"

"Yes." She turned to Charlotte. "Scotland. Fine. We'll take the risk and have someone visit because I think the place sounds perfect. Send Rick. He's been known to wear a kilt to fancy dress parties."

"The laird insisted it was you."

"The *laird*?"

"Just my little joke. I've been reading too many of those historical romances we love. I dream of being swept onto a horse by a man wearing a kilt."

"With Amy attached to your breast? That does *not* sound comfortable." There were days when she wished Charlotte, who wasn't known for her discretion, hadn't discovered her reading habit. "Please don't tell Brodie McIntyre that we read historical romance."

"Why? Read what you want, I always say."

"I agree, but I prefer to keep my personal life separate from my professional life." Also her inner self separate from her outer self. She'd been reading romance since she was a teenager. It had started off as a way of exploring emotions that were frowned upon by her mother, but then she'd discovered it was the perfect method of relaxation. She wouldn't have shared her secret reading tastes with Charlotte, but she'd happened to notice a book in Samantha's bag. The following day she'd bought a stack of books into the office, and they'd been sharing ever since. "I'm running a business, and it would be hard to keep my credibility with clients and these Scottish folk if they knew we spent our free time fantasizing about being swept into the heather by a sexy guy in a kilt."

"Exactly. It's a fantasy. It's not as if we want to do it in real life. I bet heather is prickly. And possibly full of insects. Also, I checked his photo on the internet and the laird is in his late sixties—although still very handsome in a craggy, weather-beaten sort of way."

Samantha decided it was time to change the subject. "Did he say exactly what he wants me to do on this visit?"

"No. I didn't spend that long on the phone with him because I was worried Amy was going to bawl." Charlotte adjusted her bra strap. "He said you should spend a few nights there this month, that's all. And, honestly, he did have an incredibly sexy voice."

"You think a selling point would be the owner's *voice*? It's twenty-four days until Christmas. There's no way I can fit it in a visit."

"Why don't you talk to him and try and arrange something? He even suggested Christmas itself, but I said you always spend the holiday with your sister. So then he said maybe she would like to come too, and you could test the whole family holiday thing. Which would be cool, don't you think?"

"I do *not* think."

"Are you sure? What better way to evaluate the commercial appeal of spending Christmas in Scotland than by spending Christmas in Scotland?"

"It would be *work*—and I am not working at Christmas unless there's a client emergency. I am going to travel to my sister's and then stay in my pajamas for the entire time. I'll speak to him and arrange another time."

"Hmm… You could be missing out. *Laid by the Laird* would be a good title for a book, don't you think?"

"I do not. And please hold back from suggesting book titles if you ever meet him."

"Got it." Charlotte glanced out the window. "It's snowing again."

Samantha wasn't listening. Instead she was thinking about

the hunting lodge in the Highlands. Maybe a few days in Scotland wouldn't be so bad. The Kinleven Estate looked perfect, and she could think of at least a dozen clients who would love it—and love *her* for finding it.

"Get him on the phone. I'll try and fix a date between now and Christmas. I guess I can fly in one day and out the next. Is that it?"

"Kyle rang. Four times. He sounded irritated. Said he waited for two hours in the restaurant last night."

"Oh…"

She'd been tied up with one of her favorite clients—an elderly widow who lived in Arizona and had decided to bravely embrace her new single life. So far Samantha had arranged three trips for her, and they'd spent an hour the previous evening discussing a fourth. She'd forgotten her dinner arrangement with Kyle. What did it say about her that she'd forgotten? What did it say about *them*?

"That was rude of me. I'll call and apologize."

Charlotte shifted. "He said to tell you not to bother to call unless you're ready to take your relationship to the next level."

Oh for goodness' sake!

"The *next level*? It's a relationship—not an elevator." And as far as she was concerned they hadn't made it out of the basement.

"That was kind of his point. He said you need to decide where you want to go with this. I got the impression he wanted to go right to the top floor." Charlotte gave an apologetic smile. "I think he's in love with you."

"He— *What?* That's not true. He isn't any more in love with me than I am with him."

What she had with Kyle was a relationship of mutual convenience. They were theater partners. Opera partners. Occasional bedroom partners. Only more often than not Kyle fell asleep the moment he was horizontal. Like so many people in this area, he ran a tech start-up and was busier than she was. And the most disturbing part of that…? She didn't even care.

She should care, shouldn't she?

She should care that they would both rather work than spend time together.

She should care that there was no passion.

When they were together, her mind wandered, as if searching for some more stimulating alternative to the evening she'd chosen. She looked forward to him leaving so she could get back to her book.

She knew that real life wasn't like the romantic fiction she read, but surely it should come a little closer?

"Get him on the phone," she said. "I'll talk to him."

What was she going to say? She had no idea, but she'd find a way to smooth it over and keep things the way they were.

"Before you speak to him, you should know a huge bouquet of flowers arrived an hour ago from the Talbots, who are now back from their honeymoon in Vienna and wanted you to know it was everything they dreamed it would be."

"Which is exactly how they should feel about a honeymoon." Samantha was pleased to have another satisfied customer.

"That's it! We're done. I'll make those calls and—" She broke off as Amanda, one of the junior account managers, came flying into the room.

"Samantha! Sorry, but it's urgent."

"Excuse me?"

"It's your mother."

Samantha almost said, *I don't have a mother,* but then she remembered that wasn't strictly true. Biologically speaking, she had a mother. Not a cuddly, rosy-cheeked loving mother, as portrayed by the movies, but still a mother in the most literal sense of the word.

Instinctively she kept her expression blank. She had her mother to thank for that skill—if the ability to hide the way she was feeling could be considered a skill. She had no problem with other people's emotions—just her own.

She felt Charlotte touch her arm. "Samantha? Are you okay?"

No, she wasn't okay. Mention of her mother was enough to ensure that.

"She called?"

"Not personally."

Of *course* not personally. When had her mother ever done anything personal? And Samantha hadn't heard from her in five years. Not since that last frustrating and disastrous "family gathering." She could still feel her sister's tears soaking through her shirt and remember the way her whole body had shuddered with sobs as Samantha had held her.

"Why is she like this? Why does she say these things? What did we do wrong?"

Samantha felt suddenly tired. "Who called? And why?"

Her mother would never make contact without a good reason.

"Someone called Cole. He says he's her assistant. I had no idea your mother was Gayle Mitchell. I mean, I probably should have guessed... Samantha Mitchell, right? But I just didn't—I mean, *wow*." The girl was looking at Samantha with awe and a new respect. "What a woman. She's a total legend."

Of all the words Samantha could have used to describe her mother, that wouldn't have been on her list. But she was aware of how many people—women especially—admired her.

Gayle Mitchell had a way of inspiring and reaching people. The only people she seemed unable to connect with were her daughters.

Samantha felt a pressure in her chest. How could she feel hurt? After all these years, why didn't she have that under control?

"Choice Not Chance changed my life," Amanda said. "It's brilliant, isn't it?"

Should she admit that she'd never read it? She'd used it as a drinks mat, a dartboard and a doorstop. But never once opened it. That was her choice, wasn't it?

"Did her assistant say why she was calling?"

"Well, kind of… I don't know an easy way to say this. It's going to be a shock…" Amanda sent Charlotte a desperate look. "Your mother is in the hospital."

Samantha stared at her. "What?"

"Hospital. She's in the hospital."

"That's not possible. My mother hasn't had a single sick day in her life."

"Her assistant said something about an accident. He said you need to get to the hospital because she's asking for you."

Her mother was asking for *her*? Why? Gayle Mitchell was nothing if not practical. If she was injured, she'd be asking for a doctor—not her daughter. Especially as they hadn't seen each other since that last disastrous occasion.

She glanced round as Sandra, the intern, ran into the room.

Samantha wondered if her relaxed open-door policy needed rethinking.

"Your mother is on TV!"

Samantha didn't ask how she knew Gayle Mitchell was her mother. They'd obviously all been chatting.

Sandra had grabbed the remote control and switched on the large screen on the wall. And there was her mother, tumbling from a chair, her normal poise deserting her as she flailed. What was that thing in her hand? It looked like a lump of granite.

Samantha winced as her mother crash-landed. She'd forgotten her mother was mortal. Capable of bleeding.

Anxiety washed over her. She found her mother aggravating, frustrating and many other things—but she didn't want her to actually *die*.

She shifted on the spot to try and ease the discomfort of guilt. She should have reached out. Tried to open a dialogue. Explained how hurt she and Ella were. But they'd both been waiting for their mother to apologize for being so unsupport-ive, and then time had passed, and...

What if she'd left it too late?

Numb, she stared at the screen, watching as staff scurried round, as EMTs arrived. Lying there, still and bleeding, her mother looked vulnerable. Samantha couldn't think of a single time in her life when her mother had looked vulnerable. Gayle Mitchell didn't *do* vulnerable.

"Oh my—that had to hurt," Charlotte whispered. "Why would they film this stuff? It's so intrusive. Can you sue some-one? Wow, that's a *lot* of blood. Is that normal?"

Samantha pointed the remote at the screen and turned it off.

Her heart was punching her ribs, her pulse galloping.

Had her sister seen it? Ella would be upset. Despite everything that had happened, she still yearned to be a warm, close-knit family. She'd talked about making contact with their mother, but in the end she'd been too afraid of rejection to take the plunge.

Samantha had forgotten the other people in the room until she felt Charlotte's hand on her arm.

"You're in shock—and that's not surprising. Come and sit down."

Samantha extracted herself. "I'm fine."

Charlotte exchanged looks with Amanda. "We know you're not fine, boss. You don't have to pretend with us. We're like a family here. And this is your mom we're talking about. I mean, if it was *my* mother I'd be in pieces."

If it had been Charlotte's mother, Samantha would have been in pieces, too. Charlotte's mother dropped by the office fre-quently with Amy, bringing with her homemade baked goods and a level of maternal warmth that Samantha had never before encountered.

But this wasn't Charlotte's mother. It was *her* mother.

"The phone call..." Her voice didn't sound like her own. "Did he say how bad she is?"

If she was dead, they would have said so on TV, wouldn't they?

Not dead. But seriously injured, if the film footage was accurate.

And Samantha was going to have to go to the hospital.

Her conscience wouldn't let her do otherwise.

This was her mother, and Samantha wasn't a monster.

She had to ignore the fact that her mother hadn't been present for any of the emotional highs and lows of her life. And the fact that, if it had been Samantha in the hospital, her mother probably wouldn't have come. She didn't want to model herself on her mother. When faced with a situation that required judgment, she often thought *What would my mother do?* and was then careful to do the opposite.

Which answered her own question.

She turned to Charlotte. "Call the assistant back and tell him I'm on my way. Clear my schedule. I'll go to New York tonight."

Charlotte nodded. "No worries. Totally understood. I mean, it's your mother, right?"

"Right."

Samantha ran her hand over the back of her neck.

Was she doing the right thing?

What was she going to say when she arrived at the hospital? Were they just going to ignore what had happened the last time they'd met?

Her mother probably didn't even know she'd moved to Boston.

Charlotte was making notes. "I'll book you a flight and a car to the airport, and I'll call everyone on our list and explain that you've had a family emergency and—"

"No." Samantha rubbed her fingers across her forehead. "Some of those calls can't wait. The car needs to go via my apartment, so I can pack an overnight bag. Get Kyle on the phone, because I need to apologize, and also the guy from Scotland—because we have clients who would just love his place and

I need to get that visit arranged. Tell the others I'll call them back as soon as I can."

"Are you sure? Kyle will understand if you—"

"Just get him on the phone, Charlotte. Thank you."

She knew that if there was to be any chance of saving their relationship she needed to speak to him right now. But what exactly was she saving? And did she *want* to save it? Kyle was interesting, good-looking, solvent, and he had no unfortunate habits as far as she could see. He bought her flowers. Found good restaurants. She *should* want to save it.

Except her feelings weren't engaged, and she never felt as if his were, either.

It was all so—restrained. A little cold. When they were out together she'd never felt an overwhelming desire to drag him somewhere private so that they could be alone. He'd never appeared overwhelmed by her, either. He was perfect for outer Samantha—the version of herself that she showed to the real world, but inner Samantha? The person she really was under the poise and polish? *Wild Samantha.* That woman wanted so much more.

Why did she find it so hard to be that woman? What exactly was holding her back?

Could she really blame her mother?

She sat up a little straighter.

She wasn't a toddler. There came a point where you had to take responsibility.

If something had to change, then she was the one who had to change it.

She winced, aware that her thoughts could have come straight from her mother's book. *Choice Not Chance.* That damn book that slapped her in the face every time she walked into a bookstore.

For a moment she hesitated, loath to do anything that felt like following her mother's advice.

And then she realized how ridiculous that was. This was her life and her decision. Her mother wouldn't even know about it.

She wasn't waiting until the New Year to make a resolution. She was making it right now—starting with Kyle. She wasn't saving the relationship; she was breaking up with him. Not only had she forgotten their date, she hadn't even realized she'd forgotten it. She wasn't an expert on relationships, but even she knew that wasn't good. What she had with Kyle wasn't what she wanted.

No more bland, safe, unsatisfying relationships. The next man she met, she was going to be open and honest with him. She was going to take a risk and share her thoughts and feelings, instead of keeping them locked away. Maybe if she did that, her relationships would change and she'd feel passion. She wanted that. She wanted to be emotionally involved.

Satisfied that her mother would be suitably horrified by that revelation, Samantha felt better.

"Let's make those calls, Charlotte."

"Okay...well, for the record, I think you're very brave, holding it together like this." Charlotte checked her tablet. "Just to clarify—because my brain is a little fuzzy after Amy's eventful night—I'll call your mother's assistant back and say you'll go to the hospital later. I'll tell the Mortons that you feel Iceland is the perfect choice for them, that it's your personal recommendation and that you'll call to discuss it once they've taken a look at the itinerary we suggest. I'll get the laird on the phone so you can try and persuade him that you don't need to visit, and I'll also call your sister."

"Not my sister. I'll call my sister. You get Kyle for me. And stop calling the Scottish guy 'the laird' or I'll do it by accident."

"Right. Got it."

Flustered, Charlotte left the room with the others and Samantha returned to her desk.

She closed her laptop and slipped it into her bag. She'd be

able to do some work on the flight, or maybe in the hospital. It was unlikely that her mother was going to want her hanging out in her room.

She reached under her desk, rescued her shoes and slid them on, not wanting to analyze why she needed to wear heels to break up with a guy over the phone.

The thought of seeing her mother made her feel mildly nauseated. So did the thought of speaking to Kyle. She felt the same flutter of nerves in her stomach that she'd felt before she'd done a parachute jump for charity.

She smoothed her hair, then reached across to the phone on her desk and stabbed a button. "Charlotte? If you're not feeding Amy, could you bring me a drink, please?"

"Sure! Tea or coffee?"

"Vodka. Rocks."

There was a brief silence. "Right. Coming up."

Charlotte appeared a moment later, ice clinking in the glass she held. "Here. And I'm not judging you, so don't worry about that. Your mom is in the hospital, your relationship is ending... basically your personal life is a *total* mess, so you shouldn't feel bad about needing a drink."

"Thank you."

"Was that blunt? Darn. I'm trying to be less blunt."

"*Blunt* works for me. And you're right—my personal life *is* a mess." But she was about to make a start at clearing it up.

Charlotte patted her hand. "Just to say it's okay for you to talk about it if you want to. You're always listening to everyone else, but you keep all your own personal stuff inside."

She kept everything inside. What would happen if she didn't? If inner Samantha and outer Samantha actually merged? How would that work? It would be like walking into an otherwise immaculate apartment and finding laundry on the floor.

Charlotte seemed reluctant to relinquish the glass. "Instead of vodka I could give you a great big hug. I always find a hug is the best thing when I'm scared about something."

"Charlotte—"

"And I never gossip, so you don't need to worry about that. You're probably afraid someone will go straight to the press with a story about your mom, but I would never do that."

"I know."

"You never talk about your mother, and I understand why."

"You do?"

Should she be pleased or alarmed? Could it be that someone had actually seen beneath the surface?

"Of course. It's obvious. Gayle Mitchell is a legend, and if you mention her, everyone is going to want to talk about her, or get you to pull a favor and have a book signed or something. You're afraid people will only be interested in you because of your mother—but you shouldn't think that. You're an inspiration in your own right. Look at what you've built here! Although… *Choice Not Chance.*" She beamed. "I read it three times. And I have *Brave New You* on preorder."

Samantha wished her mother had never written that damn book.

She made a mental note to store a bottle of vodka in her office. She could invent a new drinking game. One shot when someone said something flattering about her mother. Two shots when someone said those three dreaded words.

"Let's get those calls done, Charlotte."

"Right." Charlotte finally put the drink down. "And I think you're amazing, being able to focus on work at a time like this."

"Thank you."

She waited until Charlotte had left the room and then picked up the glass.

What was she doing? Was she really so bad at dealing with emotional issues that she needed a drink to get her through?

Maybe she should have said yes to the hug…

She put the vodka down on her desk. It wasn't the solution. She did not need it. She'd call Kyle, and then she'd treat herself to a double-shot espresso from the Italian coffee shop down the road before she headed to the airport.

She was nervous, and she had her mother to blame for that.

Gayle Mitchell had drummed into both her children that any relationship was the death of ambition and goals—an anchor dragging you to the bottom of the rough seas of life. Every time Samantha ended a relationship, it made her doubly uncomfortable, because part of her felt as if she was pleasing her mother. Was that why she'd stayed with Kyle for so long? Because breaking up with him felt like something her mother would approve of?

Her phone lit up and she took a deep breath. The best way to handle this was to dive right in.

"Hi, there. Firstly, I am *so* sorry about last night. I was buried in work and to be honest I didn't even look up from my desk until midnight—"

She wasn't going to say she hadn't even realized she'd missed their date until Charlotte had told her.

"Anyway, I apologize. But it did start me thinking."

She heard an indrawn breath and ploughed on.

"Before you speak, let me finish. Please. I have to be honest. The truth is, this isn't working for me. I mean, you're great company, and we always have interesting conversation and a good time, but we're not exactly setting the world on fire, are we? We have these sedate dinners, or evenings at the theater, where we behave like a middle-aged couple and you occasionally hold my hand on the way home. It's all very civilized and restrained, and that's probably my fault because we both know I'm not great at showing emotion. But I want to. You have no idea how much I want to be great at that. I want to *feel* stuff. But when you and I are together, I just don't feel it—and that's my fault not yours. I've developed this outer self, and sometimes I find it hard to connect to my inner self—" *Wild Samantha.*

She was probably saying far too much, but she couldn't seem to stop herself.

"Maybe we don't have the right chemistry, or maybe I'm never going to feel anything because I can't let go of this controlled person I've become." *Thank you for that, Mother.*

"But I owe it to myself to at least hold out for more. I'm not expecting a storm of passion, but a light breeze would be nice. And you deserve that, too. We both deserve better than this bland, neutral, polite relationship. I think we should acknowledge that something is missing."

She stared through the window at the swirling snowflakes, wondering how it was possible to feel lonely in a city that was home to hundreds of thousands of people. But among all those people how did you find that one person who was going to change your world? Honesty. That had to be a good start.

"You don't really know me, Kyle, and that's my fault not yours. I—I'm not the person you think I am. I mean I *am*, but I'm also so much more. The real me wants to have a love affair so all-consuming that I forget to go to work—instead of forgetting the man and the date because I'm *at* work. I want to sneak off in my lunch break and buy sexy lingerie, instead of eating at my desk and taking calls. I want to drink champagne naked in bed, not seated in a theater bar surrounded by strangers. I want to have wild, desperate sex without caring when or where, and I definitely don't want to think about work at the same time. I—I want to see stars when I'm kissed."

Had she just said that aloud? *Had she really just said that?*

It was all very well resolving to be more open and honest, but it had left her feeling exposed and uncomfortable. She might as well have paraded down Newbury Street naked. Thank goodness she was ending it and wouldn't have to face him again. This was what happened when she let wild Samantha take control.

That version of her needed to stay locked away inside where she could cause minimum damage.

Dying of embarrassment, she forced out a few more words. "So what I'm saying is it's over. And I don't think this will be too much of a shock to you. I know there are many things about me that annoy you—not least the fact that my sister is so important to me and we speak every day. But that is never going to change, and neither is the whole passion thing, so I think we should both just accept the way things are and agree, amicably, that it's been fun but it's time to end it."

There. She'd done it. She'd said it. In fact she'd said far too much.

Samantha closed her eyes and breathed slowly to try and slow her racing heart. She hadn't realized her feelings were quite so close to the surface.

Kyle still hadn't responded, which she took to be a sign that he was shocked by her frankness. She was shocked, too. Drinking champagne in bed, naked? Where had *that* come from?

She gave him a few moments to respond and then gave up waiting. "This is… I'm starting to feel a little awkward…" *Understatement of the century.* "Say something. Anything."

There was only silence on the end of the phone.

Samantha felt a rush of exasperation, but also a growing sense of conviction that she'd done the right thing by breaking up with him. She'd spilled every one of her emotions all over him. She'd been honest and open, the way all those relationship books said you should be, and what had she got in return? Not warmth and understanding, but silence.

"Kyle? What do you think?"

"What do I think?"

The voice on the end of the phone was deep, rough and entirely unfamiliar.

"I think you've mistaken me for someone else. We've never had dinner, boring or otherwise, and we've also never had sex, so I wouldn't know about the chemistry, but drinking cham-pagne naked in bed sounds like a pretty good date to me. And I have no idea who Kyle is, but clearly he's a guy who needs to get his act together. Because you're right—no one wants or needs a bland, neutral, polite relationship."

Samantha sat without moving. Without breathing.

Who…?

Charlotte was supposed to be calling two people for her: Kyle, and Brodie McIntyre, the guy who owned the lodge in the Scottish Highlands.

If she hadn't been speaking to Kyle, then that could only mean…

Without saying another word, she reached for the vodka and downed it in one gulp.

Ella

"**O**ne mouthful." Ella Mitchell sliced the broccoli into smaller pieces and gave her daughter an encouraging smile. "Just one."

"Want a hug, Mommy."

"Oh no—" Ella gave a firm shake of her head. "You are not hugging your way out of this one. First comes broccoli. Then comes the hug."

Tabitha screwed up her face. "Why?"

Everything was *why. Why, why, why.*

"Because it's delicious and it's good for you."

"It's yucky."

"Not yucky. It's a superfood. It will make you strong and healthy." *Using all the wrong arguments, Ella.* "Also, most importantly, it looks like a Christmas tree." Seeing Tab's frown, she held up a stalk of broccoli as evidence.

"A Christmas tree has more needles."

"True. But from a distance—"

Tab shook her head. "A Christmas tree is bigger."

Ella abandoned that line of persuasion. "How about because if you eat your veggies, I will feel like a good mom. And I want to feel like a good mom."

"I want to be a unicorn."

Ella laughed and filed that remark to share with Michael later. They'd laugh about it over dinner. *Childhood goals.* "Unicorns eat broccoli."

Tab's eyes, the same hypnotic blue as her father's, narrowed suspiciously. "Why?"

"Because they know what's good for them."

Tab poked at her broccoli. "How do you know they eat broccoli?"

Ella wasn't sure whether to be pleased or frustrated that her daughter didn't take anything at face value. "Their diet is as mythical as the creature, but it is widely assumed that in order to grow a horn and have magical qualities they need to consume good levels of Vitamin D, calcium, potassium and phosphorus."

Tab nibbled the corner of a single stalk. "Can we make more Christmas cards this afternoon?"

"I was hoping you'd want to. It's my favorite thing, and we have all that glitter to use up." Anticipation warmed her from the inside out. She loved Christmas. Loved everything about it. The chaos, the excitement, the anticipation. Most of all she loved the fact that they all spent time together.

She leaned across and kissed Tab's hair. "I love you. Do you know that?" It was important to her to say it, and she said it often. She never rationed or withheld her affection.

"Love you, too. Can we get a Christmas tree?"

"Not yet. Soon."

"Why not now?"

"Because if we get it now, it will be dead by Christmas Day." And that was the only reason. Given the choice, Ella would have a Christmas tree in their apartment all year round. There was something warming about tiny lights wound through the branches of a fir tree. It was a symbol of family time.

"Can we spend Christmas in a snowy forest?"

"I— No, we can't. Why would you want to do that?"

"It's in my book. And it looks snuggly."

"It will be snuggly here, too, I promise. We'll have a huge tree, and we'll light the fire and decorate the whole house. And Aunty Sam will be here, and we'll bake cookies—" She already had a list of all the things she planned to do. And she and Tab were going to make decorations, which she intended to store carefully and bring out every year until they fell apart.

"Will Aunty Sam be working?"

"She might have her phone because she's very busy—"

"Daddy says she's a typhoon."

"Tycoon, honey, not typhoon. Typhoon is a very big storm. A tycoon is a very powerful person."

"What's powerful?"

"It can mean physically strong, but it can also mean influential."

"What's influential?"

This went on like a cascade, question after question until Ella started to wonder if someone was testing her to see if she would finally snap.

Finally Tab seemed satisfied. "Aunty Sam is a tycoon."

And now she was expected to explain irony.

"Daddy was teasing her when he called her that—" explaining the subtleties of the exchange escaped her "—but Aunty Sam is very smart, that's true."

"Are you a tycoon?"

"No, I'm your mommy. And that makes me lucky." She had no desire to climb the corporate ladder, but that didn't mean she wasn't proud of her sister.

Fulfilment for her came in a job well done, the knowledge that she'd made a difference to someone's life, however small.

As a teacher, her reward had been seeing the delight and won-der in a child's eyes the first time they realized that letters could become words—*d-o-g dog, it's dog*!! Before that, as a barista, she'd made coffee, taking extra care, knowing that at the very least she was improving the start of someone's day, at best she was sav-ing a life. Because good coffee was lifesaving, she was sure of it. Before her barista phase she'd worked in a bookstore—*read this book, it will change your life*. The world was often a challenging place—she knew that. She couldn't change the big things, but she could improve things in a small way for others and for herself.

And now she was a mother. She wasn't building a career, she was building a family. She was building walls around their little unit that would shelter and protect.

Across the kitchen, her phone buzzed in her bag.

Ella ignored it.

Tab pointed. "That's your phone."

"I know, sweetie."

"You should answer it."

"The phone does not take priority over our conversation just because it's loud and intrusive."

"It might be important."

"But it won't be more important than spending time with you." Ella kissed Tab on the forehead, loving the warmth and smoothness of her skin. She smelled of rose and vanilla, of youth and hope. Her eyes were bright and interested. Ella loved this age, where they soaked up the world and tried to make sense of their surroundings. The *why, why, why* drove some of the other mothers into a state of ferocious frustration, but not Ella. She wanted to freeze time, to hold on to this perfect moment and never let it slip away. She wanted to always be this close and in tune with her daughter. She loathed the phone, hating the way it could intrude into a conversation, or shatter a romantic mo-ment. She resented its insistent, insidious infiltration of daily life. It was the destroyer of intimacy and the glutton of time, consuming it in greedy mouthfuls. Given the choice, she wouldn't have carried one at all, but Michael insisted.

The phone stopped ringing and she relaxed, only to tense again when it started a moment later.

Tabitha fingered the rest of the broccoli. "What if it's Aunty Sam?"

"She wouldn't ring me in the middle of the day—she's too busy." On the other hand, what if it was Sam? Or Michael? She had the phone for emergencies. What if this was it?

Ella caved and walked across the kitchen, stepping over Tab's dolls and a small mountain of dressing-up clothes as she reached for her purse.

Out of the corner of her eye she saw Tabitha hurl the broccoli under the table and was about to say something when her phone lit up with her sister's name.

She snatched it up. Her sister never phoned during the day. "Sam? If you're calling to tell me how many sleeps it is until Christmas, we have it up on the wall here. Tab made a chart. We're checking off the days."

"I— No. Not that. Have you watched TV today?"

"No. You know I never watch daytime TV." She picked up a red crayon that had been abandoned on the floor. "Tab and I started our day at Mini Musicians, where she gave a virtuoso performance on the cymbals—my ears are still ringing. Then we went for a walk in the park and came home via that cute fabric shop, where we bought an incredible gold lamé that we are going to make into a dress that Millicent is going to wear to the ball. But first we are making Christmas cards."

"Millicent? Oh, the doll. I forgot."

"You were the one who bought her Millicent. It's her favorite."

"When your favorite niece asks for a doll, she gets a doll."

Ella smiled and glanced across at her daughter, shaking her

head as she saw Tab about to hide another piece of broccoli. "You spoil her. Trouble is, I do, too."

"It's love, not spoiling. And Tab is lucky. Look, I need to—Ella, I need to talk to you."

Ella walked back to her daughter, gave her a severe look and held up another stalk of broccoli. "Go ahead. And why are you asking me about TV? What did I miss? Did they do something on your company? You found a new Christmas movie for us to binge watch?"

There was a pause. "It's our mother."

Ella dropped the broccoli on the floor.

Tab cheered and punched the air.

Ella sat down, keeping the smile on her face so that Tab wouldn't guess that anything was wrong. "What about her?"

"She's in the hospital, but she's fine." Samantha was calm and matter-of-fact. "I mean, this is our mother and she's indestructible. I'm dealing with it, but I didn't want you to see the news on TV and panic. Ella? Are you okay? Say something."

Ella felt pressure in her chest. "How do you know? Did she call you?"

"Her assistant left a message with my assistant."

Tycoon telecommunications.

"But she must have asked them to. She must have wanted us to know. How did she even know you'd moved?" Something fluttered to life beneath the layers of anxiety. Hope? "How bad? Was it a heart attack?"

"Accident."

"Car?"

"She fell off a chair and one of her awards smashed her on the head. Unfortunately she was recording an interview at the time so the footage is colorful. Don't watch it."

Tabitha frowned. "Mommy? Your face is looking funny. And a car can't have a heart attack."

Ella forced herself to breathe and behave normally. "I'm fine, honey."

"You look weird. Maybe you need broccoli. Vitamins." Tab thrust her last stalk toward her and Ella took it.

She felt weak and vulnerable, as she always did when she thought of her mother.

She also felt guilty, because thinking of her mother always induced feelings of guilt.

Guilt that she hadn't somehow made the most of her life.

Guilt that she'd disappointed a parent who had sacrificed so much for her.

I can't believe a daughter of mine would make such bad choices.

"Which hospital?" She found a pen and scribbled it down as Samantha told her. "I can be in Manhattan in under three hours."

She lived in a small coastal town in Connecticut, that was perfect for families. Far enough away from the city that her previous life there seemed distant.

"You don't have to. Focus on Tab. No sense in us both suffering. I've got this. Charlotte's already booked me onto a flight from Logan to LGA. I'll be at the hospital by this evening, and I'll stay the night in the city and call you as soon as I've spoken to the doctors and understand what's going on."

Ella was about to ask why she was planning on staying the night, and then realized that with the timing, her sister wouldn't have any choice. And unless she wanted to get a very late train home, she wouldn't have a choice, either.

Ella knew she had to go, too, but she hadn't spent the night away from Tab since she was born. Her pulse started to thump a warning. "I'll come. I just need to message Michael."

"You will not. First, you don't need to because you're not coming. And second, you don't need to because you're not coming."

It was so tempting to simply let her sister take the strain of it, but Ella knew she couldn't do that. They stuck together. They always had, and they always would. She wouldn't let Samantha do this alone any more than Samantha would let her do it. "Thanks, but I'll be okay. If she's asking for us, we should both go. And we can share a hotel room and make it fun. Hold on one moment—" She held the phone in front of her and typed a quick message. "Okay. Done."

"After what happened last time—the way she spoke to you." Samantha's voice shook a little. "Honestly, Ella. Don't go."

"She's—" Ella glanced at Tab, who was listening intently. "I have to."

"Why? Because we're her daughters? She's more interested in inspiring and lifting up a stranger, than she is in supporting us."

"I know. But I won't be like her. I won't. I wouldn't be able to live with myself. And I know you feel the same."

"I do." Samantha sighed. "All right. I'll meet you there. But please reassure me that your expectations are realistic. She is not going to clasp you to her bosom and say how much she loves you and how proud she is of everything you've achieved."

"Do you think she is finally going to apologize?"

There was a pause. "I doubt it. Not after five years."

"But she called us!" Ella lowered her voice and walked to the opposite end of the kitchen so that Tab couldn't hear every word. "That's her reaching out. That has to be a good sign."

"You are such an optimist. Which I love, but it scares me. We don't know why she's reaching out. And if you go there thinking that this is all going to end happily, you'll be hurt again and I can't bear that. I know you can't talk properly because you have Tab there, but you do know what I'm saying, don't you?"

"Yes. Are you okay?" Ella quickly glanced at Tab. "You sound stressed."

"I'm fine. Not my best day, that's all."

"Work or Kyle?"

"Kyle and I broke up. My fault and my choice, but it's still stress. This Mom thing isn't helping."

Ella kept her mouth shut. In her opinion, Kyle had been as exciting as a piece of dried fruit, but she knew better than to say so. Her sister's relationships were a no-go area. The one thing they never talked about in depth.

"How did the assistant even get your number? We've both moved since we last saw her."

"I assume they looked me up on the internet."

"It must have been a pretty shocking call."

"Yeah, I've had a few of those today."

Ella frowned. "You've had more than one bad phone call?"

"Forget it."

"I want to hear about it."

"I can't yet talk about it without wanting to die of humiliation."

Intrigued, Ella was about to ask another question when she heard the sound of Michael's key in the door. "I need to go— Michael is home. Text me the details of the hospital and I'll see you there."

Ella dropped her phone into her purse.

Hospital. Her mother. She was going to see her mother.

Michael strode into the room and immediately her tension eased and her breathing settled.

Meeting him had changed her world. She never felt less when she was with Michael. He made her feel interesting, important and confident in her decisions. He made her feel like success.

Her husband, her little girl, her big sister—they *were* her world. She'd made the family she'd always wanted.

"Daddy! Hug, hug, hug." Tab shot out of her chair and sprinted across to him. He caught her and swung her high in the air.

"How's my girl?" His gaze found Ella's, and she knew that although he was holding Tab, he was talking to her. He'd seen her message and immediately come home. He knew how difficult this would be for her.

And she wouldn't talk about it in front of Tab.

"I'm doing okay."

He shifted Tab onto his hip and held out his other arm to Ella.

She went to him immediately, and he curled her into him and held her tightly. The feeling of warmth and closeness made everything hurt a little less.

"Samantha called me." She leaned her head against his chest, feeling the rough texture of his wool coat against her cheek. It felt cold, as if winter had crept into the fibers and settled there. "I have to go into the city."

"I saw your message. Don't go. It will upset you and I don't want that."

Tab stroked her hair. "Are you sad, Mommy?"

"No. How could I be sad when I have you and Daddy?" She kissed her daughter. "Go fetch the painting we did for Daddy." She waited for Tab to leave the room and then turned to Michael. "I have to go."

"You don't *have* to, Ella, but I know you will." He hung up his coat, loosened his tie and undid his top button. He sounded tired. "If that's what you want, then I'm coming with you."

"What? No way!"

"I love you. I want to support you."

Her heart was hammering. He couldn't come with her. And she couldn't tell him the reason.

"Someone has to look after Tab. I'm not taking her to a hospital."

"We'll get a sitter."

"We've never left her with a sitter. It's fine. I don't need you to be there."

He gave her a long, thoughtful look. "You don't want me to be there. What I don't understand is why."

"I just—it will be difficult. With my mother, it always is."

"So you say." There was an edge to his voice that made her heart beat a little faster.

"Are you suggesting I'm exaggerating?"

"No, but as you've never let me meet her, it's hard for me to understand what you mean. Why are you so afraid to introduce us? We've been together more than five years, El, and apart from Sam, she's our only living family."

And that would matter to him, of course, because Michael had lost both his parents when he was in his twenties. Ella picked up a photo of them laughing with Michael and felt a tug of envy. It was a perfect family scene. They'd been older parents and he'd been an unexpected but welcome surprise. Love shone out of that photo. "I know how long we've been together. And I'm grateful for every minute." She put the photo back. "It's also been five years since I saw my mother so it's not as easy as you make it sound."

"I know." He folded her close. "And I know how much that upsets you. But I don't need to be protected from the situation."

She squeezed her eyes shut, guilt making her feel a little sick. Why hadn't she just been honest right from the start? But she hadn't, and now she didn't know how to tell the truth. "The priority is to keep everything as normal as possible for Tab. I want her in a warm, secure environment with someone she loves. And I won't be doing this alone. Sam will be there."

"Where are you going, Mommy?" Tab was back by her side and Ella caught her hand.

"Mommy has to go on a trip to see Aunty Sam. But I'll be back tomorrow."

"Is Aunty Sam in the hospital? Did she have a heart attack?" Tab missed nothing.

"She's not in the hospital. No one had a heart attack."

"Then who is in the hospital? Someone is in the hospital. You said 'which hospital.'"

"I—" Ella glanced at Michael and he shrugged. She knew he

thought she should tell the truth, but Ella didn't want to. How would she begin to explain her relationship with her mother to her daughter? She couldn't even explain it to herself. "Some-one we know—"

"What's her name?"

"Gayle." Ella swallowed. "Her name is Gayle."

Michael gave a slow shake of his head and walked toward the fridge.

The answer wasn't enough for Tab. "Is she your friend?"

"She—I—she's someone—we know—"

The fridge door closed with a thump.

Ella didn't look at Michael.

Tab wrinkled her nose, apparently enjoying this game of "de-tective." "Is she Daddy's friend, then?"

"No—he—" She wasn't going there, she absolutely wasn't. "Tab, I need to pack a bag."

"Shall I make her a card? People who are sick like cards. I want to come. I want to see Aunty Sam."

"You can't, baby. Not this time. We'll see her soon, I prom-ise."

"Christmas."

"Definitely Christmas."

"Twenty-four more sleeps. Santa and Aunty Sam." Tab danced across the room, and Michael strolled back to Ella.

"I don't want to stop you going if that's what you want, honey, but I'm not going to pretend I'm happy about it."

Tab reappeared. "I want to go with Mommy and meet her friend."

First her husband and now her daughter. How had her life ever gotten this complicated?

Michael kissed Ella and then dropped to his haunches so he was eye to eye with his daughter. "If you go with Mommy, who will watch movies and eat popcorn with me?"

Tab wavered. "Popcorn?"

"We could make it together. If you were here."

"Which movie?"

Michael laughed and flashed Ella a smile. "Do you hear that? My little negotiator. Maybe she's going to be a lawyer like her dad."

"Don't put that pressure on her! Maybe she'll decide to work in an animal shelter, or join a ballet company, or even teach kindergarten." She saw Michael's eyebrows lift. "Sorry. Ignore me. Sensitive subject."

"Of course Tab should do any job that makes her happy and fulfilled." He gave Tab's shoulder a squeeze and rose to his feet. "You and I are going to have a fun evening, Tabitha Melody Gray."

"Can we play princesses before the movie?"

Michael's expression didn't falter. "Sure." He thrust his hands in his pockets and looked at Tab. "I confess I don't know how to play princesses. Am I the prince in this scenario? Do I rescue you from peril?"

Tab gave him a look. "No, I rescue you. You're scared of the dragon because he's a lot bigger than you expected, and I chop his head off to save you. There's lots of blood. You faint."

Michael raised his eyebrows. "I'm not coming out of this well, am I? And neither is the dragon. A violent end. I obviously have a lot to learn about this game. You'll have to teach me. It's not my area of expertise."

Tab was forgiving. "You can't be good at everything."

"Are you saying I'm not good at everything?" Michael growled and then chased Tab around the house, hands outstretched to tickle her. Listening to Tab's delighted squeals, Ella's heart melted. She fell in love with Michael at least five times a day, and today was no exception.

She picked up her purse. "I'll meet my sister at the hospital. I'm sorry you had to come home early."

"I'm not. I get to see my beautiful wife and play dragons with my warrior princess." Michael caught Tab again, tickling her as she rolled and wriggled.

Ella felt a pang. She wanted to stay home and spend an evening with them. She wanted to make popcorn with her daughter and sit snuggled together in their little unit of three where she felt loved and accepted.

"I need to get changed."

Michael extracted his tie from Tab's grasp. "You look great. Why would you change?"

"Because I can't go to the hospital dressed in jeans and a sweater."

"There's a dress code to visit a hospital?"

"No, but there's a dress code to visit—" she almost said *my mother*, but stopped herself in time. "I just need to change, that's all."

She was on her way up the stairs when Michael's voice stopped her.

"Ella?"

She tightened her hand on the rail. "What?"

He joined her on the stairs. "You're changing your clothes for your mother?"

"I am." And that was only the beginning. She didn't just change her clothes for her mother, she changed her personality. And she hated the person she became.

"You should wear what you like." He stroked her hair back from her face and kissed her. "I'll come with you. If it's tough, I'll defend you. Tab has taught me some useful skills for slaying dragons. I promise not to faint no matter how much blood there is."

She tried to smile. "Thanks, but I'm better doing this alone."

"Why? I know she hurt you, but it's been five years, Ella. We have a daughter."

"I know. I know all that."

"There has to be a way to heal the rift. Whatever your relationship with your mother, she is Tab's grandmother."

"And what? Is that supposed to mean something?" The thought of exposing her daughter to her mother made Ella's heart tighten with panic. "I've told you, my mother knows how to be a CEO. She knows how to advise on your career and tell you where you're going wrong with your goals. But be a grandmother? That's not something she's qualified to do. Don't think my mother is some cuddly, caring person. That's a mistake I made constantly, still do, and I have to fight against it every day, because if I don't, I get sucked back in and what I end up with isn't a relationship, it's a bucket of disappointment and a massive ache in my chest. I won't put Tab through that for the sake of having family."

"You have family, Ella." He pulled her close. "You have me, and Tab and Samantha."

"And that's all the family I need. Quality not quantity, right?"

"I didn't mean to upset you."

"I know. And I don't expect you to understand. My mother has never, ever been proud of a single thing I've done." She swallowed. "She has never once said she loves me."

He kissed her. "I'm proud of you. I love you."

"I know. Thank you." It should have been enough, but it wasn't. A part of her, a small part that refused to be quiet, still felt like a failure. If you couldn't please your mother, what did that say about you?

"I know you were hurt that she didn't want to come to our wedding—it hurt me, too, if I'm honest because it made me angry that she wouldn't be there for you—but it was more than five years ago and maybe this is a good time to try again. It's Christmas. Season of goodwill. Is she not remotely curious about the man her daughter married?"

Ella buried her face in his shoulder so that he couldn't see her red cheeks.

How had she managed to mess things up so badly?

Ella knew her mother wasn't curious, and there was a perfectly good reason for that. She didn't know Ella was married. She didn't know she had a granddaughter.

Ella hadn't told her.

And the reason she hadn't come to their wedding was because Ella hadn't invited her.

Gayle

She was thirsty, but she couldn't reach her drink. The pain in her head sliced from forehead to jaw, a vicious stabbing so relentless she would have given anything to be able to hit Pause on it for a moment. She had no say over when she took painkillers. Someone else made that decision. Gayle hated leaving other people to make decisions for her. Decisions were personal. She hated feeling helpless. She'd vowed never to feel this way again, and yet here she was, feeling it, and it was frightening how quickly all those toxic feelings trickled back into her life. She felt weak and feeble and it terrified her. She preferred to believe she was invincible, but this whole place was a reminder she was human. The footsteps, the relentless beeping of the machine next to her or the stomach-turning smells of disinfectant and plastic. Couldn't someone at least light a scented candle? And the people around her talked in abbreviations the whole time so she only caught a fraction of what they were saying. It was all *ICU* and *TBI*, *FBC* and *MRI*. She was a patient, not a person. Why didn't people teach doctors about communication?

It turned out that as well as a head injury, she had bruised ribs. Her chest felt as if she'd been crushed by an elephant. The dizziness was terrible, as was the headache she'd had since she woke up. It felt as if someone was constantly bashing her over the head with that stupid award.

Since she'd arrived at the hospital, she'd been subjected to numerous tests and questions. Her answers had been a desperate attempt to grasp back a little control. *Yes I feel fine* (lie). *No headache* (bigger lie). Despite the fact she was sure she'd given all the right answers, no one was letting her go home.

"Can I go home?" She croaked out the question, but as she could see two versions of the nurse in front of her, she wasn't confident that the answer would be the one she wanted.

"Not yet. No one seems completely sure how long you were unconscious for, but it could have been around eight minutes. We want to keep an eye on you."

As if she was the stock market or a currency trade.

"I want to go home."

"No one wants to be in the hospital, but it's the best place for you right now."

That, Gayle thought, was debatable. Did the nurse realize how condescending she sounded? "My head hurts."

"Yes." The nurse turned as someone else appeared in the doorway. "Can I help you?"

Gayle saw a flash of bright scarlet and panicked. Blood? Was she bleeding in front of her eyes?

She heard the low murmur of voices and then the nurse returned to her bedside.

"You have a visitor, Gayle."

Gayle? As if they were lifelong friends or family. Being ill was a dehumanizing experience.

The flash of scarlet moved, and Gayle realized it wasn't blood, it was a person.

The nurse leaned closer. "Your daughter is here, Gayle."

Daughter. Gayle moved her head, a decision that caused pain to slice through her. All that red was her daughter?

The figure stepped closer, shading the bright, overhead light. Gayle saw a slender woman in a red wool coat. A few strands of fair hair had escaped from the twist on the back of her head and her cheeks were pink from the cold. Her face was expressionless, and she paused several steps away from the bed.

Samantha! It was Samantha. And she was here, at the hospital.

As her heart lifted and flew, Gayle acknowledged just how afraid she'd been that her daughter wouldn't come.

She thought back to the last time she'd seen Samantha, but it wasn't a good memory so her brain touched on it and skidded away. No point in mentioning that. Best if they all ignored it and pretended it hadn't happened. What they needed was a fresh start. Safer to talk about something safe and neutral.

But what?

What did you say when you hadn't seen someone for five years?

"That looks like a warm coat," she said, "although black would have been a better investment than red. That color will be out of fashion next season, and it will languish at the back of your closet."

"Thank you for your thoughts." Samantha's tone was controlled. "I'm capable of deciding what to wear."

"Well, of course you are. I was just—"

"Shall we talk about something else?"

"Let's do that." Gayle shrank back against the pillows, frustrated with herself for saying the wrong thing, but also frustrated with Samantha. Despite all Gayle's best efforts, she was so sensitive. You couldn't afford to be sensitive in such a hard, difficult world. Samantha had always been the same, although not as bad as her sister, of course. As a mother, it had been terrifying to see. You wanted your child to be strong and robust, not so fragile that the faintest tremor would rock their foundations.

Samantha had always been the tougher of the two girls. From the moment Ella was born, she'd taken on the role of older sister, even though the age gap was only ten months. Samantha had been Ella's protector and fairy godmother rolled into one, and it had exasperated Gayle. If Ella fell, Samantha picked her up and soothed her. If there was something Ella couldn't do, Samantha would do it for her. If it was within Samantha's power to give her sister what she wanted, then she made it happen.

Gayle had been at her wit's end. How was she supposed to teach Ella independence and self-reliance when her older sister stepped in to help and comfort her the whole time?

Talking to Samantha about it had got them nowhere.

I will always pick my sister up if she falls.

And what if you're no longer around, Gayle had said. How will she get to her feet if she has never learned how?

Samantha had stuck her chin out. *I will always be here.*

Samantha had been determined to follow her own path and ignore every single piece of advice her mother had offered, even though everything Gayle had ever done or said had been for her benefit. If Gayle had been clever, she would have given the opposite advice in order to nudge Samantha into making good choices, but that wasn't the way she did things.

Last time they'd met, Samantha had been openly hostile, which had shocked even Gayle.

She'd handled the whole encounter badly; she could see that now, but in her opinion Samantha's reaction had been an extreme overreaction. Samantha was a tigress when it came to her sister, and that hadn't changed over the years.

But she wasn't going to think about that. Move on. It was one of the key messages in her new book *Brave New You*. Leave mistakes behind. Don't carry them with you because they'll weigh you down.

Gayle felt a prickle of exasperation. All she'd ever done was try and prepare her children for life in the real world. That was a mother's job, wasn't it? It was unfair to raise a child to believe everyone was good and that the world was a sunny happy place. Better to equip them with the skills to cope with the hard and bitter blows life sent. Would you send someone into battle wearing a swimsuit? No, you'd give them armor and whatever else they might need in the way of protection, and that was exactly what she'd done. She'd done everything she could to make sure her girls wouldn't be knocked down, but if they *were* knocked down, then she'd given them the skills they'd need to get back on their feet again.

She didn't want their gratitude, but she would have settled for respect or at least some acknowledgment that everything she'd done, everything she'd taught them, had been for their own good.

Still, she knew she needed to keep that thought to herself if she wanted to heal the relationship or Samantha would simply walk out, the way she'd walked out five years previously. Her daughters didn't seem to realize that she was hurt, too.

Samantha looked at the nurse. "How serious is it? Can I talk to the doctor?"

"He's dealing with an emergency right now, but he should be back within an hour. The scan showed no bleeding or fractures. That's good news. She doesn't appear to have memory loss. She's a little irritable, but that's normal after a head injury."

Gayle thought she heard Samantha say *and entirely normal for my mother*, but she couldn't be sure.

The nurse smiled. "I'm sure you'd like five minutes alone with her."

Samantha looked uncomfortable. "Oh no, it's fine—I can—"

"It's no problem. I'll be right outside. Press the call button if you need anything." The nurse walked out before Samantha could speak or stop her.

Gayle, who had been wishing the woman gone all afternoon,

now wanted her to stay. Without the presence of a third person, the focus narrowed. It was just the two of them.

Samantha undid the buttons on her coat. Presumably she was feeling the tension, too. So many memories and unspoken words.

Underneath the coat she was wearing wide-legged pants and a turtleneck that showed off her long neck and good bone structure. Both were white.

White? In Manhattan? Gayle shuddered.

It was an outfit she wouldn't have worn in a million years, but she had to admit that with her flawless makeup and discreet jewelry, Samantha radiated success and confidence. If it hadn't been for the coat—*Red? Had she taught her nothing? It should have been black. Black worked for every situation*—Gayle would have felt gratified, although to say so would in all likelihood send Samantha straight out the door after the nurse.

"Tell me about your job, Samantha." That was a neutral topic, wasn't it? "My assistant said you're the CEO of your own company. Congratulations. You should have told me."

"Why? It's not important."

Not important? It was everything. At Samantha's age Gayle had been clawing and fighting for every morsel of success that came her way. She'd woven herself a security blanket, layer by layer. Blood, sweat, tears. It was a whole new take on patchwork.

"You've worked hard to be where you are. You should be proud of that. Never apologize for success." Suddenly she felt more like her old self. "You should own—"

"Please—can we talk about something other than my job?" Samantha appeared to be clenching her teeth. "What happened?"

"To me? A stupid accident." And just like that Gayle shrank back into the role of patient.

"Why were you standing on that chair?"

"You saw that?"

Samantha eased off her gloves. "It was on a news report."

"That damn camera crew. I'd just finished a live interview when it happened. I hope this doesn't damage my reputation."

Samantha dropped her purse onto the chair and shot her a look of naked incredulity. "You're in the hospital with a head injury, bruised ribs and a twisted ankle and you're worrying about your reputation?"

"These things matter."

"To you." Samantha draped her coat over the back of the chair, shifted her purse out of the way and sat. She didn't relax. Instead she perched on the edge, one foot forward as if she was ready to run if the need arose. "Does it hurt?"

"Knowing my reputation may be damaged? Obviously, it's unsettling, and I—"

"Your head. I was asking about your head."

"Oh. Yes. I suppose it does hurt. And my ribs." Now that she thought about it, every single part of her body hurt, but that probably wasn't surprising given the way she'd fallen. She'd tried to shut the pain out, the way she always shut out bad things. Throughout her life, she'd made a point of moving forward, dragging herself limb by limb if necessary. Pain wasn't new to her.

"Have you had painkillers? I could ask the staff—"

"No." If she mentioned it to the staff, they'd never discharge her. "Thank you, but I think they probably gave me something."

The conversation trailed off.

Samantha stared at her hands.

Gayle hunted for something to say that wasn't going to be taken the wrong way. "Did you drive?"

"Flew."

"Oh." Had conversation always been this difficult? It was a wonder they'd managed to say enough for a falling-out. "Airport a nightmare?"

"Not too bad, considering the time of year."

Gayle frowned. "Time of year?"

"Christmas." Samantha looked at her. "It's Christmas."

Gayle stopped herself asking *so what?* "Not for ages."

Samantha opened her mouth and closed it again. "In a little over three weeks. But I know you don't love Christmas."

"I've never really—" No, she wasn't going to go there. Her daughters, she knew, loved the holidays. It was another point of connection between the two of them, and contention with her. "Where did you spend Thanksgiving?"

"With Ella."

"Good. That's good." This conversation was more painful than her head injury. How much longer until the nurse came back into the room? She'd wanted her daughter to come, but now she was here Gayle didn't know what to say to her. "Thank you for coming."

"Of course."

Another awkward silence, as if they were two people who barely knew each other which, now that she thought about it, was an accurate description. Five years was a long time. What had her daughters been doing in that time? What had they achieved? Quite a lot, if the expensive watch on Samantha's wrist was an indication. She wanted to ask about Samantha's business, but was afraid her daughter might bite her head off. One injury was enough in a week.

"My assistant tracked you down. You didn't tell me you'd moved."

Samantha stirred. "No." She glanced at her watch, not a slender piece of jewelry, but a bold statement with a face that almost covered the width of her wrist.

Samantha Mitchell was a woman in charge of her time, her life.

Gayle felt a flash of pride. Maybe her decisions hadn't been all bad, even if her daughter didn't appreciate her mother's contribution to the person she'd grown to be.

"It's good to see you, Samantha. It's been too long."

"Yes."

"Almost five years."

Samantha brushed nonexistent fluff from her white sweater. "Five years, one month, a few days."

She knew the exact date?

Gayle had thought it best not to mention that last meeting, but now it was there, blazing like a neon light, and she sensed that it had to be addressed if they were ever going to heal family wounds and move forward. And she was determined to move forward. She'd say, and do, whatever it took.

"The last time we met was a little stressful. I admit I may have said the wrong thing, but it was difficult—"

"It shouldn't have been difficult." Samantha looked directly at her. Unafraid. "It was a celebration for Ella's first teaching job. She so badly wanted your approval and support, and instead you gave her a hearty dollop of judgment and disapproval."

"I was afraid she wouldn't stick at it, that's all."

"You know the impact you have on her. She was desperate for a word of praise from you, some sign that she'd finally made you proud. But instead of congratulating her, you killed any pleasure she might have had. Any sense of achievement. And it was an achievement."

"She'd finally finished something she started, and I was glad about that of course, but—"

"You have no idea how much damage you did. There was so much she wanted to talk to you about that day." Samantha stood up abruptly, knocking her purse onto the floor. Instead of picking it up, she paced to the window.

Ella had wanted to talk to her? "What about?"

"It doesn't matter now." Samantha turned. "She's coming here. Be kind."

Kind? What use was kindness when life lifted its hand and slapped you? You needed a barrier. You needed to be tough. You needed a strategy. Why couldn't people see that?

But she knew better than to say so. She'd do whatever it took to fix her relationship with her daughters. She'd praise Ella, even if she discovered she'd had ten different jobs since they last met. She'd keep her opinions to herself and tell them what they wanted to hear.

"It will be good to see her. Does she live in the city?"

"No. She moved out around the same time I did."

"You don't miss Manhattan? I would."

"But we're not you. We're different people. Individuals." Her phone pinged, and she dug it out of the pocket of her coat and glanced at the screen. "She's on her way up now. Remember— kind."

"Kind. Yes."

Why did Samantha keep saying that? What was "kind" about endorsing someone's less than ideal choices? *There, there, it's going to be a disaster and I have no idea what you were thinking when you made that stupid decision, but—*

She'd fake it.

In her time, she'd faked plenty of emotions she didn't feel.

What had Ella wanted to talk to her about?

Had she wanted advice?

No. Like Samantha, Ella had always shunned her mother's advice as if it had to be toxic simply because it came from her lips.

Samantha looked at her, long and hard. "Don't ask about her job. If she wants to tell you, she'll tell you."

"Right. Got it." She felt like a child being scolded. Was she really that bad a mother? She'd always felt as if she'd done a good job, but maybe it depended on how you measured success. If parental success was measured in hugs and emotional nurturing, then maybe she'd failed.

She felt a strange, unfamiliar feeling behind her eyes. It started as a stinging sensation and then became more of a burn. It was only when her throat thickened that she realized what this was. She was going to cry. She, Gayle Mitchell, who hadn't cried since she was nineteen years old, was about to cry because her daughter was upset with her.

There was a toughness about Samantha that she didn't remember. She should have been relieved to see it, but for some reason it made her feel even more isolated.

She tried desperately to will the tears not to fall. She stared hard. She tried to relax her throat. She clenched her jaw.

This was terrifying. She badly wanted to be back to her old confident self, sure of her choices and in command of her life.

"You're very—angry with me." Her voice was croaky but if she'd expected that to gain her sympathy, it didn't happen.

"No, not angry. I *was* angry. I—" Samantha breathed deeply. "I just don't want you to say the wrong thing to Ella this time, that's all."

Gayle panicked. She wanted to promise, but how could she promise when they had differing ideas of what the "wrong" thing was? Gayle seemed to upset her girls even when she was making small talk.

The only safe approach was not to offer an opinion. On anything.

She was going to try that.

"You and Ella are still close then?"

Samantha gave a funny smile. "We're sisters."

And you're both my daughters, Gayle thought. *But that didn't stop you from moving far away without telling me, and not once getting in touch.*

"I'm glad you have each other." She felt a stab of jealousy, imagining all the times they'd probably shared. Birthday celebrations, maybe vacations— "I'm sorry we—lost touch." She wasn't going to show how hurt she was that they hadn't been in contact. Sometimes a parent had to be the one to take the blows and the blame. "I'm glad you came."

"I was surprised that you reached out." Samantha hesitated. "I wasn't sure what you wanted."

Gayle heard the bleep of the machine, speeding up as her heart rate increased. "I wondered if we might be able to—" To what? What exactly was she asking for? "I want us to see more of each other. Maybe start again."

Samantha straightened her shoulders. "Start again? What do you mean?"

She didn't know what she meant. If only a relationship was a computer that you could return to factory settings. She wanted a fresh start. A do-over. The opportunity to make different decisions.

Should she admit that she'd started to question everything?

The thought that she might have made a mistake of gigantic proportions was too big to contemplate at that moment. There'd be time for that later, when she was back on her own in her apartment. The apartment she'd designed, along with her life. Turned out a redesign wasn't as easy as it looked.

Samantha opened her mouth, but before she could speak, the door flew open and a woman flew into the room. She was out of breath, as if she'd run all the way here.

It took Gayle a moment to realize it was Ella.

Gone was the long hair, the wild curls that her daughter never bothered to tame. Instead she wore her honey blond hair in a short, choppy, layered cut that ended at her chin. Her navy blue coat flapped open to show a classic wool dress in a shade of cranberry.

A pressure grew in Gayle's chest. *Her baby.* Her Ella. So vulnerable. So kind and giving. A tasty meal for the hyenas of the world to pick on. She'd tried so hard to protect her, and in the end all she'd done was alienate her.

Ella crossed the room to her sister. Samantha met her halfway and they hugged. They stood like that for a moment, wrapped together, a single unit.

Ella pulled away and stroked her sister's coat. "Love that red. You look wonderful."

"Is it too much?"

"What? No! It's perfect. And the white is stunning."

Gayle lay there, listening, superfluous. An outsider in her own family.

Samantha hadn't wanted Gayle's opinion on her outfit, but apparently she wanted her sister's.

She stroked the sleeve. "Well, you know how I hate black."

Samantha hated black?

Gayle wore black. Every day. It was her uniform. She hadn't known Samantha hated it.

Samantha stood back. "I love your hair that length. Suits your face shape. It's better than the bob."

Ella had once had a bob? When?

They talked, words flying to and fro, a verbal game of tennis in which each player knew the rules and was comfortable with each other. Gayle wanted to say *Hello, I'm over here*, but she was too busy registering the change in Samantha.

Gone was the tension, the stiffness, the wariness that had filled the room the moment she'd walked through the door. Instead she was relaxed and comfortable. Warm.

She took Ella's hand and gave her a reassuring smile.

Gayle wondered what it was that required such a visible gesture of support, and then realized it was her. She was the threat in the room.

"Hi, Mom." Ella walked to the bed and gave a nervous smile. "How are you feeling?"

"I've been better. Thank you for coming."

"Of course. I mean, you're our—" Ella paused and then gave a brief smile "—mother. What happened?"

"I fell. I was holding an award." That stupid award. Pride had quite literally come before the fall.

Did they even know about the award? She'd been up there on the stage, applauded by thousands. She'd given a speech on empowerment and designing her life. Her daughters hadn't even known. They weren't impressed. "It hit my head as I fell."

"Right. That's horrible." Ella fiddled with her scarf. "Are they keeping you in?"

"For tonight." Why were both girls still hovering? Were they braced to race through the door if she said something wrong? "Why don't you take off your coat and gloves and sit down?"

"I—gloves? No." Ella wrapped her arms around her waist. "I have—cold hands."

"But it's so hot in this room."

"I'm fine. I'm not hot."

Don't argue, Gayle. Don't argue.

Kind.

"Won't you at least sit down?"

Ella sat without question. She rubbed her hands nervously along her legs. "Have they said when you'll be discharged? Will you need someone to take care of you at home? We should sort something out. But only if you want that, of course."

It was the first moment of brightness in a dark, dark day.

Gayle felt her heart give a little lift.

Ella was going to offer to stay with her. It would give Gayle a chance to try and mend what she'd broken. And maybe Ella would be able to get through to Samantha.

"That's a kind offer. I—"

"I've already called a nursing agency." Samantha glanced at her phone. "My phone was on silent, but they called back a moment ago and left a message."

A nursing agency.

Some uniformed stranger would bring her a glass of water in the night and check she wasn't dead. A transactional arrangement, devoid of care or emotion.

Given the practical way she'd conducted her life up to this point, it shouldn't have bothered her, but it did.

She no longer wanted it to be like this. She wanted people to care. She wanted to have "loved ones."

But she knew that the only one who could change the situation was her.

"Thank you. I appreciate it."

Samantha looked at her, wary. "You asked to see us. Was there a reason?"

She was injured. They were her only family. Wasn't that enough?

No, no it wasn't.

"I wanted to apologize." Up until that moment she hadn't realized that was what she wanted, but she knew it now. She would do whatever it took to fix this situation. And it was true she was sorry for the way things had turned out, even if she wasn't exactly sorry for the way she'd raised them. They didn't know the truth, of course. She hadn't shared that. She'd told them all they needed to know and not a single word more. The rest she'd tucked away inside her, like crumbs under a carpet.

What mattered here wasn't the past, but the future. Today was all about putting the first stitch in the serious tear in the relationship. "I wanted to say I was sorry for what happened last time we were together. I'm sorry I upset you." Gayle desperately wanted a drink of water to moisten her dry throat. She reached for it but Ella was there first, her hands round the cup holding it steady so Gayle could drink.

"There." Ella's voice was gentle. "I presume you are allowed to drink?"

Gayle nodded and sipped, encouraged by her daughter's instinctive move to help her. Maybe there was hope.

Samantha by contrast was tense. Wary.

Gayle knew that if there was to be any chance of reconciliation, it had to be through Ella.

"Tell me about your teaching."

Ella froze. "Oh. Well…" Her gaze flickered to her sister. "I love teaching."

Too late Gayle remembered that she'd promised Samantha that she wouldn't mention Ella's job. But she was being encouraging and positive, so surely that made it all right?

"I'm glad you found something that works for you. But the most important thing is that you stuck at something. That's good, too."

Samantha's eyes narrowed. "Mom—"

"All I'm saying is that I'm sure there have been times when it has been tough. Teaching can be stressful, I'm sure, but here she is, still teaching." What had Samantha said? That Ella didn't feel her mother was proud? "I'm proud of you." She used the exact words. Said them loud and clear. "Proud that you found something you love and stuck with it."

Ella slid a finger around the neck of her dress.

Gayle could see a sheen of sweat on her brow, but still Ella kept her gloves on.

This was painful for everyone. So stiff and unnatural.

Gathering together in this sterile hospital room wasn't anyone's idea of a fun reunion. This place might heal people, but it didn't heal relationships. It didn't fix families.

What should she do? What *could* she do? The only way to convince them of how badly she wanted to fix things was to show them. Prove she was genuine and committed in her intention to heal the rift. And to do that she needed time. How was she going to engineer that?

What excuse could she make for a family gathering that lasted longer than a courtesy hospital visit?

Out of nowhere she thought about that young journalist, Rochelle.

I just love a big family gathering. Massive tree. Gifts in front of the fire.

At the time, Gayle had been typically evasive in her answer, knowing that on Christmas Day she'd be doing what she did every other day of the year. Working. Her girls had always hated that about her. Surrounded by friends whose families had yielded to commercial pressures and expectations, they'd begged her for gifts, for a tree, for a trip to the ice rink, for fairy lights and a snow globe. She'd said no to all of it, of course, because Christmas was a particularly difficult time of year for her. She handled it by working, her goal to block it out and make it seem like any other day. She didn't stare wistfully through other people's windows. She didn't allow herself to feel envious or sad, and she definitely didn't look back. Instead she made a point of focusing on her own life. Working at least had a purpose, which was more than could be said for a snow globe.

But her girls had always loved the time of year and yearned for a kind of magical Christmas they'd somehow invented in their heads.

And suddenly she knew. What better excuse was there for a family gathering than Christmas?

"You're wondering why I asked you to come." She handed the water back to Ella. "I wanted to see you in person because I want us to spend the holidays together this year."

Samantha blinked. "Excuse me?"

"The holidays. Christmas." Gayle focused on Ella. "It was always your favorite time of year. I—I'd like to join you if that's all right. I'll come to your place and we can spend quality time together."

There was a protracted silence.

Gayle could almost feel their shock.

"My place?" Ella's voice sounded squeaky and strange. "You want to come to my place?"

"I don't even know where you're living. Wherever it is, I'm sure it's wonderful. Even when you were young, you made your room cozy. I'm sure you can handle one more for Christmas.

You do have a spare room? If not, I'll sleep on the couch." She was willing to do whatever it took.

"The—couch?" Ella was balanced on the edge of her seat. "You?"

"I've surprised you." The more she thought about it, the prouder Gayle was of her idea. What better way to bond as a family than at Christmas? "But I hope it's a good surprise. You always wanted to make more fuss of the holiday season. Well, let's do it. Let's do it together. Big tree. Gifts in front of the fire. A family Christmas. All the things you used to want. Just the three of us. How does that sound?"

Samantha

"How does that sound? It sounds like the worst idea I've heard in a long time, maybe I've *ever* heard, that's how it sounds." Samantha shouldered the door of their hotel room shut and dropped her bag. They were on a high floor, and through the glass Manhattan was spread before them like a jeweler's window, all glitter and sparkle. Another person might have paused to admire the view, but this city reminded her of her mother. Of ambition. Of *Choice Not Chance*. She closed the drapes. "A family Christmas? Christmas with our mother, who makes Scrooge look like Santa?"

"She wants to come to me!" Ella's eyes were wide and worried. "She can't come to me! I'd have to explain a child and a husband, neither of which she knows about. And he doesn't know, either."

"What?" Samantha whirled round, unable to believe what she was hearing. "You still haven't told Michael? I thought—"

"I was going to, truly, but I've been waiting for the right moment and so far it hasn't shown itself to me."

All her life Ella had avoided conflict, particularly when the source of that conflict was their mother. She made herself small, while Samantha went in for the fight.

But she wasn't prepared to fight for her sister's marriage.

"That's a whole other problem. Your problem. We'll get to that in a minute. I'm still trying to handle the fact that our mother wants to ruin Christmas. What were her exact words? *I'm sure you can handle one more for Christmas.* If I'm having one more of anything for Christmas, it's going to be a big strong drink." Samantha hung up her coat and slid off her shoes.

Ella did the same. "She didn't say she wanted to ruin Christmas. She said she wanted to spend it with us."

"Yeah, and she's always been so great at making Christmas special. I'm remembering the year she told you that there was no Santa. You were four and you cried for two days." Samantha stared at her sister. "Why are you wearing a dress? Are you going for an interview tomorrow or something?"

"I wanted to look like a person who had just sprinted from work."

"You could have just told her you've chosen to be at home raising your child."

"After she said how proud she was that I'd finally stuck at something? I don't think so." Ella removed her gloves and Samantha frowned.

"Since when have you suffered from bad circulation?"

"I don't, but I didn't want to take my wedding ring off. It would feel unlucky."

"Ella, this is impossible! Do you know how hard it was to have a conversation, knowing that I couldn't talk about your marriage, your child or your job?"

"I'm sorry to put you in that position."

"It's unreal. But none of it is as unreal as the thought of spending Christmas with our mother." Samantha unzipped her overnight bag violently. "Can you believe she would even suggest it? After everything that has happened between us? And then there's the fact that she hates Christmas. She must have brain damage. It's the only explanation."

"Don't say that." Ella's forehead had been locked in frown lines since they'd left the hospital. "They're only keeping her in because she was unconscious for such a long time and they're concerned about the bruising on her ribs. And can you keep your voice down? Everyone in this hotel is going to hear you."

"I don't get it. She hates the holidays, works right the way through and always has. She thinks gifts are a waste of time, the whole thing is a commercial racket and the 'family togetherness' thing is designed to give everyone feelings of insecurity and resentment. She doesn't decorate, we never even had a tree—" Samantha forced herself to breathe and calm down. She needed a plan, not a panic attack.

She and Ella adored the holidays. It was their favorite time of year. In fact it had been their love for Christmas that had given Samantha the idea for her business. She'd realized that out there somewhere there had to be people just like them. People who looked forward to the festive season and wanted an extra special magical Christmas. People who would appreciate the Christmas markets of Europe, a cozy chalet in the Swiss Alps, or a visit to Lapland to see Santa and the elves.

She fell backward onto the bed with a groan. "Kill me now."

"No way, because then I'd have to go through this alone, and that's not happening." Ella flopped next to her and they lay, arms touching, bonded by blood and shared experiences as they stared up at the ceiling. "You should have checked in under a fake name. We could have stayed here forever and no one would have been able to find us."

"I think Michael and Tab would have something to say about that."

Ella moaned and covered her face with her hands. "Michael is going to have a lot to say about a lot of things. How do I tell him?"

"If I knew that much about how to sustain a relationship I'd be in one."

"It was just an unfortunate sequence of events. It was after one of Mom's sessions that we met. I was crying on the train station—"

"—and he came and sat with you. I know. It's adorable. And annoying that you can meet The One on a crowded train platform when the rest of us just get bruised ribs."

"He thought the wedding would be the perfect time to heal things, but I couldn't invite her. I just couldn't. He doesn't know our mother the way we do."

"He doesn't know her at all. But you're going to fix that. You have to be honest. What's the alternative? You're going to rent a house and run between your family and our mother? Pretend you're going to work?"

"Thanks for reminding me what a total mess I'm in. What am I going to do?"

"What are *we* going to do? I'm part of this 'family Christmas.'" Samantha stood up. "First we order pizza, then we take a shower, and after that we raid the mini bar." She grabbed her phone and ordered pizza to be delivered.

"I'm not sure I can eat."

"This is the best pizza in New York City. You won't be able to stop yourself. And I cannot strategize on an empty stomach."

"There's something about our mother that makes me too nervous to eat. My stomach is already bloated with panic. But I have to get over that. Maybe it will be okay. She apologized. She actually apologized."

"She did not."

"She did," Ella said. "She used those words. She said, 'I apologize.'"

Samantha pulled out her laptop and put it on the desk next to the TV. "She didn't apologize for what she said. She apologized for upsetting you."

"Same thing."

"It's not the same thing."

"But she was reaching out. Trying to make amends, even if it was in a 'mom' way." Ella sat up, too. "What did you talk about before I arrived?"

"I don't know." The whole thing was a blur. She'd seen her mother lying there and felt so many things she hadn't been able to untangle the emotions. "Nothing. Small talk. Awkward silences. It was pretty hideous."

"I guess it's bound to be awkward after what happened, and after so much time." Ella sat cross-legged on the bed. "What are we going to do? I've been looking forward to Christmas for ages. I have so many plans. It's going to be magical." She slumped. "It *was* going to be magical."

Samantha saw disappointment and desperation and knew she had to do something. "We deal with this one problem at a time. First, we kill her plan. There is no way she is spending Christmas with us. You're not the only one who is looking forward to it."

"I feel guilty saying she can't spend Christmas. It's family time." Ella fiddled with the buttons on her dress. "I know she hurt us, but she is reaching out and trying to make amends. We can't reject that."

"Fine. But we take back control. We will visit again tomorrow as planned, and tell her that we already have plans we can't change, but we can meet her for a celebration dinner in the city if that's what she'd like. I'll book somewhere fancy."

"All right." Ella uncurled her legs. "Keep talking. This is sounding good."

Samantha pulled open the minibar and removed a couple of bottles.

Ella frowned. "I thought the minibar came after the pizza and shower in your plan for the evening?"

"I'm changing the order." Samantha twisted the top off one of the bottles and emptied it into a glass. Normally she wasn't much of a drinker, but it seemed that an embarrassing phone call and an encounter with her mother could change that. "You have to tell Michael the truth before you tell Mom."

"Right. I agree. Any idea how?" Ella's phone rang and she jumped up and grabbed her purse. "That will be him. I feel guilty. Look—my hand is shaking…" She held out her hand as evidence and then dug out her phone.

"Tell him."

"I can't tell him over the phone. This is huge. It has to be in person. I'll tell him as soon as I get home." She answered her phone, a huge smile spreading across her face. "Tab! Hi, sweetheart. I miss you so much. I'm here with Aunty Sam…of course…" Ella thrust the phone at Sam. "Your niece wants to say hi."

Samantha took the phone. How did life get this complicated? "How is my princess…? You slayed the dragon? Well, go you…" She reached out and tugged Ella's hand away from her mouth to stop her biting her nails. "How many sleeps until Christmas?" She kept a tight grip on Ella's hand to stop her ruining her nails. "I am so looking forward to it…yes, you can snuggle in my bed…we will totally read that story about the rabbit in the snow that you love…" As she listened to her niece's excited chatter, she grew steadily more determined not to let their mother ruin the holidays.

They chatted for a bit longer, and then Michael came on the phone and Samantha held it out to her sister.

Ella took it. "Hi, honey… I miss you."

Samantha tried not to listen, but it was hard not to in the confined space.

Ella turned away slightly. "It was upsetting seeing her. I was literally shaking—"

Ella might be secretive about some of the facts in her life, but not about her emotions, Samantha thought. She shared the way she was feeling without hesitation.

"I love you, too," Ella said. "They're keeping her in another night. Is there any chance you could take tomorrow off, too, to be with Tab? I'm sorry. Samantha and I are going to stay another night…"

Samantha grabbed her robe and her nightdress and walked into the bathroom to give her sister some privacy.

Why was Ella worried about telling him? Michael adored Ella. Their relationship was solid.

She secured her hair on top of her head, turned on the shower and stripped off her clothes.

There was a heavy feeling inside her chest.

Envy? No. This was her sister, who she adored. She was pleased she was happy, but still…

Samantha swallowed. She *was* envious. She wanted to be the way Ella was. She wanted to be open about her feelings. She wanted to trust someone with her heart.

Because she didn't want to think about that, she thought about her mother.

Why had she reached out? Was it simply because she'd had an accident and felt vulnerable? Did she want something from them?

Gayle Mitchell's relationship with people tended to be transactional.

Samantha would have felt more comfortable had she understood what the transaction was.

Through the door she could hear Ella and Michael arguing about who loved each other the most.

Love you more…no, I love you more…

Samantha stepped into the shower and let the flow of water drown out the sound. The warmth and fragrance soothed and strengthened her. If she wanted a relationship like her sister's, then the first thing she had to do was try and be as open and honest as her sister.

When she emerged, Ella was sitting on the bed again and her phone was next to her. Her cheeks were glowing. "Michael's going to work from home tomorrow so we can spend another day here. I miss him, but it's nice to have sister time."

Samantha fastened her robe and wrapped her hair in a towel. "Next time let's hope for better circumstances."

"Are you done in the bathroom? I've been thinking—" Ella slid off the bed. "Maybe we *should* invite her for Christmas. She's our mother. What if we're being hard on her?"

"We're being cautious, which is sensible."

"But she did have it tough." Ella paused, her fingers on the buttons of her dress. "I mean our father died, and we were so little—"

"And that was sad, yes, but it happens to people and they somehow manage to move on."

"Now that I have Tab, I sometimes think about it."

Samantha eased the towel off her head. She was only ten months older than her sister, but it felt like a decade. Her sister looked so young it was hard to remember that she was the mother of an almost-five-year-old. "Think about what?"

"How I'd feel if I lost Michael. If it was just me, caring for Tab by myself. Making all the decisions alone."

"Where are you going with this?"

"I don't know. I just— Do you ever wonder what she was like before?"

"Before?"

"Before he died."

"No. Do you?"

"Yes." Ella hung up her dress. "Because big life events can change a person, can't they?"

"I guess."

"And if one big life event can change a person, then so can another."

"Are you suggesting that the accident has somehow changed our mother from ambitious robot, to warm, caring maternal human? Because she had a bang on the head, not a personality transplant. Remember last time? You were devastated."

ONE MORE FOR CHRISTMAS

"I know. But I was pregnant and emotionally unbalanced. I might have overreacted."

Samantha didn't want to think that, because if it was true then it meant she'd overreacted, too. "Did she ever reach out and apologize?"

"She just reached out. And because she did that, I think we should give her a chance."

"Dinner." Samantha took off her robe. "We'll give her the chance to have dinner with us. And forget Christmas. I'm sure she didn't mean it." Samantha frowned. "Are you going to take that shower before the pizza comes?"

Ella was staring at her. "Wow. Is that what you wear to bed?"

"Yes. Why?"

"And Kyle let you break up with him?"

"Kyle didn't have a choice. Also, he has never seen me in this. It's what I wear when I'm alone."

"You wear a sexy nightdress when you're *alone*? With no one to see it?"

"I see it." Samantha draped her wet towel over the rail and scooped her hair up.

"Are you going to tell me what happened with Kyle?"

Samantha thought about that horribly embarrassing phone call. The one good thing about seeing her mother was that the stress of it had temporarily driven everything else from her mind.

But now it was back.

Charlotte, of course, had been desperately contrite when she'd realized what she'd done.

I'm terribly sorry, Sam, I got all mixed up. My thinking is mushy. It's the baby. I think she has sucked my brains out along with the breast milk.

Samantha had reassured her that it didn't matter at all, but whichever way you looked at it Brodie McIntyre now knew more about her sex life and the inner workings of her mind than any person alive. She'd tried reminding herself of her resolution to be more open, but it hadn't made her feel better. She'd never said those things to anyone, and now she'd said them to a stranger.

She cringed as she remembered the moment she'd told him she wanted to have wild, desperate sex. Charlotte kept reassuring her that a man of his advanced years would have heard worse than that in his time, but that didn't make her feel better. She didn't like the fact that there was someone out there who now knew so much about her.

Thank goodness he lived in Scotland so there was no chance of meeting him in the street.

Unfortunately it had ruined her business plans because there was no way they would be using Kinleven now or at any time in the future, and no way she would be meeting Brodie McIntyre. They were going to have to start the search again for a place where clients could indulge their fantasy of a cozy winter in the Scottish Highlands.

Realizing that her sister was still waiting for an answer, she shrugged. "Kyle and I didn't work out."

"Was that the awkward phone call you were talking about? I am going to take that shower, get into my pajamas and you are going to tell me the whole story."

"I don't want to relive it."

"That bad?"

"You have no idea. I basically did all the talking, telling him how the chemistry just wasn't there, and how I wanted passion and sex—I said things I have never said to him before." And her humiliation hadn't faded one little bit.

"You've never said those things to me, either. I didn't know you felt that way. You never talk about your feelings."

"And if this is the way it feels, I'll never be doing it again. Turned out it wasn't Kyle that Charlotte put through on the phone." Samantha told her sister an edited version of the story, trying to deflect attention from the deeper issues.

Ella was laughing so hard it took her a moment to respond.

"So somewhere out there is a hot Scottish guy who knows you want passionate sex."

"Well, he's in his sixties, but that doesn't help. Thank you for your understanding and compassion. Makes me so glad I told you."

Ella wiped her eyes. "Sorry, but it's just such a great story."

Samantha was relieved that Ella wasn't pressing harder to find out more about the things she'd confessed to wanting. "The only good thing is that he lives on a different continent."

"But you can't let one phone call stop you using the place. You have to visit and meet him. Just make sure you're back in time for Christmas. Have you looked him up on the internet? Is there a picture?"

"Of course I haven't looked him up. Am I six years old?"

"I hope you're human. Let's do it." Ella picked up her phone and typed. "Brodie McIntyre. Oh. You're right. He isn't in the first flush of youth. But seventy is the new thirty, didn't you know?"

"I didn't know."

Ella handed the phone back. "I hope all that talk of sex and passion hasn't given him a heart attack."

"Could we stop talking about it?"

"Don't feel bad. You probably cheered him up." Ella walked into the bathroom. "This hotel is amazing by the way! Remind me to steal the mini shampoos. Tab will love them. Why have you closed the drapes? You can see the Empire State Building from the tub. How much is it costing?"

"What?" Samantha rubbed her hand over the back of her neck, still thinking about Brodie McIntyre and Kinleven. The place had looked perfect. Damn. "I don't know what this place is costing. Charlotte booked it. I asked for something central. I adore her, but the way her brain is at the moment we're lucky we didn't end up in Arizona."

"Well, look at you, Miss Tycoon, with your flashy hotels, your fancy glass office and your assistant. You're a real success.

When Mom finds out the detail of how well you've done, she'll be proud." There was a wistful note in her voice that made Sam grind her teeth.

"Success is not about staying in hotels and having a glass office. It's about meeting your own goals." Realizing what she'd said, she eyed her sister.

"*Choice Not Chance*," they chorused together, and Ella snorted.

"Some mornings my goal is simply to manage to use the bathroom without Tab asking me to explain nuclear fission. I miss her so much." Ella stripped off her clothes and filled the bathtub. "But I confess the idea of a deep bubble bath on my own is totally bliss."

Sam checked her emails, only half listening. "You don't have to visit our mother again tomorrow. I can do it. You can go home right after breakfast."

"No." Ella talked to her above the sound of running water. "If we're visiting again, then we're doing it together."

Samantha pushed open the bathroom door. Ella's head was visible above clouds of bubbles.

"I'll deal with it."

"We'll deal with it together. Don't argue because right now I'm going to soak in this tub and switch my brain off." Ella leaned back against the edge of the bath, eyes closed, cheeks pink, hair curling around her face in the steam. "This is bliss. We all need Charlotte in our lives. Is Amy sleeping any better?"

"Judging from the mistakes her mother is making, the answer to that is no." But Samantha smiled. "Even with a soggy brain, I wouldn't be without her."

"My brain was very soggy after I had Tab."

There was a knock on the door and Samantha turned. "That will be the pizza. Hurry up."

By the time Ella emerged from the bath, Samantha had the pizza box open.

They ate, chatted, watched a movie and then settled down for the night.

Ella was talking to Michael again, snuggled under the covers. "Do you miss me?"

Samantha rolled her eyes and slid into one of the two beds. She slathered cream on her face and her hands, switched off the light and tried not to hear her sister's whispered conversation.

They were both exhausted, and yet Ella was still whispering away.

What was it like to love someone so much you'd prioritize a conversation over sleep?

And what if she never found out? What if she wasn't capable of being open enough to have a real, meaningful intimate relationship?

At some point she must have fallen asleep, because when she woke the clock by the bed said it was 7:00 a.m.

Ella was still sleeping soundly.

Samantha rolled onto her side and watched her, remembering all those times they'd shared a bed as young children, keeping each other company in the dark.

"Stop staring at me," Ella murmured. "It's freaky."

"Great. You're awake." Samantha sprang from the bed and grabbed the room service menu. "How do blueberry pancakes sound?"

They chatted easily, shared breakfast, showered and eventually headed across to the hospital.

Their footsteps echoed down the long corridors, and when they reached the room their mother was in, they both paused and looked at each other.

"Dinner," Samantha hissed. "That's all that's on offer."

Ella nodded and pushed open the door, her expression suggesting she was here for major surgery, not for a visit.

Gayle was sitting up in bed.

"You look a little better." Ella walked across the room and

Samantha watched as she kissed their mother dutifully on the cheek.

Did their mother have any idea how anxious they both felt around her?

She was grateful for Ella's warm, generous nature that had her plumping pillows and fussing around with drinks.

And then she realized her sister was fussing because she was nervous.

"Did you get any sleep?"

"A little. It was noisy."

Samantha managed a brief smile. "Hospitals."

"Yes, not much fun."

The awkwardness was back.

They talked about superficial things—the weather, the traffic in Manhattan, whether there was too much construction— and just when Samantha was starting to think their mother had forgotten all about her idea of spending Christmas together, she raised the subject.

"Did you think about what I said? About Christmas? A family gathering?"

Ella sent Samantha a desperate look and she knew this was up to her. Ella would never stand up to their mother. If they didn't want Gayle ruining Christmas, Samantha had to handle this once and for all.

"A family gathering sounds—" Awful? Like the worst possible way to spend a day? Also, supremely awkward given than Ella had more "family" than she'd admitted to. "It sounds interesting. We can't do *actual* Christmas, so we thought dinner in the city would be fun. I'll book somewhere special and we'll get together the week before. Just the three of us."

"Well, of course the three of us. Who else would there be?" Gayle looked confused. "A restaurant isn't what I had in mind. It will be crowded. Noisy. And you can't come up from Boston just for an evening. I thought we could spend some quiet time together, catching up. I'm looking forward to staying with you. I can't wait to see where you're living."

Catching up on what? What they'd all been doing in the five years since they'd fallen out?

"Let's have dinner as our Christmas celebration, and then perhaps we can spend a couple of nights together early in the New Year. Maybe we could go away somewhere."

That suggestion didn't satisfy Gayle, either. "Why can't we spend a couple of nights at Christmas? That's what most families do."

Samantha opened her mouth to say *we're not most families*, and then closed it again.

"We can't do that."

Unfortunately Gayle saw the word *no* as motivation to try a different approach, and try harder.

"Why not?"

Samantha wanted to scream. It wasn't an unusual emotion to have in the company of her mother, but still a hospital wasn't the best place to vent her emotions.

Desperate, she said the first thing that came to mind. "Because we won't be here."

"You're going away?"

"Yes. I have to work." It was the one thing her mother was likely to understand.

"Work?"

"That's my job. My company arranges winter experiences around the holiday season."

It was Gayle's turn to be wide-eyed. "People want that?" The way she said it confirmed to Samantha that her mother's views on the holiday season hadn't changed, and that there was no way they were going to be spending it together.

"Yes, they want that. The holiday season is important to some people."

"They pay you to arrange it?"

"They pay a fortune." Finally Ella joined in. "And Samantha

is so good at what she does. You want sparkling snow, sleigh rides and Santa, she's your woman."

"Sleigh rides? Santa?" It was obvious from Gayle's expression that not only would she not be calling on her daughter's services anytime soon, but she was struggling to understand the mentality and motivation of the people who availed themselves of Samantha's talents.

She turned to Ella. "What about you? You've always been a lover of the holiday season. The two of us could spend it together."

Samantha felt Ella's horror.

Her sister's jaw worked and then a tumble of words emerged. "I won't be around, either. I'm going with Samantha. We thought we'd combine the trip. So we can be together."

Gayle's face brightened. "Well, that's perfect. So the two of you are already together—I'll join you."

"I—we—that's not a good idea."

"I'd like to spend time with you. As long as you don't expect me to wear a reindeer sweater, we'll be fine. Where are you going?"

Ella looked wild-eyed and desperate. "I— Scotland!" The words flew from her lips. "We're going to Scotland. Samantha has to check out its suitability for family gatherings."

What? *What?*

She wanted to slap her hand over Ella's mouth, but it was too late for that and anyway Ella was still talking.

"It's miles away. Long flight. Hazardous drive along snowy roads. It's an old shooting lodge. It will be cold. Bleak. We'll probably be snowed in with a pile of dusty books. The place is isolated." Ella sent Samantha a look of desperate apology and emphasized all the aspects of the trip that she knew their mother would hate in an attempt to recover her mistake. "There will be stags."

Gayle looked dazed. "Stags?"

"With antlers."

"Inside the shooting lodge?"

"I hope not actually inside, but—have you seen the size of those things? Terrifying." Ella was scratching the back of her head, a sure sign that she was nervous.

"Scotland. That's—" Gayle shook her head. "No. I can't do it. I can't go back."

"Oh *shame*." Ella didn't quite manage to hide her relief. "Well, never mind. We'll meet up for lunch a few times instead."

Samantha was watching her mother. "What do you mean, you can't go back? I didn't know you'd been to Scotland."

Gayle was staring into space.

"Mom?"

"Mmm?"

"Scotland. When were you in Scotland?"

Gayle shifted in the bed. "It was a long time ago."

"Well, if you've been, you probably don't want to go again," Ella said, "and that's *fine*. We understand. And we can have a celebration without it being Christmas. Samantha will pick a great restaurant, and we can—"

"Maybe it's time."

"Time for what?" Ella looked at her sister for clarification. "Time for what, Mom?"

"Time to go back to Scotland."

"No! I mean—don't put that pressure on yourself. If you fancied a return visit, summer might be better."

"No." Gayle gripped the bedcovers. Took a breath. "I'll come with you."

Samantha still couldn't think of a time when her mother had been to Scotland. "Did you go when you were a child?"

"What? No. It's fine. It will be fine."

If Samantha hadn't known better, she would have said her mother was nervous. "Where did you stay?"

"It doesn't matter." Gayle sat up straighter, some of her usual spirit returning. "That's all in the past. The place you describe sounds charming. And if you're exploring its suitability for family gatherings, what better way to do it than with your family? I'm coming. No more doubt or discussion."

For the first time in her life, Samantha wanted to kill her sister. She glanced at her and saw that Ella was crumpled by guilt.

"That's not—I don't think—" she gulped "—you can't come, Mom."

"If it's the money that's worrying you, I'll pay. I'll pay for both of you."

"It's not the money. It's—"

"Hello? Can I come in?" A deep male voice interrupted them, and Samantha and Ella spun round together to see a familiar figure standing in the doorway.

Samantha managed not to groan aloud. Was it possible for today to get any worse?

Ella gave a whimper. "Michael?"

He gave a lopsided smile. "Instead of calling again, I thought I'd come in person."

"Why?" Ella's voice was a squeak.

"You said you missed me. I wanted to be here to support you. I'm your husband, and that's what husbands do."

There was a tense silence.

Michael was the only one smiling.

"Husband?" Gayle's voice sounded thin and stretched. "You have a husband? You're married?"

"I—yes—" Ella looked so traumatized Samantha forgot that a moment before she'd wanted to kill her and took a step forward.

"Five years is a long time, Mom. Things have happened—"

Gayle wasn't listening. She was staring at her younger daughter with laser focus.

"Married. When? Why didn't you tell me?"

"Your mother doesn't know?" Michael, smile gone, glanced from Gayle to Ella.

Ella looked in desperation at Samantha.

This, she thought, *was why people shouldn't keep secrets.*

Before anyone could find a way to extract themselves from what was possibly the most awkward situation they'd ever encountered, a small figure pushed its way around Michael's legs.

Holding tightly to her father's hand, Tab surveyed the room, caught sight of her aunt and then Ella and a broad smile spread across her face.

Before Michael could stop her, she sprinted across to her mother, coat flapping, hair flying, giving Ella no choice but to swing her up in her arms.

"Hi there, bunny." Ella buried her face in her daughter's coat, presumably to take respite from a sea of stunned expressions.

"Ow, you're squeezing me. We missed you! I made your friend a card!" Tab thrust a creased card at Ella, showering the hospital floor with glitter. From the safety of her mother's embrace, she studied the woman in the bed. "I made you a card."

"Yes." Gayle sounded faint. "I see that."

Tab looked concerned. "Do you hurt? People usually stay in the hospital when they hurt."

Gayle floundered. "Yes," she said finally. "I do hurt. A little."

Tab turned to Ella, confident that she could fix this. "Mommy, kiss it better."

Samantha could have sworn Gayle made a gulping sound.

"Mommy? *Mommy?*"

"This is my mommy, and that is my daddy." Helpfully Tab gestured toward Michael, who hadn't moved from the doorway. He appeared to have turned to stone. Unimpressed by the lack of engagement from the adults around her, Tab turned back to Gayle. "My name is Tabitha Melody Gray, and I'm four and three-quarters. And I don't know your name or who you are."

There was a taut, agonizing silence and then Gayle finally spoke.

"My name is Gayle. And I think," she said faintly, "that I must be your grandmother."

Ella

"All this time we've been together, and your mother didn't know?" Michael spoke in an undertone, but that didn't conceal the steely note in his voice.

"Why did you say Scotland?" Samantha was pacing like a predator caged in a zoo.

"Mommy—" Tab tugged at her coat "—can I have this dollhouse for Christmas?"

They'd escaped from the cold into a toy store on Fifth Avenue, and Ella was fighting a temptation to crawl into the oversize dollhouse along with her daughter and never emerge. But there was no hiding from this. She needed to apologize to her sister and have the conversation with Michael. The conversation that was five years overdue.

But she didn't need her daughter to hear any of it.

Maternal responsibility took over.

She gave Tab a bright smile. The ability to produce a smile when life was collapsing seemed to have been born along with the baby. "Is there a kitchen inside that house? Go and see if there's a kitchen."

Tab didn't budge. "I don't want a kitchen I want a library."

"Then go and see if there's a library."

"I want you to come, too."

"I'll be there just as soon as I've talked to Daddy and Aunty Sam."

"I want to talk to them, too."

"But we're talking about Christmas." Ella gave her daughter a conspiratorial look and ushered her over to the dollhouse where Tab was immediately distracted by the delights of the miniature home.

Satisfied that her daughter's attention was elsewhere, Ella turned back to her husband.

Michael was looking at her with confusion. "She didn't even know you were married?"

Ella rubbed a hand over her churning stomach. "The wedding was our day. Our special day. If she'd come, she would have ruined it, the way she has always ruined and diminished every choice I've made that wasn't hers."

It was up to her to help Michael understand, but how?

She couldn't tell him that she'd been anxious Gayle would somehow have found a way to stop her wedding, the way she'd managed to use the weapon of disapproval to destroy so many of Ella's passions in the past.

Why are you wasting your time knitting? Get a well-paying job and buy a sweater instead.

"But still, you let me think—" Michael rubbed his fingers across his forehead. "I thought she had chosen not to be in our lives. I thought she had refused to come to the wedding— I didn't know you hadn't invited her."

"The last time I saw her she was relieved I finally had a job. She was afraid I was going to give it up, the way I'd given up other things." Ella moved a little farther from the dollhouse and lowered her voice. "Do you have any idea how she would have reacted if I'd also told her I was pregnant and getting married?"

Michael straightened. "I would have taken responsibility."

Ella sighed. "Michael, this isn't the eighteenth century. That isn't what I'm talking about. She thinks marriage is the worst decision a woman can make."

Michael looked at Samantha, who shrugged.

"She's not wrong. Our mother has serious issues when it comes to romantic relationships. Luckily for you, Ella doesn't seem to have inherited those."

"Issues? Because your father died so young?"

"I suppose so. She doesn't talk about it." Samantha was watching Tab out of the corner of her eye. "Or maybe we didn't talk about it because we didn't get a good reaction when we did. But she was adamant that we should always be financially independent. It's almost a phobia for her. She wanted us to go into what she saw as 'safe,' high-earning professions. Law. Medicine. Business."

And the more their mother had pushed, the faster Ella had retreated. She'd known it was wrong for her.

"Can you see me as a lawyer?" She was relieved to see Michael smile.

"No," he said. "I can't. You'd hate it."

He knew so much more about her than her own mother did.

"Also, if you'd been a lawyer it would have deprived the teaching profession of the best teacher who ever trained." He held out his hand. "Come here."

She felt a rush of emotion. "You're not angry?"

"A little hurt, maybe, that you didn't feel able to tell me the truth."

"Oh Michael—" She went into his arms and leaned on him, wrapped, warm, safe. "I was afraid you wouldn't understand."

"I don't have to understand everything about you to love you."

Could he really love the wet, pathetic creature she became around her mother?

Ella closed her eyes and pushed that thought away. Despite everything that was happening with her mother, in that moment she felt something close to perfect happiness. She had the things that mattered most in her life. Tab. Michael. Also, her sister.

Her sister.

For a moment she'd totally forgotten her sister.

At that moment she registered the rhythmic tapping of Samantha's foot on the floor.

Still holding on to the front of Michael's coat, Ella turned and faced her.

Samantha unwrapped her scarf from her neck. "While I'm touched and heartened that you two seem to have been able to push past your personal issues so quickly, it doesn't change the fact that at the moment we appear to be spending Christmas in Scotland with our mother." She unbuttoned her coat. "I'm not sure which part of that sentence is giving me hot flashes. The Scottish part, or the mother part."

Michael stepped to one side as two overenthusiastic children charged past him, closely followed by their apologetic father who clearly hadn't mastered the art of parental control.

"Because your mother didn't make a fuss about Christmas? It seems she was pretty firm with you when you were growing up, so maybe she responds to that level of directness."

Ella's insides lurched and she pulled away from him. "Can we be realistic here? Arguing with our mother is a blood sport, and I'm not into blood sports. I carry spiders outside. I can't fight with her."

"You don't need to fight with her, just be firm." He pulled her back, keeping her locked against him. "And you're not doing it alone. This time you have me."

Samantha gave a grunt and rolled her eyes. "I've been wondering what to buy you for Christmas and now I know—a suit of shining armor."

"Let her know that if she is spending Christmas with us, she has to observe our rules."

Samantha raised her eyebrows. "Spoken like a lawyer. Are you suggesting we draw up a contract? *I agree to not frown or utter a word of disapproval when I see fairy lights?*"

"She wouldn't be able to do it," Ella said. "Even if you made her sign something. Christmas is a feeling, isn't it? And she doesn't have those feelings."

"You're forgetting one thing..." Michael looked at the doll-house, where Tab was currently moving furniture around to make room for a library. "She has a granddaughter."

"Don't think that will soften her," Ella said. "She does not find young children enchanting or delightful. Christmas didn't happen in our house. Samantha and I used to have our own mini Christmas in my bedroom. Remember the twig tree?"

Samantha smiled for the first time since they'd left the hotel room that morning. "Of course."

"Mom wouldn't have a tree in the house," Ella said, "so Samantha crept into the yard next door and picked up the trimmings from their tree. Theirs was too big for the apartment, so they'd chopped off branches and left them lying around. Samantha picked them all up and used wire to fix them together. Then she decorated it. That was our tree. It was the best tree."

Michael was still. "You never told me this story. What did you decorate it with?"

The two women exchanged glances.

"Mom's earrings," Ella said. "We borrowed them."

"Earrings? Very creative."

"It was, but the point we are making is that even if our mother genuinely wanted to enter into the spirit of things, she wouldn't know how. She doesn't know how to do Christmas."

"We could teach her." Tab appeared without warning. "You

always say you can learn anything if you try. We can teach her how to do Christmas. I've read about grandmothers in stories, and they seem like a fun thing to have."

"Tab—"

"I've never had a grandmother. I think I'd like one. For Christmas." She pirouetted back to the dollhouse leaving Ella staring after her, frustrated with herself and more confused than she'd been in her life before.

"How much did she hear? Did we say something we shouldn't have said? I forget that she seems to have ears out on stalks. Now I feel bad. I've deprived her of a grandmother."

"You deprived her of a whole lot of heartache and stress. Also, she still believes in Santa," Samantha said. "One day she'll thank you for it."

She didn't blame Samantha for being wary. She was wary, too. But she was also conflicted.

"It would be awful if this was a genuine attempt to heal what happened in the past and move on, and we ignored it." She watched as Tab rearranged the beds in the dollhouse. "Maybe we should try a family Christmas."

"We're having a family Christmas," Samantha said, "just without certain members of the family present. If you invite our mother, it will be just like all the other times."

"But it won't," Ella said, "because Michael and Tab will be there."

Michael nodded. "Also, we'll be on neutral territory."

"Which brings us back to the reason I want to kill you," Samantha said. "Scotland. Why did you mention Scotland?"

"Because you'd been telling me about it, I suppose, and also because I was trying to put her off wanting to spend Christmas with us. You know she never takes time off over the holidays. I thought mentioning Scotland would be enough to have her running for the hills. Not the Scottish hills," Ella added weakly, before she was silenced by her sister's scowl.

"I was telling you that I wouldn't be going to Scotland now, or at any point in the future."

Ella was fascinated by the way Samantha managed to yell without raising her voice.

She glanced across to Tab, only to see she'd wandered to the shelves and was examining dollhouse furniture.

"Okay I shouldn't have said it. I admit it, but it was the first thing that came into my head. And I had no idea she'd say yes. She didn't at first—but then for some reason she changed her mind."

"Yes." Samantha frowned. "I didn't know she'd been to Scotland before. Did you?"

"No. And that isn't really relevant. It's now that matters."

"But—" Samantha shook her head. "Never mind. Forget it. It doesn't matter what happened, or what she thinks—we're not going to Scotland. If you recall, I said there was no way I could ever visit after I had phone sex with the owner."

Ella winced. "Small ears hearing everything—do not say the s word or I am going to have to answer a whole lot of awkward questions I don't want to have to answer for a few years yet."

Michael opened his mouth and Samantha silenced him with a stare.

"Don't ask."

There was laughter in his eyes. "Not saying a word."

"My assistant was confused. She put the wrong person through on the phone. I thought I was talking to someone else."

Michael rubbed his hand across his jaw. "It happens."

Samantha's eyes narrowed. "Are you laughing? Because if you're laughing, I'm going to have to kill you."

He pressed his hand to his chest. "Not laughing."

Ella had never seen her sister so uncomfortable. "She'll tell you about it over a bottle of whiskey when we're in Scotland."

"We're not going to Scotland," Samantha said. "And you

could buy a distillery and I would still never repeat a word of that conversation to Michael."

"But think about it. This could be perfect." Ella's mind was working. "You said the place was exactly right for your clients. You wanted to check it out. You *were* going to check it out until you totally humiliated yourself with the owner—"

"Thanks for the reminder—"

"But are you really going to let this perfect place, a place that could be the jewel in your Christmas crown, slip from your fingers just because you are embarrassed?"

Samantha tilted her head to one side. "Yes," she said. "That's a pretty accurate summary of my current strategy."

Ella couldn't believe this was her sister talking. Her sister, who had such great instincts when it came to her business. Her sister who, unlike her, was never afraid to stand up for what she wanted. "But don't you see? If we all come, then it won't be embarrassing."

"Not following your logic there. The phone call still happened. And all of you being there just provides witnesses to further embarrassment."

"You can brazen it out. Don't tell me a guy in his sixties has never weathered an embarrassing moment before." Ella warmed to her theme. "Imagine how perfect it could be. They want to sell a perfect Christmas. No one is a better judge of their skills than us." Ella had a mental image of a cozy living room with plaid and soaring sofas. She imagined sitting with Michael snuggled on a window seat overlooking the loch, sipping champagne while Tab slept safely tucked up in their room upstairs. "Think about it! Whiskey in front of a roaring log fire, Scottish gin tasting—"

"Forget tasting. I'm going to need all the gin and all the whiskey if we do this." Samantha sighed. "Everything inside me is shrieking that this is a mistake."

"The worst that happens is that you don't like the place and decide not to use it for clients."

Samantha looked at her in disbelief. "Ella, that is not the worst thing that can happen." She turned to Michael. "Talk sense into her. Tell her this isn't a good idea."

He shook his head. "I have always wanted to visit Scotland. I have two weeks' vacation booked. It sounds perfect to me."

Ella took his hand, suddenly excited. "Maybe this will work. Mom might be on her best behavior if Michael is there."

"Why? What difference will he make? He is a physical representation of your terrible decisions."

"Thanks." Michael's tone was dry. "I handle difficult people every day in my work. I'm sure I can handle your mother."

"Overconfidence is never a good thing," Samantha said darkly.

"She invited us to her place for tea once she's out of the hospital," Michael said, "so let's start with that and see how it goes from there."

"Ironic, really, that our mother is pushing us to make what will probably turn out to be the worst decision we've ever made." Samantha watched as Tab picked up a wand and waved it in their direction.

"*Macadamia,*" she announced in a forceful tone. "I'm making a wish."

"I think you mean abracadabra," Ella said. "What are you wishing for?"

"I want to spend Christmas with Nanna."

"You don't know your nanna." It felt so strange using that name. It conjured up thoughts of a kindly woman who handed out cookies. Ella couldn't square that image with her mother.

"If I spend Christmas with her, I'll know her." Ever logical, Tab waved the wand.

Gayle

Gayle stood in the middle of the toy store, overwhelmed by a sudden attack of dizziness. The doctor had said such moments were to be expected, and that full recovery would take time.

So frustrating, although on the positive side her accident had given her the excuse she needed to cancel her book tour. The promotion for *Brave New You* would take place without her, which was a relief because right now she wasn't feeling at all brave.

What made you write this book, Ms. Mitchell?

Hubris.

Perhaps it had been foolish to leave the apartment so soon after her discharge from the hospital. But her apartment had little in it to entertain a child, and she'd felt an urgent need to change that.

She had a granddaughter.

A granddaughter!

She was a grandmother.

It was an unexpected gift, and she knew, without any doubt,

that the way she handled this situation was key to any future relationship she had with her daughters. She wasn't going to show that she was hurt that Ella hadn't told her, although she *was* hurt. She wasn't going to question why she hadn't been told, why she hadn't been invited to the wedding, why they had never apologized for the things they'd said to her on that horrible day. Accusations would bring that door crashing closed again, with her on one side and her daughters on the other. She wanted the door kept open. She wanted to step through it and move forward, and if that meant leaving the past behind then that was what she'd do. She didn't have to be right. She had to be forgiving. Accepting. She could do it.

Brave New You.

She'd written about change for other people. Surely she could do it for herself?

It would be hard, but she'd dealt with harder. And the knowledge that she had a granddaughter made her all the more determined.

"Gingerbread cookie?" A store assistant dressed as an elf hovered in front of her, holding a tray heaped with gingerbread men.

The scent of warm gingerbread took her right back to her childhood, and for a moment she felt as if she was right there, standing side by side with her mother.

Can I have one, Mommy?

Of course you can. The best girl in the world deserves a treat.

The memory ripped at her insides, leaving her torn and vulnerable.

She never thought about that time. Being in this place, where her mother had once brought her, opened wounds she'd thought were long since healed.

"Thank you, no." She forced the words through stiff lips. "I'm not hungry."

But still she could imagine the flavor. The sugary sweetness. The melting softness of the gingerbread as she bit into it. Her mother laughing as she brushed sugar from her lips and pulled Gayle into a tight hug.

Gayle swayed a little, rocked by a past long forgotten. She made a point of always looking forward, but right now the world was conspiring to make her look back.

"Are you feeling okay?" The young woman frowned at her. "You look a bit pale. Is it the crowds? I can't believe the number of people who descend on New York for the holidays, can you? Total crush out there."

"There are a lot of people." To distract herself, Gayle focused on the woman in front of her. An elf? Utterly ridiculous. On the other hand she looked as if she might have exactly the expertise that Gayle needed to handle her current situation.

"No to gingerbread, thank you. But I'd appreciate help. I need to buy—" What did she need to buy? She had no idea. "Things."

"Things?"

"For Christmas." A small group of children barreled past her, thoroughly overexcited, and Gayle moved to one side. The air was filled with the scent of cinnamon and the sound of piped Christmas music. She was surrounded by a swirl of color and activity—rotating mobiles, brightly lit snowflakes hanging from the roof, a shop assistant demonstrating a paper plane, a keyboard playing with no human assistance. It was an assault on Gayle's senses and oversensitive head. "For the holidays."

She held on to the nearest shelf for support. This was a bad idea. She should have done an online shop and trusted her instincts.

But when it came to celebrating the holidays, she had no instincts.

"You mean gifts? If you tell me the ages and their interests, I'll be happy to help. Lucy? Can you take these?" The woman called to another passing elf and handed her tray of cookies over. "I'm with a customer. Thanks." Having offloaded her baked goods, she turned back to Gayle. "I'm Stacy, and it's my pleasure to help you today. And we have just about everything a child could want right here." The girl swept her arm through the air and Gayle followed the trajectory, dazzled by a kaleidoscope of fairy lights, decorations, toys and trees in vibrant colors that sparkled with glitter. Everything was so *bright*.

She was grateful for Stacy's enthusiasm. The girl didn't seem daunted, but that was probably because she had no clue as to the size of the task that lay ahead.

Gayle didn't only want gifts. She wanted proof that she could "do" Christmas and do it well. She had no idea where to start, and not knowing unsettled her. She was used to feeling in control and competent. Used to people turning to her for advice.

When it came to creating a festive feeling, she was a novice. But she could learn, couldn't she? Decorations would be the perfect way to make her apartment more child friendly without actually remodeling the place.

What had Ella always asked for as a child?

A tree. She'd wanted to go and choose a real one, and drag it home along snow-covered streets, a fantasy stimulated by watching too many Christmas movies. She'd wanted a magical Christmas. In Gayle's opinion magical Christmases existed only in the mind. The real thing not only cost a fortune, but also rarely lived up to expectations. And if it did, then it made it harder to handle the harsh reality of real life when it finally poked its ugly head through the glitter.

Gayle had never let her children believe in Santa.

Samantha had been furious when she'd sat Ella down and told her the truth.

Why did you have to do that? Why do you have to spoil everything that's fun?

Gayle had been unapologetic. She didn't believe in raising a child to believe in fantasy, when the real world was so far from magical.

But now she had to give herself to the fantasy. It was probably ridiculous to be decorating her apartment just for a couple of hours while her granddaughter visited, but she didn't care. This wasn't about tea; it was an investment in the future. She wanted Tabitha to be enchanted. She wanted her daughters to see that she was capable of change.

A tree would form the centerpiece.

Gayle had never bought a Christmas tree. Money had been so tight when the girls were young that it had felt profligate to throw hard-earned cash away on something so commercial. She'd put the money into their college fund instead and been terrified by how little she had and how much was needed. It was like filling a swimming pool, one small drop of water at a time. She'd made sure not a single cent was wasted. What was the point of toys that would be discarded after a few days? Instead she'd bought books, and activities that she'd believed would help them through life.

But this time she didn't have to worry about that.

She didn't have to worry about college funds, or how she was going to pay rent and buy food at the same time. She was in the fortunate position to be able to spend money without worrying too much about the future. And she wasn't concerned about Tabitha's expectations, because those were not her responsibility. She had parents for that.

What Gayle lacked wasn't funds or focus, it was knowledge.

"I want to decorate. For the holidays. I need a tree."

"Of course. Do you have a tree you already use from previous years?"

"No."

"You usually have a fresh tree? I love fresh trees. My mother complains about the needles dropping onto the floor, but I always think that just makes it seem more like being in a forest. And the scent when you walk into a room—well, that just makes clearing up the needles worthwhile." Stacy's enthusiasm was as bright and glowing as the decorations in the store. "Of course if you'd rather not clean up the needles, our biggest seller is the beautiful prelit pine tree, that comes with 220 multicolored lights, and it's scented."

Gayle was dragged from a distant memory of a fresh tree with spiky needles and a woody smell.

"A fake tree with fake scent?"

"That's right." The girl beamed. "These days you can buy pretty much anything."

Even your family?

Gayle managed not to ask that question aloud. She didn't even want to think it. She wasn't buying them. She was showing them that she was capable of being the person they needed her to be. This was no different to a doctor splinting a leg to offer protection while the bone healed by itself. The tree and the gifts would be the splint that held her family together long enough for it to heal.

She'd buy a fake tree, because she had no idea what to do with a real one. But she'd make it look as real as possible.

She wandered between them and selected one that looked most like the real thing. "This one."

"Would you like it with multicolored lights?"

"No, clear lights."

"Snow covered or plain?"

Children liked the idea of snow, didn't they? "Snow covered."

"Rotating?"

"Excuse me?"

"Would you like a tree that rotates?"

Her world was already rotating. "I'd like a tree that sits in the corner and behaves like a tree."

"Right. So clear lights, snow covered, nonrotating. Sounds good. I wish everyone was as good at making decisions as you." The girl made a note on the tablet she was holding. "Do you have enough decorations?"

Gayle leaned on a shelf of children's books. Her head was

throbbing. "I probably need to buy a few." Why not just confess that she had none? Since when had she cared about being judged? The feeling coincided with being beaned by an ugly award.

By the time they'd finished selecting decorations, Gayle had decision fatigue. And she hadn't even started on gifts yet. How did people do this every year?

Feeling humble and insecure, she touched the girl's arm. "I need help with gifts. For a little girl."

"Age?"

"I—" How old was Tab? What had she said in the hospital room? Four and three-quarters. "She must have been pregnant when I saw her." Gayle clutched Stacy's arm. "Was that what she wanted to talk to me about?"

"Er—excuse me?" Stacy looked bemused.

"Nothing. Never mind." Gayle let go of the girl's arm. "She's almost five years old."

Was that the reason Ella had married? She'd been pregnant?

"Are you okay?" The girl peered at her. "You look pale, and you seem a little unsteady."

"I've not been feeling too well. I had an accident. I've been in the hospital." What was wrong with her? She never admitted weakness, and she'd just done it to a stranger. She, who had never looked for sympathy in her life, was now soaking it up like a sponge.

"Oh poor you." Stacy ushered her to a chair. "Sit here, and I'm going to bring you a selection of toys. Is she a relative?"

"My granddaughter." Gayle saw shock in the girl's eyes. "I met her for the first time recently. We—"

"They live a long way away? It happens. My sister is on the West Coast and I miss her every day." The girl squeezed her arm. "We're going to give your granddaughter a Christmas she is never going to forget."

Gayle didn't mention that these preparations weren't for

Christmas itself. If she didn't pass the test during their tea, she wouldn't be spending Christmas with her family.

And maybe that would be for the best.

Scotland.

Why did it have to be Scotland?

They didn't know, of course. They didn't know any of it. They'd expected her to be put off by the distance, but if Gayle were to be put off by anything, it would be the memories, not the miles.

How would it feel being back there? Would she be able to handle it?

Her insides quivered and she straightened her shoulders.

Of course she could handle it. She could handle anything.

And maybe facing the past would help her make the changes she needed to make.

Her girls didn't need to know the details.

She'd protected them and she'd carry on protecting them, because that was what a mother did.

She watched as Stacy pulled boxes from shelves, gradually filling the shopping cart to the brim. Gayle tried not to think about the cost. It wasn't about wasting money on the holiday season, it was about spending money to make her granddaughter happy.

"Now to gifts."

"Yes." Gayle waited for all her insufficiencies to be exposed. "I'd like to buy her a range of things."

An older woman turned to smile at her. "I'm the same. If you can't spoil your grandchildren at Christmas, when can you spoil them?"

Sensing a source of reliable information and advice, Gayle leaned forward. "How many do you have?"

"Three. Two boys and a girl. My husband teases me because I buy so much for them, and in the end do you know what they play with most of the time?"

Gayle didn't even attempt a guess. "No."

"The dog."

"The dog?"

"Hamish. He's nine and half-blind. He's a rescue and no one is too sure what breed he is, but those kids love him."

Gayle's smile slipped.

Was she going to have to get a dog to win over her granddaughter's heart? She thought about it. A puppy, lolloping around her apartment. A puppy, chewing her furniture. Worst of all, a puppy relying on her for everything.

A sudden chill washed over her. She didn't want anything or anyone relying on her. She didn't want to carry that weight ever again.

On the other hand she did want her granddaughter in her life.

She winced. No need to buy a puppy at this stage. It was tea—that was all. A visit.

"Apart from playing with the dog, what else does your granddaughter enjoy?"

"Dressing up, painting—" the woman waved a hand "—pretty much anything. She's a good girl. And she loves doing things with her nanna."

"Things?"

"We bake together."

"You mean cakes?" Gayle rarely ate cake and she hadn't baked one since childhood. "Your granddaughter enjoys that?"

"Loves it. It's cozy, isn't it? Companionable."

"Is it?" A wisp of a memory uncurled itself from the depths of Gayle's brain. Her mother's hand on hers, helping her to sift flour.

"Yes. It's something we're doing together. Just the two of us. It's a chance to chat. Oh, the things she tells me while she's stirring cake mixture."

"Right." Gayle had a sudden image of her new life. It involved puppy training, cookery classes and a little girl who had interesting things to say.

Tea, she reminded herself. *They were coming for tea—that was all.*

Going over-the-top would be as bad as doing nothing.

The woman was still talking. "My granddaughter's favorite thing of all? A trip, just the two of us. We go to the ballet to see *The Nutcracker*. Have you seen it?"

"I can't say I have."

"You're missing out. You should do it."

Gayle made a noncommittal sound. The way things were with her girls, she was unlikely to be allowed to take her granddaughter out unattended. She still wasn't entirely confident they'd actually turn up for tea.

She watched as the woman selected a shimmering mermaid outfit. "Is she going to like that?"

"Like it?" The woman laughed. "I'm guessing she won't take it off for the whole holidays."

Gayle glanced at Stacy, who was still pulling boxes from the shelves. "I'll have one, too."

Stacy added it to the pile.

By the time they reached the checkout, Gayle was feeling dizzier than she had when she'd first stepped into the store.

"Would you like any of these presents gift wrapped?"

"Please. All of them. Apart from the tree, obviously." She paused. "You really are excellent at sales. You should consider doing something more with that talent."

Stacy stared at her. "More?"

"You could work your way up, I'm sure."

"Thank you for the compliment, but I love my job." Stacy scanned the gifts. "Promotion would mean being locked away in a back office somewhere, and I'd hate that. I love being out here amongst the action. And I just love the kids. Why would I want to change that?"

Why indeed? Gayle no longer had the confidence to answer that question.

She left the store, assured by Stacy that her parcels would be delivered within the next couple of hours.

She let herself into her apartment and paused, struck by the oppressive silence. Normally she treasured the quiet of her apartment, so why did today feel different? She had a sudden urge to rush back out onto the street so that she could soak up the atmosphere.

Was she really missing the cacophony of piped Christmas music? The shrieks of children whose parents were struggling to keep them under control?

She felt isolated and removed from a world where everyone seemed to be enjoying themselves.

She was Scrooge, only without the unfortunate nightwear.

This time of year had never affected her before. She'd never been the type to peep through the window of other people's lives and envy them. She'd been too busy building her own.

The conviction that she'd made all the wrong choices hadn't gone away as she'd slowly started to recover. If anything, it had grown stronger.

She poured herself a glass of water and drank it slowly. Her phone told her that she'd had twenty-four missed calls from the office, but she felt no urgency to return any of them.

Why was that?

Maybe for the same reason she'd just spent a fortune in a toy store.

She was floating in a strange place between her old life and a new life.

By the time the delivery arrived from the toy store, she'd recovered a little, which was just as well, because the bags and boxes kept coming until her apartment was piled high.

Had she really ordered so much? What was she going to do with it all when tea was over? What if they didn't want to spend Christmas with her, despite her efforts to show them she could change?

She stared at the bags and boxes, wondering where to start. Fortunately she'd never been afraid of hard work.

The tree. She'd start with the tree.

Rolling up her sleeves, she started work and she worked for four hours straight, pausing once to eat a yogurt from the fridge.

Finally she was finished, and she stared in wonder at her transformed apartment. The acres of glass which usually gave a minimalist feel, now reflected all the tiny lights she'd strung around her bookshelves and the tree itself. Under the tree were stacks of gifts in all shapes and sizes, wrapped in shiny paper and tied with bows.

Gayle collapsed onto the sofa, exhausted but satisfied.

Who said she couldn't do Christmas? This, hopefully, would be all the evidence Samantha and Eleanor would need to see that she was genuine in her desire to spend the holidays with them.

There would be no recriminations. No mentions of the past. At least, not from her.

She was going to focus on the present and the future.

Her granddaughter.

Nerves fluttered in her stomach. Had she done enough?

There was just one more thing she needed to do.

Ignoring the throb in her head, she reached for her laptop.

Samantha

"Will there be cake?" Tab danced along, joyous, hand in hand with Ella and Michael as they crossed the street.

"Unlikely." It was Ella who answered.

"Cookies?"

"Equally unlikely."

"Nanna doesn't eat?"

"She doesn't eat sweet things."

"Why?"

"Because not everyone does."

"Why don't they?"

Back and forth, back and forth, like a game of tennis. What? Why? When? How?

Samantha listened in awe as Ella tried tactfully to prepare Tab for the reality of tea with their mother. Where did her sister find her patience? Samantha adored Tab, but after five minutes of question tennis, she was done.

Enough, she wanted to yell. *Time-out.*

Her own deficiencies in patience made her wonder if perhaps she wasn't cut out to be a mother. Did she even want children?

Ella was still talking to Tab. "Nanna's apartment isn't designed for children, so you have to be very good and very careful. No running around. No hiding."

"Why?"

"Because you might break something."

"Would that make her angry and shouty?"

Ella shook her head. "No. Nanna doesn't get angry. I've never heard her shout."

Michael was quiet, and Samantha wondered what he was thinking. This whole situation must be strange for him, too.

The conversation continued, back and forth until they reached the apartment building where Gayle now lived.

Samantha glanced at her sister and Ella gave her a weak smile. They were both thinking the same thing. That the last time they'd come here, the visit hadn't ended well.

At some point they were going to have to discuss it. An explosion that big, particularly one that had caused a major rift in family relations, couldn't be ignored forever.

Tabitha craned her neck, looking at the entrance of Central Park. "Can we go for a ride in the horse carriage?"

"No."

"Why not?"

"Because that's for tourists."

"What's a tourist?"

"Someone who doesn't live here but comes for a visit."

"We don't live here."

Samantha wondered how her sister wasn't crushed with exhaustion. Tab's questions were endless, but so was her enthusiasm and her charm, fully on display as she delivered a megawatt smile to the doorman.

"I'm visiting my grandmother."

"And where does your grandmother live?" He played his

part well, and moments later they were standing outside Gayle's apartment.

"Remember what I said," Ella muttered in an undertone. "Don't touch anything."

Tab was almost vibrating with excitement, the gift she'd insisted on wrapping herself clutched to her chest. "Will there be a Christmas tree?"

"No. Nanna doesn't really celebrate the holidays."

"Why not?"

Good question, Samantha thought. *Because she considers it frivolous and a waste of time and money.*

Ella was more tactful. "Not everyone does, and there are many different reasons."

"We could buy her a tree."

Before Ella could answer, the door opened and Gayle stood there. Dressed all in black, she looked thin and a little more drawn than usual.

Samantha frowned. "Are you all right, Mom?"

"Of course. Why wouldn't I be?"

Er—head injury? A period of unconsciousness? "You've just come out of the hospital."

"It was hardly a prolonged stay. I'm feeling perfectly fine, thank you for asking."

Samantha gave up. She'd never known her mother admit to feeling weak or vulnerable and didn't expect her to start now.

She unwrapped her scarf from her neck and stepped inside her mother's apartment after her sister.

She felt so tense her spine ached.

It was impossible to be here and not remember their last disastrous family gathering. How soon could they leave without seeming rude?

She was removing her shoes and taking her time over it, when she heard Tab gasp and clap her hands.

"A *tree*! You said there wouldn't be one, but there is! Look, Mommy."

"I see it." Ella sounded a little faint, and Samantha walked into the living room and felt a little faint herself.

Her mother's stark, austere apartment—the scene of harsh words and so many bitter memories—had been transformed into a winter wonderland. If it hadn't been for the fact that her mother had answered the door, Samantha would have turned and walked out again, assuming she was on the wrong floor.

The centerpiece was the large snowy tree that glittered with silver lights, but it didn't end there. There were lights strung around the bookcases and gifts piled high under a tree adorned with decorations and candy. Her mother's minimalist white designer sofa had been accessorized with a luxurious fur throw and cheered up with a scattering of festive cushions.

If it hadn't been for the threat to her mascara, Samantha would have rubbed her eyes. Was she dreaming, or did one of them have the word *joy* picked out in flashing lights?

If there was one word she would never have associated with a trip to her mother's home in the holidays it was *joy*. And the surprises just kept coming, because leaning against those cushions was an oversize furry reindeer with an elaborate red bow tied around its neck. With its long droopy face and uneven, padded antlers, it was the most adorable thing Samantha had seen in a while.

Tab obviously thought so too because she sprinted to the sofa and hugged the reindeer so tightly Samantha expected the stuffing to pop out through its eyes.

She exchanged glances with her sister, who gave a bemused shrug.

Neither of them quite believed what they were seeing.

Tab was still squeezing the reindeer. "I love him!"

"You do?" Gayle stood stiffly in the center of the room, and Samantha glanced from her niece to her mother.

Was it her imagination or did her mother actually look nervous?

"He's the best thing ever. Is he yours, Nanna?" The word slid naturally from Tab's mouth.

"He's yours. If you'd like him."

"Mine?" Tab turned to Ella, her face glowing. "He's *mine!*"

"Yes." Ella's voice was faint. "He's— This is wonderful, Mom. I wasn't expecting— I thought—why did you—"

"It's not every day a woman entertains her granddaughter to tea. I wanted it to be special."

Why was her granddaughter more special than her own daughters?

Samantha shifted on the spot, ashamed of her own thoughts. This was about Tab, not her. She'd been afraid that Tab would be somehow hurt by the encounter, so the fact that her mother had made such a big effort should delight her, not cause pain.

The past was the past. All that mattered was that her mother had made an effort.

She watched as Tab wriggled from the sofa, still clutching the reindeer that was almost as big as her, and ran across to Gayle.

"Thank you, Nanna." Tab wrapped her arms round Gayle's legs and hugged.

Gayle stood stiff and unsure, then lowered her hand to Tab's head and gave her hair a tentative stroke.

Samantha saw tears in Ella's eyes, and her stomach dropped.

Yes, their mother had surprised them all, but Samantha didn't trust it; she just didn't trust it.

Was this another high before a massive low?

This wasn't her mother's normal behavior. They both knew that.

"I have a surprise waiting for you in the kitchen," Gayle said to Tab. "Would you like to see?"

"Yes. But I'm bringing Rudolph." Tab followed her grandmother to the kitchen, leaving the three remaining adults standing awkwardly in the living room staring at each other.

Ella shook her head. "I don't get it," she said. "Look at this—" She swept her hand around the room.

"I'm looking."

"I mean—did you have the faintest clue she was capable of this?"

"No. Why would I?" Their mother had never done anything like this for them.

"I didn't realize she even knew what a Christmas tree was."

"Mmm. And that reindeer. Did you ever see a more frivolous, useless, extravagant—"

"—gorgeous gift," Ella said. "Adorable. And no, I didn't." She turned to Michael. "This is *not* our mother. She gave us useful gifts. Gifts with purpose, designed to promote advancement in some way."

"Well, she's clearly doing better in that direction." Michael tried to be tactful.

Ella was looking at Michael. "But why? Why now?"

"Because she wants us to spend Christmas together." Samantha touched the decoration nearest to her, noticing that it still had a tiny price tag on it. "And she knows that the only way to make that happen is through her granddaughter. That's why she's making an effort." Her mother had done all this for Tab.

Michael considered. "Even if that's true, does it matter?"

Samantha peeled the price tag off the decoration and rolled it between her fingers. "Perhaps it doesn't. Except that there is no way she'll be able to keep it up. What happens then?" She felt a wave of protectiveness as she thought of her niece. There were no words to describe her love for her niece. She wasn't going to let her be hurt. "I'll check on Tab."

She wandered into the kitchen and found her icing gingerbread men.

"Here, Aunty Sam—" Tab thrust one toward her, icing dripping in tiny blobs onto the table. "Try it."

Samantha dutifully took a large bite. "Delicious." And it really was delicious. "Where did you buy these, Mom?" Maybe she should buy a boxful for the office. She knew her team would love them.

"I didn't." Gayle put a large plate in front of Tab. "I made them."

Samantha caught a piece of gingerbread as it fell from her mouth. "You? You actually baked these yourself?"

"I did. I'm a little rusty, but they seem to have turned out all right."

Rusty? Rusty implied that you used to do something, but then stopped doing it.

Samantha dissected her memory bank, trying to find a time when her mother had baked with them, or even *for* them, but she came up blank.

Tab seemed to be eating as much as she was icing, and there was as much icing on the table and the floor as there was on the gingerbread men.

Knowing what a neat freak her mother was, Samantha waited for her to say something or at least grab a cloth and start wiping up the mess, but she didn't.

Samantha reached for a knife and scraped up one of the pools of icing.

Tab added chocolate eyes to a gingerbread man. "Sometimes I bake with Mommy. Did you bake with your mommy?"

There was a long silence.

"Yes," Gayle said. "Yes, I did."

Samantha dropped the knife on the floor.

"What was your best thing to cook?" Tab added a third eye to the gingerbread man. "Mine is cupcakes."

"I made gingerbread men. Just like these."

With her mother. Samantha's grandmother.

Samantha couldn't have been more shocked if her mother had suddenly stripped naked and danced around the kitchen.

All she knew about her mother's parents was that they'd died when Gayle was in her first year of college. Ella had once found a photo of their mother with her parents, but her questions had quickly been shut down and the photo had never been seen again.

Tab was focused on the task in hand. "I'd like to make these with you, not just decorate them."

"I'm sure that could be arranged." Gayle studied Tab's gingerbread man. "You've done a great job. Well done. Although you've given that one three eyes."

"I thought he'd be able to see better with more eyes."

"It's an interesting modification." Gayle mixed more icing, to replace the mound that had landed on the floor. "Different color or the same color?"

"I want to give him a red hat."

"Then let's give him a red hat. Samantha—" Gayle glanced up "—the red food coloring is in the cupboard. Top shelf. Would you mind? Samantha?"

Samantha responded like a robot, retrieving the food coloring and handing it to her mother.

"You should probably do this part." Gayle handed the bottle to Tab who took it without hesitation.

Samantha relaxed a little. That was more like her mother. Making someone do something themselves. *If I do it for you, Samantha, how will you ever learn?*

She winced as Tab poured so much food coloring into the icing that it looked like the scene of a crime.

Gayle simply smiled. "A strong, vibrant color. Well done."

"I like red," Tab said, blobbing the mixture onto the gingerbread. "Why are your clothes all black, Nanna?"

"Because it looks businesslike, and in my work I like to look businesslike."

"But you're not at work now." Tab ate more gingerbread. "Black is a very sad color. Haven't you ever wanted to dress like a mermaid?"

Gayle was lost for words. "I can't say I have."

"You should try it," Tab said. "When my clothes are happy, I feel happy."

"I'll remember that."

"Oh Mom—" Ella was standing in the doorway, and her eyes were shiny "—this is wonderful."

Michael came up behind her, a smile on his face. "Thoughtful of you, Gayle. It's good to see Tab having fun."

Samantha saw her mother let out what seemed to be an enormous sigh of relief, as if she'd been waiting to be marked on her performance.

"I'm going to bake with Nanna when we go away for Christmas. Is there a kitchen?"

Everyone turned to look at Samantha.

"Yes," she croaked. "There's a kitchen. Not sure if guests are allowed to use it though."

Gayle slid the decorated gingerbread men onto the plate. "I'm sure you'll be able to talk them into it. You seem pretty good at that."

Samantha felt a creeping sense of dread.

It seemed she was going to be spending Christmas in Scotland, with humiliation and her mother for company.

Oh joy.

Kirstie

"I can't believe you're letting a bunch of strangers use our home over Christmas. It's—it's—" Kirstie drew breath, unable to find the right word "—cruel."

"It's practical." Her brother grabbed another log from the pile and split it with a decisive thwak. "The only viable option in the circumstances."

She didn't want to think about those circumstances.

She didn't want to think that this was the only option open to them.

Grief was a huge, dark cloud that blocked the light from her life.

"There must be another way." Deep down she knew there wasn't. She knew she was in a state of denial, but she somehow wasn't ready to admit that. She didn't want it to be this way, so she was still trying to ignore it.

He threw the log onto the growing pile. "If you can think of another, I'm willing to listen."

"No, you're not. You've made up your mind, and we both

know that when that happens you won't be moved away from it." She was being as irrational as he was being stubborn.

He'd always been the one to do what needed to be done, no matter how unpleasant or hard. When her first dog had died, he'd been the one to bury it.

He wiped his forehead on his sleeve and looked at her.

She saw the shadow of tiredness around his eyes and felt a stab of guilt. It was difficult for him, too, she knew that, but he still did it. "I'm sorry. I should be more supportive, but it's hard. Half the rooms had been closed up for a decade until you decided to open them up. James couldn't even get the window open in the garden room. I never want to make up another bed, or plump another cushion. I *hate* being indoors—"

"I know you do." There was an edge to his voice. "But there are things to be done, Kirstie, so we're doing them." His use of the word *we* added layers of guilt to the deep sadness she felt.

"It's hard for you, too, I know."

"I'm fine." He hauled another log into place. "These need to be taken inside. The Americans are going to want a roaring log fire to greet them, and for that we need logs. More logs than I can handle on my own. There are four bedrooms to heat."

"Four?"

"There's a little girl."

"You can't have a real fire in a child's bedroom."

"Good point. Three bedrooms." He nodded. "And the Great Hall, the Loch Room, the dining room and the snug."

She sighed. "And how much is all that going to cost us?"

"A fraction of what we're going to make when they start booking groups of rich Americans. Can you give James a shout and ask him to help shift this lot?"

"I'll help. James is busy trying to fix the quad bike that won't behave, and after that he is taking Bear to the vet because he ate something gross." She pushed the sleeves of her jacket up. "And what else are the Americans going to expect? Should I be in the kitchen baking shortbread?" Her sarcasm earned her a quick smile.

"Yes. After you've smoked the salmon you just pulled out of the loch and fastened those antlers to the wall. And if you could arrange a ceilidh and dust off that fiddle of yours, that would be good, too."

She caught one of the logs before it could topple off the pile. "You're annoying."

"I prefer you annoyed to upset."

"Will you be wearing your kilt?"

"If I need to." He reached for another log. "Do you have a problem with that?"

"Would it make a difference if I said yes? You wear it for weddings, graduations and now for showing off to the tourists." She sighed and folded her arms. "Tell me about them. The Americans."

"Guests," he said. "They're guests. There's Samantha, she runs the travel company in Boston. Specializes in magical winter breaks."

"Magical?" Kirstie raised an eyebrow. "Clearly she hasn't been to the Highlands in the depths of winter."

"It's up to us to make it magical. Hence the logs and the extra fur throws on the beds."

"Fur throws? Isn't that a little kinky?"

"I was going for practical and warm. And also the look I assumed they'd be expecting."

"You're turning us into a film set now?"

"That's on my list to discuss. A company from Edinburgh is coming to see us early in January. If we pass, they'll start recommending us."

"So we'll be overrun with lights and cameras, and if the movie is a success we'll be overrun with tourists coming to see the place the movie was filmed. What are you thinking?"

"I'm thinking of the money."

"This is our home. *Our home!*" Kirstie was on the verge of tears.

"And we need money to be able to keep this home. It's a big, drafty place and the cost of upkeep is enough to make eyes water. Have you taken a look at the accounts lately?"

Kirstie swallowed. She didn't dare look. "No. That's your area, not mine. You know I'm not good with numbers." She'd struggled her way through school, and it was only his help and patience that had got her through her exams with reasonable marks.

"Happy to walk you through it anytime." His expression was grim, and she shook her head and shifted the subject away from the scary topic of money.

"So is Samantha bringing her husband? Partner?"

"No partner." He adjusted his gloves and picked up armfuls of the holly he'd cut earlier. "Also coming along are her sister, brother-in-law and niece, aged four, I think. Or maybe it was five. Her mother, too."

"Five? That's young." Kirstie frowned. "We'll have to make sure she doesn't fall into the loch."

"She won't be going outside by herself."

"They're city people. What if they hate Bear?"

"Just because they live in a city, doesn't mean they hate dogs."

"A child that age will be bored here. No shops or theme parks." She knew she was behaving like a toddler in a tantrum, but she was raw inside and out. Why was life so unfair? She needed to hit out, and he was the only one she could hit.

"We'll teach her to love the outdoors. She can ride Pepper and feed the reindeer."

"No one has ridden Pepper for years."

"Then it will be a refreshing change for him." He stripped off spiky leaves from the bottom of the holly. "I thought we could use this around the fireplaces. Make it festive."

"Why not? You could add mistletoe, in case your Americans are feeling romantic."

"They're not 'my' Americans."

"It's your idea." Kirstie hesitated. "I caught Mum crying in the kitchen. She said she'd been chopping onions but that was a lie." It made her feel helpless, and she hated feeling helpless.

"She's the reason we're doing this. This is the only home she has ever known. Why can't you understand that?"

"But will it even feel like home when it's overrun by strangers?"

"One family, Kirstie! If it doesn't work, we won't do it again." There was a note of exasperation in his voice. "One family can't overrun anything. It will be personal. Intimate. We're offering a family Christmas, not a free-for-all."

"Exactly. A Family Christmas. Except, they're not our family, are they? Instead of sitting round and spending time together the way we usually do, we'll be working in the kitchen to feed people we don't know. What if they argue? What if they're difficult people? The problem with a small, intimate group is that if they're boring or rude, you can't dilute them."

"Then it will be a Christmas to remember. Can you manage those logs or do you need my help?"

She threw him a look.

"Do you know how it feels to be making our house festive for someone else?"

"For all of us. You're living in it too, Kirstie. It's going to feel the same way it always feels, only possibly less disorganized. Maybe you'll even enjoy it. It's a matter of attitude."

"No, it's a fact. You've sacrificed our family Christmas for commercial reasons."

"Practical reasons. And I haven't sacrificed anything. It will still be Christmas. We'll be cooking the same food, using the same decorations on the tree. Maybe you need to be more realistic about this time of year instead of always thinking it will be a magical time—"

Was she being pathetic? Nostalgic? "How can it be magical? It's just not the same without—"

"I know. It can't be the same. It won't be. So we need to make it different. Maybe it's a good thing to shake it up a little." His voice thickened and he stripped off another layer, his movements rough and angry.

"But spending it with strangers—"

"Since when have we refused to welcome a stranger into our home? Where's the Highland hospitality we're known for?"

She swallowed. He made her feel small and selfish and less than she wanted to be.

"Samantha is probably one of those scary, corporate types with perfect hair and nails and a no-nonsense attitude." She wrapped her arms around herself, embarrassed by her own behavior. Wishing she was one of those people who could embrace change with humor. "In case you can't tell, I'm having a bad day."

He dropped what he was holding and gave her a hug. "You don't have to apologize for that. We all have them."

"But you don't spill your feelings all over everyone." She gave a sniff and pulled away. "You need a shower. You smell of woodsmoke."

"Occupational hazard around here."

"I'm trying to be angry with you."

"I'd noticed."

"Who is prepared to fly thousands of miles from home to spend Christmas with a bunch of strangers in the middle of nowhere? It's strange."

"Not that strange. She's bringing her family with her. And don't call it 'the middle of nowhere.' I don't want to put people off coming here."

"You can't hide what we are or where we are. The nearest town is an hour away in good weather."

He dropped the branch of holly onto the pile on the floor. "If they wanted a town, they wouldn't be choosing this place. And the village is closer than that."

"One pub and a post office that sells everything? That hardly counts. Is she some kind of business machine? Forcing her family to uproot themselves over the holidays so that she can work? Because that's what this is to her, isn't it?" She swept her arm through the air, the arc of her arm taking in loch, mountains and forest. "This place we call home—it's work to her. We're a venue."

"You've never heard of mixing business with pleasure?"

"I'm worried she won't get it, that's all. I'm worried she wants fake Scotland, and that we're going to have to produce that. You want us to live as one family and eat meals together, but my tongue gets tied in a knot when I'm intimidated by someone. She'll talk about profit, loss and the bottom line. I'll talk about the problems of freezing pipes in the middle of winter and how on a bad day I can't feel my toes. And that's another thing—it will be cold."

"She lives in Boston and their winters are fiercer than ours. I should think she'll be used to the cold."

"So she is a scary corporate type?"

"I think she's human, like the rest of us." He turned away and scooped up a large bunch of mistletoe. "I think you should stop worrying about people you don't know and focus on making the place the best it can be. We make a success of this, we can fix the roof in the tower and also the windows. Then maybe your toes won't freeze at night and we can hire someone to do the housekeeping tasks."

"How about Mum crying?"

"We both know she's not crying because I've invited strangers into our house for Christmas."

"But having strangers will make it harder for her."

"Or maybe it will be a reason to get out of bed in the morning."

Kirstie thought about that and had to concede he could be right. Her mother had always been so warm and welcoming to everyone, family and strangers alike. She'd never been happier than when she was cooking and fussing over a houseful of people. "Or maybe the strain will be too much."

"I guess we'll find out. Now, are you going to take those logs to the house before they turn to mulch?"

They'd always been close, but that didn't mean there weren't times when she wanted to kill him.

Today was one of those days.

Samantha

Samantha stepped through the door of the airport and pulled her coat more tightly around her. The icy wind shocked her system. It stung her cheeks and crept through the gap between scarf and skin. A few tiny snowflakes settled like sugar on her coat.

The afternoon light was fading, but there was enough for her to see the curving line of snow-covered mountains in the distance.

Scotland.

She breathed in the clean, sharp air and felt something stir inside her.

Her clients were going to love it here.

"Wasn't he supposed to meet us?" An exhausted Ella dragged two cases and the oversize stuffed reindeer that Tab had refused to leave behind, while Michael carried the rest of their luggage and a sleeping Tab. The fact that she was finally quiet was a relief to everyone after a flight that had been punctuated by tiredness and tears.

"He said he'd be here. Be patient." Samantha wasn't in any hurry to meet him. Would he pretend their conversation had never happened? Or would he give her a wink to indicate that he knew exactly what was going on in her head? Never before had she started a business relationship feeling at a disadvantage. Resolving to be more open was one thing, but she wouldn't have chosen a client to be the recipient of her new approach.

She smoothed her hair, checking nothing had escaped from the elegant chignon she'd managed to produce in the confines of the airplane. It was a fight between her and the wind as to who was in charge of her appearance. Maybe she should have worn a hat, but then her hair would have looked wild when she'd taken it off, and Samantha didn't want to look wild. Any wildness she felt was kept firmly on the inside. She wanted to look like the person she'd been pretending to be for her whole life.

"Are you okay?" Ella steadied the case and flexed her fingers. "You seem tense."

"Not at all."

"Mmm." Ella removed her scarf and laid it over Tab, giving her extra protection from the cold. "I hope she doesn't wake up. I can't stand any more crying from her or frowning from Mom. All I need now is for her to tell me I'm a terrible mother and this Christmas will have turned out exactly the way I predicted before it's even started."

"I know you're nervous, but it's going to be fine." The words came automatically, even though she didn't really believe them. There were so many potential pitfalls, how could it possibly be fine? But the success of her business was partly down to her ability to handle the unexpected, the unplanned, the emergency, so when she said *fine* she usually meant *fine in the end*. For every problem there was some sort of solution. "And no one could ever think you're a terrible mother."

"She frowned a lot on the flight. She was judging me."

"I don't think so." It was true that Gayle had frowned a lot on the flight, but unlike her sister, Samantha wasn't convinced that Tab's restless behavior had been the cause.

"I hope he arrives soon." Her sister leaned in. "Maybe your sex conversation scared him off."

Michael turned his head. "The *what* conversation?"

"Nothing." Samantha glanced at her mother, but Gayle was standing apart from them, gazing into the distance in a world of her own. She'd been quiet on the flight. Samantha might have said nervous, except she'd never seen her mother nervous. Maybe she was as worried about spending Christmas together as they were. "Are you all right, Mom?"

Gayle stirred. "Yes. The air smells so fresh," she said. "I'd forgotten how beautiful it is here."

"When were you here? You mentioned it, but you haven't told us the details."

"Haven't I?" Gayle turned her head. "Look—vehicle approaching. I hope that's our ride. I can't feel my fingers."

Samantha had no opportunity to question her further, because a vehicle pulled up next to them and a man emerged from the driver's seat.

"Samantha Mitchell?"

She relaxed.

Not someone in his sixties. Not the craggy, weathered face of the man she'd spoken to. A younger man. Early thirties she guessed. Presumably someone who worked at Kinleven Lodge, although he wasn't at all what she'd been expecting. She'd expected a tough-looking, weather-beaten, outdoors type. Apart from the high performance winter jacket and sturdy boots, this guy looked more like a college professor.

Ashamed of herself for stereotyping, she picked up her suitcase. Just because a guy had a lean, intelligent face and wore dark rimmed glasses, didn't mean he was an intellectual. And whoever said that outdoorsy people couldn't be intellectual? The important thing was that he wasn't the man who had been on the end of that phone call. Her professional self would rather have been met by the owner, but her personal self was relieved that he'd sent someone else.

"I'm Samantha." She thrust her hand out. "I appreciate you meeting us. I wasn't sure if it would be Brodie McIntyre himself."

"I'm Brodie. Good journey? You must be tired. Do you have all your luggage?" He nodded to the rest of the group, and gestured to Tab. "There's a booster seat for the little one in the back. Also a blanket in case she's cold. I wasn't sure what to bring, so I threw everything in the car."

Ella was immediately won over. "What a thoughtful gesture."

Everyone piled toward the car, except for Samantha who couldn't move her feet.

"You're Brodie?"

"That's right." He gave her a quick smile and loaded up their luggage with ease.

Her practical side was reassured that although he might look as if he spent his time grading papers and holding large lecture theaters of students enthralled by his academic arguments, he was also the type of man who would be able to dig a client's car out of a snowdrift or fell a tree in a power outage.

"So your dad is Brodie, too?"

He waited for Gayle, Michael and Ella to climb into the car and slammed the door shut. "Cameron Brodie." His voice was rough. "My father was Cameron Brodie, but everyone called him Cameron."

"Was?"

"He died in January."

"Died?" The wind tugged at her hair, determined to unravel her dignity. "But I spoke to him—"

"You spoke to me. Is this the last suitcase?" He removed it from her numb fingers and fitted it into the car with the others.

"You were the one I—" Drenched in embarrassment, she stared at him. "I thought—"

"You thought I was my dad? I'm afraid not, although I wish it had been because then he'd still be here. This is our first Christmas without him, so if you find us less than cheery company, that will be the reason. And I probably shouldn't have told you that. A little too honest. Maybe I'm not built for a commercial enterprise." He pushed his glasses up his nose and his smile was so engaging she wondered how she could possibly not have noticed how attractive he was.

"I appreciate honesty." And she did, which made it all the more bewildering that she'd built a persona for herself that didn't reflect the person she was inside. And he knew that, of course. He knew all of it.

It was difficult to know which of the two of them felt more uncomfortable.

He gestured. "You should get in the car, before you freeze." The cold was the least of her problems.

She felt terrible. He was clearly raw with pain and she'd just hurt him. Why hadn't Charlotte's research flagged the fact that his father had died? And why hadn't she checked? Disappointed in herself, she caught his arm and then pulled her hand back.

"I didn't know about your father. My assistant searched the internet, and his picture was there—we assumed—"

"Easy mistake to make. They have his picture, with my name. Technology is fallible it seems, which won't come as news to anyone who works in that area. No harm done, Miss Mitchell."

And now he knew she'd been searching for his photo.

"Call me Samantha." She could see the rest of her family gazing through the window. Ella, mouthing, *What?* Michael with a concerned frown on his face. "First the phone call, and now this. I can't imagine what you must think of me." She didn't ask herself why it mattered so much what he thought of her.

"Phone call?" He stepped closer to her, his broad shoulders

protecting her from the worst of the wind and the curious gaze of her family. "Oh, you mean *that* phone call."

"I thought you were—"

"Someone else. I gathered that." There was a gleam in his eyes. "Do you ever get the person you actually want to speak to on the phone?"

She probably should have laughed, but right now she couldn't handle teasing.

"Those things I said—again, I can only apologize."

"For wanting good sex?" There was a hint of color on his cheekbones. "That doesn't seem to me like something you should apologize for."

Her face was probably redder than his.

It was all so unprofessional, but she'd beat herself up about that later. Right now she had more pressing reasons to apologize.

"I'm so sorry for mentioning your father. For not knowing."

"I like talking about him. Keeps him alive." He held the door open for her and she climbed in next to him.

He wiped the snow from his glasses and glanced in his mirror. "Everyone doing okay back there?"

She was glad he hadn't asked her, because she definitely wasn't doing okay.

It might have been easier had she not had such a clear recollection of all the things she'd said to him.

I want to have a love affair so passionate that I forget to go to work,
I want to sneak off in my lunch break and buy sexy lingerie,
I want to drink champagne naked in bed.

"We're great," Ella said, and Brodie gave a nod and drove away from the airport.

The car was warm and the roads empty.

"Is it always this quiet?"

"No, although I doubt it's ever as busy as the place you've come from." He drove steadily, his headlights cutting through the swirl of snow. "They're forecasting heavy snow tonight, so plenty of folks have made the decision to stay home."

On the floor of the car by her feet was a discarded newspaper, open to the business pages. Tucked into the pocket of the door was a dog lead and a book. She tilted her head to try and see the title. A biography of someone she hadn't heard of.

"Have you always lived up here?"

"Me?" He glanced at her. "No. I was working in London, but after we lost Dad I came back here to help my mother and my sister."

She looked at the snow-dusted fields, and the mountains beyond.

This place had to be a shock to the system after London, surely?

Behind her Tab woke up, sleepy and disorientated. "Is it Christmas yet?"

"Not yet." Ella pulled Tab's wool hat down over her ears to keep her warm. "But soon."

"What if Santa doesn't know we're not at home? He might leave all our presents in the wrong place."

Samantha glanced nervously at her mother, waiting for her to inform her granddaughter that Santa didn't exist, but Gayle didn't appear to be listening. Or maybe she was trying very, very hard not to say the wrong thing.

Ella tucked the blanket round her daughter. "He's going to know you're staying here."

"How will he know?"

"He just will."

"Will there be a Christmas tree where we're staying?"

"We are surrounded by Christmas trees." Brodie kept his eyes on the road, but he was smiling. "Do you like Christmas trees?"

"They're my very favorite thing."

"Good, because so far we have five in the house, but there are thousands in the forest, some of them hundreds of years old."

"Five?" Tab almost bounced out of her seat. "*Five* trees in your house?"

"Five. We need another one for the library, but I thought you might like to help with that."

"You mean help decorate it?"

"I mean help me choose one from the forest."

"I can choose it? An actual tree growing in the forest? Can we go now?"

"It will be dark by the time we get home. Tomorrow you'll probably be tired. Maybe the day after? We'll find a tree and see the reindeer."

"Reindeer?"

Brodie nodded. "We have our own small herd. They like the climate up here."

"Do they fly?"

Samantha tensed and waited for him to fluff his response.

He took his time. "Can't say I've ever seen them fly," he said finally, "but that doesn't mean they don't."

Good answer, Samantha thought, and Tab seemed to agree.

"Look, Tab, there's snow on the mountains." While Ella pointed out the scenery to her daughter, Samantha glanced at her mother. Her lack of response to the Christmas conversation was surprising. Or maybe she knew that the one sure way of killing this reconciliation dead from the beginning was to expose the myth of Santa.

Gayle was staring out the window. She was slightly hunched in her seat and she'd wrapped her arms around her upper body as if she was protecting herself.

Had she found the journey stressful? Was she regretting joining them? Was she dismayed by how remote it was?

Samantha realized how little she knew about her mother other than her business achievements. The McIntyres of Kinleven were obviously a close family. What would they make of the fragmented, dysfunctional group who were their guests?

There were times when Samantha wasn't even sure who she was. She'd molded herself into a template that fit her mother's expectations for her. She had a strong work ethic, was independent to a degree that Kyle had described as "ridiculous," although she'd never been sure what he meant by that, and she never let emotions influence her personal decisions. On the outside she was her mother's daughter. The inside was another matter entirely. Which version was the real her? The private one or the public one? It bothered her that she didn't know.

Brodie flicked on his headlights. "Is this your first time in Scotland, Gayle?"

"No, although it's been years." Gayle dragged her gaze from the view. "It's exactly the way I remembered it."

Ella reached into her bag to give Tab a drink. "When did you come here? You never told us."

"On my honeymoon."

Samantha turned her head so fast she almost pulled a muscle. *Honeymoon?*

She exchanged glances with her sister.

Their mother never talked about her marriage or their father. But it would explain why she'd hesitated before agreeing to come. The place must be full of memories.

If Brodie thought it strange that neither of them had known this fact about their mother, he didn't show it. "It's a great place for a honeymoon, although perhaps not in the middle of winter."

"Winter was perfect," Gayle said. "It was cozy. We crunched through snow in the day and curled up by a log fire at night."

Samantha tried to imagine her mother curled up on the sofa with a man. It was harder to picture because she'd never seen a photograph of her father. When they'd asked, her mother had simply said that she didn't have one. They'd assumed their mother had been so distressed by the loss of him that she'd destroyed them. Samantha felt nothing but regret that he'd died before she was old enough to have a memory of him. She didn't envy Brodie his grief, but she envied the fact that he'd had a father to grieve for.

What had her mother's marriage been like? How special had her father been, that her mother hadn't been able to entertain marrying again after she lost him?

To the best of Samantha's knowledge, her mother hadn't been involved with another man since. Coming back to the place where you spent your honeymoon had to hurt. Because Gayle didn't show emotion, it was easy to pretend she didn't have the same feelings as other people. But she had to have feelings about this, surely? Was there an inner Gayle, and an outer Gayle?

Samantha wanted to ask more. She wanted to grab hold of this tiny fragile thread and see where it led, but they were trapped in a car with a stranger and an almost-five-year-old who missed nothing.

Frustrated, Samantha stared straight ahead, watching as darkness slowly closed over the mountains.

Her mother had been widowed at the age of twenty.

That must have been hard, and yet she never talked about it except to instill into her daughters the knowledge that becoming emotionally involved could make a woman vulnerable.

"We're almost there." Brodie turned onto a narrow track that followed the course of the river. Trees rose into the darkening sky, framing the road and the river. Snow was falling lightly, floating past the windows like confetti. "This whole of this area was once forest. Some of the trees are several hundreds of years old. Kings and lairds once hunted here."

Samantha thought about the historical novel she'd brought with her to read in the privacy of her room. What had her mother's love affair been like? Had it been romantic? It was almost impossible to picture her laughing and in love. Did her mother have a whole other side to her as Samantha did?

She ignored inner Samantha and forced herself to focus. "So forest covered everything?"

"Yes. And now there's a fraction of it left, although we're working on that."

"Where did the trees go?" Tab piped up from the back seat, and Brodie glanced at her in the mirror.

"Some were chopped down for farming and timber. Some were eaten by animals like sheep and deer. We're doing what we can to change that. We're replanting trees, encouraging wildlife to return to the area."

"Rewilding?" Samantha had read about it. "You're doing that here?"

"On a small scale. We've changed our approach to land management. In the future we might explore the opportunities for ecotourism—" He glanced at her. "I'd appreciate your thoughts on that at some point, if you're willing."

"Of course." It was a relief to know that he could still picture her in a professional capacity, not just as someone who wanted to have a wild affair and drink champagne naked.

She held on to her seat as they bounced their way down a bumpy track that wound its way through the forest.

"Kinleven was originally a Highland sporting estate. It's been in our family for generations. It's only recently that we've considered turning it into a commercial venture. It's going to be a steep learning curve, for me at least." He steered to avoid a deep rut in the track. "I hope you'll be able to advise us. Ideally we'd like to attract groups who want to experience life on the estate."

"Samantha is absolutely the right person to advise you," Ella said. "There is nothing she doesn't know about what people want from a festive vacation."

They crested a ridge, and there was just enough light remaining for Samantha to see the view.

Behind her, Ella gasped. "Oh my! Will you look at that."

Samantha was looking. It was an unspoiled wilderness, and the beauty of it took her breath away.

Right in front of them was the loch, it's curving shores protected by dense forest. Behind the trees rose craggy peaks, coated with snow. And there, nestled on the shores of the loch was Kinleven Lodge, with its walls of golden stone and turrets that looked like upside-down ice cream cones. Snow clung to the roof and lights glowed from the windows.

An owl swooped in front of them, soaring through the dusky sky toward the safety of the trees, and Samantha felt a lump form in her throat. For a brief moment she forgot about her mother, about *that* conversation and how much Brodie knew about her. She focused only on how perfect the place was and how much her clients would love it. Already in her mind she was forming a list of people she would immediately contact.

Brodie glanced at her. "Say something. You think it's too remote?"

"What? No! I'm thinking it's beautiful." The word didn't begin to describe what she was seeing, but the descriptive language that came so easily to her when she was writing copy for the website had vanished.

"It is, although sometimes I forget that when the car is stuck in snow and my fingers are freezing. It's even more beautiful when the sun is shining." Brodie stopped the car in front of a set of gates and opened the car door, letting in a waft of icy air. "Just give me a minute."

While he pushed open the gates, Samantha grabbed her camera and took a few shots.

Brodie climbed back into the vehicle, snow dusting his hair and shoulders. "You must be tired after your journey, so we thought you'd probably like to go straight to your rooms to freshen up, and then we'll serve a light supper before you go to bed?"

"Sounds good. Thank you."

He drove carefully along the track that opened up as they approached the lodge.

Samantha couldn't stop looking at the house. It was even more enchanting than the photos she'd seen. "I love the turrets."

"Yes. They look charming, but they're hell when the roof needs fixing." He paused. "You like it?" There was uncertainty in his voice and she was quick to reassure him.

"I love it."

And she did. It wasn't just pretty; it was perfect. Her mind was already preoccupied with detail. Winter hiking. Drinks in front of a log fire. Maybe a poetry evening. She could easily book the place out for the entire winter season. She imagined all the people who were going to have the happiest of Christmases.

Tab clapped her hands. "It looks like a fairy castle!"

"Does it?" Brodie adjusted his glasses, as if seeing the place properly for the first time. "I suppose it does. It was built as a shooting lodge in the mid-eighteenth century by my great, great, great—" He paused and shook his head. "I lose track of how many greats—grandfather who apparently wanted to impress his wife."

"I'm sure she was more than impressed."

"She was probably cold. Place must have been drafty in the winter with an icy wind blowing down the glen." He gave a half smile. "Don't panic—we've made a few upgrades since then. Plenty of heat and hot water. You'll be cozy and comfortable."

Samantha wasn't worried. She knew she'd struck gold. Beyond the house the drive wound its way down to a neatly kept dock, past what looked like a small stable block. "You have horses?"

"At the moment there is just Pepper. He was my sister's pony. Taught us all to ride. But we're considering expanding that side of the business. Something else I'd like to talk to you about. Do you think it would be popular?"

Riding around the loch with snow-covered mountains in the distance? "For summer visitors, most definitely."

He drove up the sweeping drive and stopped outside the front of the house.

On either side of the large doorway stood two Christmas trees, each studded with tiny lights.

Samantha couldn't remember ever seeing a more welcoming home, and was relieved she hadn't allowed that one embarrassing phone call to stop her experiencing this magical place.

She stepped out of the car and took a few steps, her feet sinking into the thin layer of snow that must have fallen since the drive had been swept.

The place was extraordinary.

Her niece obviously agreed.

"It's a fairy palace," Tab breathed, clambering out of the car, holding tightly to Ella's hand. "Is there a dragon?"

"I don't believe so." Brodie rubbed his hand over his jaw, giving the question serious consideration. "I'm guessing we'd probably know if there was. We'd see droppings. Maybe a few scorched areas around the woodwork. If you see any signs of one, perhaps you would let me know. It could be a fire risk. Maybe a health and safety complication. Probably something we'd need to declare to the authorities."

Samantha managed not to smile. He claimed not to have any experience, but she could see immediately that he'd be a perfect host.

Tab seemed to think so, too. "I will go on a dragon hunt. Can we build a snowman?"

"Not right now." Ella scooped her up. "It's almost bedtime."

Michael slung a backpack over his shoulder and picked up a case in each hand, while Brodie unloaded the rest of their bags.

"You get into the warm. I'll handle these."

"I'm fine." Samantha carried her own suitcase and walked with Brodie.

She wanted to say something thoughtful about his father, but what? She'd already said the wrong thing. She didn't want to double down on her mistake.

Stuck for safe topics of conversation, she settled on the weather.

"I'm one of those rare people who love snow. I live in Boston. As well as snow, we have wind. I've actually seen snow falling horizontally there."

"I know Boston well."

"You do?"

"I've worked with a few tech starts-up there. Smart people."

"Work? What work?"

"I'm a data analyst."

"You—" She stopped dead. "I assumed you were an outdoors person who runs to the top of a mountain before breakfast."

"Ah." His smile flashed briefly. "Once I've fallen flat on my face a few times you'll realize that walking on ice isn't one of my specialities. And although I'm happy hiking up a mountain, running I leave to other people."

A data analyst.

As they stepped into the warmth, Samantha saw that the inside of the lodge was as warm and welcoming as the outside. There was a vaulted entrance hall, with a sweeping paneled staircase hung with antique portraits. A fire blazed in the hearth, and a huge tree reached almost to the ceiling, its branches decorated with green and red. Family photos clustered on tables, and there were boots and umbrellas tucked inside the porch, all signs that this was not a hotel, but a home.

Tab was absorbed by the tree. "How did you put the star on top?"

"We used a ladder." He broke off as a black Labrador sprinted toward them. "Sit! Stay! Stop—do *not* jump— Oh for—" He steadied himself as the dog planted both paws on his stomach. "As you can see, we're still working on the training." He held on to the dog's collar firmly and glanced at Tab. "He's friendly—don't worry. A little too friendly."

Tab approached the dog. "What's he called?"

"Bear."

Hearing his name, the dog wagged his tale furiously.

Tab waved a finger. "Sit."

Bear sat.

Brodie raised his eyebrows. "You have the touch. You are now officially in charge of Bear's training while you're here."

Samantha crouched down and stroked him. "He's gorgeous. How old is he?"

"About twelve months. I was driving home from my father's—" He paused. "I was driving, and there he was in the ditch."

He'd been driving home from his father's funeral. He hadn't finished the sentence but she knew.

"Someone abandoned him?"

"Left him there. I would have missed him if my headlights hadn't picked him out."

"And you brought him home." He'd rescued the dog. She had no idea why that made her feel so emotional. Jet lag. She needed sleep.

Brodie rubbed Bear's head. "He's a little out of control, but he's the most loving dog I've ever met." He straightened. "But not everyone loves dogs, I know, so if he's a problem we can figure something out."

"I love him." Tab had her arms locked round Bear, who clearly returned her feelings.

Brodie glanced up as an older woman walked into the room.

"Mum." He stepped toward her. "Our guests have arrived."

"I see that, and they're very welcome. I'm Mary." Mary held out both hands to Samantha, who took them, startled by the warmth shown to a stranger.

"Thank you for allowing us to join you."

She assumed Brodie must have taken after his father, rather than his mother. Whereas his hair was dark, hers was blond, lightened by touches of silver. The skin around the corner of her eyes was creased from years of smiling.

"You can't imagine how happy I am. It will be wonderful to

have the house full of people again." Her hands tightened on Samantha's. "It's been too quiet ever since—"

"Mum—" Brodie spoke quietly, and Mary caught his eye and swallowed.

"And you must be Tab." She beamed at the child. "It's been a while since we had young feet running around this house. When my children were your age, they used to love helping me in the kitchen. Do you like cooking?"

"Yes!"

"Good. Because with all these mouths to feed, I would appreciate help in the kitchen."

Tab still had her arms locked around Bear. "I can help. I can make cookies."

"Good. And don't worry that we're a little way from the village—" Mary glanced quickly at Brodie "—because we have everything we need right here. We're so well stocked we could feed you for a month without ever having to leave the estate. And there's plenty to do. Even if it's snowing, we can—"

"They're tired, Mum," Brodie said. "Let's save the list of activities until tomorrow."

"All I'm saying is that we're not that remote. Not at all." Mary cleared her throat. "I think people are going to love it here."

Another woman appeared in the doorway.

Brodie made the introductions. "This is my sister, Kirstie."

"Welcome to Kinleven." Her greeting was polite, but cool.

Despite the words, Samantha didn't feel welcomed. She felt tension, and a certain reserve that she didn't understand.

Sibling disagreements about having strangers join them for the festive season? Or something more?

She needed to figure it out, because she didn't want to send clients to a place where the team wasn't working well together. Family business this might be, but her clients would be paying for the very best service and that included a relaxed, smiling staff.

"Why don't I show you your rooms," Brodie said, "and then

we can have a light supper. I thought a proper tour of the place could wait until tomorrow. It's better seen in daylight."

Samantha realized how tired she was. "Sounds good to me."

They followed him up the wide staircase and along a carpeted corridor.

"Gayle, I've put you in here." He opened a door. "You should have everything you need, but let me know if I can do anything to make your stay more comfortable."

"This is charming." Gayle walked to the window. "I love the way you've put the little solar lights along the drive. It means I can still just about see the mountains and the loch. It will be delightful after the crush and noise of the city."

Samantha was starting to think she didn't know her mother at all.

Brodie flicked on one of the lamps by the bed. "Samantha?"

"It's a beautiful room, Brodie."

And it was. The room had wood paneling and high ceilings. A fire blazed in the hearth, bookshelves lined one of the walls and a comfy chair encouraged the occupants to snuggle down and relax.

Someone had taken the time to arrange branches of holly and eucalyptus in a tall vase.

Leaving Gayle to settle in, he led them through a door that led to one of the turrets.

"There are two bedrooms on this floor." Brodie pushed open a door. "I thought Tab could sleep in here, with Ella and Michael next door? Samantha, you're upstairs."

He'd taken the time to learn their names, Samantha thought, watching as Tab sprinted toward the canopy bed. He was making them feel like friends, not guests.

"It looks like a princess bed." Tab climbed onto it and bounced a couple of times. "I love it."

"I loved it, too." Kirstie walked across to the window. "This used to be my room. It has the most spectacular sunsets. Be careful of the bathroom door. It sticks sometimes."

"I fixed that." Brodie stood in the doorway, watching his sister. "Why don't you go and see if Mum needs help in the kitchen while I take Samantha to her room?"

Kirstie's gaze held his for a moment and then her mouth tightened and she walked past him.

"We're serving a light supper in the Loch Room. Do you have any allergies?"

Samantha had a feeling that the other woman would be tempted to add any allergens to whatever they were eating. "No allergies. We eat everything."

"Except broccoli," Tab announced.

"You eat broccoli," Ella said.

"Mostly I hide it." She shared a conspiratorial look with Brodie, whose wink made Samantha think he'd probably hidden broccoli himself at some point.

She followed him up a winding staircase to the room at the top.

The focus of the room was the ornately carved four-poster bed, draped in a thick velvet throw and piled with pillows and soft cushions in shades of the forest. Heavy curtains covered the windows and flames flickered in the fireplace, sending a wash of ruby light across the room.

In front of the fire was a comfortable chair, a table and a thick rug.

"There's an alcove for hanging clothes—" Brodie pulled back a curtain and then pointed to a door. "The bathroom is small, but it has everything you need."

Samantha poked her head into the alcove. "What was this used for originally?"

"No one knows. There's a rumor that the laird used it as a hiding place for his lovers."

She laughed and drew the curtain across it. "He clearly wasn't an expert on hide-and-seek. It would be the first place I'd look."

The room was perfect. Her concerns lay elsewhere and couldn't be ignored.

"How does your sister feel about all of this?"

"My sister?"

"I sensed tension." Attention to every small detail was one of the reasons she was good at her job, but still she felt a little uncomfortable pressing him for details. It wasn't as if she didn't have plenty of tension in her own family, but before she could recommend this place to people, she had a duty to understand the situation.

He paused and then closed the door so they couldn't be overheard.

For a moment the only sound was the crackle of the fire and the lick of the wind as it rattled the windows.

"Kirstie is struggling to adjust to our new reality."

"You mean taking in paying guests?"

"That and other things." He walked to the fire. "It's complicated. Families are complicated." He ran his hand over his jaw. "Or maybe yours isn't, but—"

"Mine is complicated."

"Really? Because three generations of the Mitchell family spending the holidays together is pretty impressive."

She almost told him then. She almost told him that they hadn't even been in touch with their mother for the past five years. That this "togetherness" was new to them. That she was dreading it and scared of the outcome. That she hadn't even known her mother had been to Scotland before, let alone on her honeymoon.

And suddenly she felt bad. They'd been here less than half an hour, and she was expecting him to spill all his family secrets when she had no intention of telling him hers.

Providing the hospitality was good, the McIntyre family should be allowed to keep their secrets.

"It's Christmas. A difficult time to have guests." And not the easiest time to *be* a guest. She walked to the door. "The room is beautiful, Brodie. Thank you. Did you say something about food?"

Across the room his gaze locked on hers.

She had a feeling he was about to say something more, but then Ella called up the stairs and the moment was broken.

After a delicious supper of cold cuts, salad and freshly baked bread, they all went back to their rooms.

Ella and Tab paused to say good-night to the dog, which left Samantha alone with her mother.

There was a difficult moment when Gayle paused outside her room. Samantha paused too, unsure what to do next.

Wishing her mother good-night was a new thing. She could hardly shake hands. She definitely wasn't able to hug. It was as if there was a massive physical barrier between them.

In the end she gave an awkward smile. "Sleep well. You must be tired." And without waiting for her mother to answer, she headed to the stairs that curved up to her bedroom at the top of the turret.

Inside the sanctuary of her room, she closed her eyes.

What a total nightmare.

Still, at least she wasn't expected to share a room.

She pulled herself together and was unpacking her small case when Ella wandered into the room.

"I'm so ready for bed."

"Is Tab asleep?"

"Crashed out before Michael started reading her story. This place is amazing. Can't wait to see it in daylight." She peered through one of the windows. "I bet the view is fantastic. And talking of fantastic views—Brodie is gorgeous. He reminds me of my English professor at college. Can you believe he brought a car seat for Tab, and a blanket?"

Samantha hung up two dresses. "That was thoughtful."

"He has incredible eyes. Do you think I should buy glasses for Michael?"

"Why would you buy him glasses when he doesn't need glasses?"

"Because they're supersexy. Those dark frames against light eyes—I mean, wow."

"You're madly in love with Michael!"

"I know. I'm thinking of you."

"Me?" Samantha closed her suitcase and stowed it at the bottom of the alcove.

"Yes, Brodie would be perfect for you. He's smart. Thoughtful. He has great eyes."

"And he knows far too much about me."

Ella grinned. "Exactly. He has a head start."

"Ella—"

"I know, I'm not allowed to fix you up. But you can't blame me for trying." She sat on the edge of Samantha's bed. "Does this feel weird to you? Being here as a family when we're not a real family? I keep waiting for someone to find us out. I have imposter syndrome."

"We are a family, Ella." Samantha didn't admit that she felt much the same way. "A dress is still a dress even if it's torn and the hem has fallen down."

"And a dress can be fixed. Let's hope your analogy fits." Ella lay back on the bed. "This mattress is so comfortable I might never want to get up."

"Go and sleep in your own bed."

Ella lifted herself up on her elbows. "They seem like nice people. Mom seems happy with her room, too, which is a Christmas miracle in itself because she invented fussy. Do you think she's okay? I honestly can't tell."

"I don't think she's as relaxed as she'd like us to think she is." But she wasn't alone in that. Samantha put her toiletries and makeup in the bathroom. Fresh towels lay over a heated towel rail. "Why didn't she mention her honeymoon to us before now?"

"Why would she? She never talks about her marriage. I can't even remember when we last asked her."

"No point in asking her because we never get an answer."

"I know. Losing someone she loved so much was clearly traumatizing for her. So why tell us now? And she said it so casually, as if she was commenting on the weather."

"Maybe it's part of her softening up. She's never got over him—we know that. They were so in love. Presumably the honeymoon was a special time."

Samantha closed the bathroom door. "But if the place is full of memories, why would she want to come back here?"

"Well, she didn't to begin with, did she? That day in the hospital she said no. And then she changed her mind. Maybe they're good memories. She seemed happy enough in the car."

"I thought she was quiet." Samantha would have described her mood as thoughtful and contemplative, not happy. Had she been thinking about the man she'd loved? The man she'd lost? "Do you ever think about him?"

"Who? Dad?" Ellie sat up and curled her legs under her on the bed. "Sometimes. Do you?"

Samantha put her laptop onto the small desk by the window. "Sometimes." In fact she thought of him often. She imagined the relationship she might have had with him. "I wonder what he was like."

"Mom obviously thought he was incredible because she has never contemplated a relationship since. Maybe being here will encourage her to talk about him. Maybe she'll even manage to find a photograph. Your room is gorgeous, too." Ella reached across the bed to the nightstand and picked up the book Samantha had unpacked. "*One Night with the Laird*? Is that wishful thinking?" She gave a wicked grin and flopped onto the bed, reading the back of the book and then scanning the first page.

Samantha gritted her teeth. "Can I have that back?"

"Definitely not." Ella rolled away as Samantha tried to grab it. "'Her kiss was fierce and urgent, sweeping away any polite preliminaries, demanding a response.'" She glanced up. "I like this heroine. She knows what she wants and isn't afraid to take it. On the other hand, she's hiding who she really is. Emotionally guarded. Reminds me a little of you."

"Ella—"

"'She untied the ribbon of her cloak and allowed it to fall.' Clothes were so much more seductive in those days, weren't they? It isn't easy wriggling out of skinny jeans. Maybe I should start wearing a cloak. 'She ripped the shirt from him—'" Ella flicked the page. "This is good. And hot. I want to be this woman."

"It's a book, Ella."

"So? The emotions are real enough. He wants her. She wants him. Mutual passion right there on the page. It happens."

"People don't rip each other's clothes off in real life. Not in a romantic way."

"Sometimes they do. Michael ripped my shirt off once. Weirdly enough Tab found one of the buttons in the living room the other day when she was crawling around the apartment, which probably says a lot about my cleaning skills. Don't tell Mom, although a lack of domestic ability is probably the one thing that wouldn't bother her."

"In the living room?"

"Yes. We didn't make it to the bedroom."

Her sister's casual confession made her feel a little strange. Kyle had never ripped her clothes in his haste for intimacy. They'd always undressed themselves. He'd carefully hung up his clothing before joining her in the bedroom. They'd never resorted to having sex in the living room. Never had sex in the kitchen, or on the stairs, or in any other room other than the bedroom. The prelude to sex had all the excitement of unwrapping a gift when you already knew what was inside.

"Michael did that?" Why was she asking? Much as she liked him, she wasn't sure she wanted that much detail about her brother-in-law.

"Yes. He'd been out of town for a week and we were both a bit—desperate." Ella shrugged, not remotely embarrassed. "You know—when you don't want to wait."

Samantha didn't know. And she badly wanted to. She'd always told herself that type of urgency only happened in novels, but here was her sister telling her it happened in real life.

Maybe she just wasn't the type of woman men wanted to unwrap.

"He—ripped your shirt?"

"To be fair it was a particularly annoying shirt. I struggled with the buttons myself, so it was probably more impatience than lust, but still—" Ella was still absorbed by the book. "Can I borrow this when you're done? I'm starting to think I might want a night with the laird. And you *definitely* need a night with the laird. Do you think he keeps his glasses on when he makes love? They make him look incredibly sexy."

There was a tap on the door and they both turned to see Brodie standing there.

Ella gave him a bright, unapologetic smile, but Samantha felt color rush into her cheeks.

Had he heard? Yes, probably. It seemed she was destined to be permanently embarrassed in front of this man.

He glanced briefly at Ella. "Just checking you have everything you need?" He didn't look at Samantha, which made her think he'd definitely heard.

Why, oh why, hadn't she packed Dickens, or *War and Peace*? When she'd tucked the book into her luggage, she hadn't thought anyone would see it but herself. She couldn't imagine ever being without a book, and the romances she loved were perfect for escape and relaxation. She'd figured that spending Christmas with her mother would mean she needed both in spades.

What if her mother had seen the book? She could just imagine the reaction.

I can't believe you're filling your head with romantic nonsense.

And yet her mother was here, back in Scotland where she'd spent her honeymoon, so at some point in her life, presumably she'd believed in romance.

Samantha lifted her chin, refusing to apologize for her reading choices. "We're fine, thank you."

"The only thing we seem to be missing is a sexy laird in a kilt ready to sweep us away into the heather. Do you have one available through room service?" A grinning, unrepentant Ella sprang from the bed, the book still in her hand. "Samantha has been conducting some in-depth research on the mating practices of the local population."

Samantha snatched the book from her sister's fingers and slapped it facedown next to the bed, even though she'd abandoned all hope of maintaining a professional appearance.

Somehow, tomorrow, she would try and make a fresh start. In the meantime she just wanted this day to be over.

"We have everything, thank you."

Brodie finally looked at her, and she saw that her sister was right about his blue eyes looking good with the dark framed glasses.

"Right." He cleared his throat, turned and banged his head on the door frame. "Ouch." He touched his fingers to his head and pulled a face.

"Are you all right?" Ella reached out, as if to save him from any more disasters.

"Fine. I'm completely fine." He rubbed his head and gave Ella a rueful smile. "I need to remember to duck my head in these old rooms." He backed away, stumbled slightly as his shoulder caught the door. "Oops—still fine—I hope you sleep well, Samantha." His gaze met hers for a brief second and then he turned and bumped his way out of the room.

She knew there was absolutely no chance of her sleeping. None.

"Did you see that?" Ella's whisper was so loud, she might as well have yelled. "He couldn't take his eyes off you. He kept banging into things."

"He banged into things because he couldn't get out of the room fast enough. The man was terrified. Between the phone call and now this, he's probably wondering if it's safe to sleep in the house with me."

"He is adorable." Ella sighed. "And if you don't want to unwrap the incredible gift that is that man this Christmas, you're not the woman I know you are."

Ella

Ella woke to darkness and was disorientated. She reached out blindly, found her phone and checked the time.

Three o'clock in the morning.

She put the phone down, flopped back against the pillows and waited for her mind to wake up properly.

It was almost Christmas, and they were in snowy Scotland.

She waited for the familiar warm feeling to creep through her body, but nothing happened. What was wrong? Where was the tension coming from?

She was here with her family. Michael, Tab, Samantha. And—

Her mother.

She sat up, breathing hard. Her mother. She was the one who had suggested her mother join them. What had she done? Christmas was always so smooth. An indulgence, as sweet as chocolate cake. Adding her mother into the mix could, and probably would, disrupt the balance.

What if she'd ruined Christmas?

Beside her, Michael stirred. "What's wrong?"

"Nothing." She lay back down and he pulled her against him.

"I know it's not nothing. Is this about your mother?"

"Yes. It all feels so—wrong. She still hasn't said anything to me about the fact that I didn't tell her I was married with a child."

"Maybe she realizes that is in the past now, and it's time to move on."

"My mother isn't like that. She doesn't let my bad decisions pass without comment."

"You haven't seen her in five years." Michael's voice was rough with sleep. "She could have changed."

Or not. "What if this whole thing is a mistake?"

He pressed her back against the bed and kissed her. "We are going to have the best Christmas ever."

Were they? He didn't know their mother.

He slid his hand from her hip to her thigh, and then higher, and she decided that for now at least she'd leave him to his fantasies because she was having a few of her own.

"Are you making a move on me?"

"Several moves." His mouth was on her jaw, her throat, her breast. She felt the softness of his mouth and the rasp of stubble over sensitive skin.

Desire, warm and wicked, unraveled inside her. He wasn't her first lover, but she'd known from that first heated kiss they'd shared that he'd be her last.

Michael.

She slid her arms round him, curved her legs over his. "I love you."

"Of course you do. You're a woman of taste. Ouch!" Michael winced as she moved her knee. "If you think you'll ever want a second child, you should be careful."

"I don't know if I want a second child. Would it turn out like you?"

"You mean smart and wickedly handsome? We're a rare breed. I can't guarantee it." He kissed her, smothering her response.

She put her hand on his shoulder, ready to push him away and carry on talking, but then he deepened the kiss and she forgot what it was she'd wanted to say. The kiss turned from soft and deliberate to wild and urgent.

She felt the skilled glide of his fingers and the erotic stroke of his mouth against the most sensitive parts of her.

Only when she was pliant, writhing, desperate, did he finally ease into her. She wrapped her legs round him but he held himself still, kissing her until she was almost in a frenzy. When he finally started to move, it was a slow, rhythmic teasing of her senses, controlled to the point that she might have thought he wasn't as desperate as she was, except that she knew him. She cupped his face in her hands, saw the feverish glitter in his eyes and knew the effort it was taking him to hold back.

"I love you." She whispered the words against his mouth. "Love you. Love you."

He held her gaze, and she squirmed at the sheer pleasure of it, urging him to *please, please just*—

He thrust deeper, and she would have cried out but his mouth was on hers, the erotic intimacy of his kiss stoking her pleasure. Sensation built and built until she felt herself tighten around him, her body beyond her control as she reached the peak and fell.

She felt him shudder, burying his face in her neck to muffle the sounds. Finally he lifted his head and cupped her face in his palm. "Love you, too." He kissed her gently. "Very much."

Her heart was full, but she gave him a teasing smile. "Of course you do. You're a man of taste."

Acknowledging her comeback with a smile, he rolled onto his back and pulled her against him. "Now go back to sleep."

She did, and the next time she woke there was a pale streak of sunlight poking through the windows. Michael still had his arm locked around her, and she lay for a moment feeling utterly content.

"What time is it?" She reached for her phone and groaned. "It's late. How could we oversleep?"

"Blame the incredible sex." Michael tugged her back against him but she pulled away.

"I can't believe Tab slept this late. She always crawls into bed with us at 5:00 a.m."

"Remembering what we were doing at 5:00 a.m., I'd say it's a good thing she overslept."

Ella kissed him and slid out of bed. Her head felt as if it had been stuffed with down.

"I'll just check on her."

"Don't. You'll wake her up."

"What if she woke early and wandered off? She could have been eaten by a reindeer—"

Michael rolled onto his back, giving up on sleep. "Reindeer are herbivores."

"Stabbed by their antlers, then."

"They always seem like pretty docile creatures in the movies. Would Santa really use them to pull his sleigh if they were so lethal?"

"I'm just going to check on her." She tugged a sweater over her nightdress and tiptoed from the bedroom into the room next door.

She pushed gently at Tab's door, opening it just enough for her to peep into the room.

The bed was empty.

She opened the door fully. "Tab?"

There was no sign of her daughter.

Panic knotted in her stomach.

"Michael! She's gone!" She ran back into the bedroom and tripped over her shoes. "Get dressed. We have to search for her." She grabbed her shoes from the floor and her jeans from the back of the chair. "How could I have slept so late? I *never* sleep late."

"Ella—"

"Why didn't I hear her? We should have stayed home and not come here for the holidays. I hope they lock the doors in this place." She pulled off her nightdress and dragged on her jeans. "She could have wandered anywhere—"

"Calm down." Michael forced himself out of bed. "I've never seen you like this."

"Well, now you're seeing me." Her heart was thumping, her pulse racing. He was right that she had to calm down. "We need to find Brodie McIntyre. We need to—"

"Breathe." Michael ran his hand over his face, waking himself up. "You need to breathe. Then we return to our usual parenting style, which favors logic over panic. She's probably downstairs playing with the dog."

"Or maybe she took the dog for a walk and she slipped into the loch and drowned."

"Why would she do that? And why would you think that?" He grabbed a robe. "Okay, let's go find our daughter." He glanced out of the window and paused. "Ah—panic over."

"What? Why?"

Ella joined him at the window and saw Tab in the distance, a tiny figure against a vast snowy landscape. Next to her was a larger figure. An adult, dressed in a bulky down jacket.

"Who is that she's with?"

"Looks like your mother."

"That's not my mother. My mother only ever wears black. That jacket is—" she squinted "—peacock?"

"Well, maybe she fancied a change. It's definitely your mother."

"But black is her color. Still—" She flopped down onto the edge of the bed. "It's a relief that Tab's okay."

Michael sat down next to her. "Are *you* okay?"

"I'm always like this around my mother. You know that."

"I don't know that. I've never seen you with your mother. And I don't understand why you'd be any different in her company."

"We all act differently around different people, Michael. Have you seen my gloves?"

Michael handed them to her. "I'm the same with everyone. There's just the one version of me. Admittedly it's an awesome version."

She finished dressing. "You're a different person at work than you are at home."

"No." He shook his head. "I'm still the smart, supersexy, good-humored guy you fell in love with."

She threw her sock at him. "At least you didn't include *modest* on the list. And this is the version of me when I'm around my mother, so I guess you'll just have to get used to it. Are you coming, or am I doing this on my own?"

He pulled her into his arms. "It's going to be okay, honey. We just have to figure out a way for you to be you again. And now relax. Tab is fine."

"She might not be fine." The source of her anxiety had shifted. "How can she be so thoughtless?"

"She's not even five years old, honey."

"I'm talking about my mother. She could at least have left a note. Tab doesn't even know her. Why would she just take off with her like that?"

"Presumably because she wants to get to know her. Seems pretty obvious to me. Also, they did sit next to each other on the flight. You mother was a saint on the journey. Tab was hard work, and your mother read to her and did endless puzzles."

"Are you trying to make me feel bad?"

"No, Ella." He sounded tired. "I'm trying to explain why your mother might have taken Tab outside on her own. She's trying to bond with her, and I think it's important that we let her."

"She has no idea of what Tab is capable of. That child is so curious. She climbs everything, sticks her nose in everything, wants to have fun—"

"There's nothing wrong with wanting to have fun."

"I know. But my mother doesn't believe in fun. She believes in self-improvement."

Michael strolled back to the window. "Are you sure about that? Because it looks as if she's having fun to me. They're building a snowman."

"No way. My mother wouldn't know how to build a snowman, and—oh—" She joined Michael at the window and stared. Even from this distance she could see her mother scooping up another handful of snow and adding it to the ball that Tab had already created. "I don't believe this."

"What don't you believe? Why all the hysteria and yelling? I could hear you up a flight of stairs. At least tell me you saw Santa and his reindeer flying across the mountaintops." Samantha's voice came from the doorway. "Where's Tab?" She walked up behind Ella to see what they were looking at. "Oh."

"Yes." Ella tried not to be hurt by the "hysteria" comment.

"I must be more tired than I thought. I'm hallucinating." Samantha rubbed her eyes. "For a moment there I thought I saw our mother building a snowman with Tab."

"She is. And she's laughing."

"Is Mom wearing a—*blue* coat?"

"I thought it was more peacock." Ella shrugged. "I keep telling Michael how unlike her that is."

"Well, that's a good sign." Samantha was still staring out of the window.

"Sign of what?"

"Sign that she can change. She wears black. All the time. But today she's wearing peacock."

"Which will no doubt please our daughter," Michael said, "as it's close to a mermaid color. It's thoughtful of her. And now that I know our daughter is safe and happy, I'm going to take a shower and wash away the drama." He disappeared into the bathroom, leaving the two sisters alone.

It's thoughtful of her.

Ella felt a sizzle of frustration. He made her feel as if she was making a fuss over nothing, but her difficult relationship with her mother wasn't nothing.

She rubbed her chest with her hand, and then she saw Samantha's wistful expression and knew that whatever she was feeling, her sister was feeling the same way. "It hurts, doesn't it?"

"What?"

"You know what."

"I don't." Samantha straightened. "I don't know what you're talking about."

"Oh come on! You feel fine? No emotions at all seeing her out there building a snowman?"

"Ella—"

"Why do you do that? Why do you always hide your feelings? I share everything with you. It hurts my feelings that you don't talk to me."

"I talk to you all the time. We talk about feelings all the time."

"You've never talked to me about Kyle."

"I—there's nothing to talk about."

"See? That's what I mean. I talk about my feelings and you listen. You listen to everyone. You're great at that. When it comes to talking about your own, you're not so great. This is me! Your sister! You can tell me how you feel."

"About Mom building a snowman with Tab? I feel pleased. Relieved. I was as worried about this Christmas gathering as you. I don't understand why you're not relieved, too. What did you want, Ella? Did you want her to ignore Tab?"

"No, and I *am* relieved that she seems to be making an effort. But I also feel a little weird about it." She was going to have to be the one to say it. "She never did that with us."

"But she's taken Tab outside to play with her. That's massive."

"Yes, and it hurts because she is out there playing with my daughter, trying to make her happy, and that is something she never did with us."

Samantha stood up and hugged Ella. "I understand why you're upset."

"Do you? And are you not upset?" Ella extracted herself. Why was it that her sister could comfort her, but not admit her own feelings?

"It's different. I'm not Tab's mom."

Ella gave up. "I'm going outside to join them. Do you want to come with me?"

"This is a professional visit for me. I need to explore the estate, talk to Brodie about the types of activities we can offer, work up some plans and numbers. I'm going to take photographs, investigate transport options. I also promised to explore with him other ways that he could monetize the estate."

Ella looked at her sister properly for the first time and realized how groomed and professional she looked even in warm, practical clothing. "Is that sweater new? You look amazing. How long have you been awake?"

"A few hours. I was working. I had some preparation to do for today."

Ella was about to ask her sister if she was looking forward to spending the day with Brodie when Michael emerged from the bathroom.

"Am I the only one around here who is starving?" He picked up his watch from the nightstand. "I'm willing to test the full Scottish breakfast for you, Samantha. I will give you my considered opinion on every element."

Samantha smiled at him. "Your sacrifice is duly noted."

"Always willing to take one for the team. Are you coming for something to eat, Ella?"

"Later." Ella pulled on extra layers and found her coat. She felt isolated. No one, not even her sister, seemed to understand the way she was feeling. "I want to check on my daughter."

"Our daughter." Michael's tone was mild. "She's our daughter."

"True. But she's with *my* mother. She's probably telling Tab never to get married, or to make sure she only ever takes a well-paid job. Or maybe Tab has fallen over and she's telling her to pick herself up."

Samantha exchanged a look with Michael. "You need to relax, Ella, or this Christmas gathering is never going to work. You can't hover over Mom, watching her every move."

Nothing stung quite as sharply as criticism from someone you saw as an ally. "How can you say that? You know what she's like. Just look at the impact she's had on you."

Samantha's mouth tightened. "What's that supposed to mean?"

"It's our mother's constant dire warnings that are responsible for the fact that you're single and focused on work. You're terrified of feelings, which is why instead of experiencing wild abandoned passion, you spend your nights reading about wild abandoned passion. Which, now I think of it, could be the very definition of safe sex. It's certainly safer than opening up and trusting someone." She saw the wounded expression in her sister's eyes and tried to backpedal. "All I'm saying is that our upbringing had a powerful effect on us. I'm afraid to tell our mother the truth about my life, and you don't form intimate relationships because Mom told us never to build our lives around a man."

Samantha stood in frozen stillness. "Are you finished?"

"I just think—"

"And I think you should stop talking now."

Ella swallowed. "You're acting as if this is all normal, but before this we hadn't spoken to our mother for five years. So forgive me if this whole thing is a bit sensitive. We're pretending we're a normal family, and we are not a normal family."

"I'm going to see if I can find the McIntyres and some breakfast and if I can't, I'll retire to my room with my romantic fantasies." Samantha left the room and Ella stared after her miserably.

"Now I've upset her." And she felt terrible. She and Samantha never fought. Her sister was her comfort blanket, and she knew Samantha felt the same way about her.

"She'll be fine." Michael picked up his phone. "Your relationship will survive one tactless comment."

"You think I was tactless?"

"I think you're not yourself. And if this is how you are around your mother, then perhaps this is a good time to look at that."

"What's that supposed to mean?"

He put the phone in his pocket. "If there are things you want to say to your mother, then say them."

"I've told you, she makes me feel like—"

"A child. Yes. I get that. And I get that it's hard, but it's up to you to rewrite that narrative. We're always children to our parents. We'll probably be the same around Tab when she is thirty and fully independent—but if you're truly going to reestablish a relationship with your mother, then both of you need to put the past behind you."

"How am I supposed to do that?" How could he make it sound so easy? If it were easy, she would already have done it.

"You could start by telling her that you're not teaching right now. That you've chosen to stay home and raise our child. Surely a woman who writes books encouraging people to make choices will understand your need to make a few of your own?"

Ella could just imagine how that would play out.

"She's fine with other people's choices. But she's only good with her daughter's choices if they align with her ambitions for us."

Michael picked up her scarf and put it round her neck. "Then you need to make it clear that accepting your choices is going to be part of your relationship moving forward." He kissed her forehead. "She doesn't have to like your choices, but she does need to accept them."

Ella thought back to that awful day five years before. *You're a terrible mother.* They were all carrying on as if those harsh words had never been said. But she hadn't forgotten the words, and she was sure her mother wouldn't have forgotten them, either.

Could they really move forward and heal their relationship without addressing what had happened?

"I'll talk to her when I feel the time is right."

"That time is now. Do you want me to be with you for that conversation?"

"No, of course not. I'm not that pathetic."

Or maybe she was that pathetic. But if she was, she didn't want him to see it.

She sat down on the bed. "I was so looking forward to Christmas. It was going to be magical."

"Honey, have you looked out of the window? It is as magical as can be out there, and your daughter is laughing. Sure, it's not the way we planned on spending the holidays, but I think it will turn out to be better. I know you're worried about your mother, but maybe this will be a turning point in your relationship."

He always saw the potential and not the pitfalls.

"When you drown me with optimism I don't know whether to hug you or hate you." But he was right, of course. Tab was laughing, they were staying on the edge of a snowy forest and beyond the doors of the house were real reindeer. It was a child's idea of a winter wonderland.

He tugged her to her feet. "Give it all you've got. If she doesn't respond, then at least you know you did all you could."

She knew he was right. She was a grown woman with a job she loved and a family she adored. She was proud of what she did and who she was, so why was she so afraid to be honest with her mother?

"I still want her approval. Why do I need that?"

"I think it's called being human." Michael nudged her toward the door. "Join in. Maybe Tab is exactly what both of you need. She might bring you together."

Ella wasn't so confident.

She walked with Michael down the wide, sweeping staircase, feeling as if she was being judged by all the ancestors staring down at her from the paintings. What was it like to have family stretching back for centuries? She didn't even have a photograph of her father, and her mother refused to talk about him.

Maybe Ella should push the issue and try and get her to talk. If she'd come here on her honeymoon, then maybe that was a good place to start.

Kirstie stood stiffly in the hallway. "We've laid breakfast in the dining room."

"Thank you." Ella turned to Michael. "You go ahead. I'll go and get Tab and Mom. Oh wait—do you have a carrot?" When Kirstie looked blank, Ella smiled. "My daughter is building a snowman."

For the first time since they'd arrived, Kirstie smiled. "I'll fetch one from the kitchen."

She was back moments later with a suitably shaped carrot, and Ella left Michael to continue thawing the frozen Kirstie, and stepped out the front door.

The overnight fall of snow had turned the grounds into a magical shimmering landscape. The storm had left the trees thickly coated, the driveway and the lawns leading down to the loch transformed into a field of white streaked with silver as the sun danced across the ice crystals.

Ella breathed in the crisp air and curled her hands into fists to warm them against the icy bite of the winter weather.

She smelled woodsmoke and the sharp aroma of pine and fir. She was dazzled by silver and snow and realized that this was the atmosphere they all tried to re-create in their homes. People bought fake trees covered in fake snow in an attempt to reproduce the wintry charm of the forest. Only now did she realize what a poor imitation it really was.

She glanced back at the lodge. Snow clung to the turrets and a curl of smoke emerged from one of the chimneys. It was a completely perfect place to spend Christmas.

If she could find a way to heal things with her mother, then maybe everything would turn out well.

Two pairs of footsteps, one much larger than the other, wound their way through the otherwise pristine surface, and she followed the trail around the house and found Tab and her mother engrossed in the construction of their snowman.

"He needs a bigger head." Tab smacked the snow with her hand and then glanced up. "Mommy!"

Ella's heart melted. "Hi there! Having fun?"

"Yes. I wanted to bring Bear but we couldn't find him." Tab stroked and smoothed the snowman.

"You've been busy."

Her mother's cheeks were pink. "You didn't have to join us. You could have slept in. I thought you and Michael could probably use some time together."

In any other circumstances it would have been a thoughtful gesture. But her mother wasn't a regular babysitter, and this wasn't a normal situation.

"I woke up and found Tab's room empty." Ella dug her hands into the pockets of her coat. "I didn't know where she was."

"She was with me."

"But—" *She doesn't know you.* "I was worried, that's all."

"She's not likely to come to much harm in a place like this."

Ella glanced around the snowy wilderness. It would take a year to list the number of potential accidents. She took a deep breath and remembered Michael's words.

Explain to her in a rational, mature way, that you were concerned.

She opened her mouth and closed it again.

Why, when it came to her own mother, was it so hard to vocalize the things that mattered to her?

"Tab is very active. Unpredictable. She loves to climb and explore."

"That's good. It's how a child gains confidence and a sense of the world."

Ella wanted to explain to her mother how hard she had worked to stay balanced on the tightrope that stretched between encouragement and caution.

Should she confess that when her instinct failed her, she thought about her mother's parenting style and did the opposite? No. Despite the choppy past, she genuinely wanted to heal their relationship. And their situations had been different. Her mother had been alone. Ella couldn't begin to imagine how she would have coped in the same circumstances.

"It is good, but it's also a little scary. She doesn't know her own limitations."

"Limitations are often in the mind. They're what stop us from moving forward. Fear is a powerful set of brakes."

The comment was so typical of her mother. *Push your boundaries. Never listen to no.* As if everything was a battle. Man against life, or in this case Woman against life.

It could have been taken straight from *Choice Not Chance*, not that Ella had read it. Like her sister, she'd decided it would leave a bitter taste in her mouth.

Maybe it was time to push her own boundaries.

"Not knowing your limitations isn't a good thing when you're playing close to a deep lake and a dark forest." It sounded as if she was reading from a children's book designed to thrill and scare young minds. *There was a deep lake and a dark forest.* "She needs to be watched."

Her mother was about to scoop up snow, but she paused and straightened. "I've been watching her every second. I'd never let anything happen to her."

And now she felt mean and small. "Of course you wouldn't intentionally. But you don't—I mean you're not—" How should she handle this? *We have very different views on child-rearing.* "You're not used to handling very young children, and she doesn't know you. And you don't know her." *And you don't know me, and how I want to raise my child, which is very different from the way you raised us.*

She waited, braced for a comeback, but her mother gave a tentative smile.

"You're right, but that's what this holiday is for. Getting to know each other better. So far we're getting along just fine. I'm being guided by her." She scooped up another handful of snow for Tab. "She asked if we could come out here and build a snowman together. I gave her a little breakfast. Just a slice of toast. She told me she likes toast. I presume that was the right thing to do?"

Ella was taken aback. "Yes, that's—it's great that you thought to give her something to eat."

"She didn't eat a lot on that journey. She wasn't interested in food. We did a lot of puzzles together. Read a heap of books."

"You were good with her." Patient. Attentive.

"She's a smart girl."

Ella relaxed a little. This was more familiar. No doubt her mother's next sentence would be, *She's going to be a doctor or a lawyer.*

"She is smart. Sometimes too busy to eat."

Her mother nodded. "I expect her body clock was all churned up. I tried to get her to eat more breakfast this morning, but she was desperate to be outdoors. I put plenty of layers on her. We held hands the whole way here." She looked at Ella, troubled. "Did I miss something? Did I do something wrong? Because I thought I had everything covered."

All her life Ella had desperately longed for her mother's approval. *Look what I've done, Mom. Look what I've made.* Never before had her mother sought her approval.

"You've been great." And maybe they were making headway. Maybe things could be different.

"You're right that it's been a while since I've been with children Tab's age." Her mother scooped up more snow for Tab.

"I did some research, but that doesn't really prepare you for the individual."

Research? Her mother had done research? What type of research?

"Mom—"

"She's smart and strong. She knows what she wants, but she has good manners. She's a credit to you, Ella."

Her mother had praised her. Her mother had actually praised her.

It made her feel light-headed.

"It's mostly her." It was a struggle to keep her voice normal. "And she has her moments when she's tired."

"Of course she does. And she asks a lot of questions."

That was something Ella wasn't going to disagree with. "She'll question you until the battery in your brain dies."

"Is this the age group you teach?"

And just like that they reached a junction. Left or right?

This was the perfect moment to tell her mother the truth, but she didn't want to do anything to shatter this new, fragile truce.

She chose the safer of the two paths.

"Yes. I've always loved this age. They're learning so much every single day."

The wind picked up, bringing with it a flutter of snowflakes. They spun and swirled, light as dust.

Her mother was hunkered over the snowman, her coat a splash of color against the snowy landscape, her hair wind-blown and her face free of makeup. The wound on her head had healed, but there was still a scar. The mother she knew always wore black, and a fierce expression. She strode through life with her mouth pursed, eyes fixed forward, as if not one single body part was allowed to deviate from its brief. This new version of her mother, this peacock-colored, smiling, soft-as-butter, attentive version, wasn't someone she recognized.

An icy wind snaked through the collar of her coat, and Ella

was about to step forward and zip Tab's coat up to the neck, when her mother leaned across and did exactly that.

"Are you warm enough, honey?"

Honey? *Honey?*

Her mother never used pet names. Her communication when they were growing up had always been practical. *Have you brushed your teeth? Don't forget your reading book. Pay attention in class. Learn something new every day.*

"Yes, thank you, Nanna. I'm like toast. I've finished the head." Tab pushed, pressed and patted. "What do you think?"

The snowman was possibly the most misshapen object Ella had ever seen.

She held her breath, waiting for her mother to kill Tab's joyful moment with a careless remark about how she should keep trying until she was perfect at it, but instead Gayle clapped her hands.

"I think it's *wonderful.* You have a real talent."

Ella was so shocked she forgot about the cold.

She'd always believed her mother wasn't capable of being warm and encouraging with her family. She'd made excuses— assumed that something inside her had died when she'd lost the man she loved. But it seemed she *was* capable of it.

Her insides churned with a cocktail of emotions she couldn't identify.

Regret? Even a little envy? She straightened her shoulders. Whatever it was, she was going to ignore it. This was *good.* Really good.

Her mother was trying hard and Ella would try hard, too. Sometimes in life it was important to stop thinking about what might have been, and think about what could be.

Tab pressed more snow onto the body, her breath steaming the cold air. "Can we build a snowman every day that we're here?" She glanced up. "Nanna?"

"Yes, we can."

Tab brushed the snow from her mittens. "Next we need twigs! For arms."

"I'll find the arms." Ella headed toward the trees, her feet punching through the thin crust and sinking deep.

Pinecones poked through the layer of snow and she stooped and picked a couple up, tucking them into her pocket. Then she found twigs and a stone that she thought might make a good mouth.

She took her time, enjoying the winter wonderland, and then walked to the edge of the trees and watched the two figures tending the snowman and laughing together.

Her mother waved at her and she waved back.

She felt a burst of hope. Christmas was going to be all right after all.

Michael was right that Tab might be the bridge between her and her mother.

She imagined her mother finally opening up and telling her and Samantha about their father.

She imagined them all gathered together round the large Christmas tree, enjoying each other's company in a way they never had before. If her mother had photos somewhere, maybe she'd agree to share them.

"Here." She walked back and dropped her forest finds at Tab's feet. "Plenty of options there."

Tab, always particular, discarded a couple of twigs and then selected two.

She pushed the "arms" into the body of the snowman, and then the tiny stones became its eyes. "Who built the first snowman?"

Ella, who was used to Tab's endless questions, settled in for what was probably going to be a lengthy conversation.

"No one knows exactly who built the first one, but we know that people have been building snowmen for a long time. Back in the fifteenth century a very famous artist and sculptor called Michelangelo built a snowman for the man he worked for."

"Was it a good one?"

Ella reached out to help with the arms of the snowman. "I think we can be pretty confident it was exceptional."

Tab pushed the pinecone into the snowman's face. "Were you alive in the fifteenth century, Nanna? Did you see the snowman?"

Ella heard her mother make a choking sound.

"I was not alive."

"That would make Nanna more than four hundred years old," Ella said patiently. "Humans don't live to be four hundred."

"Although there are mornings when I *feel* four hundred."

Ella couldn't remember them spending a more enjoyable hour together. It was like discovering sugar, when you'd only ever tasted salt.

"Brodie said some of the trees in this forest are hundreds of years old. So they're older than humans." Tab stepped back to admire her snowman. "Building a snowman might be my favorite thing."

Ella crouched down next to her daughter. "Last week baking cookies was your favorite thing. And the week before that it was dancing."

Gayle shaped the snowman's neck with her gloved hand. "Do you have ballet classes?"

Tab shook her head. "I dance with my mommy. We dance round the house." Tab sprang up like a bouncing ball. "Let's do a snowdance, Nanna!"

"Aren't we going to finish your snowman?"

"Let's dance first. We can make footprints." Tab grabbed both Gayle's hands but Gayle stood looking helpless.

"I don't really—I don't dance. I can't dance."

"Everyone can dance." Still holding her grandmother's hands, Tab proceeded to demonstrate, leaping around awkwardly, her movements hampered by padded winter clothing and snow boots. "Mommy join in, too."

Ella laughed and took her daughter's hand, twirling her. It was a moment of pure joy. Spontaneously she reached for her mother's hand but Gayle snatched her hand away with a quick shake of her head.

"I prefer to watch."

Ella almost wavered, checked by her mother's response, but instead she took both Tab's hands. She wasn't going to let her mother's judgment impact on her relationship with her daughter. That wasn't happening. "You're lucky it's just dancing, Mom." She spun Tab, then scooped her up and swung her round with a few whoops of joy that Tab echoed. "Last week's fun activity was nail polish. She used bright red. I had to stop Michael calling an ambulance when he saw the result."

She'd expected her mother to laugh at that, but all Gayle managed was a weak smile.

Which probably proved that one's children were never quite as funny and endearing as one thought they were.

Despite her best efforts, Ella felt self-conscious. She put Tab down and turned back to the snowman.

"Are we going to finish this snowman? He needs a nose, and I happen to have one right here." Ella produced the carrot from her pocket, and Tab's face lit up as she took it. Ella waited. "What do we say, Tab?"

"Thank you." Tab pushed the carrot into place, sending an avalanche of snow sliding off the snowman.

"I never would have thought of bringing a carrot." Gayle shifted position and rubbed her ribs with her hand.

"Mom, are you *sure* you're all right?"

"Yes. Just not used to bending down scooping up snow."

"Nanna has hurt ribs." Tab tugged off her hat and balanced it on top of the snowman's head. "Did you know Nanna hasn't made a snowman since she was my age?"

"No. I didn't know that." She didn't know her mother had ever made a snowman. She couldn't begin to imagine it. Building a snowman required a carefree, childlike enjoyment, something she didn't associate with her mother. The truth was she knew very little about her mother's past, but it seemed she'd talked about it with Tab.

Ella looked at her mother, but Gayle's eyes were focused on the snowman while Tab carried on chatting. "She made one with her mommy. It had a red scarf. Nanna didn't want to build one with me at first. She thought she'd forgotten how, but I reminded her."

Ella tried to imagine her mother as a little girl, eyes bright with excitement as she'd built her snowman.

"Did you build it in Central Park, Mom?"

Gayle stirred. "No. We had a large garden."

"But you were living in an apartment in Manhattan."

"Not back then. We didn't move to Manhattan until I was sixteen, although we often visited of course. When I was young we lived in Vermont in a large house with lots of land. We always had deer eating our plants, which frustrated my mother."

Ella handed Tab another twig. "You never mentioned that you lived in Vermont."

Her mother had built a snowman. Why had she never built one with them? What had happened?

She had so many questions, and no answers.

She was about to ask a few of those questions, when Michael appeared. He wore a wool coat, collar turned up, hands thrust into his pockets.

"How's it going here?" He was calm and relaxed, but his presence told Ella he'd rushed breakfast in order to be here for her. "How are my girls?"

"We're having fun," she said. "The snow is the perfect consistency for building snowmen."

"Then it's lucky I'm here to judge the snowman contest." He turned his attention to his daughter.

"It's not a contest," Tab said. "It's just me. So I win."

"You do. I officially declare this snowman the best in Scotland. Possibly the best in the whole of the Northern Hemisphere."

"You're silly, Daddy."

"Not silly. That is an excellent snowman." He leaned toward Ella. "Should I mention that he might need a nose job?"

She raised an eyebrow. "You think a parsnip would have been better? How was breakfast?"

"Worth taking a break from snowman building to sample. That's why I'm here. You should eat something. I recommend the full Scottish breakfast."

"I had toast," Tab said. "I want to play in the snow." She was busy scooping up more snow, only this time she was constructing something new next to the snowman.

Michael dropped into a crouch next to his daughter.

"Another snowman?"

"It's a snowdog." Tab patted and shaped the mound. "To keep him company."

Michael rose to his feet and smiled at Ella. "You and your mother should go and have breakfast together."

"No hurry."

"Go—" he held her gaze "—seize the moment."

He was encouraging her to spend quality time with her mother, and that was probably a good idea, particularly as everything was going so well.

"Where's Samantha?"

"Last seen vanishing into the library—great library by the way—for a meeting, and then I think the plan is that Brodie is going to take her round the estate so they can discuss business."

Was her sister still angry with her? And how did she feel about spending the whole day with Brodie? Had she managed to get past the embarrassment of their earlier exchange?

"I'll wait until Tab finishes the snowdog."

"Go. I've got this." He tugged her toward him and kissed her.

"No kissing." Tab pressed two small stones into the dog's face. "They're always kissing, Nanna."

Ella, remembering her mother's presence, stepped away.

Michael handed Tab a twig for the dog's tail. "Daddy loves Mommy. Nothing wrong with kissing."

"It's yucky."

"Yucky? You think it's yucky?" Michael made growling monster sounds and leaned in to kiss Tab's neck.

She squealed and tried to escape, giggling so hard she fell backward into the snow.

He scooped her up and Ella shook her head, torn between laughter and exasperation.

"Now she's covered in snow, Michael."

"And she loves it."

Ella brushed the snow from Tab's coat, removed her scarf and wrapped it around her daughter's neck. "You need this to keep warm." She caught sight of her mother's face and saw a look of such intense pain that she stopped breathing. Even when she'd been in the hospital, Gayle had seemed strong and in control. Her mother's reaction to life was so combative and gladiatorial and she so rarely showed her feelings that Ella had at some point assumed she didn't have them. What had caused that reaction? Was it seeing Ella and Michael with Tab?

"Mom?" She said it gently and then louder because her mother didn't seem to hear her. Finally Gayle blinked.

"Sorry? What did you say?"

"I— Nothing." She couldn't probe more deeply into her mother's emotions with Tab so close by. It was something to be done in private. "You're right, Michael. I'm starving. You finish off here with Tab. Mom and I will go and eat breakfast and we'll see you in a while."

She turned and started to trudge through the snow, her mother keeping pace by her side.

How should she handle this? It wasn't as if she and her mother usually shared anything emotional. How should she start this conversation?

Hey, Mom, just now you looked as if your child had died in front of you. What's that about?

Her mother spoke first. "He seems like a good father."

"Michael? He's amazing. Fun. Interested. Tab is lucky."

"Mmm. Is he good to you?"

"To *me*? Of course. Why would you ask that?"

"Why wouldn't I? You're my daughter. Your welfare doesn't stop being important to me, even though you're an adult and married."

"I should have told you about Tab. And Michael."

"I wish you had, but I understand why you didn't." Gayle turned up the collar of her coat. "I don't blame you."

"You…don't?"

"No. I handled our last meeting badly. I hurt you, and I'm sorry for it. All I've ever wanted was to protect you and your sister. I don't expect you to understand that."

"Then help us understand it." Ella stopped walking. They were five minutes from the house and she didn't want a conversation this important to be interrupted. "What were you protecting us from, exactly? Is it because of Dad? I don't understand how it feels to lose the person you love so young, but I do understand how it feels to want to protect your child." Maybe that was common ground. A good place to start.

Gayle glanced back toward Tab and Michael. "You must have been pregnant that last time we met."

"Yes." Was her mother going to simply ignore her question?

"It explains why you were so emotional, and why Samantha was so protective."

Exasperation licked at the edges of her patience. "I was emotional because—" *You upset me.* Keep it neutral. No accusations. "The conversation upset me."

"I was concerned about you. You didn't seem able to settle at anything. Before you trained as a teacher, you had four different jobs in two years."

"But those jobs helped me figure out what I wanted. And what I wanted to be was a teacher. I know I disappointed you. You wanted me to be a doctor, or a lawyer."

"I wanted you to be secure and financially independent. And you didn't disappoint me. You scared me."

"*Scared* you?" They stood there, shoulder to shoulder, and yet the distance between them felt huge.

"You're a mother." Gayle turned to look at her. "You must understand how it feels to be afraid for your child. You want to protect them from the world, but deep down you know you can't protect them and the next best thing is to make sure you equip them to fight whatever life sends through the door. I tried to give you those tools. I made sure you could swim. I taught you to read, so that by the time you started school you were already an independent reader. I took you to martial arts classes so that you could handle yourself with confidence."

Ella thought of the number of times she'd begged to learn ballet. "I wanted to dance."

"I couldn't afford ballet and martial arts. I chose the one I thought might be most useful. No one ever danced their way out of trouble." Her mother stirred. "I wasn't afraid of you being a teacher. I was afraid of you giving it up and moving on to the next thing. Sampling, and not sticking. I needed you to stick. I wanted you to be able to always support yourself."

"I was trying to find a job that made me happy."

"Happiness doesn't pay the bills."

"Life has to be about more than paying the bills, but I understand that being widowed so young must have been frightening."

"It was. I relied on your father financially. That was a mistake."

"You never talk about him."

"Excuse me?"

"Dad. You never talk about him. You never talk about your

marriage. Until last night Sam and I had no idea that you'd come here on your honeymoon."

"Why would you?"

Did she really need to spell it out? "I would have thought that might be something you might have mentioned before." Ella put her hand on her mother's arm. "Is being here difficult for you?"

"Difficult?"

"The place must have memories." Because her mother was contributing nothing to the conversation, she made a guess. "It must have been a special time."

Her mother stared into the distance. "I try not to think about it."

"Because it hurts so much?"

"Because thinking about it is a reminder of how very foolish I was." Her mother extracted herself from Ella's grip and continued toward the house.

Foolish?

"There's nothing foolish about love, Mom." She hurried to catch up. "Love is the most important thing there is."

"Oh Eleanor—" her mother turned "—I had hoped that age and maturity might have made you less romantic and more practical, but it seems that hasn't happened."

Eight minutes, Ella thought. *Eight minutes of conversation and they were locking horns again.* She felt small and insignificant, as if her opinions didn't matter. Her mother wasn't telling her that they thought differently. She was telling her that she was wrong.

There was no discussion. No acceptance of a differing point of view. Just judgment.

Her instinct was to stalk off, to protect herself, to accept that this relationship was never going to change.

But then she remembered the look on her mother's face when she'd seen Tab with Michael. She'd been feeling *something*, even if it was something she denied and wouldn't talk about.

It was like following a few bread crumbs and hoping they'd

lead you out of the forest. She wasn't sure where that information would lead, but she felt that it had to lead somewhere. She wanted to follow it right to a dead end if necessary.

"It must have been terrible for you, being widowed so young and raising two young children alone. But losing someone doesn't mean that loving them was wrong."

"Please stop, Ella—" her mother looked tired "—you have no idea what you're talking about."

An hour earlier she'd thought this was a whole new start. And now it seemed they were back at the beginning.

"Not all relationships go wrong, Mom. And even when a relationship does go wrong, that doesn't mean it wasn't worth having."

Gayle stopped again. "I don't want you to have to struggle, Ella, that's all. I don't want you ever to lie there wondering how you're going to support yourself and your baby. I'm sure that by the time you've paid for childcare, there isn't much of a teacher's salary left. But at least you're still part of the workforce, maintaining your skills in case you should ever need them."

She should confess that she wasn't paying for childcare. That she'd chosen to stay at home. But even if she'd chosen to go back to work and have most of her salary eaten by childcare, that would have been her decision, too. She hadn't because she didn't want to miss a single moment of these early years with Tab. Why would she give that precious gift to a stranger? The atmosphere was already so fragile it was like stepping onto the frozen surface of a pond, knowing that the ice could crack at any moment. "Life isn't all about money, Mom." It was a limp version of what she should have said.

"Life is never about money until you don't have any. Then it becomes a rather glaring priority." Gayle took a breath. "You think I'm boring, don't you? That my focus is in the wrong place. That all I think about is work and self-improvement. But love doesn't provide any of the practical things you need in life. And it can blind you to reality. Tempt you to make yourself vulnerable."

Was there any point in confessing that love was the only thing she truly needed in her life?

No. Her mother's comment was so obviously driven by personal pain, and Ella was trying to learn more about her, not alienate her. "It must have been very hard for you when Dad died. We were so young. And you were on your own. I can't even imagine."

"I don't suppose you can. And that's my fault because I always tried to protect you from it."

Protect them from what? The pain of grief? The struggle of lone parenting?

Her mother started walking again, heading to the warmth of the lodge.

Ella hurried to catch up. How had she ever thought that spending Christmas with her mother might heal their relationship? They weren't a family. They weren't a unit. Ella felt defeated, her earlier optimism punctured by sharp reality.

"We're freezing to death out here." Gayle opened the front door and tugged off her boots. "I don't know about you, but I'm ready for breakfast."

That was it? That was all she was going to say?

Ella considered herself to be pretty good with people, but she had no idea how to connect with her mother. If anything, her attempts to get closer seemed to have driven them further apart.

How could you have a proper relationship with someone when you didn't really know anything about them?

Gayle

Had she made a mistake returning to Scotland?

She'd come here to build a relationship with her granddaughter and rebuild her relationship with her daughters. She badly wanted to bridge the gap, but how? It seemed that in order to achieve that closeness that Ella clearly wanted, and which she also wanted, she was going to have to think about things she didn't want to think about and talk about things she didn't want to talk about. Why did Ella want to know about her father when he'd been gone from her life before she was even born?

Gayle had been six months pregnant, and Samantha had been just seven months old.

She'd trained herself not to think about that time. It was all too upsetting, and she'd learned that emotion clouded the brain and stopped you focusing on the important things like surviving. Talking just wasted time that was precious when you were raising two children alone.

She'd never been the gossipy type. Instead she preferred to

examine her problems and either solve them or learn to live with them.

And as for talking about their father—

Maybe it *had* been a mistake coming back here. If she wasn't careful, she was going to make her relationship with her daughters worse, not better.

Why had she mentioned that she'd visited Scotland on her honeymoon? That was a detail that had inevitably attracted the attention of romantic Ella.

Truthfully, she hadn't expected it to be this difficult. She'd thought she'd be able to handle it, the way she handled everything in her life. Nothing defeated her.

And yet here she was with shaking hands and a sick feeling in her stomach simply because her daughter had asked about her honeymoon and wanted details of her father.

The years had fallen away, along with all the layers of defenses she'd carefully constructed over time.

Did she remember her honeymoon? Oh yes, she remembered it. Every moment. She'd been flying high, and still at the point in her life where she hadn't realized that flying high simply made the fall harder when it came.

She'd paid a price for naivety, and optimism.

Feeling fragile, she removed her scarf, and then her coat and handed them to Kirstie, who was hovering near the entrance. The young woman was trying hard to compose her features into a pattern that looked friendly and welcoming, and instead she looked like someone with severe toothache. Gayle wondered what was making her so miserable and opened her mouth to talk to her about finding her power and using it, but her heart wasn't in it. Right now she wasn't sure she could access her own power, let alone help anyone else find theirs.

She needed to sit down. She needed a moment on her own to pull herself together and rediscover her own strength.

She walked into the dining room, where she and Tab had eaten toast together earlier that morning.

Now a fire blazed, and silver gleamed against dark green linen. It took her right back to that first morning of her honeymoon. Ray had been awake before her and had been sitting by the fire with a coffee and a newspaper. For a brief, disturbing moment Gayle could see his face. The confidence of his smile. The flash of perfect teeth. The crinkling at the corners of his eyes.

Usually her memories were fuzzy and indistinct, but this one was sharp and so real it unsteadied her.

A wave of dizziness barreled into her, and she swayed. She reached out to steady herself and found herself clasping someone's hand.

"There. Come and sit down." It was the woman from the night before. Brodie McIntyre's mother. What was her name? She never forgot a name, but this morning her mind wasn't behaving the way it usually did. She was trying to focus on the moment, but her mind kept dragging her back to the past.

Gayle wanted to reject her help, but she didn't dare. Without someone to hold on to her, she had a feeling she'd end up on the floor and that would be even more embarrassing. "Thank you. I'm feeling just a little—"

"Wobbly? Jet lag does that for you."

"Yes." Jet lag and visions of dead people. And unsettling exchanges with her daughter.

"And you were up early and playing with your little granddaughter. That burns energy. She's a lively one. You need food and a hot drink, and then you'll feel more yourself."

"Thank you." Gayle accepted the help gratefully, something she hadn't done for several decades.

She could hear Ella's voice outside in the hallway, presumably talking to Kirstie, and she was grateful that her sharp-eyed daughter hadn't witnessed this particular episode or the questions would never end.

"Drink some coffee, warm yourself in front of the fire, and I'll be right back. I'm Mary, by the way. I don't think we were properly introduced last night."

Mary. That was it.

"I'm Gayle."

With the minimum of fuss, Mary poured a cup of hot coffee for her and then disappeared toward the kitchen. She was back moments later, this time carrying a bowl.

"Eat a few mouthfuls of this. You'll soon get your strength back."

"What is it?"

"Porridge, made to my special recipe. My mother always said to me 'porridge should be nothing but oats, water and a little salt,' but I couldn't persuade mine to eat it that way so I made a few adaptations. I've always enjoyed experimenting with food."

"I don't usually—"

"Try a mouthful." Mary put the spoon in her hand, as if Gayle were a child. "I think it's what you need."

Gayle felt too weak to put up a fight, something else that probably should have worried her.

Breakfast was always black coffee. She ate all her food within an eight-hour window and was ruthless about managing her calorie intake. It was a regime she'd started when her babies were young, and she couldn't afford to grow out of her clothes. She could afford all the clothes she wanted now, but the ruthless self-discipline had become a habit. Still, flexing on this one occasion was hardly going to kill her.

She took a small spoonful to be polite and paused, savoring the texture—smooth creaminess and the crunch of sugar. "Oh my—"

"Good, isn't it?" Mary seemed not at all surprised by Gayle's reaction.

"It's better than good." She took a larger spoonful, tasting other flavors that she couldn't immediately identify. "What's in this?"

"Oats, together with a little McIntyre secret."

Gayle cleared the bowl, and not because she was being polite. "It's the most delicious thing I've tasted. And that's coming from someone who never eats breakfast."

"While you're staying here you'll eat breakfast. It's freezing out there with more snow forecast. You'll need the fuel. Is the bairn still outside?"

"Yes. She's with her father."

Mary nodded. "She's a happy, inquisitive little thing. A credit to you. And she looks so like her mother."

Gayle put the spoon down.

Why hadn't she seen that? "They're similar in many ways. My daughter had the same happy, bubbly, inquisitive personality." It had terrified her. Ella had always been so trusting. She had no fear of strangers. She'd happily chat with anyone. Tab seemed to be the same. "Have you worked here long?"

Mary straightened cutlery and gathered up a used napkin. "I married Cameron McIntyre when I was nineteen and I've lived here ever since. Sometimes I feel as if I know every tree and rock in the Glen. There's not a blade of grass I haven't walked over at some point."

"You own the place? I apologize. I didn't realize—"

"No need for apology. How could you have known? Losing my Cameron last year was the hardest thing I've ever had to deal with, but when I realized I might lose the home we'd lived in together for all of our married lives—" Mary took a deep breath. "Life going wrong is the real test of a family, isn't it? Brodie had a great job in London, but he moved back here and took this on. He gave up a lot for us, and that makes me feel guilty, but not so guilty I'll tell him to sell this place and live his own life. Which I suppose makes me selfish. But when

I'm here, I feel as if part of Cameron is still here with me. And now I'm talking too much."

"Not at all." It was a relief to listen to someone else's problems. It stopped her focusing on her own.

The thought made her flush with shame. When had she become so selfish?

This was Mary's house. Her dining room, where she'd laughed with her husband and enjoyed meals with her children. She was entertaining strangers in order to keep her family home.

Gayle thought about her own bruised and fractured family. She'd done everything she could to make her daughters independent, to the point of pushing them away. She'd believed that to be more important than protecting the family unit. She'd taught them to rely on themselves and not need anyone. And where had that got her? Regret flashed through Gayle, along with the doubt she'd felt that day in her office when she'd been hovering on the edges of unconsciousness. It wasn't a comfortable feeling. What was the point in wondering if you'd made mistakes as a parent when there was nothing you could do to fix it?

She decided to follow Mary's example and ignore her own thoughts. "It must be difficult having strangers in your home."

"I can't tell you what a relief it is. There is nothing I love more than having a house full of people. Noise drowns out thoughts, don't you find? Right now I don't much like my thoughts. Hearing your granddaughter laughing this morning was one of the best things I've heard in a long time. Being a grandmother must be a wonderful thing. I envy you."

Gayle was used to being envied, but not for that.

She thought about her morning with Tab. The innocence and simplicity of it. Tab's small hand tucked trustingly into hers. There was no history. No judgment. Just the moment.

Did you know that every snowflake is different, Nanna? Mommy says they're like people.

"It is a wonderful thing."

And she wasn't going to lose it. She'd do whatever it took.

Her relationship with her own children had been about preparing them for the world.

What was her role with a granddaughter?

She didn't have one, which was perhaps why she'd found their brief time together that morning so lighthearted and refreshing. She'd been able to enjoy the moment without that soul crushing sense of responsibility.

Focused on scooping up snow with one very excited little girl, she'd briefly forgotten all her problems. That exhausting tension had eased. Her brain had cleared. Life had seemed simple.

And then Ella had arrived, anxious at first because she hadn't trusted her mother with her child.

She wasn't trusted with her own grandchild.

The pain of it was shocking. Worse than the bang on the head.

Maybe she hadn't done everything right, but did they really think she was that bad a mother? Or maybe it was part of life that everyone chose to do things differently from their parents.

She thought of Ella, crouched down eye level with her daughter, listening. Attentive.

Had she given her daughters that much time and attention?

Probably not, because she'd been working to build a safe financial future for them all.

Excuses, excuses, excuses.

Didn't she always urge people to own their actions?

Mary was still nursing the coffeepot. "I'm longing for one of my two to give me grandchildren, but these days it isn't the done thing to ask, is it? I daren't raise the subject. I did it once and I was soundly scolded by both my daughter and my son. Do you have to watch what you say with your girls?"

Gayle gave a hysterical laugh. Every conversation with them was like walking over broken glass. If you trod too heavily, you'd be lacerated. "I certainly do." She felt an unusual sense of kinship. "Why don't you sit down, Mary? Join me."

"I shouldn't." Mary paused. "Brodie probably wouldn't approve."

"He's not here, and we are. Also, our children can't have everything their own way, however old they are. Please." Gayle waved a hand toward the door. "I have no idea where my daughter has gone, and I don't want to eat breakfast alone. If anyone complains, you can blame me."

Everyone else seemed to blame her for everything, so more blame would barely register.

The thought annoyed her.

Since when had she been so self-pitying? That wasn't the way she operated. She looked at the facts and did what she could. It was like opening the fridge and making a meal based on the ingredients available.

"I think she was talking to my daughter. I hope Kirstie doesn't say something she shouldn't. Was she rude to you?"

"Rude?" How honest should she be? "Not rude at all. She looked—"

"Miserable?"

"Serious. As if she has a lot on her mind."

"She does, but I'm worried she's going to scare away the guests. I think Brodie is afraid of that, too. She's struggling with this new direction for our family. All she wants is to be outdoors with the reindeer. The fact that she isn't is my fault, although it's poor Brodie that she's blaming."

"Why is it your fault?" Gayle hoped Ella wouldn't join them in the next few minutes. Talking with Mary had eased the tension that had been with her for the past month. "Pour yourself a cup of that delicious coffee. Join me. You'll be doing me a favor."

Mary poured one and topped up Gayle's cup. Then she sat down in the chair next to Gayle. She was poised on the edge, as if she wasn't quite committed to staying. "I shouldn't be talking to you like this."

"Talking can help." She was glad Ella wasn't around to hear

that. Given the conversation they'd had, she'd no doubt add hypocrisy to the never-ending list of Gayle's sins. "And sometimes it's easier to talk to a stranger."

"That's true. I'm always acting a part around the children. I don't want them to know how bad I feel, because then they'll feel bad. So I put my best smile on with my dress in the mornings. Have you ever done that?"

Gayle thought about all the things her children didn't know about her. "Many times."

"It's part of being a parent, isn't it? You're the support, not the supported. The only time I allow myself to cry is in the shower and the kitchen because I can hide it there."

"How do you hide in the kitchen?" Gayle had visions of Mary crouched under the table, howling into a napkin.

"I don't hide myself, but I can hide tears. I chop a lot of onions." Mary fiddled with her cup. "Onion soup, onion gravy—onions in everything. They're a marvelous cover-up for red, watering eyes."

"I'd never thought of that." Gayle didn't cry. And generally she didn't have to hide her emotions because she lived alone. She wasn't wrapped up in her children's lives the way Mary seemed to be. *But she wanted to be.* She thought about Tab's happy smile, and how much fun they'd had building that snowman. "Why do you think it's your fault that Kirstie is struggling?"

"Because I'm supportive of Brodie's idea of opening our home to guests. I think it's a good way to solve our financial difficulties, but Kirstie feels as if it's a betrayal. She thinks there must be a different way. Wants a magic bullet. But life isn't like that, is it?"

"No. And people are generally afraid of change, even though sometimes it can be good."

If it weren't for the fact that the past few weeks had shaken her faith in her own beliefs, she would have given Mary a copy of her book.

"You're right, and the truth is sometimes we have no choice but to change. I'm willing to do whatever it takes to stay here."

"Your daughter doesn't feel the same?"

"Kirstie is upset with her brother for even contemplating allowing strangers into our home. Film crews. TV. He's thinking about doing weeks for hikers, and weeks for artists, writers and musicians." Mary smiled. "He's a mathematician. Very clever. When he was a teenager, the school used to tell me that they'd never taught a pupil with a mind like his. And he's musical. Plays the cello and the piano. But his creativity stops there. Trying to come up with solutions that aren't numerical is half killing him I think, so the last thing he needs is his sister fighting him."

Gaye thought about the man who had picked them up from the airport. Practical. Dependable.

"You must be proud of him. And of Kirstie. She's here by your side, helping you, even though she'd rather be out there with the reindeer."

"Yes." Mary finished her coffee. "I did wonder if it would be easier for everyone if we sold the place and I moved to an apartment in the city. I wouldn't need to worry about a leaking roof and frozen pipes. But I don't think I'd survive. We go for the day sometimes, and I can't breathe with so many buildings crowding in on me. I'm staying here until we've tried everything. And that means Kirstie adapting, too. So that makes me feel selfish. But it also means I don't have the privacy for those quiet, difficult moments when grief swamps you."

"Does it matter if they witness that? Your children must know you're upset. It's natural to grieve."

"I want to protect them from that. Even when your children are grown, you still want to protect them, don't you?"

Yes, Gayle thought. You did. Even when they didn't thank you for it.

"Maybe we protect them too much. I don't know." She took a mouthful of hot coffee. "I'm not the right person to pass an opinion on that. I'm not a very good mother." She felt her voice falter and then felt Mary's hand on hers.

"That's nonsense. You're an excellent mother."

"I'm really not. And lately I've been questioning some of the parenting decisions I've made." Had she really just said that aloud? And to a relative stranger? "Ignore me, I'm—"

"You do that, too? It's a relief to know it's not just me."

"You question your parenting decisions?"

"Of course. You do what you think is best at the time, based on the information you have available, and it's only later when you look back that you wonder if you made the wrong choices." Mary leaned forward. "What we have to remember is that looking back doesn't give you the same picture you were looking at when you made those decisions. All we can do is our best, based on the information and circumstances of the time, and I'm sure you did that."

It was reassuring that Mary, who seemed to have a close loving relationship with her family, sometimes felt the way she did.

"You feel doubt, too?"

"Constantly. Welcome to parenting. The hardest thing you'll ever do in your life. And the thing they don't tell you in any of the books is that it gets harder, not easier. At least when they were toddlers you could control their world to an extent. It was tiring of course, relentless on occasions, but it was also fairly predictable. You were in charge." Mary shook her head. "Then they become adults and you realize that the stress of parenting doesn't ease. If anything, it gets worse."

"It does." She hadn't thought about it before, but Mary was right. The child side of things had certainly been simpler in many ways.

"My two don't seem to think I can possibly understand anything about their lives."

"Tell me about it."

Mary sat up a little straighter. "Could you eat a Scottish breakfast, Gayle?"

"The porridge will keep me going for hours, but thank you. My son-in-law—" she stumbled over the still-unfamiliar words "—Michael, told us how delicious it was. I'm sorry we didn't all sit down together this morning. We've made work for you. You must have been in the kitchen for hours."

"And I'm loving every minute. I'm so happy you're here." Mary topped up Gayle's coffee. "I was dreading Christmas. It was always my favorite time of year, because no matter what was going on in people's lives, they always came home for the festive season. But the house has felt so quiet and empty without Cameron. I even started to think that maybe I *should* sell it, but it isn't just the house you sell, is it? You sell all the memories that go with it. You can't put a price on those."

There were memories that Gayle would happily have sold. "I hope you won't have to sell."

"I'm scared that if I sell, I'll regret it. There's nothing worse than regret."

As someone who had plenty of regrets of her own, Gayle wasn't about to argue with that. "I understand."

"What do you usually do at Christmas?"

"I don't do anything." Gayle put her cup down. "When the children were young, it was just me and it was all a bit of a struggle—" *Oh the understatement.*

"Just you? You and their father—"

"He died. Before Ella was born."

"Oh Gayle! And here am I complaining that I've lost the person I had more than forty happy years with. I feel terrible."

"Don't. I'm pleased you had those years with someone you loved."

"But to be widowed when you had two babies—how did you cope?"

"A day at a time. A decision at a time. Christmas was an expensive time of year." And that wasn't all of it, of course, but it was all she intended to share. "I suppose I became used to not celebrating. Even now I take the day off because the office is closed, not through choice. Usually I catch up on work."

"Your girls don't come home?"

"No, but that's my fault. I've never made a fuss of the holidays." This was the perfect time to confess to the messy nature of their family relationships. To tell Mary they'd been estranged for five years. But she, who so rarely cared what anyone thought of her, didn't want Mary to judge her harshly. "They're busy with their own lives."

"That's hard, isn't it? Because you don't want to pressure them, but at the same time you want them to know they're welcome. And family matters. I always think that whatever else it does, Christmas gives families a nudge to get together no matter how busy their lives. I suppose that will change when they're seriously involved. Neither of mine are in serious relationships. Brodie was seeing someone in London for a while I think, but it ended when he had to come back to Scotland."

Gayle gave a vague murmur of sympathy. Her girls had never involved her in their relationships, and that was her fault. And now she could understand why Ella hadn't felt inclined to invite her to her wedding.

She'd already been pregnant that last time they'd met. She'd been afraid that her mother would have said or done something to spoil the happiness of her special day.

Would she have said the wrong thing?

Possibly. Probably.

She would have worried that her daughter was pregnant. And worried that she was getting married for the wrong reasons.

But the fact that Ella hadn't felt able to tell her didn't make her proud.

Mary was still talking about Brodie's last relationship. "Not that I thought she was right for him. He brought her back here for a weekend, but she found it remote and isolated. She wanted shopping, and there's not a lot of that around here. And then Bear, who was a puppy then, jumped on her coat with muddy paws and poor Brodie spent an entire day driving it to the dry cleaner."

"The dog?"

"The coat. They broke up soon after. Not that he ever discussed it. But I think she was one of the other reasons Kirstie was nervous about this plan to have guests. She was left with the impression that city people weren't going to like the wildness of this place."

"Or maybe the wildness is exactly what they will like," Gayle said.

"I don't know, but Brodie is convinced your daughter Samantha *does* know and should be able to help. Do you think she will, Gayle?"

Should she admit that she knew almost nothing about her daughter's business? She'd done an internet search, of course. The website was impressive. The testimonials equally good. Really Festive Holidays.

Who would have thought that would be a sound business proposition?

"My daughter will be able to help—I'm sure of it."

"I hope so. Brodie is my strong one. He does what has to be done. But I know when he's hurting. He's pinning a lot of hope on your daughter. He showed me her website. The photography alone made me want to book something myself. You must be very proud of her."

"I am proud."

"Did she always love Christmas as a child?"

Gayle put her cup down. "Yes."

And she'd never understood it. Her girls had imagined it to be a mystical, magical time of year. Gayle saw it as part of a commercial conspiracy designed to tempt innocent people to

spend a fortune in order to create the type of holiday celebration showcased by the media. *Buy this and your Christmas will be
perfect.* Life was rarely dreamy, and you did a child no favors by
pretending that it was. The one gift she hadn't wanted to give
her girls was that of unrealistic expectations.

She still remembered the moment when her rosy view of life
had been exploded by reality.

But apparently there were people prepared to pay what seemed
to Gayle to be outrageous sums of money to experience her
daughter's vision of a romantic winter vacation.

She'd looked at the website and almost been tempted to book
a week visiting the European Christmas markets, an activity
that would normally make her want to run fast in the opposite
direction.

Mary stood up and cleared the cups. "If you don't normally
spend Christmas together, this trip must be extra special for you."

"It is." Extra special and extra stressful.

"Well, we'll do what we can to make it memorable. Do you
work, Gayle?"

Gayle thought about the award in her office—*that wretched
award*—the book sales, her enviable list of clients. Her agent had
called her several times in the past few weeks to let her know
that her new book was outselling her last.

For once, she had no desire to talk about her work. "I run a
boutique consulting business." It was clear from Mary's interested expression that she had no idea what that would involve
but was too polite to say so.

"That sounds impressive."

"Not really." Normally she'd be asking questions and helping Mary examine and possibly redefine her life. But right now
it seemed to her that Mary was far more confident about her
choices than Gayle was.

There was no chance to say anything more because at that
moment Ella walked into the room.

Gayle tensed but Mary gave a quick smile.

"You must be hungry after being out in the snow. I'll fetch you a cooked breakfast." She made a rapid, tactful exit. Gayle almost begged her to stay. She wasn't sure she could handle more questions at the moment.

Ella hesitated. "Good breakfast?"

"Delicious."

"I'm sorry if my questions made you feel uncomfortable, Mom." She sat down in the empty chair next to Gayle. "You seemed upset and I wanted you to feel able to talk about it, but I understand that not everyone wants to do that. And given that I didn't talk to you about Michael, it's hypocritical of me to expect you to do the same about Dad. I'm sure there are many things that you want to keep private, and I'm going to stop asking you. But I want you to know that if you want to talk, then I'm here to listen."

Gayle was totally wrong-footed.

How did Ella do that so easily? She'd apologized, unreservedly, for making Gayle feel uncomfortable. And perhaps her questions were understandable. Both her daughters deserved answers. But how, when you'd covered something up for such a long time, did you begin to tell the truth?

Samantha

Samantha sat in the suffocating intimacy of the car, gripping her phone.

She kept her gaze fixed forward, but avoiding awkward eye contact did nothing to dilute the tension. Did he feel it, too? Was he nervous to be sitting next to a self-confessed sexually frustrated woman?

Or maybe he wasn't tense. Maybe he was feeling pity that her sex life was so unfulfilling. Maybe he was wondering if it was her fault.

Even her sister seemed to think that was the case. *You're terrified of feelings, which is why instead of experiencing wild abandoned passion, you spend your nights reading about wild abandoned passion. It's the very definition of safe sex.*

The words hurt, but words often hurt more when they were true.

Her head was fuzzy with jet lag. Her heart beating just a little too fast.

The coffee she'd drunk at breakfast might have been a mistake.

She was painfully conscious of Brodie McIntyre sitting within touching distance in the driver's seat. It would have been easier if she hadn't been so ridiculously attracted to him. It was enough that he knew her innermost thoughts in embarrassing detail, without having to deal with the added layer of complexity that came with sexual chemistry.

Laid by the Laird.

Samantha closed her eyes briefly. She was going to kill Charlotte.

In the meantime, she'd handle this situation the same way she handled any other crisis. She'd stay calm and work the problem.

Her body felt hot. Tight. Appalled, she sat up a little straighter and felt him glance at her.

"Everything all right?" His attention stoked the heat a little higher.

"Perfect. I'm excited to see what you have to offer—" *Oh Samantha.* "I mean on the estate, obviously."

There was a pause.

"Is there anywhere in particular you want to start?"

"You decide. You're the local expert." She grabbed her phone from her lap and opened a notes file. She typed Brodie and then immediately deleted it and changed the heading to Kinleven, Day 1. She was going to focus on the place, not the person next to her.

Professional Samantha was going to smother wild Samantha.

He adjusted the heater. "This is the only vehicle we have that can handle the snow and rough terrain, but it's pretty basic. No heated seats. Are you cold?"

"No. I'm hot. I mean—I'm warm enough. These are ski pants, and I have lightweight thermals under my sweater. I know a great deal about dressing for winter. Advising on appropriate clothing is one of the things we offer as part of our service to clients. We try not to recommend specific brands, but we give examples and—"

"Samantha—" he stopped the car in front of the gates "—could you relax? Your tension is making me tense." Without waiting for her to reply, he sprang from the car and pushed open the gate.

Relax.

As if that was something one could do on command. As if she had chosen shallow breathing and tense muscles over the infinitely more comfortable alternative.

She watched as he secured the gates, then stamped down a pile of snow. He looked so comfortable in his surroundings it was hard to picture him living in a city, spending his days hunched over a computer screen.

Data analyst.

He climbed back into the car, drove through the gate and stopped so that he could close it behind them.

Needing air, Samantha opened the door. "My turn." She dragged the gates shut, grateful for the freezing air that cooled her heated skin. She'd never minded cold weather. Others complained, but she found it invigorating. Deep in the Highlands it was also clean and fresh. Snow in Boston meant inconvenience and dangerous driving, and snow darkened by footprints. Here it meant quiet.

When they'd arrived, the beauty of their surroundings had been shrouded by dusky light, but today they'd woken to bright sunshine. There was a clarity to the view, and a sharpness to the outline of the mountains.

She had an urge to walk a few steps, to feel her boots break through the hard top layer to the softness beneath, but Brodie was watching, hands resting on the wheel as he waited for her to climb back into the vehicle.

She checked the gate was secure and then joined him.

"Thanks for that." He waited for her to fasten her seat belt before pulling away. "In an ideal world we'd have electric gates, but this isn't an ideal world and round here we end up doing a fair amount of manual labor."

"I guess that explains your muscles." And now it sounded as

if she'd been staring at his body. "I mean, it must be a great way of keeping in shape." *Shut up, Samantha.*

"Are you always this nervous?"

"Nervous? I'm focused, that's all, and maybe that sometimes comes across as nervous energy. This is me. This is who I am."

"So this isn't about that phone call?"

"What phone call? I'm thinking about work. I take it seriously. I assume that's why you invited me here."

"It is, but if we have an issue then I think we should address it, don't you?"

She did not.

"There's no issue."

How was she going to survive a whole day of this? On the other hand, the alternative was spending the day with her mother, and that was an even less appealing option. She didn't envy her sister, having to smile and build a snowman as if nothing was wrong.

Not for the first time in her life, Samantha was happy to use her work as an avoidance strategy.

She'd done her best to prepare herself, using makeup as armor. Ella was right that she'd taken ages over it, but not because she was hoping to attract Brodie McIntyre. Dressing in a professional manner made her feel professional. People judged on appearances—that was a fact of life. She was confident that no one looking at her would guess that her personal life was a hot mess. Her "natural" look had taken so long to achieve she thought she might have visibly aged during the process. She'd half expected to have to deal with crow's feet and wrinkles.

"Tell me more about your reindeer herd. They are going to be a real draw for clients. Are we going to see them?"

"That's the plan." Brodie drove along the narrow track that followed the winding river to the loch. "In the summer they roam wild, but in winter we keep them fairly close. We might have to walk a little way but the boots you gave me to put in the car look pretty sturdy."

"I don't have a problem with snow." She glanced up from her notes. "I'd like to see as much of the surrounding area as possible. My objective today is to get a real feel for the place so that I can evaluate our options."

"Right." He hesitated. "It's pretty wild around here. I'm sure not all of it will be a draw."

"You're worried it's too remote? I picked up on that last night."

"Because of my mother?" He fiddled with the heater. "She was trying a little too hard to convince you, wasn't she? How did she describe this place...?"

"I think her exact description was *the hub of civilization.*"

He groaned. "She won't be in charge of marketing, I promise."

"I thought she was charming." She was quick to offer reassurance. "And Kinleven might not be the hub of civilization but I can assure you that's a benefit."

"You're sure about that? We *are* pretty remote."

"Yes, I'm sure." She smiled. "This is my job. This is what I do."

"Not all of the estate will appeal to visitors. I need to know what you think will work and what won't."

"You'd be surprised what appeals to people. That's why I'd like to see as much as possible. When I've had time to digest the information, we'll talk about it. I'll prepare a full proposal. And we'll need to consider costings of course." She made a few notes on her phone. "We need to discuss your staffing, and logistics in the event of severe weather. In the meantime, show me everything, unfiltered, including Rudolph and his teammates. Although it seems a shame not to include Tab for that part."

He drove carefully as they hit a bumpy part of the track. "We'll make sure she spends time with them. The forecast is good for the next few days. I have an idea that might work."

"If it's anything to do with reindeer, she'll love it."

He glanced at her. "You're a doting aunt."

"You've met her. How could I not be? Also, being an aunt is perfect. I get all the fun and none of the responsibility."

"You and your sister are close."

"It's obvious?"

"Yes. And also you mentioned it on the phone. You said you spoke every day."

Was there anything about that phone call that he'd forgotten? She felt herself blush. "Kyle used to get a little frustrated that Ella and I were always talking."

Brodie made no comment.

But what was there to say?

"Ella and I are close in age, too." She made no reference to the rest of that conversation. "There's only ten months between us, although I'm still the oldest and the bossiest. You're the oldest, too?"

"By four years. But Kirstie is definitely the bossiest. So I know you're the protective older sister. I know you run a successful company. What do you do when you're not working?"

"Not working?"

"I assume there are moments when you do other things." He gave her a quick smile. "I already know you like opera and champagne."

She sighed. "Mr. McIntyre—"

"Brodie. And I like opera and champagne too, by the way."

"Brodie—if we could just forget that conversation ever happened, I'd appreciate it."

"Why? That conversation is part of the reason you're here."

"Excuse me?"

"Did that sound suggestive?" It was his turn to be embarrassed. "I apologize. What I meant was, you were open and honest. Authentic. It was unbelievably refreshing. These days people filter everything, as if only perfection is acceptable even though we all know that doesn't exist. Flaws are not allowed.

Before you got in touch, I was contacted by another company who were interested in using the lodge for house parties."

"You were?"

"Yes. I turned them down. They didn't understand what we're trying to do here. Kirstie always accuses me of being insensitive and responding to nothing but numbers, but it isn't true. I know that if this plan is going to bring in what we need financially, then we have to look beyond the numbers. We need someone who understands this place. Someone who will bring in the right people. People who will love what we have here and want to come back. People who will appreciate it the way it already is. The company I contacted weren't interested in our goals, or in the history of this land. They asked questions about Wi-Fi signal, phone signal, how we handle snow clearing, how we could try and minimize the fact that we're remote."

"That's where your anxiety about the location came from?"

"It was part of it. I don't want this place to be presented through a filter, and then have to deal with people who were expecting something different."

"Sensible. It's the way to ensure satisfied clients."

"And that's what we need. I know nothing about your job, but presumably it's a relationship. Like all relationships, to be successful it has to be based on trust and honesty. If you're hiding who you really are, how is that ever going to work?"

Were they still talking about Kinleven?

She swallowed. "You're right."

"I don't need someone to do numerical calculations. I can do that part." He looked at her. "What I need is someone who can see the human side. Someone who can offer an honest assessment of our strengths and weaknesses, because I can't make a mistake."

"Because of your family."

"Yes. It's tough when you're inviting strangers into your home—you want to know it will be sensitively handled. In my case it was even more important because Kirstie has been dead against the idea from the start, even though she can't come up with an alternative. I have to show her this is going to work. That it's possible to find a way to share what our family has built here, without changing it. After my conversation with that company, I doubted my strategy. I was having second thoughts. And then you contacted me to express interest."

"I read an article. It was a couple of years old."

He nodded. "The one about my father? He sent me that one. It was good. After you contacted me the first time, I looked you up. Read a few interviews. You talked about passion and the importance of having life experiences that would stay with you and how much you love organizing that for people."

"Memories are forever. They're important."

"True, but I admit I did wonder if it was a clever marketing spiel. Anyone can use words that sound impressive. But with you, I didn't think it was verbal manipulation."

"But you thought it might be," Samantha said. "Which is why you insisted on meeting in person."

"It's hard to judge someone unless you can look them in the eyes while they're talking. And then your assistant Charlotte said you were on the phone for me, and—"

"We don't have to relive that part."

"You're still embarrassed? Don't be. That accidental phone call proved to me that you were the right person to advise us even before I met you. You weren't applying a filter to yourself."

"Please don't remind me." *Wild Samantha.*

The car bumped over a rut in the track and with a soft curse, he pulled to the side of the road and stopped.

"Would it help if I told you that compared to my life experience, that phone call was nothing?" He killed the engine and rubbed his fingers over his forehead. "What if I told you that embarrassment has been my life partner?"

"Brodie—"

"I was the kid who was never picked for sports. Last one standing on the field. Had to be allocated by a teacher. I was the nerd. The geek. Call it whatever you like. My attempts to try and be cool and fit in didn't work, because that wasn't where I fitted. And this was before technology was big, so I couldn't even impress anyone by fixing their laptop or their printer." His humor and honesty were disarming. "Helping my dad round the estate, I was more of a liability than an asset. If we chopped down a tree, I'd almost kill us. All I wanted to do was get back indoors and play with numbers, because numbers made sense to me. That's when I discovered that you have to play to your strengths." He watched as a bird fluttered across the snow, searching for food. "I learned then that it's better to excel at being who you really are than fail at being what you're not. I started helping everyone with their maths homework. And then my father brought home a computer. That was it for me. My degree was in maths, but I became interested in computer science and data analytics. Before that I always felt like a misfit in everyone else's world, and suddenly this was my world and I was the king."

She was silent for a moment and then gave a half smile. "You can fix my printer?"

He laughed. "Maybe. Although I sometimes think those damn things seem built to break."

"You obviously love what you do. Was it difficult giving it up to move home?"

"I haven't given it up." He removed his glasses and rubbed his fingers over his eyes. "I moved myself up here, and currently I'm working freelance. It means I can do what I love, while still trying to sort out this mess."

"So you have an office somewhere on the estate?"

"Yes." He let his hand drop. "I need you, Samantha. Forget embarrassment. I need you because if you can't help me, I don't know who can. I have the knowledge to predict that financially we're screwed, but no skills with which to fix it." He slid his glasses back on and she noticed that his hand shook a little. "I'm waiting for you to tell me I'm deluded and that this is never going to work. Maybe I'm as deluded as my sister, because I've been hoping for a miracle."

"It's Christmas, Brodie." Samantha leaned back in her seat, relaxed for the first time in weeks. "Miracles happen at Christmas. And I can immediately put your mind at rest about this place. It has huge commercial appeal, and once you've shown me everything there is to see, we'll sit down and talk through the options and produce a plan that everyone in your family will be able to live with."

"And if you hate something, you'll tell me?"

"Yes." She hesitated. "I'm sorry about your dad… I really am. And I'm sorry this is a tough time for you."

"It's life, isn't it? Reminds me of this road. Full of holes and ruts and places where you can blow out a tire." He swung the car back onto the track and carried on driving.

"Kinleven is stunning. The landscape is beautiful. You have a winner here, Brodie, and I'm excited about the reindeer. Tell me more about them. How did they come about?"

"My father introduced them to the estate about thirty years ago." He slowed down as he negotiated an icy patch on the track. "It wasn't easy at first, but he talked to various people, and fortunately our local vet had knowledge and was interested. They adapt well to the Scottish climate. Kirstie and I grew up with them. Can't remember a time when we didn't have the herd. Kirstie trained as a vet nurse, but all she really wanted to do was work here on the estate, so she came back a few years ago. She's out on the hills whenever she gets the chance."

"Helping out in the lodge must be tough for her."

"Yes, that's one of the problems." He glanced at her. "She'd rather be outdoors. But this is a family business. We all have to do what's needed."

"Who is looking after the reindeer while Kirstie is working in the lodge?"

"We have James, who retired from a big city job and moved up here for a different lifestyle after his wife died, and several local volunteers who come up to the estate to help."

"And people come and visit?"

"Not generally. My father used to give talks in local schools, and he'd take a couple of the reindeer along—the better behaved ones. But nothing formal. Taking the reindeer out is pretty time-consuming."

"But you could hold an event right here in this beautiful place. Their home." Samantha stared out the window at the snow heaped at the side of the track. It gleamed and dazzled in the sunlight. "Imagine traveling along this track in a sleigh pulled by reindeer."

"I don't have to imagine it. I've done it. Confession?" He gave her a brief, conspiratorial smile. "It's not as romantic as it looks, at least not for the person in charge. Reindeer are animals. They can be damn stubborn. They don't always seem to understand that they're making someone's dream come true however much you try and reason with them."

Samantha laughed. "I can imagine. I'm a city girl. Not much experience with animals. Certainly wouldn't know how to negotiate with a reindeer."

"You've always lived in cities?"

"New York and now Boston."

"And Ella?"

"She and Michael moved to a small town in Connecticut. They have a house on the water. Very pretty." And was she envious? Yes, she was. "He was a hotshot lawyer in Manhattan, and then he met Ella and both of them decided they wanted a different life."

"I suppose as long as you both want it, that works. You see them often?"

"Yes. She's only a couple of hours from me so every few weeks I pile my work into my bag and head down there on a Friday night." It was the closest she came to enjoying family life. "You were living in London?"

"London based, but I spent weeks at a time in Boston. Then my father died, and I came home to support my mother and Kirstie. Intended to stay until after the funeral, but things got complicated."

"You mean financially?"

"All of it." He pulled the car off the road and parked. "We walk from here."

She left the car and slammed the door. "We're seeing the reindeer first?"

"Yes. And then we'll hike up through the forest a little way because there is a great view of the whole estate from the top. I'd like you to see that. I'd like you to see all of it."

They changed into hiking boots, zipped up down jackets, hauled on backpacks and then headed along the trail that wound its way through the forest.

The air was crisp and cold, numbing her face and turning her breath to mist.

His stride was longer than hers and she found herself walking a little way behind him, which gave her a perfect view of wide shoulders and ruffled dark hair.

She looked away quickly. "What's the fence for? Keeping guests in or unwanted guests out?"

He turned and waited for her to catch up. "It's to keep deer out of this section of the forest. Overgrazing stops the forest from regenerating, so if we keep the deer away it protects the seedlings and gives new trees a chance." He glanced up through the branches to the sky. "Two thousand years ago this place was covered in the Caledonian Forest. Oak, birch, aspen, rowan, juniper and Scots pine. Hard to imagine."

She stopped to pull a hat out of her backpack. "But you're replanting?"

"We're part of a project that aims to restore the forest. It's not just about trees, it's about the whole ecosystem. And the deer aren't the only species to blame. The forest was cleared for agricultural land and to meet a demand for fast-growing timber. But now we're planting native trees, removing invasive species, putting up fences. There's a strong local interest so we're not short of volunteers."

They followed the trail as it twisted its way through the forest and then they left the trees behind and ahead of them was nothing but the loch, framed by mountains.

Samantha pulled out her camera and took a few shots. "That's incredible."

"It is." Brodie stopped next to her. "You see the little cottage?"

"Cottage?" She lowered the camera and scanned the snowy slopes. "I don't see anything except stunning scenery."

"At the end of the loch, on the left. Not far from the lodge. Stone building." He stepped closer and pointed. His arm brushed against hers. His body blocked a little of the biting wind.

"I see it. Tucked away by the trees. It blends into the surroundings. That's a cottage?"

"One of my ancestors built it originally as a shelter. Climbers and hikers used it if they were caught in a storm. It was basic back then. My grandfather made it habitable. My father fixed it up into something special, thinking that he might rent it out as another way of getting income. He proposed to my mother there."

"That's romantic."

"You think so?" He smiled, and she felt a sharp tug of response inside her.

She wondered if he had any idea how attractive he was.

"It sounds romantic to me."

"He always joked that he did it there because it was impossible for her to get away. It had been snowing all day and they were

trapped. Watch your footing here—the snow is covering rocks."
He held out his hand and she took it, picking her way carefully.

"And are you considering renting it out?"

"No. That's not part of the deal. It's currently my office."

"Your office?" She let go of his hand and stopped walking.
"You work in that remote cottage?"

"It's not that remote. Five minutes drive from the lodge if the
track is kept clear, but far enough that no one is going to come
in and clean, move empty mugs, or pieces of paper."

"I understand. I don't like people moving things on my desk.
I assume your mother loves the mountains as much as your father did?"

"Yes. She was born and raised around here. They met at school
when they were both six years old. They used to hike and spend
the night in the hut every year for their anniversary." He stared
into the distance. "They did it last year."

"It must be very tough for her. And on you."

He turned. "Is your father in your life?"

"No. He died when I was a baby." It wasn't something she
usually talked about, but they'd talked about so much already it
seemed pointless to hold anything back. "My mother was pregnant with my sister. It must have been a hideous time for her."
She'd never thought much about it, but now she was thinking
about it and with the thoughts came guilt. She remembered how
protective she'd been when Ella was pregnant. Who had taken
care of her mother?

"She never married again?"

"No. She didn't have a career at that time, so she went back
to college and then worked to support us." How hard must it
have been for her, raising two children, grieving the love of her
life and being frightened about finances? The guilt grew worse.

"At least she had you. You're lucky you're a close family."

This was the point where she should tell the truth. That her
relationship with her mother had always been difficult. That

they hadn't spoken for five years. And yes, it was true that her mother hadn't contacted her either, but now Samantha wished she could turn back time and reach out. She couldn't believe it had been so long, but it turned out the longer you left it the harder it was to bridge that painful gap. And how could she have reached out without revealing everything that Ella had chosen to hide? She'd been in an impossible position.

"Samantha?"

She pushed her thoughts away. They might have talked about everything else, but she wasn't ready to talk about that. "So how far are the reindeer herd from here?"

"They're over there." He pointed and she stopped walking.

It was so cold she'd lost feeling in her nose, but that didn't stop her reaching for her camera and taking a few shots. Reindeer against fresh snow. Did it get any better?

"Should I have brought food to prove I'm friend not foe? Lichen? Grasses?"

"I'm impressed." He zipped his coat a little higher. "Most people want to feed them carrots."

"Ah, but this isn't my first reindeer herd, although they are definitely the prettiest. I've seen them in Lapland, and I spent time with a reindeer herder in Norway."

"And here was I thinking that your job was all about fairy lights and Santa."

"Parts of it are, of course. Taking children to Lapland is always magical. But I have plenty of other clients who visit because they want a taste of life in the Arctic Circle. Some people want to experience the Polar Nights."

"A holiday in darkness?"

She leaned on the gate, watching the reindeer. "That's what I expected the first time I visited at that time of year, but it wasn't the case. It wasn't pitch-black. Hard to describe, but a bit more like twilight. Beautiful, although a little eerie, perhaps. The snow reflects the stars, and there were times of the day when

I found there was enough light to be able to read. And it's the perfect time to watch the aurora borealis."

"So you don't only cater for Christmas addicts. Do you want to get closer?" He opened the gate. "They're pretty friendly."

"I've never associated reindeer with the Highlands."

"Thousands of years ago they lived here. Now they're native to Arctic and subarctic regions."

"*Rangifer tarandus.* We call them caribou, but reindeer is more romantic somehow." The reindeer herd were grazing, heads down as they foraged. Sunlight glinted off the snow behind them. It was the most calming, peaceful thing she'd seen in a long time. "They have such big hooves."

"Spreads their weight and stops them from sinking into the snow." Brodie secured the gate behind them. "Also useful for digging into the snow and finding food. Perfect design."

"What happened to him? He only has one antler." She pointed. "Did he get into a fight?"

"The males cast their antlers after the autumn mating season. The females keep them until the calves are born in May."

Samantha decided she might have to find an excuse to come back in spring. "Can I take photos?"

"Go ahead."

She retrieved her camera and snapped away until one of the reindeer wandered toward them.

She took a few close-ups and then put her camera away. "Can I stroke him?"

"This one is a she. We call her Wren."

"You recognize them individually?"

"I grew up with them." He looked a little embarrassed. "All the reindeer are named after birds. Because they can fly, obviously."

"Obviously." She shared a look with him and then reached out and tentatively stroked the reindeer. *He knew the reindeer by name.* He'd told her he was out of his depth here, and yet he recognized them. Something thawed inside her. "This might be the most exciting thing that's happened to me in a long time. I feel about six years old." And if she felt this excited, how would her clients feel?

"You're never too old to enjoy reindeer. And the setting doesn't hurt. It's better than a meditation session being out here in the winter."

"You don't miss the city?"

"Not particularly, although I miss being close to an airport when I need to travel. Also, I miss feeling confident about what I'm doing." He rubbed the reindeer's neck. "I like to think I'm pretty good at my job. This? Not so much. But being here has its compensations. No commute. Great air quality. There's a simplicity to life that I missed when I was in the city."

Samantha smiled as the reindeer nudged her. "And many people would agree with you. Do you have any idea how special this is? I'm sure it's a lot of work to do events, but how about people coming to you? That way you don't have to take the reindeer anywhere, and you're still taking advantage of these fabulous surroundings."

"You mean as well as house parties?"

"Yes. It must be possible to do both." The reindeer nudged her again and she tugged off her glove so that she could sink her fingers into his fur. The warmth of the animal contrasted with the bitter cold of the wind. "What you have here is very special."

"The reindeer?"

"All of it." She smiled as another reindeer approached. "Who is this?"

"Goose."

"You look nothing like a goose." She rubbed the animal's neck. "You're right about it being relaxing. Do you think reindeer therapy could become a thing?"

"You tell me."

"I think it could. Right now I want to sell my apartment

and live in the mountains with a herd of reindeer." It was all she could do to tear herself away, but they headed back to the car and bounced and bumped their way back along the rutted track until they reached the road. "Where are we going next?"

"To the village. This will be the closest thing we have to civilization in case your guests feel in need of that during their stay. We have a small school, a post office that sells everything from tea to hiking boots and a pub. Highland pubs have a long tradition of great hospitality."

The pub overlooked the river and was surrounded by pine trees.

Samantha paused by the door to take a few photographs— snow piled against a stone wall, the pub sign swinging slightly in the wind—then she stepped through the door and was enveloped by warmth, the hum of conversation and the smell of good food. There was a crowd of people gathered round the bar, and it was obvious that almost everyone in there knew each other.

The conversation stopped as she entered. Heads turned.

She smiled and hurried across to Brodie, who had grabbed a table close to the open fire.

"Have I done something wrong?"

"Wrong?" His glasses had steamed up, and he pulled them off and dug around in his pockets for a cloth.

She handed him one from her purse. "They're staring at me."

He polished his glasses and squinted toward the bar. "Probably those ski pants you're wearing."

"They're the wrong thing to wear around here?"

"No. The pants are great. You look great in them. Better than great. I mean, that's probably why... Forget it." He colored, fumbled with his glasses, dropped the cloth. "I shouldn't have said that. I didn't mean to make you uncomfortable."

"You didn't. And thank you for the compliment." She retrieved the cloth, feeling a strange sweetness spread through her. "I assume it was a compliment?"

"Yes. Menus." He shot to his feet. "I'll get menus."

She watched as he strode to the bar. That feeling of awkwardness and embarrassment that had been with her since that phone call had faded during the morning, probably because he was more awkward and embarrassed than she was. The difference was that he seemed to accept it as part of who he was.

She unwound her scarf from her neck, feeling warm. It was the fire. It had to be the fire. Nothing else.

Heat flowed from the huge stone hearth. She grabbed her camera and took a few interior shots for her newsletter. A basket of logs. The walls hung with ice axes and other pieces of climbing equipment.

Brodie returned with menus. "Forgot to ask what you wanted to drink. Single malt? They have about ninety-four different ones to choose from."

"Tempting, but I'm not a lunchtime drinker. Diet cola is fine, thank you." She slid her camera back into her backpack and a moment later heard laughter.

Brodie was in conversation with three men who were leaning on the bar.

They appeared to be teasing him because his face was pinker than usual, but he handled it with his usual good-natured laughter. He seemed completely comfortable with who he was. Even on a short acquaintance she sensed there was no outer Brodie and inner Brodie. Just Brodie. He knew he was a little clumsy and awkward, and accepted it with laughter. But equally he knew his strengths. He didn't play down his professional skills. He was a man who knew exactly who he was and was happy to own all of it.

She felt a twinge of envy. She would have given a lot to be half as comfortable with herself as he was.

"So Really Festive Holidays—" He put the drinks down on the table. "Tell me how that happened. How did you become the Christmas expert?"

Samantha had a vision of Ella, five years old, glowing with excitement as she'd delved into the "stocking" Samantha had made her.

"I always loved this time of year. I used to dream about the perfect way to spend Christmas, and when I started working in the travel industry I realized that I could make that a reality for people, although what we offer isn't exclusively Santa focused. Some people don't want a traditional family gathering over the holidays, but prefer to travel. Lapland is popular, so are the European Christmas markets. I've sent people to Iceland, but also to Paris and London if they want a city break."

"London? Not that I don't like London, but I can't imagine anyone booking it for a special festive break. What's in London that would be attractive to tourists at that particular time of year?"

"Christmas lights. *The Nutcracker* ballet at the Royal Opera House in Covent Garden. Champagne afternoon tea at one of the exclusive London hotels. For you, London is probably about crowds, commuting and work stress, but that isn't what a tourist experiences. My job is to bring out the magic of a place and focus on that." She curved her fingers around her glass. "I bet I could make you fall in love with London again."

He smiled. "I think you could make a person fall in love with any place you wanted them to love. Which is good news for me. I'm grateful you're willing to spin that magic of yours over our little patch of the Scottish Highlands."

"I don't think it's going to take much work to turn this place into something magical."

"No?" He took a mouthful of his drink and then set his glass down. "So what do you think so far?"

"I'm excited." She pulled her phone out of her coat pocket. "I made a few notes when we were in the car, and I know we still have plenty to see, but I'm already in love with the place and I know others will feel the same."

"What if we let people book rooms and they don't get on well?"

"I think the way forward may be to offer exclusive hire to individual parties. It would be lucrative and less disruptive for you. We can sell it as an intimate, authentic experience living as part of a Scottish family."

"Fights and moods included?"

She laughed. "I suggest we make those an optional extra."

"Exclusive groups. Won't that be expensive?"

"Yes, but there are people who will pay well for something special that they can't experience elsewhere. And they can't experience what you're offering here. We'd need to refine it of course, but your basic offering is unbeatable."

"On the strength of that, I'll buy you lunch."

"No, lunch is on me." Samantha glanced at the menu. "What do you recommend?"

"It's all good, but the burger is the best you'll ever eat."

"Well, that's a challenge I can't refuse."

He stood up. "Soak up the atmosphere while I'm gone."

She did as he suggested, glancing from the crackling log fire to the pictures on the stone walls. There were black-and-white photos of mountains, of the pub itself through the decades, framed newspapers and an old pair of wooden skis. She was surrounded by laughter and conversation, the atmosphere warm and welcoming.

She pulled out her phone and checked her emails while she was waiting, surprised to have a good signal.

She had a bunch of emails from Charlotte that she swiftly dealt with, and a few from clients, thanking her and sending her photos from their travels.

"What did Kyle say when you eventually talked to him?" Brodie sat back down at the table. "Did he rise to the challenge? Show up at your office, whisk you away to the nearest five-star hotel and pop open a bottle of champagne?"

She should have felt defensive, but it seemed she'd moved past that with this man. Her inner and outer self had merged, temporarily at least.

"None of that." She put her phone on the table. "And I didn't say everything I said to you. Saying it wasn't easy and I guess I lost my nerve."

"But you still broke up."

"Yes. I mumbled something about busy lives, and different priorities—blah, blah."

"So everything but the truth."

She shrugged. "I ended it. The 'why' didn't matter in the end." She broke off as their food arrived.

"There you go, Prof. That should boost the brain cells." The chef put the food on the table, winked at Samantha and headed back to the kitchen.

"Prof?"

"It was my nickname at school." Brodie shook salt over his bowl of fries. "I could tell you that it was because I was the best and brightest in my class, but as we're being honest here I'm going to confess that they called me Prof because I wore wire-rimmed glasses that were invariably bent out of shape. That's why I moved on to something more substantial."

And they suited him. Ella was right about that. Those dark frames against his light eyes—

She took a mouthful of burger to distract herself and nodded approval. "You didn't lie. This is good."

"Yes. People battle snow and ice to eat these burgers." He took a bite. "Did you and Kyle date for long?"

"A year."

He raised his eyebrows. "A year is a long time to be with someone who doesn't excite you."

She put the burger down. "There are other things that matter, too. Mutual interests. Reliability." *Safety.* But she didn't say that one aloud. It embarrassed her to admit that she was afraid.

Afraid of feeling too much. Afraid of being hurt. In everything else she was the strong big sister, but not in this. When it came to love and emotions, Ella was fearless. She opened her arms and her heart, *here I am, come and break me.*

"You can get those things if you join a hiking group or a book group."

"What do you know about book groups?"

"I know they can end a relationship." He gave a quick smile. "The woman I was seeing insisted that I join her at her book club. She thought I needed to broaden my reading. She was constantly substituting my crime fiction and biographies for literary fiction."

"You went to the book group?"

"Me and ten women." He took another bite of his burger. "Sounds better than it was."

"It didn't go well?"

"Well, there was wine—" he shrugged "—so that part was fine. But then we had to talk about the book. Which I was alone in hating, and alone in admitting to hating. Apparently, I should have kept my views to myself. I embarrassed her." He finished his fries.

"Because you hated the book?"

"Yes. Apparently she'd been boasting about—" he paused "—how brainy I was." He reddened, embarrassed, and she smiled.

"And you ruined it by admitting to reading books that smart people aren't supposed to read?"

"Something like that. She wasn't impressed, but I don't read to impress people. I gave up on trying to impress people decades ago. I read what entertains me, and what interests me."

"What does interest you?"

His gaze lifted to hers and lingered there. Suddenly she couldn't breathe properly. Her throat tightened. Her skin heated. She could feel her own heartbeat. She kept wondering what it would be like to kiss him.

For a long moment neither of them spoke. And then finally he stirred and turned his attention back to the food.

"What interests me? Apart from good crime fiction, World War II. Code breakers. Bletchley Park. Fascinating stuff." He reached across and helped himself to one of her fries and she pushed her bowl into the middle of the table.

Had she imagined that moment? Was it just her? Was she so desperate for a wild affair that she was no longer able to have a conversation with a man without wondering what it would feel like to kiss him?

He paused, his hand hovering over the bowl. "Sorry. Shouldn't have done that without permission."

"What—? Oh, you mean the food. It's fine—fries are best when they're shared."

"Shared? You mean when I eat all of mine and half of yours?"

"That works for me. And they are good." Even though her stomach was too full of nerves to leave room for food. "So that relationship died?"

"Mutual agreement." He helped himself again to her fries. "You're sure about this?"

"Go for it. You weren't brokenhearted?"

"No. Which says a lot, doesn't it? As you said on the phone, in a good relationship you want to feel things. Mostly we felt—" he paused, thinking as he finished her fries "—irritation I suppose. And my father died and my priorities changed. I wasn't in the right frame of mind to work at a relationship while I was grieving for my father and supporting my mother and sister. You're obviously pretty close to your mother."

She could lie, or at least gloss over the truth. She could make some glib comment about the distance between Boston and New York, pressure of work, busy lives. There were any number of ways to redirect the conversation, but the hours they'd spent together had softened her, like butter left in the sun.

"Up until last month, we hadn't seen each other for five years."

"You had a falling-out?"

"I suppose you could call it that. It's always been a difficult relationship." She tugged a corner off her burger. "We disappointed her. She had a very clear idea of what she wanted for us, and neither of us wanted that. I didn't realize it had been five years. Time passes—you wait for the other person to contact you, then things change in your life and you're in a different place and you're not even sure how to move on from there—"

"So what brought you back together?"

"There was an accident—" Samantha told him all of it, and he listened with no visible signs of surprise or judgment.

"I haven't read her book, although the title is familiar. Seems ironic that she writes about choice, and yet didn't encourage you to make your own."

"I know. I grew up thinking that, and I suppose it stopped me looking deeper. I suppose it all stemmed from losing my father when she was so young. She had no family support so it can't have been easy. But she doesn't talk about it, so it's all guesswork. Until you asked her that question, we didn't know she'd been to Scotland on her honeymoon."

"So she only discovered she had a granddaughter a few weeks ago, and you've gone from nothing to spending Christmas together."

"That's right. And now you're probably wishing you'd never invited us."

"What I'm thinking," he said, "is that this is the most relaxed I've been in a year." The way he was looking at her made her feel breathless and sixteen years old.

"We are not an average family."

"Does such a thing exist? I could have pretended that everything was perfect here and that my whole family is excited and positive about welcoming strangers into our home. As I said, honesty works better for me. Whether it's reading, feelings, skills—I prefer people who are what they seem to be."

She thought about her mother not knowing about Michael and Tab. The fact that she still didn't know that Ella had chosen to be a stay-at-home mother. The fact that Gayle didn't talk about her marriage. Filtering your life was exhausting.

"You're right. And the truth is I'm still anticipating a disaster. We're very different from our mother in so many ways." She realized that her stomach muscles had been tense since she'd stepped off the plane in Inverness. "My mother's style of parenting is very different from my sister's. At some point, there is going to be a major clash. I'm braced for it. I've had a knot in my stomach since the airport. My sister is totally focused on her family. It's everything to her. Building that nest and making it cozy. Me? I'm more about work, and—damn." She pushed her plate away, appetite gone. "I guess I have my mother to thank for that. So maybe we're not so different after all." Ella was right. It was unsettling to admit it. "I've turned into my mother, and I didn't even see it happening. I might need that whiskey after all."

"Because you like your work? That doesn't make you like your mother. From what you've told me, your mother virtually cut herself off from personal relationships. You spend your weekends playing with your niece. You've supported your sister for all of her life. And you're running a company with a small team who all love you and have been with you from the beginning. Do you know how unusual that is?"

"How do you know so much about my company?"

"If you want the best job done, you choose the best people." He cleared his throat. "And I might have talked to—er—Charlotte a few times."

"You talked to Charlotte? About what?"

"An astonishing array of subjects. She's very chatty."

Samantha laughed. "She is. Clients love her. I love her, too."

"I can understand why. And Amy is adorable. She sent me

a photo." He pushed her plate back toward her. "Eat. It's cold out there. You need food. I shouldn't have finished your fries."

He'd remembered the name of Charlotte's daughter.

"I'm not that hungry. Talking about my mother reminds me of all the things that can potentially go wrong while we're here."

"There's always a possibility that your mother really has changed."

"You think people can change?"

"Maybe *change* is the wrong word. I think people have an ability to adapt to different circumstances. I hope they do, or I'm not sure how my mother will cope." He finished his burger and wiped his fingers. "I think she'll be fine as long as she is living here, in familiar surroundings, along with all the memories of my father. I'm determined to make that happen. It would be easier if I wasn't fighting my sister."

She badly wanted to help, and not just for professional reasons. "Let's talk numbers." She reached into her purse and pulled out a notepad and pen. "Let's figure it out together. I've seen enough to know what you have to offer, and I have a good idea about what people will pay. You know what you need. Let's bridge the gap. If you can present facts to your sister, she might find it easier to accept. Maybe she'll be able to adapt to new circumstances, too."

And she should probably follow her own advice.

Being with her mother at Christmas was definitely going to require some adaptation, on everyone's part, but that didn't mean it wasn't going to work.

Talking to Brodie had reminded her that all families were complicated, even apparently functional ones.

Perhaps everything would be all right after all.

Of course it would help if she could stop imagining Brodie naked.

Ella

"Where are we going?" Ella stifled a yawn as she grabbed her coat. She was still feeling the effects of jet lag. "And what did you do all day yesterday? You were back so late we didn't have a chance to chat."

"I was working." Samantha gathered up all her outdoor gear. "Did you have fun?"

"Mmm." Ella wasn't sure how to answer that, so she ignored the question. "What's the plan for today?"

Michael had shut himself in the bedroom with his laptop and two brimming mugs of coffee, dealing with a work emergency so it was just her, Samantha and Tab.

"We are going on a trip and you need to dress warmly." Samantha was on her knees next to Tab, zipping her coat and tugging her hat down over her ears. "Where are your gloves?"

"In my pocket." Tab produced them with the drama of a magician pulling a rabbit out of a hat. "Are we going on a secret trip?"

"It's a secret trip."

"Will we see Santa?"

"Better than Santa." Samantha scooped her up and swung her, and Ella wondered what had happened to her sister, because *something* had happened, she was sure of it.

"You're raising expectations. Where are we going?"

"Patience. You're worse than your daughter." Samantha helped Tab with her snow boots and rose to her feet. Her hair slid smooth and silky over the shoulders of her white jacket. She was energized. Glowing.

Intrigued, Ella tugged her sister to one side. "What is going on?"

"I've told you, it's a—"

"I'm not asking about the trip. I'm asking about why you're glowing inside. It's as if someone has changed your batteries, or—or—rebooted you. And where were you last night? You and Brodie didn't come back for dinner."

"He was showing me the area. We ended up at the far end of Loch Ness, so stopped for something to eat." Samantha tilted her head. "Am I glowing? I'm excited about this place. My clients are going to love it." She was smiling, and Ella was smiling too even though she had a suspicion that it wasn't thoughts of her business that had put her sister in such a good mood.

"You're not angry with me after yesterday?" She glanced at Tab, but her daughter had gone in search of Bear, who was her new best friend. "I thought maybe you were planning on burying me in a snowdrift after the hurtful, tactless thing I said."

Samantha reached for Tab's scarf. "You didn't say anything that wasn't true."

"None of it was true. I was upset about the whole Mom thing, and I felt you were judging me for overreacting about Tab, and—I don't know. I don't know what made me horrible."

"You weren't horrible—you were honest. Sisters should be able to be honest with each other. And you were right. I have closed myself off. But I'm trying to change that. Tell me what happened with Mom yesterday. And don't give me 'mmm.' I want details."

Ella was starting to wonder if her sister had bumped her head. She'd been reluctant to come on this trip, but now she was behaving as if she was having the best time ever.

"It started off okay. Great, actually. She was like a different person."

"She was good with Tab? Didn't say the wrong thing?"

"She would have won grandmother of the year."

"That's great. That's hopeful."

"I thought so, but then I messed up. But nothing new there. There is so much about her that we don't know, and I tried asking—I thought it might help if we got to know each other a little better. Did you know she lived in Connecticut before moving to Manhattan?" Her sister's surprised expression answered that question. "Me neither. But these little gems keep emerging, like the fact she thought her honeymoon was foolish. Or maybe she thought she was foolish."

"Foolish?"

"Don't ask me for clarification, because I don't get it. I was trying to piece together a puzzle based on nothing. I tried asking her about Dad, but she shut down. Wham. It was like a door closing on my hand."

"She's not used to talking to us about personal things." Samantha laced her boots. "We need to persist. Is she joining us today?"

"I think so." What if her mother spoiled the trip? On the other hand, she'd been great with Tab the day before, and if this was truly going to be a family Christmas then it was going to take some flexibility on everyone's part. "Which could be good or bad."

"She's trying. I think we should try, too. People can change."

Was this really her sister talking?

"You're very upbeat all of a sudden." Ella glanced around to

check where Tab was. Giggles and barks from the library answered her question. "What exactly happened yesterday? You
and Brodie came back laughing and comfortable together. It
wasn't awkward?"

"It was hideously awkward, at least to begin with."

"But?"

"But we spent an excellent, productive day together. We
have a plan."

"A plan?"

"For this place. Brodie talked about his plans and ambitions,
and I talked about what I believed was possible."

Ella knew her sister, and knew it had to be more than that.

"What else did you talk about?"

"Everything. I am so excited about adding this property to
our portfolio. I almost called two of my favorite clients to tell
them I've found their perfect vacation for next year, but then
I realized I'm getting ahead of myself. We still have things to
figure out. But Brodie is a genius with numbers so I think between us we'll have this thing nailed in no time." She laced her
other boot and stood up.

"By things to figure out, I assume you mean how to sell the
idea to Kirstie."

Samantha glanced up. "You talked to Brodie?"

"No, I talked to Kirstie. Long chat yesterday."

"Yes? How did that come about?"

She'd been avoiding their mother. "It was a bit awkward, actually. I walked into the library to try and find a new book for
Tab, and she was hiding in there."

"Hiding?"

"She was upset. Trying not to let her mother see, I guess. Anyway, we talked a bit. She misses her dad, but she's worried about
upsetting her mother so she doesn't talk about that part. Hence
hiding away in the library. This whole thing is tough on her."

Tab reappeared with a newly devoted Bear following her, and Ella immediately censored her conversation.

"Are you ready for your surprise treat?"

"Yes. Can Bear come?"

"I don't know." Ella glanced at her sister. "Can he?"

"I'm sure he can, but I'll check with Brodie."

Brodie was part of this treat?

She was about to ask for details, but Samantha scooped Tab into her arms.

"Okay, I need you to close your eyes tightly. No peeking."

Tab slapped both hands over her eyes. "I'm not peeking."

"Are you sure? Keep those eyes closed and don't open them until I say so." Samantha carried her niece outside and Ella snatched up all the extra layers they were likely to need and followed.

"It's all very exciting going on a mystery trip, but it means I don't have a clue what to take and—oh—" She stopped dead. *"Oh!"*

"Can I look? I want to look." Tab still had her hands over her eyes and Samantha pulled them away.

"You can look."

Tab opened her eyes and then her mouth fell open wide, as if she was at the dentist. No words emerged.

Ella exchanged looks with her sister. "You've silenced my daughter. That's a first."

Samantha looked pleased as she walked Tab down the steps, where she finally found her voice.

"Reindeer. Are they real?"

"Yes, real." Samantha put her down and crouched down beside her. "This one is called Goose. The one behind is Sparrow."

Ella saw the look on her daughter's face and felt a lump form in her throat. "You're the best aunt. The best sister."

"Can I stroke them?" Tab stretched out her arms, and Samantha looked at Kirstie, who was holding the reins of the leader.

"Of course. They would love that." Kirstie was noticeably more relaxed and friendly, and as Ella drew close she gave a quick smile. "I'm sorry about yesterday. Thanks for listening."

"Don't apologize. It was good to talk. I'm just sorry things are tough for you." Ella reached out and touched her arm. "It's a difficult situation."

For all of them, she thought.

Samantha lifted Tab again so that she could stroke one of the reindeer.

The little girl reached out. "Is this one Rudolph?"

"This one is called Finch." Kirstie held him steady, a million times more happy and relaxed with her reindeer than she was serving breakfast. "He was born here."

"Hi, Finch." Tab stroked the reindeer's fur. "Can I sit in the sleigh? Are we going for a ride?"

"You can. We're going on a trip into the forest to find the perfect Christmas tree."

Tab squirmed out of Samantha's grasp and skipped toward the sleigh. Bear bounded after her, but as no one called him back, Ella assumed that was allowed.

She turned to her sister. "I don't know what to say. This is magical."

"I'd like to claim the credit, but it was Brodie's idea." Samantha stroked Finch absently. "We're going to offer this to guests. What do you think?"

"A trip into the forest in a sleigh pulled by reindeer? I think you'll be flattened in the stampede of clients wanting to book it." Hearing voices, Ella glanced over her shoulder and saw her mother and Brodie walking toward them. "She's laughing. He's making our mother laugh."

"He's an easygoing guy."

Ella wanted more detail of her sister's day with Brodie McIntyre, but there was no opportunity to ask, so she joined Tab and Bear in the back of the sleigh, and her mother climbed in next to her.

"This is fun."

"We're going to find the perfect tree, Nanna!"

Gayle, who had never before shown enthusiasm for a Christmas tree, clapped her hands. "What fun."

Ella felt faint. She hadn't known her mother could recognize fun, let alone enjoy it.

Samantha joined them in the sleigh, and Brodie and his sister walked with the reindeer, guiding them as they plodded along the trail that led away from the lodge.

Ella sat cuddled up close to her daughter under the blanket as the sleigh moved through the forest. The only sounds were the dull thud of the reindeers' hooves as they hit the snow.

It was crisp and cold, and the trees stretched upward, creating a snowy canyon of native pine and spruce.

How could she have doubted that coming here was a good idea? It was perfect.

And today she wasn't going to push her mother to talk about the past. She was just going to enjoy the day.

Confident that there would be no awkwardness or conflict, Ella relaxed.

Gayle was chatting with Tab, listening carefully and answering the endless questions without a hint of impatience.

She'd been wrong to think her mother couldn't change, Ella thought. So wrong.

They followed the trail for about half an hour and then stopped.

Kirstie grabbed a backpack from the back of the sleigh and opened it up.

She pulled out a small, prettily wrapped gift and handed it to Tab.

"For me?" Tab stared at it in wonder and then unwrapped it with the speed and desperation of the average five-year-old.

Inside the package was a small reindeer carved from wood. "I love it."

"That's adorable." Ella examined it and looked at Kirstie. "Did you make it?"

"My dad made them." There was no missing the pride in Kirstie's voice. "He used to give them to the kids in the local school. We had a few left. I thought Tab might like one as a souvenir."

"That's so thoughtful and kind. Thank you."

Brodie appeared by the sleigh. "I need some help locating the perfect tree. Is there anyone in this sleigh who could help me with that?"

Tab scrambled toward him, still clutching her reindeer. Bear followed, as smitten with the little girl as she was with him.

Holding tightly to Brodie's hand, she trudged through the snow, giving each tree her close attention.

The process of choosing took a good twenty minutes and then finally she pointed.

"This one."

"Good choice." Brodie studied it. "It's about the right size."

"How will we get it home?"

"We'll drag it home behind the sleigh." Brodie returned Tab to Ella. "Better keep her here while I chop it down."

"I'll help you." Samantha sprang out of the sleigh and Ella saw her sister and Brodie exchange a smile.

Interesting, she thought, and caught Kirstie's eye.

"This is fun. I haven't seen my sister this relaxed in a while."

Kirstie stroked the reindeer, but her eyes were on her brother. "I haven't seen Brodie this relaxed, either. I like your sister. She seems straightforward."

"She is." Ella was only half listening as Tab started firing another series of questions at Gayle.

"Why does that reindeer only have one antler?"

Kirstie turned her head. "They cast their antlers—that means they fall off—every year and then they grow a new set."

"Does it hurt?"

The questions continued.

"Why does Santa come at night, Nanna? How does he see? Are there lights in the sky?"

"No." Gayle looked vague. "There are no lights in the sky."

Ella watched as Brodie chopped down the tree. He and Samantha were laughing together, exchanging a few words here and there as if they had a long-standing, comfortable relationship. Watching them closely, Ella decided it was more than that. Comfort, with edge. There was a chemistry between them that she could feel even from a distance. She'd never seen her sister so relaxed.

"Does the sleigh have headlights?" Tab was determined to solve the mystery.

"No, of course not."

"Does he carry a flashlight?"

"I—no. Enough questions about Santa now, Tab."

"But how can he see? What if he has an accident like you did?"

"He isn't going to have an accident."

Ella watched as Samantha and Brodie dragged the tree back together. Brodie said something she couldn't hear, but she saw her sister blush and laugh and realized they were flirting.

When had she ever seen her sister flirt?

"If he can't see," Tab said, "then he *could* have an accident. I don't want him to have an accident."

"He won't!" Her mother's voice rose.

"But how do you know?"

"Because there is no Santa." The words exploded out of Gayle. *"There is no Santa!"*

"No Santa?" Tab looked flummoxed. "You mean he doesn't come to Scotland?"

"He doesn't come anywhere. He doesn't exist."

Tab's distressed howls dragged Ella from her fantasy of her sister having a wild love affair.

"Mom!" Appalled, she almost erupted with fury and frustration. Had her mother truly just said that? She was so angry she couldn't breathe, but she reached for her daughter, scooped her up and tried to calm her. "Stop crying, honey. Stop crying, and we'll talk." She couldn't make herself heard over Tab's screams, and she winced as a particularly shrill scream connected with her inner ear. She sent her mother a furious look over Tab's squirming, writhing body.

Just when she'd started to relax. Just when she'd thought that maybe, *maybe*, her mother had changed and this could possibly work. It was her childhood all over again.

The commotion reached Samantha.

Abandoning Brodie, she hurried back down the track, her feet slipping and sliding on the snow. "What's wrong? What's happened? Did she fall? Is she hurt?"

Because Ella was trying to calm Tab, Gayle spoke first.

"She's fine. Totally fine."

"She doesn't sound fine. Why is she crying?"

"Because I told her there was no Santa. She wouldn't stop asking, and—"

"Stop!" Ella intervened, cradling Tab as her crying intensified. "Stop talking right now."

Tab howled, inconsolable, her sobs reverberating around the forest until finally the energy left her and she slumped, exhausted, on Ella's shoulder, her little body still juddering. "Nanna—says there is no—Santa." She hiccuped her way through the sentence. "He—doesn't exist."

Ella met her sister's appalled gaze for a fleeting second and then Samantha took Tab from her.

"Well, of *course* there's a Santa." Cuddling Tab, she threw their mother a blacker look than the one Ella had already given her. "What Nanna meant was that she hasn't actually *seen* him. But just because you haven't seen something, doesn't mean it doesn't exist."

Tab rubbed her swollen eyes. "So how does he see? Nanna says there are no lights in the sky."

"There are lights in the sky," Samantha said, "and I've seen them. There are stars, and then the moon—and also the aurora borealis—the northern lights. When we're back in the warm, I can show you photos on my phone."

"So you've seen him?"

"No, I haven't seen him. I was always in bed asleep when he came. Which is exactly where you will be."

Ella relaxed a little, but Tab still wasn't convinced.

"But how does he get round the whole world in one night?"

"Exactly." Gayle stood stiff and miserable. "It isn't mathematically possible."

"It could be, although some factors remain unconfirmed of course." Brodie dug his hand into his pocket and pulled out a pen and a scrap of paper. He pushed his glasses farther up his nose and then focused on Tab. "The earth rotates—did you know that? It turns. Slowly, so you'd never know."

Still clinging to Samantha, Tab shook her head and he stooped and picked up a pinecone.

"We'll pretend this is the earth. This is where we live. And it moves like this—" He turned the pinecone and then handed it to Ella and scribbled on the paper in his palm. "If you do a calculation, taking into account the rotation of the earth, wind direction and—er—" he cleared his throat as he scribbled down a series of complicated equations "—speed and relative weight of the vehicle, in this case a sleigh, it's possible."

Tab stopped rubbing her eyes and stared at Brodie's scribbles. "What about the weight of the presents?"

"Smart question." Brodie changed a couple of numbers. "But the weight of the load carried is part of the overall weight calculation. So it's all good." He was so convincing that Ella almost believed it herself.

She was breathless with gratitude and admiration, but Tab was still suspicious.

"So why doesn't Nanna believe?"

"This is—er—very complicated maths." He sent Gayle an apologetic look. "Not always easy to understand—"

Gayle opened her mouth but Samantha spoke first.

"Which of the reindeer is Buzzard again?"

Tab pointed, her arm wavering. "The one with half an antler."

"Shall we go and stroke him?" Samantha whisked Tab to the reindeer at the front, protecting her from whatever it was Gayle had been about to say.

Brodie followed, which gave Ella the chance to speak up.

She couldn't let this pass. She just couldn't.

She wasn't sure where to start, but Gayle made it easy.

"I know you're angry with me, but I was thinking about what's best for Tab. She asks these endless questions and you're doing her no favors by offering up lies in response. It's not right to encourage her to believe that life is a fairy tale."

"I decide what's right. I'm her mother, and I decide." Ella's voice shook as much as her hands. "I don't care what you think. It doesn't matter what you think." She couldn't believe her mother would say such a thing, although why should it surprise her? This was her childhood all over again.

Her mother was tense. "All I'm saying is that bringing up a child to believe in a magical benevolent being creates false expectations. You think I'm the killer of joy, but I'm trying to protect her."

"The difference between us is that you try and suppress joy because you're so afraid of losing it, whereas I want to savor joy wherever I find it. Yes, life sends dark times, but that's all the more reason to feast on the happy times and store them up. I'm not teaching her to believe a lie—I'm teaching her to enjoy the moment."

"I think—"

"It doesn't matter what you think. Tab isn't your child, and this isn't your decision." Ella stood her ground. She'd never set boundaries for herself before, but she discovered it was remarkably easy when it related to her daughter. "This is my life, Mom. My choices. My decisions. You don't get to decide for me. I don't need or want your opinion on my career choice, my relationships or the way I raise my daughter."

Her mother was pale. "But if you—"

"There is no 'but' on this one. If I want to indulge Tab with a Christmas stocking and tales of Santa and flying reindeer, then I'll do it. And if one day I regret taking that approach, then that's on me. But in the meantime, you'll go along with it. It was your choice to spend Christmas with us, Mom. You insisted. So these are the rules. That's it. That's all. If you don't like it, then perhaps this isn't the best place for you to be."

Her heart was thudding so hard she felt dizzy and faint.

She expected her mother to come back at her, to deride her choices, but instead Gayle swallowed hard.

"I think it's best if I go back indoors. I feel a little tired. It's the cold air." She turned and stumbled along the forest trail that led back to the house, leaving Ella feeling hot with frustration and misery, but also strong. She'd said what needed to be said. Yes, it was hard doing that, but that didn't mean it was wrong.

For the first time in her life, she'd insisted that her mother respect her choices. She felt furious, but also empowered.

But none of those feelings changed the fact that the chances of having a happy Christmas were looking less likely by the minute.

Gayle

She'd been trying so hard to change, and it mattered so much that she did. There was a delightful simplicity to being with her granddaughter. Maybe it was because they had no history. It really was a fresh start, and that freshness—that feeling that this truly was a second chance—had infected Gayle with optimism. But she'd made a mistake. In that one fatal moment she'd been her old self, not the self she'd promised herself she'd be in order to glue together those fractured family bonds. It turned out that change was nowhere near as easy as she made it sound in her books. Right now it felt as painful as having a sharp object stuck in her side. Her old self had shoved her new self out of the way when confronted by something as contentious as Santa. Now she wished she'd said nothing, or at least murmured something vague.

Christmas had always been a breaking point in their family.

She'd found it difficult—impossible in fact—to pretend. And Ella didn't understand. Why would she? Gayle had never told the truth. And Ella had always been impulsive and dreamy. Oblivious to the dark that lurked at the edges of the happiest life.

Santa? Flying reindeer? Not in the life she'd lived.

Gayle stumbled through the front door of the lodge, desperate to reach her room. Her throat ached. Her eyes stung. She hadn't cried for decades. And yet here she was, ready to bawl like a baby. It was because she was tired and despondent. Her carefully constructed, familiar life no longer fitted, and this new life didn't seem to fit, either. It was as if she'd tried to squeeze herself into someone else's clothes.

She put a foot on the stairs and heard her name.

"Gayle!" Mary's voice came from behind her, low and lilting, full of warmth. "I've just made tea and baked cookies. Would you come and sample it?"

The sanctuary of her bedroom lay round two turns of the wide staircase. There was a lock on the door. A view of the mountains. She could use the space to recalibrate and figure out how to handle this latest setback.

Was this it? Had she ruined everything before it had properly begun?

"Gayle? Is everything all right?" The kindness in Mary's voice was more appealing than the judgmental silence of her room.

Right now, she didn't like herself very much. She wasn't sure she wanted to be alone.

She blinked several times and then turned. "Did you say cookies?"

Mary McIntyre wore an apron tied around her broad waist, and there was a dusting of flour on the sleeve of her sweater.

This was the mother she should have been, Gayle thought. This was the mother her girls had deserved. Soft and rounded, radiating warmth like a blazing log fire. Instead they'd had Gayle, whose softness had been worn away by life.

Feeling weak and tired, she walked with Mary, following the delicious smells of baking. The kitchen was at the back of the

house. It was a large room with windows overlooking the mountains. A room filled with sunlight, heat and family history. There
were coats hanging on pegs, and boots lined up by the door.
The large stove kicked out warmth. Everything about the place
was comforting, from the herbs on the windowsill to the stack
of neatly folded tea towels on the freshly scrubbed countertop.

One glance told Gayle that this place was a haven, the very
heart of the home.

Every available surface was covered. Pies lay cooling on wire
racks, the pastry thick and golden. Muffins, their domed tops
studded with berries, were lined up alongside slabs of sugar-
dusted shortbread. The kitchen smelled of cinnamon and chocolate, of warmth and love.

"You've been busy. Are you expecting extra guests?"

"No. I may have overdone it, but baking helps me." Mary
opened a cupboard and pulled out cake tins and freezer con-
tainers. "After Cameron died, the neighbors brought food every
day. They thought I wouldn't want to be cooking. What they
didn't know is that I find cooking to be the best therapy. Not
that I've ever had any other type." She gave a tired smile and
waved a hand. "Sit down, Gayle. It's good to have company.
I've been feeling a little—wobbly today."

So not just her, then.

Gayle settled herself down at the large table and ran her hand
over the surface. Little cracks and tiny dents spoke of years of use
and a lifetime of family meals. Gayle thought of the table in her
Manhattan apartment. Glass. It had no history, but she hadn't
wanted to bring anything from the past with her.

To Gayle, the kitchen had always been a practical place. Somewhere to prepare food with as little fuss and bother as possible.
A necessary task, one of many to be ticked off a long list. In
order to manage everything, she was ruthless about deleting un-
necessary tasks. If she'd had the choice, she would have deleted
eating. The kitchen had never been somewhere to linger, and

never a source of comfort. Both would have been an indulgence. She certainly wouldn't have considered cooking to be therapy.

Mary put a mug of tea in front of her and lifted a few of the warm cookies onto a plate.

"You've been out with the reindeer?"

"Yes." How much should she say?

"Judging from your expression, you didn't have a good time."

"I—made a mess of things."

"With the girls?"

Gayle stared at the cookies. She'd never been the type to gossip with anyone. She didn't chat. She didn't confide. So why did she find it so easy to talk to Mary? "I've always struggled with the whole concept of Santa. Is it right to encourage children to believe in a mythical, magical being who delivers gifts down the chimney?"

"I suppose most people don't even think about it. It's something fun and joyful. We just go along with it."

"And that's what I should have done. I've been trying hard to get it right, to say the right thing—"

"No one can say the right thing all the time—we've already agreed on that. And what the 'right thing' is changes according to the day and the person. It's subjective." Mary offered no advice, and no judgment. Just understanding.

"This wasn't subjective. I messed it up. When Tab asked me about Santa I said he didn't exist—" She shook her head. "There is no excuse. I see now that the decision on how to handle Christmas should be my daughter and son-in-law's. It's not my place to decide something like that. Ella was furious—"

"Oh you poor thing. No wonder you seemed so upset when you walked through the door."

"I don't blame her. The irony is that I used to praise myself for being such a great mother in what seemed like dire circumstances. There were so many times when I doubted my ability to carry on. I talked to myself. I waited until the girls were asleep and then I'd stand there, lecturing that pale frightened young woman I saw in that mirror. I reminded her that big goals are achieved through numerous tiny steps." It was something she'd never told anyone. Never revealed to anyone. "I was basically doing for myself what I try and do for people now, in my work. I encourage them to look inside themselves and bring out the best. I tell them that we can almost always do more than we think we can. And all these words, everything I say to people now when I'm asked to speak, they were all things I said to myself." She sniffed. "I suppose you could say I turned misfortune into fortune."

"What an inspiring story. To be able to do all that when you had lost the man you loved." Mary put her cup down. "Did you have no one to support you? Talk to you?"

"I'd moved to a new area, and I didn't know anyone. And I'm not sure I would have talked anyway. I think I knew, even then, that I needed to listen to my own voice."

Mary broke a cookie in half. "I don't know how I would have managed in those early days if I hadn't had my friends and family. Someone from the village dropped by every day for the first two months. And it's true that I didn't always want the food, and there were times when I wished they'd leave me alone so that I could just grieve in peace, but I'm glad they didn't. It forced me to get up and live life, even though that life had shrunk to less than half its original size." Mary sighed. "You should have had that support, Gayle. No one should have to cope with the death of a loved one alone."

She could change the subject. She probably should change the subject.

"He didn't die. At least, not then." She didn't know what made her speak about something she'd never spoken about before. Maybe it was Mary's kindness. Maybe it was simply that this new shift in her life had torn open something she'd kept safely inside her. "I left him." She glanced at Mary, expecting to see shock and instead saw sympathy.

"That can't have been an easy decision to make."

"In fact it *was* an easy decision, although not so easy to execute." Gayle's mouth felt dry. "The first time he hit me was right here in Scotland, on our honeymoon."

"Oh Gayle." Now there was shock, and also a glimpse of anger that didn't seem to fit mild Mary.

"I probably should have walked out right there and then, but it's so easy to make excuses and to convince yourself it won't happen again. I met him at college. I was in my second year, and I'd just lost both my parents in a traffic accident. We were very close. The closest family you could imagine. Only child. Treasured daughter. I was their princess." Gayle rubbed her hand over her neck, wondering how it was possible to still miss her parents when it had been so many years. "I had an idyllic childhood, which at the time was wonderful, but it in no way prepared me for the harsh reality of life. Losing them together like that, so suddenly, was like being marooned on an island with no survival skills. I felt alone. Afraid. I had no idea how to cope. I went back to college because I didn't know what else to do, but it felt like a different place and I felt like a different person. I had no idea how to function. I'd been truly loved, and now I had no one. And then I met Ray. He was fifteen years older than me. Maybe that was what drew him to me. A cliché, I know, but I wonder now if I was looking for some sort of parental type support." It had taken her years to figure that out, but Mary didn't seem surprised.

"That makes perfect sense. You were lost with no map. He offered a safe place." She topped up Gayle's tea and pushed the cup toward her. "Drink something."

Gayle took one sip and then another, then closed her hands round the mug taking comfort from the warmth.

"I leaned on him. You're right that with him I felt safe, which is ironic looking back on it. Most of the students I mixed with seemed as flaky as me, and then there was this guy with money and an apartment, who seemed to have all the answers. He was patient, kind, and he took care of me. And then I found out I was pregnant."

"That must have been a frightening thing."

"It was. I wanted to finish college, I knew I *needed* to finish college. I had to make a life for myself. And I think I knew then that although on the surface I was coping better, I wasn't really. I wasn't really caring for myself, so how could I care for a baby? I'd gone from one cosseted life to another. Being with him absolved me of the need to take control and be a responsible adult. But he was delighted by the fact I was pregnant. He didn't want me to worry about finishing college. He would look after me. With hindsight, I should have seen a red flag, but I was an emotional mess and I took the easy path. I married him."

"And you came to Scotland."

"Yes. It was beautiful, and I remember being happy. Until the day he hit me—I don't even remember why. Something I did. Something I said. And I was shocked. No one had ever hit me before. My parents were loving, if anything they were overindulgent. I had no experience of abuse of any kind."

"You didn't walk out then?"

"No. He was mortified and apologetic. Blamed it on work stress, drinking too much—I don't know. I can't remember that part, either. But I accepted his promise that he would never do it again." She was almost too embarrassed to admit her stupidity. "I believed him."

"Why wouldn't you?" Mary thumped her mug down on the table. "You'd never been given reason not to trust people before." Her visible outrage made Gayle feel better about something that had troubled her for decades.

"Reflecting on it later, I decided I just didn't want to see it. He was the one who had supported me after I'd lost my par-

ents. I had no confidence in my ability to be self-sufficient."
She breathed. "Things seemed to settle down. He had angry
moments, but he didn't hit me again. Until Samantha was seven
months old. I was six months pregnant with Ella when he threw
me down the stairs. I don't know how I didn't lose the baby.
Somehow I managed to twist myself and landed on my back
and not my stomach. Samantha was screaming and I saw him
pick her up and shake her. That was it. That was the moment I
knew I had to get away. It wasn't just me who was in danger, it
was my daughter and my unborn child. So I left. It was Christmas, and from then on I always associated Christmas with that
awful day." She reached for her tea, but her hand was shaking
so badly most of it slopped on the table. "I'm sorry. I'm—"

"Don't." Mary reached for a cloth, her movements calm and
quiet. "Don't apologize for being upset about something that
would have broken most people."

"It was right then, at the lowest point of my life, that I realized the only person I could rely on was myself. I had no loving parents to cushion me from life. No partner—because in
no way were Ray and I ever partners. I had no qualifications
and no career prospects. I'd thought about working, of course,
but Ray had insisted it was better if I stayed at home with the
children, and as he earned plenty there was no need for me to
work. I hadn't finished college. It didn't even occur to me that it
would be sensible for me to have a way to earn a living in case I
needed to do that one day. Without the girls I don't know what
I would have done, but I had them and they were my motivation for everything."

"So what did you do?"

"I was lucky that I had a small amount of money that my parents left. Fortunately I'd never told Ray about it. Three months
after I left him, the police came to my door. He'd wrapped his
car around a tree. He'd been drinking. I went into labor that
night. They put the baby in my arms, and I felt this tiny scrap of

flesh and a ton weight of responsibility. I had a ten-month-old and a newborn. That was the point in my life when I grew up."

"I would have been crushed by it," Mary murmured. "Flattened."

"I was. Thinking about the enormity of it, the hugeness of what lay ahead, froze me. So I narrowed my field of vision. I dealt with the problem that was in front of me. And then the next problem. I found a home day care provider who lived in the same block as me, and worked two jobs to pay for it. Hardly saw the girls, but I did what I had to. I finished college, and spent every moment of every day applying for jobs. To start with I got nowhere, and then I was offered a job on a graduate program with a consultancy firm. They'd decided they needed to hire more women. It was a box ticking exercise, but I didn't even care. It grew from there. I constructed a new life from the rubble of the old one."

And maybe that was something to be proud of. Maybe not all her choices had been bad.

Mary didn't seem to think so.

"And you did that while raising two beautiful girls." She paused. "Did you tell them the truth about their father?"

"I told them he died. I didn't think they needed to know the rest. I've never told anyone, not a single soul. Until today. You're easy to talk to, Mary McIntyre."

Mary's hand tightened on hers. "In your situation, I think I would have done the same. Not told them all of it."

"Truly?" She, who had navigated the past three decades without seeking anyone's approval, was pathetically grateful to have one of her decisions endorsed.

"Their father was dead. What was the point?"

"That was my reasoning, but now they're asking—or Ella is. She's a romantic. She wants to know about my relationship. My honeymoon. She thinks I'm traumatized because I lost the love of my life. They think the fact that I have no photos, and no memorabilia of any kind, is a sign that I can't think about him. Which is true, but not for the reasons they think. And now I'm trapped by my own lies."

Mary frowned. "You didn't lie. You just didn't disclose the truth of what your life was like before he died."

"And maybe I should have done. Although I don't know how, or when, I would have done that. What would I say? *By the way girls, that father you never met? He liked to push me down the stairs.*"

Mary shook her head. "At what point should we stop protecting those we love? That's the question."

"One of many questions." Gayle fiddled with the cookie in front of her, facing an uncomfortable truth. "Maybe I'm the one I'm protecting. I survived by not looking back. You'd think after all these years I'd be ready to look, but I'm not."

"Why would you want to look at something as ugly as that? You don't have to apologize for it or feel guilty. You have a right to protect yourself. I think it's called self-care."

"The irony is that I was determined to be the best parent possible. I was determined that the girls would have all the skills they needed to survive in life. Not pony rides and ballet lessons, not that I could have afforded those anyway, but classes that would help them. Extra tuition in math, reading programs. When I bought gifts, it was always books and puzzles. I didn't wrap them in padding, even though I wanted to. I taught them to pick themselves up when they were knocked over. I taught them to heal their own bruises. I wanted to teach them self-reliance." She rubbed her fingers over her forehead. "I wanted them to know their own strength, so they would never lie awake in the dark trembling, afraid they couldn't meet life's challenges."

"You're a wonderful mother, Gayle. The girls are lucky to have you."

She was a fraud. A total fraud. "Up until a few weeks ago, the girls and I haven't spoken for five years."

There was a protracted silence and then Mary reached across the table and took her hand. "Oh Gayle—"

"Our last meeting—I upset them. I said the wrong thing. It wasn't just wrong, it was hurtful. My own experiences have made me—inflexible. And afraid." It was so hard to admit it. So hard. "Everything I've achieved—everything I am, was driven by fear. I was afraid to love, so I stayed single. I was afraid to trust, so I did things alone. I was afraid of not being able to support my family, so I put everything I had into my work. Fear. All of it was about fear. And if that wasn't bad enough, I let my fear dictate the way I raised my daughters." She could see everything so clearly now. "I didn't know it, but Ella was pregnant that last time we met up. Because I was always so judgmental and disapproving of her choices, she was afraid to tell me. And Samantha was so angry with me—protecting her sister. I see that now."

Mary stood up and fetched a glass of water. "Here. Drink this."

She picked up the glass and drank. "I was upset. They were upset. I expected them to reach out and apologize, but they didn't. And I was too stubborn, and lacking in self-insight, to reach out to them. I was convinced I was right and they were wrong." Regret poured into her. "I pushed my own children away because of the way I was. And the gap grew wider, and Ella, my sweet Ella, didn't know how to bridge it because so much was changing in her life. At what point do you tell your mother that you're married with a child? It doesn't get easier to do that—it gets harder. And she should have been able to tell me that." A great lump wedged itself in her throat. "I wasn't with her for the biggest events of her life. I wasn't with her when she married Michael, I wasn't there to help her when she was pregnant, and I wasn't there for her when she gave birth. I'm a terrible mother."

"That's not true, Gayle. Not true."

"It's true. I thought I was doing the right thing, but now I see I wasn't." The lump grew bigger. Emotion filled her, starting in her heart and spreading through her body. "I was scared, and it's a terrible, horrible, awful feeling. I didn't want them to feel that way."

"How does that make you a bad mother?" Mary's hand tightened on hers. "And as parents our responsibility is to make our children independent. You did that. You did a good job. Your daughters are strong, capable, admirable women."

Gayle's chest felt full. "Yesterday I watched my daughter playing with her daughter." Tears filled her eyes. Mary's face blurred in front of her. "There was no purpose to it. No educational goal. They were simply having fun together, enjoying each other's company. They laughed. They hugged. They talked to each other about everything and nothing." She almost choked on the words. "There were no teachable moments, just joy for the sake of joy. I never made time for that. I used to think there *was* no time for that. But how can we be too busy for happiness? How?"

The tears spilled over, big fat tears of regret that stung and scalded. She tried to stop them, but the barrier she'd built had weakened and now there was nothing holding them back. She felt raw and vulnerable. A drowning swimmer with no life preserver. A skydiver with no parachute.

"Gayle—"

She felt Mary's arm come round her, but that simple act of kindness simply accelerated the outpouring of emotion. She'd never talked to anyone like this before, but now she'd started she couldn't stop.

"I never built a snowman with them. I never did that." She was drowning in her own tears. Choking on them. She couldn't catch a breath. Her head was filled with all the things she hadn't done and hadn't said. "Not—once. No—" She hiccuped, sucked in air. "No snowman. We didn't—" it was hard to breathe "—bake cakes together at weekends—we didn't dance—I don't know how to dance." All the things she hadn't done multiplied in her head, replacing every last good opinion she'd ever had about herself. She felt Mary's grip tighten, and instead of pulling her hand away, she clung, holding tight, the arms of her new friend the only thing preventing her from falling right to the bottom of the dark pit lined with her own maternal failures.

Mary rocked her like a child, and she cried until she felt sick from crying, until her body went limp.

"There." Mary's voice soothed. "You've been through so much, and frankly I don't know how you've held it together. You're a true inspiration."

"How can you possibly think that?"

"How can you *not* think it?" Mary sat down next to her, but kept hold of Gayle's hand. "I don't know what I would have done in your situation, how I would have coped, but I know I wouldn't have achieved what you've achieved."

"Two children who resent me?"

"I doubt they resent you. It sounds more as if they don't understand you. And if we're to blame for anything in this complicated game called parenting, then maybe it's that."

"We?"

"You don't have the monopoly on frustrating your children, you know." Mary gave her hand a final squeeze and then stood up and walked across the kitchen. She opened a drawer, pulled out a clean cloth and dampened it. "You protected your girls, and the downside is they have no idea of the reasons behind all the decisions you made. Maybe you should tell them." She sat back down and held the cloth to Gayle. "For your eyes. They're swollen."

"Thank you." Gayle took the cloth and held it to her face. She'd experienced emotional lows before, but always on her own. At the beginning, when life had fallen apart, there hadn't been anyone she could lean on and then she'd become so used to handling things alone, she'd forgotten how to reach out. She'd forgotten how it felt to feel supported. "What's the point of telling them now? It feels like excuses."

"You're not making excuses. You're saying 'these are the reasons I made the choices I made.' And you made plenty of good choices. No one is perfect, Gayle. I'm not, you're not, and I'm sure your girls aren't, either. No person is perfect and no relationship is perfect."

"Your relationship with Cameron sounded perfect. You had more than four decades together."

"Perfect?" Mary sat back and laughed. "No one can be perfect for four decades. That doesn't happen. I loved Cameron. I loved him as much as it's possible to love another person, and I know I was lucky. He was a good man, but he was far from perfect. When people talk about him—not just friends and neighbors, but the children—they talk about the good bits. *Do you remember when Cameron did this? Dad was great at that, wasn't he?* They never mention any of the frustrating or irritating things. And that makes me feel alone. It makes me feel as if I was the only one who really knew him. They never mention how he was always losing his glasses, or how many times we had to turn the car round because he'd left his wallet in the house. They mention his optimism, and how inspiring it was to be with someone who always believed there would be a great outcome to everything. They never talk about how frustrating that could be, or maybe they just didn't see it. *It will be fine, Mary,* he'd say, even when I knew for sure it wasn't going to be fine." She shook her head. "He refused to entertain the possibility that something might not work out. It almost drove me to drink. One of the reasons we're needing to take in paying guests now is because he thought some magical being would sprinkle fairy dust on our home and solve all our financial problems. And maybe he knew he could be that way because I was firmly rooted in reality. He knew I was holding the string of his balloon, and I wouldn't let him float away. Living in a dreamland doesn't prepare you for reality. You'll understand what I mean by that." There was a wobble in Mary's voice, and this time it was Gayle who reached out and took her hand.

"Sounds as if you had a great partnership despite those things."

"We did. And there were plenty of things about me that frustrated him, too. I'm cautious. I can't leave the house in the morning unless the kitchen is cleared up and sparkling. I never throw anything away. But we fitted. Was our marriage perfect? Definitely not. But it was perfect for us. A relationship is like a jigsaw, isn't it? Whether it's with a partner, with friends or with your children—it's made up of hundreds of tiny pieces, some perfect, some imperfect. Those characteristics unique to each one of us, the genes we inherit, our life experiences, the way we behave. Tiny, misshapen little pieces that make us who we are. And when you make a life with someone, you have to somehow find a way to make all those pieces fit. If you're lucky, they come together into something that makes sense as a whole. Cameron and I made sense." Mary blew her nose. "And you have no idea how good it is to talk about him this way. Remember him properly, without having to protect the feelings of the person I'm with."

"You've brought him to life for me." Gayle had never made room in her life for friendship, but now she wished she had. "You chose well, Mary."

"I was lucky."

"No. You recognized a good man when you saw him. You understood what mattered to you, and what didn't. You made a choice. That's not luck." Gayle folded the cloth neatly and put it on the table. "I don't think my family has fitted together well for a long time."

"But that doesn't mean it can't happen. You're here, building a relationship with your granddaughter, even though being back in Scotland must be hard for you."

"I was hoping it would happen. It's the reason I'm here. But I've messed it up."

"And you don't think your daughter will forgive you for that?"

Gayle thought about how important Christmas was to Ella. "I'm not sure that she will. I said the wrong thing."

Mary sat up straight. "Have you never said the wrong thing before?"

"I'm sure I have. Many times."

"And when you do, do you fold and give up?"

Gayle looked at her. "No. At work I take responsibility. Apologize. Learn. Try and move forward. But this is different. Family is different. More complicated."

"Stay there. Don't move." Mary stood up, left the room for a moment and then returned a couple of minutes later and slapped two books on the table. "I recommend you read these. I think they'll help you."

Gayle glanced at them.

Choice Not Chance, and *Brave New You*.

She didn't know whether to laugh or cry. "Where did those come from?"

"I ordered them. Brodie said you were a top businesswoman, and frankly I found that a little intimidating."

It was the first time she'd found her achievements uncomfortable. "Mary—"

"It's true. You're an impressive woman, Gayle. Which is why I know for sure you'll be able to find a way through this. What would you say if I was in your situation and you were advising me?"

"I don't know. I don't know anything."

"That's because you're having a wobble, but if you read Chapter Six in this one—" Mary pushed *Choice Not Chance* in front of her "—you'll remember to take your own advice and never make your choices when you're feeling tired, low or any way less than at full strength."

Gayle put her hand on *Brave New You*. "I'm embarrassed to open this. It seems so smug and self-satisfied to me now. A whole book telling people how to embrace change and cope with change, and here I am not handling change at all."

"I don't see a section in this book where you tell people change is easy. You're honest about how hard it is. That's part of what makes it so valuable. This is written by someone who understands that change is hard."

"You probably haven't read enough of it to know."

"I've read the book twice, Gayle, and I can't tell you how much it has helped me. I woke up this morning feeling stronger than I have in a long while. Since before my Cameron died. I woke up with hope, and a tiny bit of excitement for the future. And you're the reason why. Do you know how many books I've flung at the wall in the past year?"

"You've read other books?"

"Yes. I grabbed onto everything, like a drowning woman clinging to logs in the hope that they'll keep her above the surface. I wanted to find a way to rebuild my life, but all I could see was what lay behind me, not what lay ahead. Your book changed that. And I'm not the only one you've helped. I went online and saw the reviews, and also some of the comments from people who have heard you speak. Women whose lives you changed. You should feel proud. Do you know how many people you've inspired? You've changed lives, Gayle."

She was going to cry again, and her face was still swollen and blotchy from the last time. "I think we might need some of those onions you mentioned."

"Your family are out in the forest. They won't be back for a while, and when they are we'll hear them. Read your own books, Gayle. That's my advice." Mary gave Gayle's shoulder a squeeze. "You've talked a lot about your girls, and about your career, but nothing about yourself. Your personal life. Your needs."

"My girls and my career were my life."

"You never fell in love again?"

"I never let myself." Gayle blew her nose hard. "I'm not saying there weren't men. There were a few over the years, but never for any length of time. And that was my choice. It took every drop of my energy and willpower to build what I had, and I couldn't risk it all." She paused. "That's what I tell myself. I suppose the truth is I was scared of relationships, too."

"And who wouldn't be, after coming through what you came through?"

"I always thought of myself as fearless, but I never moved outside the safe little bubble I'd created for myself."

"Enough self-blame and regret, Gayle. You probably feel awful after all that crying. You should eat something more. Try my shortbread. My grandmother taught me to make it when I was the same age as your granddaughter. She swore it could make everything better. I used to come by after school with skinned knees and she'd sit me down right here at this table with a glass of milk. It was years before I realized shortbread didn't really have magical healing properties."

"That's a great story."

Mary put a slice on a plate and gave it to Gayle. "And it's not too late, you know."

"For what?"

"For a relationship. Intimacy. Fulfilment."

"I've had a very fulfilling career. I've been lucky." Listless, Gayle broke off a corner off the shortbread. She had no appetite, but she didn't want to hurt Mary's feelings. She couldn't remember a time when she'd been shown such kindness. She didn't operate in a world where people were kind. In her world you had to fight for a place and then you had to fight to keep it. In the land she inhabited if you showed your weaknesses, especially if you were a woman, they'd be used against you.

"But your career doesn't laugh with you, understand you and hold you when you're scared or tired."

"What I can't do for myself, I've learned to do without." She ate a piece of shortbread and closed her eyes. It was still slightly warm from the oven, and she tasted sweetness as it crumbled in her mouth. A montage played through her brain—baking with her mother in the kitchen, hands dug deep into soft flour. Arriving home from school and immediately heading to the kitchen for a snack. Was it the food itself that was a comfort, or the memories that came attached like a sugar coating? Did we love food because food meant love? "This is perfect. I've never tasted anything better. Except perhaps your porridge. Also the soup you served last night. And the lamb. In fact everything you've served us since we arrived here." Having thought she wasn't hungry, she now realized she was starving. She broke off another piece of shortbread. "I think your grandmother might have been right about it having healing properties. Have you thought about writing a cookery book?"

Mary laughed. "To teach someone to make shortbread? It's a staple in thousands of kitchens around here. No one needs my recipe."

"I disagree." Gayle glanced at the cakes and pies cooling on the countertop. "What you do here is special."

"I make ordinary food. These days no one is interested in ordinary food."

"I disagree. You could call it *Tastes from a Highland Kitchen*. No, wait…" Gayle paused. It was a relief to feel some of her energy returning. "*Tales from a Highland Kitchen*. You include personal stories about the recipes, like the one you just told me. Maybe interspersed with photographs of the estate."

"Who would be interested in that?"

"In good, traditional recipes with human interest and family stories thrown in? A lot of people. Think about it. If you're keen, I can make a call to my publisher."

"Your—" Mary plopped down on the chair. "Are you serious?"

"Yes. I'm not promising they'll go with the idea of course, but I like to think I can spot potential and you have it in spades. Maybe later, when I've washed my face and done something to get rid of this headache, we can sit down and brainstorm ideas. You can feed me more of your excellent food, which definitely does have magical properties, and you can tell me more stories of growing up here and your grandmother. And here's another thought—" Gayle's mind had gone from feeling sluggish and soaked with regret, to alert. "How would you feel about teaching cookery?"

"Teaching?"

"Talk to my daughter, because this is more her field than mine, but I could imagine that there would be a big demand for small groups of people to come and stay for a few days of cookery."

"A cookery week?"

"Maybe not a week. Short breaks. They can cook what they're going to eat while they're here. So basically you'd have help in the kitchen. Or maybe you offer that as an extra when they're here for their house party. *Cook with Mary.*"

Mary laughed. "I'm starting to understand how you've done so well in life."

"I don't think I've done well at the things that matter."

"You're focusing only on what you didn't give the girls, instead of looking at what you did give them."

"Maybe." It was humbling how badly she needed to hear someone tell her that she hadn't made a complete mess of things. Inside she felt doubtful, crumpled and insecure.

And maybe Mary realized that.

"Here's something else to think about." She offered another slice of shortbread. "It's never too late to build a snowman, Gayle. It's never too late to dance, or laugh, bake cookies or date a man. It's never too late."

Samantha

"I have no idea where she's gone. She's probably taken a taxi to the airport," Ella said, "because I refused to let her make choices for me. I've probably upset her."

Samantha clasped her hands behind her back to hide the fact they were shaking. She was so angry with her mother. Gayle was the one who had insisted on spending Christmas with them. Why do that, if she didn't want to make it a happy time for her granddaughter? How could she intentionally upset little Tab? The shaking grew worse. She kept her focus on her sister. "I'm proud of you. It's the first time you've drawn a line and forced her to accept your choice."

"Yes." Ella stood a little straighter. "And it feels good in principle, but also bad, if that makes sense."

Samantha managed a nod. "Of course. You don't change who you are overnight. It's a process."

"I still can't believe she actually said that, can you?"

"I—yes, I suppose I can." Her lips were dry. Her mouth was dry. Tab's crestfallen expression was stuck in her head, and suddenly she was reliving all those childhood Christmases where her mother had ripped away the cloak of mystery that surrounded Santa. It had been a tug-of-war between her and Samantha, who had desperately wanted her sister to experience the same magic as her friends. And doing that for her sister had made it magical for her, too. But it had come at a cost, and she'd been the one to pay that price. She'd been the buffer between her mother's beliefs and her sister's joy.

Ella was oblivious. "Brodie saved the day—that man's a god, by the way. How did he come up with that mathematical model? I almost believed him!"

"Math is his thing. He's supersmart."

"And supersexy, but we'll talk about that another time." Ella rubbed her forehead, tired. "I was starting to think the holidays might be okay after all, but now I'm not convinced. Do you think Christmas is ruined?"

"No. We're not going to let it be ruined." She spoke automatically, reassuring her sister the way she always did. "We're going to make this work. Tab is going to have a wonderful Christmas."

Maybe, since her sister had finally been honest with their mother, she should do the same.

She and her mother hadn't discussed that last gathering. They hadn't dealt with the past; they'd left it behind. Bitter words, and then nothing. Samantha had chosen to ignore it, which is what she so often did of course. Outer Samantha ignored inner Samantha.

But no more.

"I'm going to find her. It's time I talked to her about a whole lot of things, including what happened five years ago." Samantha headed for the stairs. "I'll check her room."

"I'll come with you. And don't try and talk me out of it." Ella was only a few steps behind her. "I know I'm the one who caused the rift between us in the first place."

"I was the one who—"

"Said the words. I know, but you were defending me. You were protecting me, the way you always have. You're incredible, but I shouldn't have put you in that position. I can't change the past, but I can make sure it doesn't happen again. We'll talk to her together. We'll have an adult discussion, and if we can't agree on a way forward that works for everyone, then we'll need to rethink the rest of this holiday break." Ella seemed strong and confident, which was more than Samantha did.

She felt raw and vulnerable. Right at that moment she would have given anything just to escape outdoors and hug a reindeer. Or Brodie.

The fun they'd shared the day before felt as if it had happened in another life.

She paused outside their mother's room. The door was ajar.

Ignoring the sick feeling in her stomach, she tapped on the door, gave it a little push and immediately saw that the room was empty.

"She's not here." And the relief was incredible. The conversation she didn't want to have was going to have to wait.

"But all her things are still here, so I don't think she's left." Ella followed her into the room. "Maybe Brodie will know where she is. Unless he arranged a car for her, she has to be somewhere in the house, right?"

"Right."

"I can't stop thinking about how fantastic he was. All that talk of ratios, pi, angles, velocity—what a hero. I've never heard a more convincing argument for the existence of Santa. I ended up believing it myself. I'm going to have to hang up a stocking."

"You always hang up a stocking." Distracted by the books on her mother's nightstand, Samantha was only half listening.

"I know. And you always fill it. Which is why you're Santa Sam. I think you're— What? What are you looking at?"

Samantha picked up the stack of books and sat down on the bed. "Have you seen these?"

"No. Don't tell me she's reading Highland romance, too?"

Samantha didn't answer. The anger drained out of her and she handed the first book to her sister.

"*Be the Best Grandparent Ever.*" Ella stared at it and then sat down next to her. "Oh."

"And then there's this one *Grandparenting Skills for Beginners—*" Samantha passed it over. "And this one. *Nanny or Nanna? A Guide to Building a Relationship with Your Grandchild.* She's really been trying." And it didn't make sense. Why then had she been so careless around Tab?

"Have you seen this?" Ella was flicking through one of the books. "She's written notes in the margin."

Samantha glanced over her shoulder. "And underlined passages. 'Remember you're not the parent.'"

"'Be careful not to impose your views.'"

"I should have paid more attention to that part." Their mother's voice came from the doorway, and they both turned, guilty, books still in their hands.

Gayle stepped inside the room. "I ordered those books the day you came to my apartment in Manhattan. I was determined to get it right, but I underestimated how hard that would be. I'm sorry for what I said about—" their mother broke off and glanced over her shoulder, checking that Tab wasn't nearby "—you know who. I promise I'll find a way to join in with the magic. I'll try harder. I can do this."

Ella made a sound, dumped the books on the bed and hurried across to their mother. "I know you can. We'll find a way. I overreacted, because I'm protective of Tab." She put her arms round their mother, while Samantha sat there, stiff and awkward, envying her sister's ability to show her emotions so readily.

She watched, feeling out of her depth as her mother patted Ella's arm.

"You don't have to be sorry." Gayle pulled away. "You wanted to give your baby a magical moment, and I almost ruined it. Hopefully I didn't. Brodie seems to be a quick thinking person."

Had her mother been crying?

Her eyes looked a little puffy and swollen.

Ella obviously thought so too, because she gathered up the books from the bed and then put them down again. "Are you all right, Mom? You look—your eyes are a little red."

"Allergies. Probably the dog. I've taken medication." Gayle paused and then closed the door of the room. "Actually, that isn't true. I have been crying."

"Oh Mom!" Ella's voice thickened. "I am sorry I upset you so badly."

"Not you. I managed it all by myself. And I think it's time I talked to you both. Properly." Gayle sat down on the chair. "I should have done it a long time ago."

"Talk to us about what?"

"About your father."

Ella sent a guilty glance toward Samantha. "Honestly, you don't have to. I shouldn't have asked. I—"

"Sit down, Ella." Gayle spoke quietly. "This isn't going to be easy to say, but it isn't going to be easy for you to hear, either. Let me speak, and when I've said everything I want to say, you can ask your questions. And I promise to answer them. All of them. Anything you want to ask."

Ella sat back down on the bed next to her sister.

Samantha couldn't shift the sick feeling in her stomach. Was she the only one finding this uncomfortable? Her mother was about to make some sort of confession, but she couldn't help thinking that they didn't have a solid enough relationship to support that level of intimacy. It meant adding another dubious ingredient to the already unpalatable soup of emotions that were sloshing round inside her.

Gayle kept her hands in her lap. Fingers locked. Knuckles white. "There are things I haven't told you."

"About Dad?" Ella shifted a little closer to Samantha.

Instinctively she took Ella's hand and gave it a squeeze. Looking out for her sister stopped her having to think too hard about her own feelings.

"Just tell us, Mom." She wanted facts, so that they could deal with them and then talk about the past. And she was determined that they would talk about the past.

"Your father died in exactly the way I described, but what I haven't told you is everything that happened before that."

Samantha held tightly to her sister's hand as her mother started to talk.

Next to her, Ella gasped, reacted, made sympathetic noises, responded to everything their mother told them. At one point she stood up and poured her mother a drink, the water sloshing over the sides as she poured with a shaking hand.

There, drink something, take a break, this must be so difficult for you.

Still Samantha sat, feeling like an observer not a participant, not knowing what to say.

All these years when she'd pictured her father, she'd imagined a benign, loving figure. She'd imagined how her life might have been different had he lived. She'd thought that maybe she and her father might be close. That he might have been more approachable than her mother.

The clash between her childish dreams and the reality was so violent she didn't know what to do with the pieces.

"I didn't want the two of you to ever feel the fear I felt. I never wanted you to feel vulnerable. I wanted you to be self-confident." Her mother blew her nose on a tissue Ella had handed her. "I wanted you to feel you could cope with anything."

Samantha imagined her mother, pregnant and with a toddler, bruised physically and emotionally, walking out on the only security she knew.

All the times I blamed her, she thought. *All the times I thought she was a machine.*

"I wish you'd told us." Ella was crying now, her arms round their mother. And Gayle hugged her back.

"I was trying to protect you. If he hadn't died, maybe I would have told you the truth, but he did, and then I couldn't see the point. It would have hurt you. I didn't want to hurt my girls."

"I understand." Ella rocked her. "I understand all about wanting to protect your child. It's what a mother does. In your situation I probably would have done the same. I'm grateful."

Samantha said nothing.

How was it protecting a child to hide the truth? She didn't feel protected. She didn't feel grateful. She felt confused.

She should say something. But what?

I would have liked to have known, Mom.

What was the point of saying that when there was no undoing the past?

She felt so many different things it was hard to untangle them. She felt guilt that she and Ella had never questioned if there was more going on, and anger and frustration that her mother hadn't told them, and therefore hadn't helped them understand. Would her own relationship history have been different if she'd known about her mother's past?

And then there was her father.

Samantha swallowed. She felt as if she'd lost someone. She tried to picture the man she'd imagined all these years, but this time her brain wouldn't cooperate. He'd gone, the shadowy figure who had lurked in her imagination as absent as the real person had been. She felt a profound sense of loss, which was ridiculous because how could you lose something you'd never had?

Ella was asking questions now, about those early days, about how her mother had managed, information flowing until Samantha found it hard to breathe.

"It happened at Christmas." Gayle spoke quietly. "I think that's why I was never able to see Christmas as magical. I associated it with the worst time in my life. But being around Tab made me remember the Christmases I'd had before that time. With my parents. Happy times. I don't know what happened today—habit, I suppose. She was asking a lot of questions, and the words came out before I could stop them. Have I ruined everything?"

"No." Ella shook her head. "Thanks to Brodie, she is still happily anticipating the arrival of Santa."

Gayle slumped. "Thank goodness for that."

"She does ask a lot of questions, and sometimes it does wear you down, so I do get it. But I can't bear to think you went through that at Christmas. And you emerged from it this strong, independent person. I could never in a million years have been as brave as you've been." Ella choked, scrubbed her palm over her cheeks.

Gayle stirred. "I think you're one of the bravest people I know."

"Not true. And as we're all being honest here, there's something I haven't told you—" Ella's gaze skidded to Samantha, but she felt too exhausted and confused to give her sister any direction.

She was on her own with this decision.

Ella sat up straighter. "I'm not working at the moment. I haven't worked since Tab was born. My choice. I wanted to be a stay-at-home mother, and Michael supports that. And me. He supports me, financially at least. Although I do intend to go back to teaching in the future. Not because I don't feel our relationship is secure, but because I love it so much. And I'm good at it."

There was a long silence.

Finally Gayle spoke. "You didn't tell me."

"No."

"You didn't feel able to tell me. That's on me."

"No, it's on me, for not being braver. For not owning my decisions. I avoid confrontation."

Gayle stirred. "There are many different types of bravery. You

love without hesitation. You leap, even when there is no promise of a safe landing. You encourage your daughter to explore
her world, but you don't hold her back. You offer a safety net,
but not a restraining harness. You made your choices and were
sure of them, even when I tried to make you doubt yourself."

"But now I understand why you were afraid for me." Ella
took her mother's hand. "It makes sense."

"Maybe, but it doesn't excuse it. From now on I will be re-
specting your choices, starting with your family life. He's a good
man, your Michael."

"Yes, he is." Ella sat a little straighter. "I love him… I respect him. I need him, but if something happened to him, I'd
survive. It would be unspeakably hard, but I know I'd survive.
I never doubted my ability to handle what life threw at me. I
have you to thank for that. And I should have said it sooner. I
should have recognized what you gave us."

Samantha stood up abruptly, trying to get her head above the
surface before she drowned.

Was she the only one struggling to process all this?

"I have to—I'm sorry—I need air."

Ella jumped up. "Are you—"

"Fine!" Samantha held up her hand like a stop sign and backed
away toward the door. She didn't want a hug. She didn't want
conversation. She'd already had more than enough, and now
she needed to be on her own. Ella and their mother would
bond and heal all those cracks, but she felt removed from it all.
"I need—I just need—"

"Time to process." Her mother caught Ella's arm to stop her
following Samantha. "Take as long as you need. When you're
ready, we can either talk, or not. Whatever works for you."

She wasn't used to her mother being so understanding.

She knew she still owed her mother an apology for the things
she'd said that last time they met, but she couldn't handle that
right now. She couldn't handle any of it.

All the things they hadn't known—

All the things they might have done differently—

Her father—

She mumbled something, left her mother and sister to continue their conversation and headed down the stairs with no particular destination in mind. The emotions inside her grew, the pressure building until she was dangerously close to exploding.

Air. She needed all the air she could breathe into her lungs.

The front door was an escape hatch at the end of a dark tunnel, and she headed straight for it.

"Samantha?" Mary's voice stopped her. "Are you all right, dear? It's late to be going out."

The door was a few steps away. Within reach. She had no energy for conversation. She had nothing left to give anyone. She'd reached breaking point.

She might have crumbled right there and then, but Brodie emerged from the library and crossed the hall in long strides.

"Oh hi, Samantha—I've been wondering where you were. Don't worry, Mum. This is work. Samantha and I have plans for tonight." Without pausing, he grabbed his coat and hers.

"Work? Plans?" Mary was astonished. "You're going out? What about dinner?"

"We're having a working dinner. Samantha is only here for a few days, and I intend to use every one of those days. If we're going to turn this into a commercial success, then we need all the advice she can give us." He shrugged on his coat. "She's being generous with her time. I'm taking her for something to eat in the village—because that's something our guests might want to do—and then I'll show her the estate by night. After that we'll go to my office to run some numbers. We'll be late, so don't wait up."

"The estate by—night?"

"Yes." Brodie draped Samantha's coat around her shoulders

and urged her toward the door. "I thought we could offer... starlight strolls."

"Star—but Brodie they're forecasting more snow, and—"

"My office is warm. We'll be working out of there. Don't wait up—we have a lot to get through." Brodie propelled Samantha through the door before his mother could think up a suitable response.

She heard the door close behind her. Ice-cold air cooled her face and bit through her clothing.

She was grateful to him for removing the need for a conversation with Mary, but now she had another problem. She didn't really want to be with Brodie, either. She didn't want to be with anyone.

"I can't—"

"I know. Don't talk. I've got this." He steered her toward the car, his hand firm on her back. "Don't slip. It's icy here."

She stumbled, tears blinding her. She didn't even care that he was there to witness it. She was beyond caring.

"Why don't you—" He saw her tears and the breath hissed through his teeth. "Damn. Hold on. Just for a few more seconds." He unlocked the car and lifted her into the car. "Stay there."

He slithered his way to the driver's side, slammed the door on both of them, closing them in.

"Seat belt." He reached across her and fastened it. Then gave her leg a squeeze. "I'm driving us away from here. Then we can talk or not talk—whatever you prefer."

Now the tears had started she couldn't stop them and with them came sobs, great tearing sobs.

"Hold on—just hold on—" He accelerated, spun the wheels, cursed and slowed down. "Just need to get through the gate, and then no one can see you, or follow us."

She couldn't hold on.

She sobbed. She sobbed for her mother. She sobbed for her

father. She sobbed for herself—for the person she was, and the person she wished she was.

She choked on her tears, on her feelings, on a flood of remorse and regret.

She had no sense of time passing but was dimly aware that the car had stopped, and then he was unfastening her seat belt and pulling her against him.

He said nothing. Just held her tightly and let her cry.

She cried until she had nothing left, and then gradually the tears slowed and then stopped, and she flopped against him, so depleted of energy that she couldn't have moved even if she'd wanted to. But she didn't want to. She wanted to stay here in this warm, safe place.

His arms were locked around her.

His coat scratched her face.

Brodie.

Her head throbbed. She felt terrible, and yet at the same time better for having let all the emotion out.

She forced herself to pull away from him.

She had no idea where they were. How far they'd driven.

"Well." She dug her hand in her pocket and found a tissue. "That was professional."

"We're not in office hours now. You don't have to live up to those high standards you set for yourself. Here—" He handed her another tissue. "You must have one hell of a headache. I've got something for that in the cottage."

"Cottage?"

"You looked as if you needed privacy. I thought I could drive you somewhere more isolated. Somewhere you can scream without anyone hearing you."

She blew her nose. "That sounds like a tagline for a horror movie, Brodie."

He brushed her tears away with his thumb. "I thought I was making you an attractive offer."

"Is it a line you use often with women?"

"You're the first. You don't think I should use it again?"

She took another tissue from the packet. "I think maybe the promise of isolated places and screaming might not have the appeal you think it has."

"No? Because statistically speaking, the chances of being murdered in a remote Scottish—"

"Enough! When I said I wanted to be kept awake at night, it wasn't with horror stories." But he'd lightened the mood, which was no doubt his intention.

"All I'm saying is that you're more likely to trip and fall into—"

"Brodie!"

"Not helping?" He sat back and pushed his glasses up his nose. "Right. I'll be quiet. I'll simply drive you somewhere no one is going to disturb us. Where you can safely be upset without witnesses."

"I've already been upset. You were a witness."

"I'm not a witness. I'm simply your driver. Your tour guide, on our starlight stroll."

"Starlight stroll." She pressed her palms to her cheeks, trying to cool her hot face. Her eyes were stinging. "It actually sounds good. I'd book that."

"Not tonight. Tonight isn't about what everyone else wants and needs. It's about you."

"You think you know what I want and need?"

"Well, I was on the end of a rather revealing phone call. But I promise not to take advantage of that inside knowledge." He was adorably awkward, but at the same time kind and incredibly decent.

"Brodie—about tonight—I don't know how to thank you—"

"Nothing to thank me for. If you're sure you're all right for a few minutes, I'm going to drive us to the cottage. Just sit tight."

Sooner or later either her mother or Ella would come looking for her. And she didn't want to be found. She'd thought she wanted to be on her own, but now she discovered she was perfectly happy being with Brodie.

"The cottage—that's the cabin you showed me? The place you use as your office?"

"Yes. Five minutes drive from here. Just far enough to stop people disturbing me when I'm working."

"Is it big?"

"There's enough space for screaming, if that's what you're asking. Damn, my glasses are steaming up." He hit the brakes and grabbed his glasses and a lens cloth. "Don't ever ask me to be a getaway driver."

"Noted." He hadn't even asked her why she was crying, and she was grateful for that.

They bumped their way along the track, the lights picking out ruts and heaps of snow.

Her face burned and her eyes felt swollen. "Does the cabin get cut off?"

"In theory, but not in practice because we clear the snow. I work from here. I need access."

He turned off the main track and headed for the loch.

She could see a soft glow of light in the window of the cottage.

"I can see what you mean about no one hearing you scream."

"I scream regularly when my code doesn't behave."

"It's gorgeous. Perfect. I can see why you don't want to rent it out."

He pulled in next to the cottage. "That's more practicality than sentiment. I have tens of thousands of pounds worth of computer equipment here. It's my office. I don't share my office with anyone. I felt guilty appropriating it, but I needed somewhere I could focus without someone opening the door and offering me food."

"You don't like food?"

"Generally, yes. When I'm working, no. I hate to be disturbed when I'm concentrating on something."

"You don't eat when you're working?"

"Snacks. Junk food. Stuff I can eat without taking my eyes off the screen. Stay there. I'm going to come round and help you."

"I'm hysterical, Brodie, not injured. I can walk." But she was touched by how attentive he was.

"I can't let you walk around here while you're upset. It's dangerous." He sprang out of the car and reappeared by her door, hand outstretched.

She took it while her feet found purchase on the slippery surface. "You're quite the gentleman, Brodie."

"I am?" He cleared his throat. "Maybe I was thinking about the insurance risk. You could fall into the loch, or trip over in the forest."

"You think I suffer from coordination issues?"

"No. I don't think that. I think you seem like—well, a very capable person. Capable and coordinated." Flustered, he adjusted his glasses and gave her a sheepish smile. "It's possible that I'm describing what would happen to me. I'd crash, probably break a limb and definitely break my glasses. I'm sure you'd glide across the ice, and if you slipped it would be an elegant affair."

She hadn't thought it possible that she could feel like smiling given her current state of mind, but it seemed she'd been wrong about that. "I'd land on my butt, Brodie. And it would not be elegant."

"You'd look great. Even on your—um—butt." Color streaked across his cheekbones and he gestured to the cottage. "But I suggest I save you the possible pain—you hold on to me."

"But you've already told me that you have a tendency toward clumsiness."

"True. I'm probably dangerous to be around."

He wasn't wrong about that, but not for the reasons he thought. He was the only man who'd ever met inner Samantha.

"I'm kind of relieved we're not going to the pub." She closed the car door. "Not that I didn't love it, you understand—"

"But the last thing you need right now is a bunch of cheery locals. I know. I only said that because if I hadn't, my mother would have asked more questions about how I intended to feed you. As if I'm six years old and can't find a meal unless it's put in front of me." He flashed her a quick smile. "Also, you needed space, and generally speaking mothers don't understand the concept of wanting space. I've found it's best to pretend you want something specific."

"How did you know I needed space?"

"Your face."

"I planned on taking a walk."

"But then you'd be focusing on your problems, rather than your walking. Which brings us back to—"

"Insurance?"

"Insurance. Exactly. And the bruised—er—butt."

She couldn't hide her amusement. "You don't use that word a lot, do you?"

"I've used it more in the past two minutes than I have the rest of my life, but practice makes perfect. Wait there while I grab those boxes and bags from the back seat. I have some things I need to take in."

"I can help. Give me a couple of those."

He did, and she glanced down and saw snacks, fruit and, judging from the clinking sound, there were a couple of bottles in the bottom.

Brodie headed for the door, his vision half obscured by the boxes he was holding.

He fumbled with the lock, and then the door opened and light flooded over the snow.

She followed him inside and dumped the bags. They were in a small open plan living room and kitchen. Huge windows overlooked the loch, and the room was dominated by a big sofa and very little else. She glanced at the kitchen area. "You want me to put this stuff away?"

"I can handle that." He closed the door and gestured. "Sit down. Make yourself at home. Are you cold? Do you need warming up?" He coughed. "I mean, there are blankets—"

"I know what you mean." For some reason she couldn't tease him. "I'm warm, thanks. I hadn't expected it to be warm."

"I've rigged it up so that I can control the heating from the main lodge. And I was over here earlier. Put in a couple of hours after our reindeer trip. I'm not going to ask what you did. It obviously didn't end well. Excuse me while I dump these boxes—" He walked toward a door and pushed it open with his elbow.

She was too intrigued not to follow. "Is this your office? Can I— Holy crap, Brodie." She stopped in the doorway and glanced around her. Multiple computer screens lined the walls, all of them flickering with incomprehensible lines of code. "You could run a space program from here."

"I need the processing power." He put the boxes down and then grabbed a couple of unwashed mugs. "This is embarrassing. Didn't know I'd be entertaining guests when I was here earlier. I was concentrating on something and didn't clear up."

There was a waste bin overflowing with paper, and more mugs abandoned on the floor. More sheets of paper, each covered in endless numbers written in his dark scrawl.

She didn't care about the mess. She might not understand data analytics, but she understood focus.

"What's this?" The only wall that wasn't lined with monitors was a giant whiteboard covered in equations.

"I was figuring something out. I should fetch you a drink. You looked as if you needed one earlier. Are those more mugs?" He scooped them up so that they were all dangling from the fingers of one hand. "I swear they breed. I'll wash them. I think I have a couple of new ones in the cupboard. Unused. If I promise to use those, can I tempt you to coffee? I know you like coffee."

"Not this late in the day. Don't worry. I'm fine." There was a stack of papers next to a keyboard and she noticed the signature on one of them. "*Doctor* McIntyre?"

"Oh that's just—" He dismissed it with a wave of his free hand. "PhD. Maths, not medicine."

"Why don't you call yourself Doctor?"

"I don't know. Because I'm always afraid someone is going to ask me to save a life? Because the sight of blood makes me nauseous? Also, it sounds a little pretentious, don't you think?"

"I do not. You're obviously a very smart guy, Dr McIntyre." But she knew that already of course. Smart. Kind. Sexy. She thought about the way he'd propelled her out of the house and into the car without hesitation.

"Can we stick to Brodie? Please."

"I'll try. Can't promise." She was too fascinated by her glimpse into his world. A table was pushed against the wall and on it was a half-built model of a spaceship. The complexity of it made her head ache. "So this *is* mission control. I knew it."

He gave an awkward laugh. "Fiddling with tiny bricks helps me think."

She turned to leave and caught her foot on something.

She would have landed on her face, but he shot out a hand and steadied her.

"I need to clear up. I know. So many ways to die here, and none of them would make sexy headlines."

She clutched at his arm until she'd regained her balance. She could feel the swell of muscle under her fingers. *Strong biceps, Dr McIntyre.* "You're doing it again, Brodie. Pushing that horror theme. Good job I'm not the nervous type."

"In this place you're more likely to be killed by bacteria than a serial killer." He let go of her and gestured with the hand holding the mugs. "I'm going to wash these. Just—pick up that blanket and throw it somewhere."

Blanket? That thing on the floor that had almost broken her neck was a blanket?

"You don't have a bedroom?"

"Next door, but sometimes I don't want to walk that far. I just nap where I'm working and then work again. Sorry. Damn, I shouldn't have brought you here."

"Why not?"

"Because normally people don't see this side of me. It's a bit too—undiluted."

She thought about that phone call. "Then I guess we're even."

He nodded. "I guess we are. If you don't want coffee, then we'll go for wine. In fact I should have thought of wine to begin with."

She followed him to the kitchen and took the mugs from him. "I'll wash those."

"No, you can't do that. I don't want you—"

"You rescued me, Brodie. The least I can do is help." She ran the water until it was hot and soaked the mugs. Through the window the moon sent a wash of ghostly light across the surface of the loch and the snowy peaks. "This place is a jewel."

"You're not nervous? Most people would find it too isolated."

"I'm not nervous, which is weird because in Boston if a man wanted to drive me to his shack in the middle of nowhere, I'd definitely say no."

"Good. Sensible." He unloaded the food from the bags into the fridge. Juice. Butter. Eggs. Bacon. "I would hope you'd have a strong sense of self-preservation."

"So what am I doing here with you?"

"Escaping your family who make you want to scream." He lit the woodburning stove. "That's also a kind of self-preservation. I'm the least threatening of the two options."

He wasn't wrong about that.

She finished cleaning the mugs, and when she was satisfied that nothing toxic had been left alive, she put them to drain.

Then she hung up their coats and made herself comfortable on the sofa, watching as he lit candles. "You don't have lights?"

"I do, but I look better by candlelight."

Would it fluster him if she said he looked good in every light? "I probably do, too." She brushed her fingers under her eyes. "Do I have mascara all over my face? I probably look like a panda."

"You look good to me." His voice was rough. "And a panda happens to be my favorite animal."

"An hour ago I wanted to scream, but now I want to laugh. You're a funny guy, Dr McIntyre."

"That's not good, is it? Funny guys don't usually get the girls."

She looked at the curve of his mouth and the way his dark hair fell across his forehead. "I'm sure you do just fine." Her heart kicked against her chest. "Thank you for bringing me here, Brodie. It was kind."

"It was selfish. I need you to have a good time so that you recommend this place to all your rich clients."

"Whatever happens, I'm going to do that."

"You are?" He dropped the box of matches and retrieved it. "Best if I don't burn the place down, then. This is a little nerve-racking. You're only the second woman I've ever brought here. And the first time didn't go well."

"What happened to the first one? Don't tell me—her bones are buried in a shallow grave under the cottage."

"No, but I think she would have done that to me if she'd had the tools." Candles lit, he put the matches back in the drawer and grabbed two glasses from the cupboard. "I intended it to be romantic."

"It didn't turn out that way?"

"She saw a spider. Screamed." He put the glasses down on the table. "Her scream made me jump and I dropped the bottle of expensive white I'd been saving for a special occasion."

She grinned. "That must have shocked the spider."

"Never seen anything run so fast. And she was close behind." He poured wine into the glasses and handed her one. "To us. May we survive everything our families throw at us."

He sat down next to her and she tapped her glass against his.

"To starlight walks and survival skills. And to you, for rescuing me."

He took a mouthful of wine and put his glass down. "Not sure what you mean by that, but you're welcome."

"If you hadn't bundled me into the car and brought me here I would either have gone alone and died of frostbite, or I would have had an embarrassing meltdown in the house in front of your mother. Neither of those outcomes would have been great." Her phone buzzed and she sighed. "I should have anticipated that." She grabbed her coat and found her phone. "It's my sister."

"Wondering where you are?"

"Something like that." She replied to the message.

Am fine. With Brodie, working. Don't wait up for me.

A few seconds later, the reply came back.

Laid by the Laird?

She shut her phone off before Brodie could see it and dropped it back into her pocket, hoping he didn't notice her blushing.

"Is your sister okay?"

"I think so. We had a big, tell-all, confessional conversation with our mother tonight, so that was a load of fun."

"Ah."

"Exactly." She took another sip of wine. "Ella is probably fine. She's the sort of person who likes things to be fixed. Likes people to get along."

"You don't?"

"I think I'm more—complicated." She finished her glass of

wine. "Sometimes I think I don't have great insight into my own feelings."

"And that—er—has nothing to do with the wine?"

"No. Maybe wine would give me more insight."

"Sounds to me as if you knew what you wanted when we talked on the phone that night."

"You didn't talk to me. You talked to inner Samantha."

The corners of his mouth flickered. "I like inner Samantha a lot. She's a hell of a woman. Would inner Samantha like to talk about tonight?" He topped up her glass. "No pressure. But I'm happy to listen if you need a nonjudgmental ear. We don't have to tell outer Samantha."

"How did you know there's an outer Samantha?"

"I've met her. She's a hell of a woman, too. A little scary though."

"Scary?"

"Massively efficient. Competent. Driven. No flaws. And she dominates inner Samantha, which is a shame."

She ran her finger over her glass. "So there isn't an inner and outer Brodie?"

"There probably was at one time, but they merged."

"I wish I was more like you." She leaned back against the sofa, nursing her glass. "As for my meltdown tonight—I think it's been coming for a while. Ella leaks emotion all the time, but I store it up inside where no one can see it." She took a sip of wine. "I built a life that didn't have my mother in it, and then suddenly she's back in it. Only it's complicated, because my sister didn't tell our mother she was married, or that she had a child, or that she's currently at home and not working and I'm expected to remember who knows what about who at what point, and that is blowing my brain. And now, tonight, I discover that apparently my father didn't die the way my mother said—I mean he did die, but only after she'd left him because he was abusive."

"That's—" He adjusted his glasses. "I'm starting to understand your need to escape."

"I can't even tell you why I'm upset—it's all a tangled mess. But I feel like a bad daughter for not entertaining the possibility that there might have been more to my mother's story. I feel selfish."

"You're not a mind reader, Samantha. Aren't you being a little hard on yourself?"

"I don't think so. I thought she was this tough, ruthless workaholic, but it turns out that she became that way because she had to. And then there's my father—I had this image of him in my head. I'd sometimes picture him taking me to the park, or reading to me, or visiting me in my office. Being proud. And tonight that image was shattered forever. And I feel as if I've lost him, which makes no sense at all because all I've lost is the false pictures I painted for myself. Does this make any sense?"

"Perfect sense. You didn't have a father, so you imagined one."

"And boy did I get it wrong. Actually, maybe I don't want to talk about it." She sat up. "I thought I did, but I don't. Just for tonight I'd like to forget the whole thing and pretend I'm a normal person, with a normal family."

"That exists?"

"I want to think it does."

"Fine." He stretched his legs out and together they stared at the view. "Family gatherings often have an interesting dynamic. I remember the year my uncle Finlay—he wasn't really my uncle by the way, more a friend of the family—arrived with his twenty-two-year-old girlfriend."

"Was that a problem?"

"It was a big problem for his wife, who he'd left at home. She turned up in the afternoon and we had to smuggle the girlfriend out of the house."

Samantha laughed. "We didn't really do Christmas when we were kids. You probably gathered that, as you've already had to intervene to save Santa's reputation. Thank you for that, by the way."

"You're welcome."

"Did any of that fancy math actually make sense?"

"Not a word of it."

She grinned, finished her wine and put the empty glass back on the table. "That's good. Is there more?"

"More? I—yes. Yes, there's more." He grabbed the bottle and filled her glass again. "You're thirsty."

"More trying to numb myself."

"Should I try and stop you?"

"Why would you stop me?"

"Headache. Lowering of the defenses. Potential liver damage in the long term. What? Why are you laughing?"

"I love the way you spell out the facts with no filter."

He emptied the rest of the bottle into his own glass. "I should keep quiet?"

"No, because it turns out that the only thing that distracts me from my crazy family is you talking. The wine isn't doing it." She sighed. "Take my mind off it, Brodie."

"Me?"

"Unless there's someone else hanging around here I don't know about?"

"Just the body buried under the cottage. Any preferences for how I—er—distract you, or am I allowed to use my initiative?"

"Whatever works for you, but it's only fair to warn you that taking my mind off the crap in my life is going to be a challenge."

He put his glass down.

"You don't have to stop drinking, Brodie."

"I might need both hands."

Laid by the Laird.

And now she'd stopped thinking about her mother and was thinking about sex.

"Stand up." He took her glass from her and tugged her to her feet.

"What are we—" The wine had made her head a little fuzzy and she swayed a little as he tugged her into her coat. "Where are we going?"

"We're going on a starlight walk."

"Why? So you don't feel you've lied to your mother?"

"No. Because I think you'll like it."

"What I like," she said, "is being in the warm." With him. Chatting like this. It was effortless.

"Short walk." He opened the cottage door, and she whimpered as the cold air slapped her in the face.

"Brodie—"

"A few steps. I want to show you something." He pulled the door shut and took her hand. "It'll be worth it, trust me. Close your eyes."

"You're kidding. It's dark, snowy, and you want me to close my eyes. That requires a level of trust I don't even give to people I've known for years."

"That's outer Samantha talking. Shut her up. I've got you."

A warm feeling spread through her insides. *If only.*

Oh, what was wrong with her? This was real life, not one of her novels.

She closed her eyes, wondering why she was going along with this. "I feel compelled to point out that I won't be able to see the stars with my eyes shut."

"Stop talking. Listen."

She heard the crunch of their feet breaking through the thin crust of undisturbed snow. The occasional soft thud as branches shook off their winter load and snow met more snow. She heard her own breathing, and the beat of her heart. Could he hear that? He had to be able to hear it, surely.

She walked gingerly, gripping his hand tightly, terrified of slipping. "I don't hear a thing."

"Precisely." He urged her forward, and they walked for about five minutes and then he stopped.

"Can I open my eyes now?"

"Not yet."

"That is the last time I ever tell you to distract me."

"Okay, stop here. Tilt your head back."

"Brodie—"

"Just do it. Then open your eyes." He steadied her, hands on her shoulders.

She opened her eyes. And saw stars. What seemed to be hundreds of tiny stars embedded in the sky above them. It was magical. So completely perfect that for a moment she almost expected to hear sleigh bells and see Santa and his reindeer speeding across the night sky.

"Wow." She tipped her head back farther, looking at it from different angles. She could feel his hands, strong on her shoulders and was surprised by how good it felt. "Well, who knew a starlight walk could actually be a thing."

"I only do this for special guests."

She turned to look at him and for a split second saw the same heat in his eyes that she was feeling inside her. Anticipation was sharp and sweet, and then he pulled her in and kissed her.

There was a moment of shock, and then she sank down into a world that was nothing but sensation. She felt the brush of his thumb across her cheek, the gentleness of his touch a contrast to the deliberate purpose of his mouth. This kiss wasn't tentative or questioning. It was a declaration of intent. A teasing, tantalizing promise of more to come.

They kissed until she lost all sense of place and time, until there was nothing in her world but Brodie, and stars, stars, stars.

And then finally the cold penetrated and she gave an involuntary shiver.

He felt it and lifted his head, cursed softly and dragged her close, hugging her and warming her.

Dizzy, she put her hand on his chest to steady herself. Her first coherent thought was that Brodie McIntryre might be clumsy at a number of things, but kissing wasn't one of them. Her second was that she didn't want this to stop. "Do you only do that for special guests, too?"

He cleared his throat. "That's a bespoke activity. You said you wanted to see stars when you were kissed. That kind of thing puts a lot of pressure on a guy, so I thought I'd hedge my bets. If you hadn't closed your eyes when I kissed you, you would have seen stars over my shoulder."

She rested her head against his chest, laughing. Then she wrapped her arms round his neck and looked up at him. "So tell me—where did you learn to kiss like that?"

"I don't—I'm not—ah—" He gave a quick smile. "You're teasing me."

"Teasing you is fast turning into my favorite activity."

"I can go along with that. I might even do some teasing myself." His gaze dropped to her mouth, his head lowered again as if drawn by some magnetic force, and then he shook his head. "No." He drew back. "We have to get indoors."

"Brodie—"

His eyes darkened. "We have to— Oh hell—" His mouth slanted over hers again in a brief, hungry kiss. "We shouldn't—"

"Don't stop—" But her shivering grew more pronounced, and he pulled away and yanked the zip of her coat up higher.

"Here—" He pulled off his scarf and wrapped it around her neck. "You're freezing—I'm selfish—let's go. We're going inside. Right now. It would help if you didn't look at me. Definitely don't kiss me." He grabbed her hand and half pulled her back through the snow to the cottage, following the tracks they'd made.

It was a good thing he was the sensible one because she would happily have stripped off her clothes right there and then.

She had no idea how her skin could feel cold when she was burning inside.

They reached the cabin and she tried to tug him toward her.

"In a minute—" His mouth grazed hers and he groaned. "You taste good."

Her hand crept inside his jacket, and he powered her through the door and slammed it shut with his foot.

"Okay, we should probably—"

She grabbed him and hauled him against her, lifting herself on her toes to kiss him. His lips were cool, but there was nothing cool about the erotic heat of his kiss.

Melting with frustration, she fumbled with the zip of his jacket, and he did the same with hers. Mouths fused, they stripped off clothes, hands tangling, fumbling as they stumbled their way to the sofa.

They fell onto it, misjudged because neither were paying attention, and tumbled onto the floor with him underneath.

She heard his head crack and winced.

"Brodie! Are you—"

"It's good. I'm good. I crack my head several times a day. It comes from being tall. As long as I'm conscious, don't stop—" His hands drew her head back to his and she nibbled at his lips.

"But the sofa—we could—"

"A flat surface is safer." There was a rasp of desire in his voice. "Nowhere to fall."

He sank his fingers into her hair, kissed her, his breath warm against her mouth as she slid over him. She traced his body with her hands—*strong shoulders, the swell of muscle*—and then she felt him grasp her hips and draw her down.

She felt the hardness of him brush intimately against her, and then he paused, breathing rapid, jaw tense.

"We should probably—"

"Yes—" She could barely think. "Where—"

"Wallet—"

They talked in unfinished sentences, too desperate for each other to concentrate on words, but she found what they needed, and then there was no more holding back.

They joined together in a single smooth movement that brought a gasp to her lips and a groan to his. It was fast and furious, the pressure and the pleasure building to a peak that intensified as pleasure ripped through them both at the same time.

She felt him scoop her up and deposit her on the sofa. Then he came down on top of her, and this time he took it slowly, exploring her with his mouth, kissing his way down her body leaving no part unexplored, and it was the most intimate, intoxicating experience of her life.

When he took her for the second time, she arched and wrapped her legs around him, feeling the pleasure build again until every nerve ending in her body was screaming for release. It was wild and hot and wickedly good, and she lost track of time as they made love over and over again.

Finally, when they were both exhausted, he pulled a blanket over them and she lay in the curl of his arm, eyes closed, wishing she never had to move.

"I've never had sex on the floor before."

He tugged her closer, making sure she didn't tumble off the sofa. "Can I ask you something?"

"Mmm." She nuzzled his neck. "What?"

"Were you thinking about work just then?"

"I—what?"

"Work. I need to know if you were thinking about work."

She was barely aware of where she was or who she was, and he was wondering if she was thinking about *work*? "No. I haven't even— Just no."

"Good."

She lifted her head and saw a smug smile spread across his face. "Why would you ask that question?"

"Because the first time we spoke, you said you wanted to have a love affair so consuming you would forget about work."

She thought back to the conversation and then laughed. "Are you kidding?"

"No. In any other woman, trying to take her mind off work might be a low bar, but not you. You eat, dream and sleep work. And then there's all the other stuff—"

"What other stuff?"

He cleared his throat. "Your reading habits."

She slid her hand over his chest, her smile teasing. "The title was *One Night with the Laird*."

"Right. And I'm hoping this might be more than one night, but either way you have to understand that a book like that would give any guy performance anxiety."

"'A book like that'?" She moved her hand lower. "You haven't even read it."

"In fact I have, but even if I hadn't, I had the dubious pleasure of hearing your sister reading from it."

"You've read it?"

"I downloaded it that same night. I told myself that if you had certain expectations of what it would be like here in Scotland, I needed to know what they were. I confess I found his sexual prowess a little daunting. I may have spent the intervening time thinking of all the reasons I shouldn't kiss you."

"The main one being that we're working together?"

"That didn't even feature."

"What then?"

"For a start I don't own a carriage and horses." He pulled her closer. "I did consider buying a carriage to enhance my rakish appeal, but a four-wheel drive is more practical on these roads. And it seems I'm supposed to have an unhappy relationship with alcohol— I have to confess that currently my relationship with alcohol is more than happy."

She glanced at the bottle and the empty glasses on the table. "Mine, too."

"You, of course, should be showing a certain ruthlessness toward me and creeping off in the dead of night in order to conceal your identity."

"It's a little late for that part. And if I slunk out of this cottage you'd find my naked body dead in a ditch tomorrow."

"Which would be a terrible waste. Also difficult to explain. I did consider throwing you over my horse and galloping away with you, but Pepper is eighteen and has arthritis so that might not be the romantic ending you're searching for."

"Noted." She kissed his cheek and then his jaw. "Anything else?"

"You should probably tell your sister for the record that I generally do remove my glasses before I make love."

She lifted her head. "You heard that?"

"Your sister doesn't have a little voice."

Samantha grinned and kissed his shoulder. "I should be embarrassed, but I think I've moved beyond it."

"Good." He ran his hand gently down her back. "Do you want to go back to the house?"

"Do we have to?"

"No. We could spend the night here and then creep back in like thieves before anyone else is awake which, now I think about it, could be a scene right out of your Regency romance."

"It could, although if that's the way we're going, you should probably find a way for me to climb unnoticed through my bedroom window."

"Given that your bedroom window is on the fourth floor and I'm notoriously bad on ladders, I would propose the stairs, madam."

She propped herself up so that they were face-to-face. His eyes were sleepy, hooded, and without his glasses she could see that his lashes were thick and dark.

"Right now you look more rakish and real than any hero in my books."

"I shall be careful not to move or speak. That way I can't shatter the image." He put his arm round her and pulled her closer so that their mouths were almost touching. "I should have had champagne chilling in the fridge, so we could have dealt with all your fantasies at once."

"Tonight has been better than any fantasy. I just wish we didn't have to go back to reality."

He tucked the blanket round her. "We could move to the bedroom. Despite the blanket on the floor of my office, I do actually own a bed."

"I like it here."

"You're not cold?"

"I'm snug." She lay still for a moment. "You said that if you fell, you'd break your glasses. Does that happen often?"

"Mmm." His eyes were closed. "This is my fourth pair in two years."

"Wow, now I'm intrigued." She kept her arms locked around him. "What do you do to them?"

He turned his head to look at her. "The last pair was damaged a month ago when I was leaving the Stag's Head."

"The pub where you took me for lunch? What happened?"

"I had a little disagreement."

"You mean a fight?" She couldn't imagine it.

"Not exactly." He cleared his throat. "I mean, it was a fight of sorts, although no other humans were involved. Just me. And a patch of ice. We went about four rounds."

"Ice? You slipped?" She started to laugh and he gave her a severe look.

"Is this your idea of sympathy? Because if so, it needs work."

"Was there any damage?"

"You mean apart from to my glasses? Yes. I took a severe blow to my pride. It's a particularly soft, sensitive part of me, and the damage was immeasurable."

She couldn't stop laughing. "Your honesty is—"

"A passion killer?"

"I was going to say refreshing." She leaned down and kissed the corner of his mouth and then his lips. "And adorable."

"Adorable? Is that a good thing?" He hooked his arm around her, trapping her against him, and there was nothing soft or sensitive about the way he held her.

"I'm naked and in bed with you, and I've known you about— actually, forget it. I'm not going to think about how long I've known you. I'll freak myself out. I don't do this. I mean, not that there is anything wrong with sex you understand, but usually I have to really know someone before I get into bed with them."

"I know. You told me."

"Don't remind me. I still can't think about that without wanting to die. It was the worst, most embarrassing conversation I've had in my life."

"It's undoubtedly the best conversation I've had in *my* life."

"You were embarrassed, too."

"No. I've often dreamed of a woman telling me she wants to drink champagne naked in bed. You really messed with my sleep." He lifted his hand and pushed her hair back from her face. "Especially after I looked you up. Cute photo, by the way."

"You looked at my photo?"

"I might have peeked. Once or twice."

"This is so unprofessional."

"We're not working. And technically, we haven't agreed to work together yet, so there is nothing to be professional about." He paused. "I don't do this, either."

"You don't?"

"My last relationship was a disaster. We made you and Kyle look like Romeo and Juliet."

"They both died."

"Ah—a reminder that I should steer clear of literary references."

"Why were you a disaster?"

He paused. "I suppose we didn't like each other that much."

"Not a good basis for a long, happy relationship." She slid out of his arms and wandered naked to the kitchen to pour herself a glass of water. She drank it looking at the reflection of the moon on the water. "Do you know how weird this is?"

"What exactly?"

"Me, being naked with you, telling you everything. Being one hundred percent inner Samantha. I don't do that." But apparently she did do that.

So maybe he was right. Maybe change was possible.

Brave New You.

She filled another glass and took it back to him. "Unbelievable."

"Are we still talking about you being naked?"

"No. We're talking about the fact that I think I may actually have to read my mother's book."

Ella

"This is the first time I've seen you baking." Ella sat at the kitchen table as her mother and Tab sifted flour into a large bowl, their movements uncoordinated and uneven.

"And it may be the last," Gayle said, "because although the idea of baking is comforting, the truth is I don't have Mary's skills."

"But you baked those delicious gingerbread men when we visited you in Manhattan, and Tab iced them."

"Mmm. Truth?" Gayle glanced at her. "I made two batches that I threw away before I finally managed to produce something edible. Baking was something I did with my mother, and that was a long time ago. I never flew solo. I'm not pretending to be good at it."

And no one watching her would have had reason to argue with her. She was floundering in the unfamiliar, every maternal muscle straining as she tried to be the best grandmother possible. There was something endearing about the way she gripped the sieve, as if unsure whether it should be held like a weapon or a utensil.

This was a new version of her mother. Not just being in the kitchen, but being unsure of herself. Her mother was always sure.

"It's just a question of following a recipe." Mary tactfully wiped up some of the flour that had landed everywhere other than the bowl. "And if you're cooking with children, it's about keeping it fun and simple. The end result isn't important."

Knowing what a perfectionist her daughter was, Ella could have pointed out that the end result probably would turn out to be important, but she didn't. It turned out Tab had definitely inherited some of her grandmother's characteristics.

All that mattered was that they were all doing this together. Laughing. Exchanging anecdotes, creating memories. *Remember that Christmas in Scotland when we baked with Nanna?*

Outside the temperature had dropped and it was snowing. The mountains were no longer visible through the window, obscured by swirling flakes of white.

But there was no chance of her active, inquisitive daughter being bored.

Here in the warm, cinnamon-scented fug of the kitchen, there was plenty to entertain and distract.

It was a scene straight out of one of Ella's "family fantasies," as Samantha called them. Still it felt strange. Her world felt bigger than it had a few weeks ago. It had been the three of them, and Samantha. Now the walls had expanded to include her mother. The long and frank discussion they'd had the night before had resulted in a sense of connection she'd never felt before. She no longer felt watchful and tense. She was no longer braced for her mother to say the wrong thing, but she knew that if that moment came, then they'd handle it. They'd talked until the early hours, holding nothing back. Not parent and child, but two women. Adults. And Ella had discovered that understanding a person, knowing them and the path they'd walked, changed everything.

Mary was whisking egg whites for a more complex recipe, while supervising the others. "You're doing fine there. Might want to add a spoonful more flour to compensate for what's on the table." Like a conductor bringing together a large orchestra, she coordinated tasks. She was the king of the kitchen, and Gayle obviously thought so, too.

"Don't devalue your own skills, Mary. You have a special gift. And we're going to use that. As soon as Samantha is here, we're going to talk to her about it. Where is she?" Gayle sliced butter into the mixture. "It's unlike her to sleep this late. Do you think we should check? I'm a little concerned about her." She glanced at Ella, the only other person in the room who knew there might be a reason to be concerned.

"No." Ella knew for a fact that her sister wasn't in her room, and she knew that because she'd looked in on her in the night. The bed had been undisturbed, and Ella had paused for a moment and then rumpled it, just in case their mother happened to decide on a heart-to-heart in the middle of the night.

"She's been working hard." She covered up and deflected, the way her sister always had for her, and she realized that her relationship with her mother wasn't the only thing that had changed. Samantha had always protected her and fought her battles, but now she was the one protecting Samantha. And she was going to be fighting her own battles from now on.

She had a feeling that her new sense of strength would have pleased her mother.

When Samantha had stumbled from the room the night before, Ella had been worried about her. She'd been torn between her mother and her sister. She'd chosen her mother, but doing so had made her feel as if she was letting her sister down, and she'd felt nothing but relief when the text had arrived from Samantha, telling her that she was working.

She'd felt instinctively that if Samantha was with Brodie, then nothing bad could happen. From what she'd seen, he seemed like a man who could handle things, and she was hoping that skill would extend to her sister.

"I'm sure she's tired and sleeping late. She's a hard worker, your Samantha. She and Brodie were out late last night, planning starlight walks." Mary fetched a bag of sugar from the cupboard. "I don't see the appeal myself, but they both seemed to think it would be a winner."

Ella kept her expression neutral. *Starlight walks?*

In other words, Samantha had been in a hurry to leave the lodge. She'd needed fresh air and space, something her sister always did when she was stressed.

How she'd linked up with Brodie, Ella didn't know.

Gayle pushed the bowl closer to Tab. "Your turn. Now you need to rub it all together."

Undaunted, Tab dived in with glee. Moments later she was elbow deep in flour and smiles.

While they were occupied, Ella sent a quick text to her sister.

Where are you?? And why didn't you sleep in your bed last night? Should I be worried?

She'd give her sister half an hour to respond, and then she was going to go and find her.

In the meantime she was going to steer the conversation away from Samantha.

"Your mother—" she looked up "—my grandmother—she was a good cook?"

"Some people have a knack for it. She was one of those. Like Mary." She smiled at Brodie's mother. "Did you always cook?"

Mary had whisked egg whites into soft peaks. "From a child, side by side with my mother. There's no better place to spend your time than a well-equipped kitchen."

Gayle washed flour from her hands. "I admire you, Mary, but you're not going to find me agreeing with that one. I can think of plenty of rooms where I'd rather be than the kitchen."

"What was she like?" Ella slid her phone back into her pocket. "Your mother."

"Now I think about it, she was very like you. Creative. Warm. She had a way of making people feel better when she spoke to them."

The compliment made her glow.

"Did she work?"

"No." Gayle dried her hands. "She wanted to stay home with me, just as you've chosen to do with Tab. And Tab seems to be loving spending time with you as much as I loved spending time with my mother."

She no longer needed her mother's approval for her choices, but that didn't mean she wasn't pleased to have it.

"I think you're ready to add ginger to that." Mary measured it and handed the spoon to Tab.

"Cookery classes for kids," Gayle said. "We should probably add that to our list of ideas."

"Instead of gingerbread men, can we make ginger reindeer?" Tab stirred and poked at the mixture.

"We can. I even have a cutter the right shape somewhere." Mary delved into a cupboard and emerged victorious. "Here it is!"

Ella discreetly checked her phone again, but there was nothing from her sister.

She was about to make an excuse and leave the kitchen to find her when the door flew open and Samantha strode in carrying a stack of papers and her laptop, with Brodie right behind her.

Her hair was pulled back into a neat ponytail, and her makeup freshly applied. On the surface she looked like someone who had slept soundly all night, but something about the glow in her cheeks and the shine in her eyes made Ella think that wasn't the case.

Last time she'd seen her sister, she'd been worried she was on the verge of a major meltdown, but here she was looking strong and in control.

Ella was relieved. Also puzzled.

"We have a plan." Samantha chose the end of the table that wasn't being used as a production line for gingerbread reindeer.

Brodie sat down next to her.

They didn't seem to be looking at each other. Was that good or bad?

Kirstie poked her head round the kitchen door. "You wanted me for something?"

"Come and join us." Brodie pulled out the empty chair next to him. "We've some things to say, and you're part of this."

Samantha spun her laptop round so that they could see the screen.

"Winter in Kinleven." Mary read the heading and then sat down. "That photograph is stunning. I haven't seen it before."

"Samantha took it. She's a talented photographer." Brodie shuffled the papers in his hand, most of which seemed to be covered in numbers. "Show them the rest."

"This is very rough at the moment. And it's private—the public can't access this page. But I wanted to give you an idea of what we're offering. I want you to see it from the point of view of your guests." Samantha moved through the photographs. Sunrise over the loch, the light turning the snow from white to gold. A reindeer posed against a snowy background. The lodge, with its fairy-tale turrets. Tab, her face alight with laughter as she sat in the back of a sleigh. There was even a photograph of Bear, his glossy black coat standing out against the snow falling around him. There was a pub, looking warm and inviting. A shot that took in the forest floor and the snowy branches of fir trees. And then there were the internal shots—the Christmas tree in the library; Mary's shortbread dusted with sugar; a glass of whiskey, the color deepened by the glow of the fire behind, hints of tartan, the shimmer of red ribbon.

As she scrolled through the photographs, Samantha started to talk.

She painted pictures of hikes along the loch trails, of sleigh rides and reindeer encounters, of trips into the forest to cut the perfect Christmas tree.

Then she talked about her clients, about the type of people they were and what they wanted from the winter holiday season.

Kirstie was the first one to speak. "It looks great, but what if the guests don't get on? We're not a hotel."

"And that is what is special about Kinleven." Samantha focused her attention on Brodie's sister. "Not everyone wants a hotel. What we're offering them is more personal. And we will be offering this exclusively to family groups, or groups of friends. They have to book the whole place. I've done some calculations, based on what I know people have charged for something similar—although not around here. It's difficult to match what you have here, which is, of course, part of its value."

Mary looked overwhelmed.

"You've put in a lot of work," Ella said. "You must have been at it for most of the night."

Samantha didn't react, but Brodie blushed up to the tips of his ears.

Charmed, Ella took pity on him. "I want to book it," she said. "I want to spend the holidays doing all of these things. Have I told you lately that you are so, so good at your job?"

"She is. Which is lucky for us." Brodie passed the pages to his mother. "I printed them out. Circled the numbers you need to look at. Ultimately this is your decision, Mum."

"I need my glasses." Mary stood up, found them next to the toaster and slid them on. She picked up the papers, studied the numbers Brodie had marked in red, and looked up. "No way would anyone pay that."

Samantha glanced up. "They would. Trust me."

"But you don't—"

"I've already contacted two of my most long-standing clients in confidence, testing their interest. One is ready to book for ten days over Valentine's Day, and the other wants two weeks at the beginning of December."

Mary looked at Brodie and he nodded.

"We've run the numbers together. This whole thing works."

Kirstie sat tense and stiff. "We'd have strangers in our home every Christmas." She was the only one who wasn't looking excited.

"If Christmas itself is an issue, then we can avoid those dates. But from the end of November through to Christmas Eve, we can offer festive holidays."

Kirstie took a deep breath. "I'm hating being indoors. It's killing me."

"Which is why your responsibility will be outdoors, mostly with the reindeer." Samantha pulled out a couple of sheets of paper from the pile and passed them across the table. "This is just a start. You'll have many more ideas I'm sure, but basically there is so much potential there. It's going to grow. You're going to be busy."

"You want me to be in charge of the reindeer?" Kirstie flicked through the papers, reading the plans. "You don't want me to work in the lodge?"

"That would be a waste of your talents. Also, if this is going to work you have to love what you do."

Ella only half listened as Samantha outlined the rest of their plans for Kinleven. She was more interested in the detail of her sister's blossoming relationship with Brodie. They talked as if this was something they'd planned together and discussed at length. They passed pages of notes between them, fingertips brushing, exchanging the occasional brief glance that seemed to exclude everyone else. Ella was willing to bet that if she peeped under the table she'd see Brodie's leg pressing against her sister's.

"There's something else we wanted to talk about, Samantha."

Gayle spoke for the first time. "What Mary produces in this kitchen is nothing short of magic. Can we use that?"

"You mean apart from offering great food?" Samantha tapped her pen on the table. "You mean cookery classes?"

"Yes. Small numbers—"

"Make it personal."

"A weekend in a Highland Kitchen—"

"They eat what they cook. Add in whiskey tasting." Samantha nodded. "That would work. We could offer it as an optional extra to guests, but also a few special weekends during the year."

"And for guests who are staying here, maybe a cookery morning for children. But one parent has to be included, because Mary can't spend her time trying to stop children poking their fingers into the oven. And Mary and I have been putting together a cookery book—" Gayle was casual. "My agent already has a publisher interested."

Mary gasped and dropped the papers in her hand. "Really?"

"Early days of course, but we're pulling together a proposal, and I'm feeling hopeful."

Mary pressed her hand to her chest. "This is—I don't know what to say—it's so *exciting*."

"We could gift a copy to guests." Samantha was quick to spot the commercial opportunity. "Include dishes that Mary serves during their stay."

"It's a lot of work for you, Mum." Kirstie handed the pages back to Samantha. "But it's what you love doing, right?"

"I'm already excited."

Bored, Tab pressed a pastry cutter into the gingerbread mixture. "Can we cook them yet?"

Mary stood up. "We certainly can. Let's get them in the oven."

Gayle stood up, too.

"Mom?" Samantha closed her laptop. "Could I talk to you for a few minutes?"

"Of course." Gayle removed her apron. "Shall we go to the library?"

"I want to go with Nanna." Tab abandoned her gingerbread reindeer.

Ella wanted to go with her mother, too. She wanted to be there for her sister in case she was upset. In case she needed her. But she knew it wasn't the right thing to do. Ultimately, everyone had to fight their own battles. They had to find their own strength. Her mother had been right about that.

Ella scooped up Tab. "We have so much to do here, and Nanna will be back soon."

Her sister needed to spend time with their mother in private.

Gayle

The library was possibly her favorite room in the house. Bookshelves rose floor to ceiling, and elaborate twists of glossy greenery framed the fireplace. Ivy twisted into holly. Feathery branches of fir.

The space folded around you like a comfort blanket, drawing you into another world, which made sense to Gayle because didn't books do the same thing? She'd sneaked into this room several times over the course of the past few days, settled herself in one of the comfortable reading chairs, secured her headphones and listened to her beloved Puccini while watching the snow drift soundlessly past the window. Occasionally she'd paused to respond to emails, but Simon had stepped up into the role and most of the content was updates. After much thought she'd emailed Cole, apologized that he'd missed his grandmother's funeral and promised to be more flexible moving forward. Remembering some of the things they'd said when she was lying semiconscious in her office still made her face burn. She didn't want to be the woman they thought she was. She still had to figure out how her work fitted into this new version of her, but for now work wasn't her priority.

Two deep sofas faced each other across a rug, but Samantha walked past them to the window.

Gayle took one look at the rigid set of her shoulders and closed the door behind her.

Whatever was about to be said, needed to be said in private.

Samantha had been upset when she'd left the room the night before. Unlike Ella, whose reactions had been open, honest and immediate, Samantha had revealed nothing.

My fault, Gayle thought as she watched her daughter struggle with how to frame a conversation she didn't want to have. *This is all my fault. I taught her to be guarded. To depend on no one. To protect herself.*

And now she was protecting herself from her mother.

There was a wall between them. It was up to Gayle to dismantle it, brick by brick, and make sure, somehow, that their relationship wasn't caught in the rubble.

"You don't have to choose your words, Samantha. Just say whatever it is you want to say. I'm listening." Too little, too late? She hoped not.

Samantha turned. Gone was the efficient businesswoman who had drawn up a comprehensive plan to turn Kinleven from a money draining liability to a viable commercial business. Instead there were nerves and vulnerability.

"I'm sorry I walked out like that last night. You must have thought—"

"I thought you needed time. You were the same as a child. You had to think things through carefully. It's a quality." *Listen, just listen. Let her do the talking.*

She couldn't coach her way out of this one. She couldn't open a book at a certain chapter and say *read this.*

Samantha stood, hands clasped in front of her as if she was about to give a presentation to a roomful of people.

"We haven't talked about that last meeting."

Did they have to go back that far? Now that she'd started moving forward, she wanted to carry on doing that.

"If that's what you want, then of course, let's start there."

"I'm sorry for the things I said that day." Samantha's fingers were interlocked. Tense, twisted, like Gayle's insides.

It was the apology she'd waited for, and yet now she found she didn't want it.

"You have nothing to be sorry for."

"I said—" Samantha swallowed. "I called you a terrible mother."

As if she'd forgotten. Those words had ripped the fragile thread that held their relationship together. An impenetrable barrier had formed, and she'd allowed her own hurt feelings to get in the way of finding a way through.

"Maybe I was a terrible mother." She thought about Mary and their conversation about the complexity of parenting. Perhaps you had to be a parent to understand it. "It's no defence, but that wasn't my intention. I had your best interests at heart from the moment you were born."

"I can see that now. We didn't have the full picture. I shouldn't have said what I said."

"No, you were right to say what you said. I was inflexible and judgmental. I upset Ella terribly, and instead of apologizing, I drove you both away. You were protecting your sister."

"I thought so, but now I wonder if I was enabling her. I've thought about it a lot. I should have encouraged her to be honest with you about her life, and then supported her afterward." Samantha was basically saying that her sister would have needed supporting after she'd told her mother the truth.

It wasn't flattering.

"The blame was all mine. I shouldn't have put you in that position. I should have seen what was happening."

"I should have reached out afterward—" Samantha stumbled

slightly over the words. "I would have reached out, but it became—complicated."

"Because your sister had a baby. And a husband." Gayle tried to lighten things a little. "*Complicated* is probably an understatement."

"Not only that." Samantha paused. "I'm not good at talking about my feelings. I find it—hard. I do *have* feelings. I feel plenty of things—" She gave a tentative smile that made Gayle wonder if that was a recent discovery.

"Of course you do. And I'm the reason you don't find it easy to express them, so don't blame yourself for that."

Samantha shook her head. "I'm an adult. Whatever happened in the past, I'm responsible for the way I behave now. It's a choice, isn't it?"

Gayle smiled. "Maybe, although that makes it sound simple and we both know it isn't."

"I feel terrible, Mom."

"Why would you feel terrible?"

Samantha ran her hand over the back of her neck. "Because it was so hard for you, and we had no idea and we just assumed you were this cold, working machine—that we couldn't ever be what you wanted us to be. And also that all these years I've been imagining what my father might be like and it turns out he was nothing like that—" Samantha pressed her palms to her cheeks, breathing deeply. "We—didn't understand. I wish you'd told us."

"I could say 'so do I,' but I'm not sure it's true. I'm not sure I would ever have been able to burden my children with my problems."

"What you achieved—" Samantha's eyes were swimming. "It's incredible, Mom. I read your book."

"Which one?"

"Both of them. I read them last night. You're probably shocked that I hadn't read them before."

Was she shocked? Not really. There had been times when it

had felt as if Samantha had rejected everything Gayle had of-fered.

"It doesn't matter. You don't have to explain." She didn't say that she'd lost all confidence in her own beliefs and words after her accident. Or that it was her blossoming friendship with Mary that had rekindled a little of her self-confidence. The fact that she was standing here now, able to have this conversation was at least partly down to Mary.

"All my friends hero-worshiped you. They thought you were an inspiration. A fearless champion of women and a cool mom." Samantha gave a half smile. "They envied me. Wanted what I had. And I wanted what they had. Mothers whose achievements weren't quite so measurable. Who didn't make them feel infe-rior. I was angry with myself for never managing to be what you wanted me to be no matter how hard I tried. I kept comparing myself and falling short. I assumed that everyone felt sorry for you, having a daughter like me."

"Oh Samantha—" The pain of it was indescribable. The knowledge that she'd hurt the child she'd been trying to pro-tect. She'd had no idea. She hadn't seen how vulnerable Sa-mantha was.

She'd offered advice on so many aspects of life and change, and yet had no words of advice for herself on how to stop want-ing to somehow undo the decisions she'd made. What it was like to want to take all the experience she'd gained over her years of life and apply them to the beginning. Hindsight wasn't just a matter of timing, it was a matter of wisdom and that was gained with experience.

Gayle closed the distance and took her daughter's hands, pry-ing those tense fingers apart and smoothing them. "I was proud. Even when you fought me, I was proud, because I could see that you had strength and would always be able to handle what life threw at you. I should have told you that every day, so that you never had to doubt it. I was always proud of you, and I'm proud of the way you love your sister, and how hard you've worked to try and help this family."

"I wish I'd done things differently."

I wish I'd done things differently, too.

"You protected yourself, and I was the one who encouraged you to always do that. And you protected Ella. You're a wonderful sister." She kept hold of her daughter's hand. "When you become a mother, they tell you about feeding and sleeping, but what they never tell you is that one day you might want to turn the clock back and make different decisions."

"I don't know—" Samantha shook her head. "I don't have children. I can't begin to understand how you felt. It must have been so, so hard. I'm proud of you, Mom. I should have said it before." Tears fell, and Gayle wrapped her in her arms, something she hadn't done since Samantha was a child.

"There." She held her daughter, stroking her hair, soothing, until eventually Samantha pulled back and sniffed.

"Is this something we can put behind us? I really want to."

Gayle, always so practiced at handling her emotions, discovered that she'd lost the art. "I want that, too."

"I'm sorry—" Samantha sniffed again and scrubbed at her cheek with her palm. "You raised me not to be a crier."

"And that was wrong. I taught you not to let emotions drive your choices— Here, use this." Gayle found a tissue in her purse. "Luckily your sister ignored my advice and did her own thing. But you find it hard to show your feelings."

Samantha blew her nose. "I'm trying to change that. Another choice."

"Indeed. And I'm doing it, too." Gayle gestured to her sweater, which was a soft shade of heather. "I'm learning to wear something other than black."

"You look good in it."

"And you looked good in that red coat you wore to the hospital that day. Stunning."

"You said—"

"I know what I said, and it's embarrassing to remember it. You have an enviable sense of style." Gayle stood up straighter. "If you'd be willing to help me choose new clothes, I'd appreciate it. I've gone with 'mermaid' for this trip, but I need business wear that doesn't look as if I'm either about to swim the ocean, or go straight from work to a funeral."

"Of course." Samantha gave a tentative smile. "You could come and spend a couple of days in Boston with me, and we could go shopping."

Gayle had to fight back emotion. She was going shopping with her daughter. She was going to stay with her daughter. "I'd like that very much. You live alone? Ella told me you'd recently broken up with someone."

"She's right—I did. But the breakup was pretty mutual and we never lived together. He—wasn't the one for me."

Gayle wondered about Brodie but didn't say anything. Her relationship with her daughter didn't allow her to ask those questions yet. But one day, hopefully.

Samantha looked at her. "What about you? Have you ever thought about relationships?"

"At the beginning I didn't even think about it. It wasn't an option. I was too busy building a life for us." Gayle walked to the window. "And I had no faith in myself. I'd made a terrible choice, once. How did I know I wouldn't do the same thing a second time? It would have been a risk. Not just for myself, but for you, too. And after you left home—well, I guess I just got out of practice." She'd built a life that didn't include anyone else.

Samantha helped herself to water from the jug that was kept on one of the small tables. "If you tell Ella that, she'll sign you up for online dating."

Gayle laughed. "That sounds terrifying."

Samantha put her glass down. "I'm glad you joined us for Christmas."

"So am I." And despite a few rocky moments, it was going well.

She was feeling truly hopeful for the first time since she'd arrived. She and her daughters were talking. Properly. For the first time in their lives. Providing that dialogue continued, she was optimistic about the future.

Perhaps she would contact her publishers and suggest adding a chapter to *Choice Not Chance*. She needed to address the fact that choices might change throughout life. Maybe add a chapter on parenting choices. Mary felt the way she did—there had to be other people who questioned the decisions they'd made. Maybe guilt was an unavoidable aspect of parenting. Guilt about the choices you'd made. Guilt about the choices you hadn't made. Working mothers, stay-at-home mothers. Strict parents, liberal parents. Did anyone ever feel they'd got things right? And how did you ever really know? There was no way of predicting how things might have turned out if you'd made a different choice. You didn't get to walk the same road twice. And into that mix came the child, an independent being. A unique individual.

Maybe this was a whole new book. She felt a ripple of excitement, as she always did at the advent of a new project. What would the title be?

Her thought process was disturbed by Tab bursting into the library, clutching the stuffed reindeer Gayle had given her. Bear followed, tail wagging. "Nanna! Will you buy me a dog for Christmas?"

"No, Nanna will not buy you a dog for Christmas." Ella was hot on her heels, trying to control her daughter. "Sorry to disturb you. She's getting thoroughly overexcited. Mary wants to talk to you with Kirstie and Brodie, Samantha. She has a few questions."

"Not a problem." Samantha was back in professional mode. She smiled quickly at Gayle and left the room.

"Can you watch Tab for half an hour, Mom?" Ella looked frazzled. "Michael and I need to wrap some presents."

"Presents?" Tab bounced on the spot. "I want to wrap presents!"

"You're going to stay with Nanna."

"But—"

"Sometimes we negotiate, but this is not one of those times." Ella kissed her daughter on the head. "Stay with Nanna. Be good."

As Ella left the room and closed the door behind her, Gayle selected a book from the shelf. A few minutes of quiet time with her sweet granddaughter was exactly what she needed. "Come and sit with Nanna. We'll read together."

"I don't want to read. I want to wrap presents." Tab sprinted to the door and Gayle just caught her before she opened it.

She swept the little girl into her arms.

Her daughter had asked her to mind Tab, and that was what she was going to do.

"But I have lots of fun things I want to do with you."

"I want to wrap presents!" Tab wriggled and squirmed until Gayle was forced to put her down or drop her.

She said the first thing that came into her head. "If you don't want to read, then maybe we could make a card for Mommy and Daddy."

"I don't want to make a card." Tab headed for the door again, and this time when Gayle grabbed her, she launched herself on the floor, screaming.

Gayle was aghast. Her sweet granddaughter had vanished and been replaced by a monster.

She tried to pick her up and received a kick in the face as a reward. "Ouch." She rubbed her hand over her jaw. "Tab, you need to stop that."

"I want Mommy!" Tab writhed, kicking one of the decorations from the tree. It shattered into pieces on the oak flooring.

"Tab! Calm down. You're going to cut yourself." She had to sweep up the remains of the decoration before one of the shards was buried in Tab or the dog. She tried picking Tab up, but the child was a moving target and surprisingly strong. She grabbed a cushion from the sofa and put it over the shattered ornament.

She was out of her depth. It had been decades since she'd handled a child of this age. Tab was usually so enthusiastic and cooperative, but today she was tired and cranky.

Ignoring her aching jaw, Gayle tried love. "You poor thing. Come and hug Nanna."

"I want Christmas to be *now*."

"Well, tomorrow is Christmas Eve, so it's not long."

Tab's face crumpled. "I want Santa to come right now."

So did Gayle. She wanted someone to come now and save her. Anyone. Santa would be fine. Never in her life had she felt more inadequate. She had no idea how to calm the child down, and she didn't want to disturb Ella. What sort of a grandmother was she that she couldn't occupy one almost five-year-old for thirty minutes?

"I want Mommy!"

"Mommy's busy right now, but—"

Tab kicked her again, this time hard enough that Gayle almost lost her balance.

"Enough! Tab, behave yourself. You're being very naughty."

Tab burst into noisy howls that brought Ella running.

"What is happening here? Why all the noise?"

Tab's yells grew louder. "Nanna cross. Nanna says I'm naughty."

Gayle felt a wash of despair. Just when she'd thought everything was going well. If she told her daughter that Tab had kicked her, she'd sound like a toddler herself.

She started it.

She was desperate to show Ella that she could handle this. "Tab—"

"Go away! I hate you, Nanna. I hate you and I don't want to play with you ever again."

Gayle felt as if her heart had been skewered.

"Tab." Ella knelt down next to her daughter and hugged her, ignoring the flying fists and drumming heels.

"Be careful of the broken ornament—I'm worried about your knees and the dog's paws." Gayle tried to collect the pieces in her hand, while Tab shuddered and then went limp.

"I don't want to play with Nanna."

"Hush." Ella rocked her, and Gayle slid silently from the room, feeling like a complete failure.

She wasn't entirely sure what she'd done wrong, but she'd obviously done something very wrong and now Tab hated her.

Just when she'd thought things were going well. Just when she'd started feeling hopeful. She'd tried so hard to knit the family back together again, and now they'd been wrenched apart and it was all her fault. She'd been a terrible mother, and it seemed she was also a terrible grandmother.

Thirty minutes. Was it really so hard to look after a child for thirty minutes?

What must Ella think of her? And what now? Should she leave? Was that even possible so close to Christmas? She didn't want to ruin their family Christmas, but she couldn't bear the thought of leaving them and spending the holidays alone in her apartment.

She closed the bedroom door, dropped the ornament fragments into the bin and sat on the edge of the bed.

The books she'd bought on being a good grandparent mocked her from their place on the window ledge.

I hate you, Nanna.

She sat, marinating in her own failures for what felt like hours. Leave? Stay? Which?

She was still weighing up the best course of action when there was a knock on the door.

"Mom?" The door opened. It was Ella. Gayle sat up a little straighter, bracing herself.

"Come on in. Ella, I don't know what to say. I—"

"Well, Tab has something to say before you do." Ella pushed the door open and Tab slunk in next to her. Her face was blotchy with crying. "Tab?" Ella's voice was level and calm. "What did you want to say to Nanna?"

Tab flew across the room and flung herself on Gayle, almost knocking her flat on the bed in the process.

"I'm sorry, Nanna." She buried her face in Gayle's neck and clung tightly. "I'm sorry I said mean things."

Ella waited. "What else, Tab?"

Tab shrank against Gayle. "I'm sorry I kicked and hurt you. That was wrong."

Gayle hugged her, the relief indescribable. "That's a very nice apology. What a grown-up girl you are."

"I love you, Nanna. Do you love me?"

"Yes, I do. I absolutely do."

Tab looked at her mother and Ella smiled.

"You can go and find Daddy now."

Tab sped off, leaving Gayle alone with her daughter.

"I'm probably the one who should be apologizing." Gayle's insides were liquid with relief. "All you wanted was half an hour, and I didn't manage to give you ten minutes."

Ella laughed and sat down next to her. "You did well to last ten minutes. Handling an active, excited Tab this close to Christmas isn't easy."

"But you're brilliant at it. You don't overreact and you're so calm."

"It isn't easy. I'm always thinking, *Is this going to work? Is this the right thing to do?* But all you can do is make the best choice you can in the situation you find yourself in." Ella paused. "Which is exactly what you did with us."

"But did I do the right thing? Maybe I got it wrong. Maybe I was a terrible mother. Maybe I'm going to be a terrible grand-mother."

"No!" Ella squeezed Gayle's hand. "I know Tab hurt your feelings, and I'm sorry about that, but she's just a child, Mom. She spouts these things when she's tired. She's still very young, and struggles to control her emotions. You can't attach too much meaning to what she says. Sometimes it's best just to let it pass and not examine it too closely."

"I keep thinking I should have—"

"Well, don't. Looking after young children isn't easy. I love being a mother, but that doesn't mean there aren't days when I am desperate for Michael to walk through the door so that I can have five minutes to breathe. How did you do it on your own? I have no idea. I'm exhausted. I'm going to need Santa to bring me headache pills." Ella flopped back on the bed and closed her eyes.

"You're a wonderful mother, Ella. Tab is a lucky girl." Gayle rubbed Ella's shoulder. "Can I fetch you headache pills?"

"No, I'll be fine, but thank you." Ella sat up. "Nothing that five minutes peace with my own mother won't cure. I'm so glad you came. Are you? Or has that horrifying glimpse into the other side of my daughter made you book a flight home?"

"I'm pleased I came."

"When we get back home, will you come and stay with us? We have a pretty house near the river. Big garden." Ella paused. "No pressure. You'll probably be too busy getting back into work after your injury. I know you've already taken more time off than you have in a decade."

"I'd love to come. Thank you. I can't wait to see your home. And work won't be a problem. I think I've earned the right to ease up a little, and I've already decided I'm going to delegate more. I'd like to spend more time learning to be a grandmother. I'd like to be there for you so that when you need five minutes to go to the bathroom without Tab firing questions through the door, you know she's safe. I'm going to read up on handling tired children. What do you think?"

Ella smiled. "I think Tab is a very lucky girl to have a grand-mother who cares as much as you do."

The approval and validation wiped out all the doubt and in-security that Gayle had been feeling.

"I hope so." She sat, side by side with her daughter. "I'm going to make it so."

Kirstie

They sat in the kitchen, the way they so often had when they were growing up and wild weather had kept them trapped indoors. Her mother was stirring something on the stove, her brother had his head down, focusing on a calculation. The air was filled with the scent of freshly baked bread, which took her straight back to childhood.

It was all so familiar, and yet unfamiliar because her father should have been there, too, sitting in his usual place at the end of the table, newspaper spread out in front of him, steaming mug of tea by his hand.

Kirstie was still getting used to the fact that they were no longer four. That they would never be four again. It had been almost a year since her father had died, and still she walked into the kitchen and was shocked not to see him.

She hadn't known it was possible to miss someone this much.

"Eat something, Kirstie." Her mother put a plate in front of her. "You didn't eat earlier, and you need your strength."

Tempting her on the plate was a mound of fluffy scrambled

eggs flecked with ground black pepper, and hot slices of toast, the bread freshly cut from the loaf that was still scenting the kitchen.

Her mother thought food cured everything.

Not wanting to offend or draw attention to herself, she took an unenthusiastic bite, tasted perfection and decided maybe her mother had a point.

"She seems to know what she's talking about, I'll give you that." She took another mouthful. "But if I focus on working outdoors with the reindeer—" and she wanted that so badly; she wanted to go back from tending people to tending her animals "—that's going to make a lot of work for you, Mum." And she felt guilty about it. She should be working in the lodge with her mother, sleeves rolled up. The thought of it was a ton weight pressing down on her. Whenever she was indoors she kept gazing out the window, wanting to be out there.

"I've already spoken to Eileen in the village." Her mother joined them at the table, coffee in hand. "She thinks her niece would love to come and help me out. If the work is for her, then we'll formalize it."

"It will be hard."

"When have you ever seen me afraid of hard work? I never wanted to work in an office, that's true. I never wanted the nine to five. You understand that, because you never wanted it, either. I can't imagine a life without this place, and these mountains. This way, I get both. And you get to be with the reindeer. Seems they're going to be an important part of what we're doing here."

"If you're sure." Released from the pressure of guilt, Kirstie felt the first stirrings of excitement. No more stripping beds. No more polishing windows, plumping cushions or washing dishes. She was going to be outdoors. She'd have cold toes instead of wrinkled hands, and that suited her just fine.

Her mother put her cup down. "I am sure, although I'd be grateful if the two of you could cover the place for a few weeks in April if we happen to be busy then."

Kirstie took a bite of toast. "What's happening in April? Where are you going?"

"I'm going to New York, to stay with Gayle. She's invited me, and I said yes."

Kirstie put her toast down. "New York? But—" she exchanged a glance with her brother "—you've never traveled outside Europe. You and Dad always—"

"We always stayed close to home. I know. But it's just me now. And I'm going to America, to see Gayle. She's going to show me the sights. We're going to spend some time together. She's going to set up a meeting with her publisher to discuss our book idea. I'll probably cook a few Scottish treats to take to that meeting." She slid her hands round the mug. "Am I nervous? Yes, I am, but I'm doing it anyway."

Brodie smiled. "Good for you, Mum. That's great. Inspiring."

"Gayle is an inspirational woman." Mary abandoned her coffee and pulled a book out of her bag. "*Brave New You*. I read it to be polite, because I wanted to know more about the family, and I ended up underlining passages." She pushed it across the table to Kirstie. "You should read it. But I'd like it back when you've finished it."

Kirstie took the book but didn't look at it. She was too busy looking at her mother. "You seem different. You've been so sad—"

"I'm still sad. Part of me will always be sad, and there are days when I'm crushed by it. But the truth is that sometimes life sends you change that you wouldn't have chosen, and this was one of those times. I had no choice about losing Cameron, but I do have a choice about what I do with my life from now on. I miss him terribly, but I intend to get out of bed and keep living, no matter how hard that feels. And all the memories can come along with me."

They all handled it in different ways, Kirstie thought. She

handled it by being outdoors. By throwing herself into hard, physical work. She'd missed that.

And now she desperately wanted it back.

"Will this work, Brodie? Truly?" She'd been against the whole idea, but now she badly wanted it to work.

"Are you talking about the finances?" He pushed at his glasses. "You've seen the numbers. Yes, it will work, providing guests will pay what Samantha thinks they'll pay. And providing enough people book."

"And will they?"

"There are no guarantees, but she knows what she's doing. She's impressive."

"You should know. You've spent enough time with her over the past few days." She saw his face redden and was pleased, not because she had a sadistic streak—although who didn't love teasing their sibling?—but because it proved she hadn't been wrong. Those glances she'd observed, the brief brush of fingers as they'd passed papers between themselves, it had meant something. He cared, and she wanted him to care. She knew what he'd sacrificed to come back here, and she wanted everything good for him. "Relax. I like her. A lot. And you're right—she is impressive. She knows what she's talking about, she isn't afraid to break a nail and she didn't overreact when Bear got excited and peed on her leg by accident. So she gets my vote."

"Your vote for what?"

"For—" she had to be careful not to overstep, because she didn't want him to back off "—whatever position you choose to give her."

"Consultant." Brodie dropped the papers he was holding. Picked them up again, flustered. "She's our partner in this, I suppose."

"Partner. Right." Kirstie tried to hide her smile, and he sighed and put the papers down.

"Is this going to be a whole new thing? Insinuation and sly winks? Because it will earn you a snowball down your neck."

"It might be a new thing. Too early to say." She finished her breakfast and pushed her plate away. "Depends on how much fun it is."

"For me, it's no fun at all."

"But it's doing my romantic heart good."

"You have a romantic heart? I didn't know that. Promise me you're not going to embarrass me on Christmas Day."

Enjoying herself, Kirstie thought about it. "Can't promise that." She saw her mother smile. "What's funny?"

"The two of you bickering, the way you always used to. It does my heart good."

"Seeing us fight does your heart good?"

"Yes, because it's normal. It's how it should be. I've missed it."

Sister-brother banter, the type they'd always had until grief and the pressures of life had smothered it.

"So that's confirmed, then. This is a whole new thing, because it makes Mum feel good."

Brodie gave a resigned laugh. "Happy to take one for the team, but please don't let Samantha hear you."

Mary stood up and headed back to the stove. "While we're talking about it, you should know that I like her, too."

"Were we talking about it? I thought it was a Kirstie monologue. But if we are talking about it, perhaps this is a good time to point out she lives in Boston. Also, she's just come out of a relationship."

Kirstie beamed. "Which leaves her free for another relationship."

"And you love Boston." Mary opened the oven and pulled out a tray of cinnamon cookies. "You've always loved Boston."

"Not that we want you to move there," Kirstie said quickly, "just pointing out that you can visit."

"Good to know I have your permission."

She felt a lightness that she hadn't felt in a long time. And a glimpse of a future that might hold change of the good kind. Change that wasn't shadowed by darkness.

She reached for *Brave New You*, flipped it over and read the back cover.

Maybe she'd try just one chapter. Where was the harm in that?

Samantha

She waited in her room, jumpy and on edge, keeping her phone on long after everyone else in the house had fallen asleep. She kept glancing at it, but the screen didn't light up.

Would he come? Should she have said something to indicate she wanted him to? But when? They'd been surrounded by people all day, cooking, planning, playing games.

Once or twice she'd caught his eye and he'd smiled, but she, who was so bad at relationships, didn't know what the smile meant. She didn't know what any of it meant.

And it wasn't as if she was completely without experience. She'd dated other men. She'd dated Kyle for a whole year and hadn't once felt like this. Not even at the beginning when it was supposed to be exciting. Not once had she felt a fraction of the things she felt when she was with Brodie.

She flopped back on the bed, carefully reliving every exciting moment because it seemed she might never get to experience it again. For the first time in her life she'd let herself go, held nothing back. She'd given him access to all that she felt, and all that she was. *Inner Samantha.* At the time she'd thought he'd done the same, but maybe she'd been wrong about that?

The questions fought each other in her head until eventually, exhausted, she fell asleep.

When she woke it was Christmas Eve and she was still alone in the bed. There had been no tap on the door in the darkness. No reprise of what had happened in the cottage by the loch.

She rubbed her eyes and looked out the window.

The storm had cleared, leaving fresh snow and blue skies, and she had to get up and get on with her life. And she had to do it without showing any of the emotions swirling around inside her.

Which she would, because this was what she did.

The day passed in a noisy, busy, joyful flash of snowman building, sleigh rides and present wrapping.

Tab's excitement levels shot through the stratosphere, thanks partly to the impending prospect of Santa's visit, and also to the steady volume of sugary treats that Mary kept producing in the kitchen. Ella, Michael and Gayle kept Tab busy, with Kirstie doing her bit with the reindeer.

There had been no sign of Brodie all day.

Kirstie had mentioned that he'd driven into the village for something and was now working in the cottage by the loch. She imagined him, coffee cooling in mugs as he focused, and considered hiking through the snow to surprise him. Common sense stopped her.

Imagine how awkward that could be. He'd be too polite to rebuff her, and she had too much pride and dignity to put them both in that position. She didn't want to spend Christmas Day hiding behind the Christmas tree, trying to avoid an embarrassing encounter. She didn't want it to feel awkward whenever they had to call each other in the future about a client.

The fact that he hadn't joined her the night before was presumably his way of saying that for him it had just been a one-night thing.

He'd only taken her to his cabin because she'd been upset.

He was a kind, decent guy. He'd been helping.

She'd told him she wanted to see stars, and he'd given her stars. She'd never forget it. Not the clarity of the night sky, or the skill of his kiss. At some point the whole experience had merged and she wasn't sure which of the stars were celestial and which were conjured by her thoroughly oversensitized body.

Rather than feeling sad, she should feel grateful that they'd had that one night. It was something to remember. Something to measure other relationships by, because she knew now that what she wanted wasn't a dream, or a fantasy, or something that only happened between the pages of a book.

If you were lucky enough to find the right person, it could happen in real life too, as it had for her sister.

Exhausted with smiling, she hid herself away in the library under the pretext of wrapping gifts. While she was there, she also caught up with emails, the whole time trying to listen to the voice of reason in her head.

That one night they'd spent together had been just that. One night.

She tucked a gift into the paper, wrapped it neatly and measured a length of ribbon.

Two consenting adults. That was a perfectly legitimate type of relationship.

She wrote neatly on the label, pushed the gift to one side and started on the next one until finally she had a neat pile, ready to be transferred to the tree in the living room, where it had been agreed they'd be opening their gifts the following morning.

Tab had already hung up her stocking, and Samantha had filled a stocking for her sister, as she'd done every year since Ella was born.

With no more gifts to wrap, she was tempted to stand in the window and see if she could catch sight of the cottage from here, but she forced herself to stay seated and instead reached for her laptop.

She sent messages to all her staff and clients, dealt with a few issues, made a note to deal with others once the holiday season had passed. Through the closed door she could hear Tab's excited shrieks and Bear's barks as her niece and the dog chased each other round the house.

She could hear her mother's voice.

"Tab? Shall we leave a treat for Santa? One of Mary's cakes, perhaps? A drink?"

Samantha glanced up from her email. Had her mother really just said that? Her mother finally embraced the magical fantasy of Santa? Maybe miracles really did happen at Christmas.

Just not for her.

Determined not to feel sorry for herself, she returned to her emails, only half listening as Ella answered Tab's questions.

"Yes, I'm sure he'll be hungry."

"But will he have time to stop and eat? Won't that make him late?"

"It won't make him late."

"He doesn't have a schedule?"

Samantha closed her laptop, unable to concentrate for the first time in her working life.

It could wait. It could all wait. There was more to life than work.

She stood up, scared. Where had that thought come from? What was happening to her? For once, inner Samantha seemed to be getting the better of outer Samantha.

She moved to the window seat, staring at the snow, pretending to herself that she wasn't hoping to see Brodie striding toward the lodge wanting to talk to her about something.

What had he needed so desperately on Christmas Eve that he'd had to drive to the village?

When she could no longer justify staring, she joined her family in the living room and played with Tab, until finally the little girl went to bed and a contented hush fell over the house.

"Drink." Ella collapsed on the sofa and waved a hand. "Michael, I need a drink."

He grinned, poured her one and handed it to her. "Tired?"

"After all that fresh air and running around?" Ella curled her legs under her, the picture of contentment. One-handed, she typed a message into her phone. "It's already the best Christmas ever and we haven't had Christmas Day yet. To Nanna. And Santa." She lifted her glass to Gayle, who had collapsed in a chair opposite her.

She envied her sister's contentment. She'd never had that. She'd spent her life striving and driving herself, trying to be more, working to reach a goal that she hadn't even defined. She'd been there for everyone but herself.

At least, thanks to Brodie, she now knew what she wanted.

Her phone pinged, and when she checked it, she saw a message from her sister.

So? Was it as good as the books you read??

Samantha gave her a look and Ella grinned and raised her glass in a silent toast that was just between the two of them.

"Tab insisted we put milk out for Santa," Mary said, "but I think he would probably prefer a good single malt." She replaced the milk with a glass of something stronger and winked at Michael.

Gayle stood up. "We need a boot. And ash from the fire."

"Excuse me?"

"We need to make a big boot print on the hearth so that Tab can see where Santa stepped after he came down the chimney."

Ella gave her a curious look. "That's a great idea—what made you—"

"My father used to do it. One year I caught him at it. He wasn't even wearing the boot. Just pressed it hard onto the hearth with his hand and made a few footprints."

Ella smiled. "And just like that the magic was ruined. Did you say something?"

"No." Gayle shook her head. "I could see from his face that he was loving every minute of what he was doing for me. That, to me, was the magic."

Love.

Samantha's throat stung and right at that moment, when she was straining every muscle to hold back the emotion that was threatening to overwhelm her, Brodie walked into the room. He wore jeans and a sweater that made his eyes seem bluer than ever, and Samantha didn't think she'd ever seen a more delectable, incredible man in her life.

She wanted that night back. She wanted to do the whole thing again so that she could savor every moment, and linger over every touch and taste.

Because she wanted to fling herself at him, she shrank back in the chair and curled her fingers round the arm.

Mary was fussing over him, handing him a drink, encouraging him to warm up by the fire, and all Samantha could think was that if her body heated up even a fraction of a degree more, then she'd probably combust. She heard the conversation going on in the distance and pretended to be paying attention, all the while trying to seem normal when she didn't feel normal.

She saw him deep in conversation with Michael, the two of them talking and laughing together as if they'd known each other forever. When Brodie glanced at her, she made her smile a little wider, telling herself she was fine, totally fine.

She took another mouthful of her drink and saw Ella cross the room and say something to Brodie, something that made his face turn red to the tips of his ears.

She had no idea what her sister had said, and she decided she didn't want to know because it was obviously something horribly awkward and embarrassing.

By the time she eventually headed to her room, the effort to seem normal had given her a pounding headache.

She swallowed a couple of pills with a glass of water, took a long hot shower, and curled up in bed. She'd barely opened her book since that first night, but hopefully it would be the distraction she needed.

Downstairs she could hear the creak of stairs and doors closing as her family settled down for the night. Somewhere at the other end of the lodge, Brodie would be settling down, too.

Samantha rolled onto her side and opened the book, willing herself to concentrate on the words on the page.

> *She would close the door and walk away and forget all about him. She would pretend this had never happened...*

Samantha put the book down. Good luck with that. Hopefully the heroine would have more success than she was having.

She gave up on reading and was about to pull on a robe and go downstairs to the kitchen when there was a light tap on the door.

Presuming it was her sister, Samantha almost didn't answer, but then decided that talking to her sister might actually be what she needed. Being closed off had got her nowhere, so it was time to try the opposite.

She pulled open the door.

Brodie nudged his way past her and closed the door behind him.

A thrill shot through her. "Brodie—"

"Shh—" It was only as he turned the key in the lock with his right hand, that she realized his left hand was holding a bottle of champagne.

"What are you—" The words died as he pressed his fingers to her lips and then lowered his head and replaced his fingers with his mouth, kissing her until she couldn't remember her question and wouldn't have cared about his answer even if he'd given one.

He kissed her the way he'd kissed her under the stars that night. And this time it was even better, and she knew that at least some of the stars she'd seen that night had come from inside her. She didn't know what she was doing, or what he was doing, or where this was going, or even what she wanted, but if someone had asked her if she'd like to feel this way forever, she would have said yes.

"I can't believe you bought champagne."

His hands were in her hair, his gaze fixed on hers. "I had to drive for an hour to buy it."

"That's why you drove to the village?"

"In the end I drove a bit farther than that. I decided that when you're trying to make someone's dream come true, you need something superior to the one they stock in the village."

His hands moved down, his fingertips tracing the line of her shoulders and sliding under the thin straps that were keeping her decent. The straps surrendered under the determined pressure of his fingers and so did her nightdress, ivory silk and never before worn in anyone's company other than her own. He didn't rip it from her body, but she discovered that a slow undressing could be equally seductive.

"What are you doing?"

"You wanted to drink champagne naked in bed and it sounded like a great idea to me, so let's do it."

It didn't occur to her to argue. Instead she helped him undress, their fingers tangling in their haste, and then her arms were around him and he was kissing her while simultaneously trying to open champagne.

"Wait—let me—" He pulled away long enough to ease out the cork.

There was a loud pop. The cork hit the ceiling, champagne cascaded over both of them and they both fell onto the bed, smothering laughter with kisses and soft words as he struggled to keep the bottle upright.

She grabbed it from him while there was still some left in the bottle. "Did you happen to bring glasses?"

"You already know I don't need glasses for sex."

"I meant the sort you drink out of."

"Oh—" He lifted his head briefly. "*'I want to drink champagne naked in bed.'* That's what you said to me. No mention of glasses. You need to be more specific in your brief."

She wriggled upright and sank back against the pillows. "I have never drunk out of the bottle before in my life." But it felt like the right thing to do. She wanted her life to be full of things she'd never done before, and this was a good place to start.

"There's not much left in the bottle anyway. We're wearing most of it." He kissed her shoulder. "This fantasy is working well for me. How is it for you?"

"Damp." She lifted the bottle with both hands, giggling like a teenager. That was a first, too. When had she last laughed until her ribs ached? She couldn't remember.

"You need to giggle quietly, or we'll have people knocking on the door. I like your family, but right now I'm not in the mood for company."

"Talking of family, what did my sister say to you earlier?"

"Ah. That's between me and your sister. But she did threaten various parts of my anatomy should I ever cause you a moment's unhappiness."

"She threatened you? I'm so sorry!"

"Don't be. She loves you." He took the bottle from her, took a mouthful of champagne and then put it down next to the bed.

"What are you doing?"

"We're reaching the *wild desperate sex* part."

"We already did that."

"I don't need reminding. I haven't been able to concentrate all day." He kissed his way down her neck to her shoulder and lower, until his mouth brushed the tip of her breast. The thrill of desire overwhelmed everything, and they came together, wild and frantic.

She moved beneath him, blood pounding, heartbeat racing, and it was as intoxicating as it had been the first time.

Afterward she lay in his arms, and if she'd been given a choice she would have stayed there forever. "I can't believe this is happening. Last night I thought—"

"Yes. Last night. I lay awake waiting for you." He turned his head. "Where were you?"

"Me? I was here. Awake. Hoping you'd knock on my door."

"I almost did, but then I reasoned my way out of it. I thought you might have regrets. I kept wondering if I'd taken advantage of an emotionally unstable woman."

"Excuse me?" She lifted herself on her elbow. "Are you calling me emotionally unstable?"

"No need to be defensive or embarrassed. My family makes me emotionally unstable, too."

She lay back and sighed. "You're right. I was emotionally unstable. This has been a weird Christmas. But that wasn't why I slept with you."

"Good. But in that case why didn't you come and tap on my door?"

Why hadn't she? "Firstly because I'd managed to convince myself that you'd had pity sex—"

"Pity sex?"

"Yes. You felt sorry for me and were trying to make me feel better."

"I'm putting my back into this hospitality thing, but even I wouldn't go that far. There was no pity involved." He stroked his finger along her cheekbone, as if memorizing her face. "You said 'firstly.' What was the second thing?"

"I don't know where your room is."

He paused. "You don't?"

"No. You've never shown me the private side of the house.

If I'd plucked up courage to sneak through the lodge in my robe—which I probably wouldn't have done—then I wouldn't have known which door to knock on. I might have ended up walking in on your mom."

He lay back and pulled her closer. "I'm going to put a note on my door. Just in case."

"I wish we could stay like this." She felt like a child, wanting Christmas to last forever except in this case it wasn't Christmas she wanted. "I wish we could freeze time."

"But then we'd miss all the moments in the future that are going to be even better than this one."

"You think we have a future?" The words were followed by embarrassment. "Ignore me. You don't have to answer that."

"Why wouldn't I answer it?" He ran his fingers lightly down her arm. "I suppose the answer to whether or not we have a future depends on us. Do you want one?"

"The logical side of me says it isn't practical."

"Ah. Outer Samantha. I like her, but right now I'm talking to inner Samantha. What does she say?"

"She says go for it. Do whatever it takes."

"Then what's the problem?"

"I don't usually listen to her. My logical side has the loudest voice—" She kissed his shoulder. "I'm scared."

"Me, too. But that's a good sign."

"It is?" She liked the way his fingers felt on her skin. Gentle, but possessive. In a good way. A very good way. She'd never been able to sit still long enough to contemplate a massage, but she would have sat for a week while he touched her like this.

"Yes, because it shows we *do* want this. We both care. We're emotionally engaged."

"Yes." She'd never been scared with Kyle. Never once been nervous that it might not work out. "I'm glad you're not doing this out of pity."

"I may occasionally break my glasses and lose my wallet, but that doesn't mean I don't know what I want."

"You live in Scotland and I live in Boston."

"Meaning?"

"I'm giving you reasons why this probably won't work."

"How about giving me reasons why it *will* work? Like the fact that we both want it to and are willing to make it work. I can fly to Boston. I'm willing to clear space on my desk for you to work when you come and spend time here. I'll even wash up a few mugs."

It wasn't logical. It wasn't sensible. But it sounded so good. She snuggled closer. "You'd make space for me in your office?"

"As long as you promise not to touch anything."

"Can I touch you?"

"That's allowed." He rolled her under him, kissing her again, and it was another hour before they finally finished the champagne.

"This might be the best Christmas ever." She took another mouthful and handed it to him.

"It's the best so far. There are going to be plenty more. Champagne from the bottle on Christmas Eve can be our first tradition."

The future was theirs. Whatever they chose to do with it. At some point they'd have to make choices, but they didn't have to make those choices tonight. Tonight all they had to do was enjoy their time together.

And that's what they did.

Gayle

"Nanna! Wake up."

Gayle woke to find Tab jumping on her bed holding a bulging stocking and Bear, her ever-present guardian, sitting patiently by the door.

Ella appeared in the doorway. "Sorry! Tab, I told you that you weren't to wake Nanna."

"But I want to open my stocking with her."

Gayle sat up and pulled Tab into the bed so she wouldn't be cold.

"Ella, you might want to check the end of my bed because there is something there."

It had been gone midnight when she'd finally finished wrapping, and she hoped she'd done the right thing.

Tab checked and found the two stockings. "They're for Mommy and Aunty Sam. Santa must have come into your room, Nanna. Did you see him?"

"I was sound asleep the whole night."

Samantha appeared in the doorway. "Did someone say Santa?"

"He left a stocking for you!" Tab pushed it toward her and Samantha glanced at her sister, and then at Gayle.

"Santa filled a stocking for us?"

Aware that Tab was watching, Gayle mirrored Ella's excitement. She wasn't going to blow this. "It seems that way."

"A stocking." Ella sat down on the edge of the bed and pulled it onto her lap. "I can't believe—"

"Can I open it for you?" Tab bounced on the bed. "Can I?"

"No you can't," Michael said. "You have your own to open. This one is for Mommy."

Tab started opening her presents and Ella took wrapped packages from the lumpy, bumpy stocking with her name on it.

"I feel about six years old. I can't believe Santa did this for us." Ella pulled a dome-shaped parcel out of her stocking and gave her mother a knowing look.

"I can't believe it, either." Samantha was opening her own. It was full of extravagant treats, and watching their faces, Gayle wondered why she'd ever thought that fun for fun's sake was a waste of money. She pushed aside regret. The past was done.

"A snow globe!" Ella pulled it out of the wrapping and shook it, watching as snow swirled around the winter scene inside. "I always wanted one."

"And I predict you will play with it for five minutes," Michael murmured, kissing her on the neck as he headed for the door to get dressed.

After breakfast, Gayle pulled her daughters to one side.

"There's something I'd like us to do." She'd been thinking about it since that conversation in the kitchen with Mary. "We're going to build a snowman."

Ella grinned. "Great idea. I'll call Tab—"

"Not Tab. Not this time. Us. The three of us."

Samantha frowned. "You want to build a snowman?"

"Yes, because we never did it and we should have done. And

you're probably thinking that it's too late now, that we can't turn the clock back—"

"We don't think that, do we?" Ella glanced at Samantha, who shook her head.

"It's never too late." Something about the way she said it made Gayle wonder if she was thinking about more than simply building a snowman. There was a new lightness to Samantha that Gayle hadn't seen before. And although she was no expert on romantic relationships, she was sure it had something to do with Brodie.

"Let's go while Tab is playing with Michael." Ella grabbed the coats and they spilled outside into the snow and crystal clear air, shivering and wrapping up as they walked.

"This place is fantastic." Ella spread her arms and did a twirl. "Can we just book it ourselves every year?"

"I've already costed it and we wouldn't be able to afford it. Ironic, no?" Samantha scooped up snow and threw it at her sister.

"Oh you—" Covered in snow, Ella retaliated, and soon the two of them were throwing snow and Gayle found herself caught in the crossfire.

"And here was me worrying you were too grown-up to enjoy playing in the snow." She wiped snow out of her hair. "Good to know I was wrong about that."

Ella shivered as she freed snow from the neck of her jacket. "She started it." And then she realized what she'd said and burst out laughing. "Let's build that snowman, before we get frostbite."

They did it together, the three of them, layering snow onto snow and as it grew Gayle realized they were building more than a snowman.

"I've been thinking—" She paused to take a breath, watching as Samantha smoothed more snow onto the snowman's head. "If you wanted to see a photograph of your father, I could probably find one." She'd decided that it wasn't what she wanted that mattered, it was what they wanted.

Ella paused, snow cupped in her two hands, cheeks glowing. "I don't think I want that." She glanced at her sister. "But if you do then—"

"No." Samantha shook her head. "I thought I did, but I don't. It doesn't seem to matter anymore. I'd rather focus on the future rather than the past."

"Me too. And your future has snow in it." Ella threw the snow at her sister just as Tab came running toward them, a carrot in one hand and twigs in the other.

"We brought you arms and a nose."

By the time they went back indoors, they were all freezing, but Gayle couldn't remember ever having so much fun with her daughters.

Mary had been right. It was never too late.

And when they moved back into the house and gathered round the Christmas tree, she was sure of it.

Mary was next to her. They looked across the room to where Michael was swinging Tab, now dressed in the mermaid costume Gayle had bought her. Samantha and Brodie were sitting side by side, deep in conversation, and Kirstie and Ella were still having fun with the snow globe. "I never thought Christmas could look like this."

"Me neither."

Gayle saw Samantha laugh at something Brodie said, noticed those little touches that said *I know you. You're mine.*

Mary saw it, too. "You have a wonderful family."

"Yes." And she felt grateful for what she had. For second chances. For new friends. She was even grateful for that award and the bang on the head because who knew where she'd be without that.

Some of the decisions she'd made might have been the wrong ones. She had no real way of knowing, and it was pointless to dwell on it now. What mattered were the decisions she made moving forward.

The future was hers to design.

★ ★ ★ ★ ★

ACKNOWLEDGMENTS

Occasionally I'm lucky enough to go to my publisher's offices and raise a glass with the publishing team to celebrate the release of a new book, and I'm always reminded of just how many people contribute to the complex process of getting my books into the hands of readers. I'm grateful for their collective enthusiasm, and for the care and attention they show, so thank you to team HQStories and HQN books. You're the best.

I'm deeply grateful to be able to work with my brilliant editor Flo Nicoll, and also my agent Susan Ginsburg and the whole team at Writers House.

Writing a Christmas story usually extends well past the festive season, so thanks to my family for tolerating my mini Christmas tree well into March, and for only occasionally complaining when I make them watch a Christmas movie while everyone else is eating Easter eggs.

I'm grateful to my friends, writers and nonwriters, for occasionally making me live in the real world, not a fictional one.

My biggest thanks go to my readers, who continue to buy my books, send me supportive messages, and are so patient when I manage to film myself sideways on Facebook Live. I'm so lucky to have you. I hope this book makes you smile.

Love Sarah

x

Turn the page for a sneak peek of The Summer Seekers,
the delightful new book from
USA TODAY *bestselling author Sarah Morgan!*

Kathleen is eighty years old. After a run-in with an intruder, her children want her to move into a residential home. She's not having any of it. What she craves—*needs*—is adventure.

Liza is drowning under the daily stress of family life. The last thing she needs is her mother jetting off on a wild holiday, making Liza dream of a solo summer of her own.

Martha is having a quarter-life crisis. Unemployed, unloved and uninspired, she just can't get her life together. But she knows something has to change.

When Martha sees Kathleen's advert for a driver and companion to take an epic road trip across America, she decides this job might be the answer to her prayers. She's not the world's best driver, but anything has to be better than living with her parents. Traveling with a stranger? No problem. It couldn't be worse than living with her parents again. And anyway, how much trouble can one eighty-year-old woman be?

As these women embark on the journey of a lifetime, they all discover it's never too late for adventure…

1

Kathleen

It was the cup of semi-skimmed milk that saved her. That and the salty bacon she'd fried for her supper many hours earlier, which had left her mouth dry.

If she hadn't been thirsty—if she'd still been upstairs, sleeping on the ridiculously expensive mattress that had been her eightieth birthday gift to herself—she wouldn't have been alerted to danger.

As it was, she'd been standing in front of the fridge, the milk carton in one hand and the cup in the other, when she'd heard the sound of breaking glass. A faint shattering, brittle and out of place here in the leafy darkness of the English countryside, where the only sounds should have been the hoot of an owl and the occasional bleat of a sheep.

She put the glass down and turned her head, trying to locate the sound.

The moon sent a ghostly gleam across the kitchen and she

was grateful she hadn't felt the need to turn the light on. That gave her some advantage, surely?

She put the milk back and closed the fridge door quietly, because she was absolutely sure now that she was not alone in the house.

Moments earlier she'd been asleep. Not deeply asleep—that rarely happened these days—but drifting along on a tide of dreams. If anyone had told her when she was twenty that she'd still be dreaming of that affair when she was eighty she would have been less afraid of aging. And it was impossible to forget that she *was* aging.

People said she was marvelous, but most of the time she didn't feel marvelous. The answers to her beloved crosswords floated just out of range. Names and faces refused to align at the right moment. She struggled to remember what she'd done the day before, although if she took herself back twenty years or more her mind was clear. And then there were the physical changes—her eyesight and hearing were still good, thankfully, but her joints hurt and her bones ached. Bending to feed the cat was a challenge. Climbing the stairs required more effort than she would have liked, and was always done with one hand on the rail *just in case*.

She'd never been the sort to live in a *just in case* sort of way, and it annoyed her that she was doing so now. This new cautious approach was partly because of her children. She'd never been an anxious person, but their anxiety had infected her.

Her daughter Liza wanted her to wear an alarm. One of those medical alert systems, with a button you could press in an emergency, but Kathleen refused. In her youth she'd traveled the world, before it was remotely fashionable to do so. She'd sacrificed safety for adventure without a second thought. Most days now she felt like a different person.

Losing friends didn't help. One by one they fell by the wayside, taking with them shared memories of the past. A small part of her vanished with each loss. *This is the person I was.* It had taken decades for her to understand that loneliness wasn't a lack of people in your life, but a lack of people who knew and understood you.

She fought fiercely to retain some version of her old self—which was why she'd resisted Liza's pleas that she wear an alarm, remove the rug from the living room floor, stop using a step ladder to retrieve books from the highest shelves and leave a light on at night. Each compromise was another layer shaved off her independence, and losing her independence was her biggest fear in life.

Kathleen had always been the rebel in the family, and she was still the rebel—although she wasn't sure that rebels were supposed to have shaking hands and a pounding heart.

She heard the sound of a door being quietly opened. Someone was searching the house. For what, exactly? What treasures did they hope to find?

Having fiercely resisted all suggestions that she acknowledge her own vulnerability, she was now forced to acknowledge it. Perhaps she shouldn't have been so stubborn. How long would it have taken from pressing the alert button to the cavalry arriving?

In reality, the cavalry was Finn Cool, who lived three fields away. Finn was a musician, and he'd bought the property precisely because there were no immediate neighbours. His antics caused mutterings in the village. He had rowdy parties late into the night, attended by glamorous people from London who terrorized the locals by driving their flashy sports cars too fast down the narrow lanes. Someone had started a petition in the post office to ban the parties. There had been talk of drugs, and half-naked women, and it had all sounded like so much fun that Kathleen had been tempted to invite herself over. Rather that than a dull women's group, where you were expected to bake and knit and swap recipes for banana bread.

Finn would be of no use to her in this moment of crisis. In all probability he'd either be in his studio, wearing headphones, or he'd be drunk. Either way, he wasn't going to hear a cry for help.

That left the police. But calling the police would mean walking through the kitchen and across the hall to the living room, where the phone was kept. She didn't want to reveal her presence. Her children had given her a mobile phone, but it was still in its box, unused. How did you even switch it on? She had no idea and no interest. Her adventurous spirit didn't extend to technology. She didn't like the idea of a nameless faceless person tracking her every move. And why did she need a mobile phone when she had a perfectly good landline?

Unfortunately that landline was of no use to her in her current crisis.

There was a crunching sound, louder this time, and Kathleen pressed her hand to her chest. She could feel the rapid pounding of her heart. At least it was still working. She should probably be grateful for that.

When she'd complained about wanting a little more adventure, this wasn't what she'd had in mind. What could she do? She had no button to press, no phone with which to call for help, so she was going to have to handle this herself.

She could already hear Liza's voice in her head: *Mum, we warned you!*

If she survived, she'd never hear the last of it.

Fear was replaced by anger. Because of this intruder she'd be branded Old and Vulnerable and forced to spend the rest of her days in a single room, with minders who would cut up her food, speak in overly loud voices and help her to the bathroom. Life as she knew it would be over.

That was *not* going to happen.

She'd rather die at the hands of an intruder. At least her obituary would be interesting.

Better still, she would stay alive and prove herself capable of independent living.

She glanced quickly around the kitchen for a suitable weapon and spied the heavy black skillet she'd used to fry the bacon earlier.

She lifted it silently, gripping the handle tightly as she walked to the door that led from the kitchen to the hall. The tiles were cool under her feet—which, fortunately, were bare. No sound. Nothing to give her away. She had the advantage.

She could *do* this. Hadn't she once fought off a mugger in the backstreets of Paris? True, she'd been a great deal younger then, but this time she had the advantage of surprise.

How many of them were there? One? Two? More?

More than one would give her trouble. She only had one pan.

Was it a professional job? If it was kids hoping to steal her TV, they were in for a disappointment. Her children had been trying to persuade her to buy a "smart" TV, but why would she need such a thing? She was perfectly happy with the IQ of her current machine, thank you very much. Technology already made her feel foolish most of the time. She didn't need it to be any smarter than it already was.

Maybe they wouldn't come into the kitchen. Maybe she could just hide here until they'd taken what they wanted and left.

They'd never know she was here.

They'd—

A floorboard squeaked close by. There wasn't a crack or a creak in this house that she didn't know. Someone was right outside the door.

Her knees turned liquid.

Oh, Kathleen, Kathleen.

She closed both hands tightly round the handle of the skillet.

Why hadn't she gone to self-defence classes instead of senior yoga? What use was the downward dog when you were dealing with an intruder?

A shadow moved into the room, and without allowing herself to think about what she was about to do she lifted the skillet and brought it down hard, the force of the blow driven by the weight of the object as much as her own strength. There was a thud and a vibration as it connected with his head.

"I'm so sorry—I mean—" Why was she apologizing? How completely ridiculous was that?

The man threw up an arm as he fell, in a reflex action, and the movement sent the skillet back into Katherine's own head. Pain almost blinded her, and she'd just braced herself to end her days right here, thus giving her daughter the opportunity to be right, when there was a loud thump and the man crumpled to the floor. There was a crack as his head hit the tiles.

Kathleen froze. Was that it? Was he suddenly going to spring to his feet and murder her?

No. Against all odds, she was still standing while her prowler lay inert at her feet.

Her heart was racing so fast she was worried that any moment now it might trip over itself and give up.

She held tightly to the skillet.

This might not be over.

Did he have an accomplice?

She held her breath, braced for someone else to come racing through the door to investigate the noise, but there was only silence.

Gingerly she stepped toward the door and poked her head into the hall. It was empty.

It seemed the man had been alone.

Finally she risked a look at him.

He was lying still at her feet, big, bulky and dressed all in black. The mud on the edges of his trousers suggested he'd come across the fields at the back of the house. She couldn't make out his features because he'd landed face-first, but blood oozed from a wound on his head and stained her kitchen floor.

Feeling a little dizzy, Kathleen pressed her hand to her chest.

It was all rather alarming. What now? Was one supposed to

administer first aid when one was the cause of the injury? Was that helpful or hypocritical? Or was he past first aid and every other type of aid?

She nudged his body with her bare foot, but there was no movement.

Had she killed him?

The enormity of it shook her.

If he was dead, then she was a murderer.

When Liza had expressed a desire to see her mother safely housed somewhere she could easily visit, presumably she hadn't been thinking of prison.

Who was he? Did he have family? What had been his intention when he'd forcibly entered her home?

Kathleen put the skillet down and forced her shaky limbs to carry her to the living room. Something tickled her cheek. Blood. Hers.

She picked up the phone and for the first time in her life dialed the emergency services.

Underneath the panic and the shock there was something that felt a lot like pride. It was a relief to discover she wasn't as weak and defenceless as everyone seemed to think.

When a woman answered, Kathleen spoke clearly and without hesitation.

"There's a body in my kitchen," she said. "I assume you'll want to come and remove it."

2

Liza

"I told you! Didn't I tell you? I *knew* this was going to happen."

Liza slung her bag into the back of the car and slid into the driver's seat. Her stomach churned. She'd missed lunch, too busy to eat. The school where she taught was approaching summer exam season and she'd been halfway through helping two students complete their art coursework when a nurse had called her from the hospital.

It had been the call she'd dreaded.

She'd found someone to cover the rest of her classes and driven the short distance home with a racing heart and clammy hands. Her mother had been attacked in the early hours of the morning, and she was only hearing about it *now*? She was part frantic, part furious.

Her mother had always been so cavalier. Had she even locked

the French doors that led to the garden? She'd probably invited the man in and made him tea.

Knock me over the head, why don't you?

Sean leaned in through the window. He'd come straight from a meeting and he was wearing a blue shirt the same color as his eyes. "I presume I don't have time to change?"

"I packed a bag for you."

"Thanks for that." He undid another button. "Why don't you let me drive?"

"No, I've got this." Tension rose up inside her and mingled with the worry about her mother. "I'm anxious, that's all. And frustrated. I've lost count of the number of times I've told her the house is too big, too isolated, that she should move into some sort of sheltered accommodation or residential care. But did she listen?"

Sean threw his jacket onto the back seat. "She's independent. That's a good thing, Liza."

Was it? When did independence morph into irresponsibility?

"I should have tried harder to persuade her to move."

She should have told her a few more tales about the rate of accidents in the home amongst the elderly. But the truth was, she hadn't really wanted her mother to move. Oakwood Cottage had played a central part in her life. The house was gorgeous, surrounded by acres of fields and farmland that stretched down to the sea. In the spring you could hear the bleating of new lambs, and in the summer the air was filled with blossom, birdsong and the faint sounds of the sea.

It was hard to imagine her mother living anywhere else, even though the house was too large for one person and thoroughly impractical—particularly for someone who tended to believe that a leaking roof was a delightful feature of owning an older property and not something that needed fixing.

"You are not responsible for everything that happens to people, Liza."

Sean settled himself in the passenger seat as if he had all the time in the world. Liza, who raced through life as if she was being chased by the police for a serious crime, found his relaxed demeanour and unshakeable calm occasionally maddening.

She thought about the magazine article folded into the bottom of her bag. *Eight signs that your marriage might be in trouble.*

She'd been flicking through the magazine in the dentist's waiting room the week before and that feature had jumped out at her. She'd read it, searching for reassurance.

It wasn't as if she and Sean argued, or anything. There was nothing specifically wrong. Just a vague discomfort inside her that reminded her constantly that the settled life she valued so much might not be so settled. That just as a million tiny things could pull a couple together, so a million tiny things could nudge them apart.

She'd read through the article, feeling sicker and sicker. By the time she'd reached the eighth sign she'd been so freaked out that she'd torn the pages from the magazine, coughing violently to cover the sound. It wasn't done to steal magazines from waiting rooms.

And now those torn pages lay in her bag, a constant reminder that she was ignoring something deep and important. She knew it needed to be addressed, but she was too scared to touch the fabric of her marriage in case the whole thing fell apart—like her mother's house.

Sean fastened his seat belt. "You shouldn't blame yourself."

She felt a moment of panic, and then realized he was talking about her mother. What sort of person was she that she could forget her injured mother so easily?

A person who was worried about her marriage.

"I should have tried harder to make her see sense," she said.

Men just didn't seem to feel the same sense of responsibility and associated guilt that women did.

Her brother was the same. *"Stop stressing, Liza."*

What was it like to be so relaxed? To leave the worrying and responsibility to someone else? Would Matt even have thought to drive to the cottage to see their mother this weekend if she hadn't called and spoken to her sister-in-law?

What would happen now? If her mother needed someone to stay with her next week, then it would have to be Liza—but that would mean arranging cover for her classes, and this close to exams it really wasn't fair on the students. She could ask Matt to take time off, but he would in all likelihood revert to childhood and go out to kick a ball on the beach, leaving their mother to take care of herself. And what about the coming weeks?

They would have to sell the house—there was no doubt about that. Although Liza desperately hoped it could wait until later in the summer. It was only a few weeks until school ended, and then the girls had various commitments until they all went on their annual family holiday to the south of France.

France.

A wave of calm flowed over her.

She was counting the weeks. Crossing off the days on her calendar.

Relaxation. Sunshine. No pressures.

France would give her the time to take a closer look at her marriage. They'd both be relaxed, and away from the endless demands of daily life. She and Sean would be able to spend some time together that didn't involve handling issues and problems. Until then, she was going to give herself permission to forget about the whole thing and focus on the immediate problem.

Her mother.

Oakwood Cottage.

Sadness ripped through her. Ridiculous though it was, the place still felt like home. She'd clung to that last remaining piece of her childhood, unable to imagine a time when she would no longer sit in the garden or stroll across the fields to the sea.

"Dad made me promise not to put her in a home," she said.

"Which was unfair of him. No one can make promises about a

future they can't foresee. And you're not 'putting' her anywhere."
Sean was ever reasonable. "She's a human being—not a garden
gnome. Also, there are plenty of really nice residential homes."

"I know. I have a folder bulging with glossy brochures in
the back seat of the car. They make them look so good I want
to check in myself. Unfortunately, I doubt my mother will feel
the same way."

What if her mother refused? It would mean driving to Cornwall every weekend to check on her, and that wasn't going to
work. Liza had her job, Sean and the twins. Not to mention the
house and a never-ending list of things to do.

The only other option would be to invite her to live with
them. But their house was already crowded with the four of
them. And how could that possibly work? Her mother was something of a maverick, and quite capable of encouraging the twins
to be the worst versions of themselves and they were doing pretty
well without help. It would be horrendous. And then there was
the privacy aspect—or lack of it.

Sean was scrolling through emails on his phone. "In the end
it's her choice. It has nothing to do with us."

"It has a lot to do with us. It's not practical to go there every
weekend, and even if they weren't in the middle of exams the
twins wouldn't come with us without complaining. *'It's in the
middle of nowhere, Mum.'*"

"Which is why we're leaving them this weekend."

"And that terrifies me, too. What if they have a party or
something?"

"Why must you always imagine the worst? Treat them like
responsible humans and they'll behave like responsible humans."

Was it really that simple? Or was Sean's confidence based on
misplaced optimism?

"I don't like the friends Caitlin is mixing with right now.
They're not interested in studying and they spend their weekends hanging out in the shopping mall."

He didn't look up. "Isn't that normal for teenage girls?"

"She's changed since she started hanging out with Jane. She answers back. She's stroppy, when she used to be sweet."

"Hormones. She'll grow out of it."

Sean's parenting style was "hands off." He thought of it as being relaxed. Liza thought of it as abdication.

When the twins were little they'd played with each other. Then they'd started school and invited friends round to play. Liza had found them delightful. That had all changed when they'd moved to senior school and Alice and Caitlin had made friends with a different group of girls. They were a year older. Most of them were already driving and also, Liza was sure, drinking.

The fact that she might not like her teenagers' friends was a problem that hadn't occurred to her until the past year.

She forced her attention back to the problem of her mother. "If you could fix the roof in the garden room this weekend, that would be great. We should have spent more time maintaining the place. I feel guilty that I haven't done enough."

Sean finally looked up. "What you feel guilty about," he said, "is that you and your mother aren't close."

It was uncomfortable, hearing the truth said aloud. It was something neither she nor her mother acknowledged. Not being close to her mother felt like a flaw. A slightly grubby secret. Something she should apologize for.

But she'd tried so *hard*.

Liza tightened her hands on the wheel. "We may not be close, but that doesn't mean I don't love her." She clamped her teeth together, knowing that she couldn't say what she really felt. That she felt overloaded—as if the entire smooth running of their lives was *her* responsibility. The weight of it was crushing. Sean had a busy architectural practice in London. When he wasn't working he was using the gym, running in the park or playing golf. Liza's time outside work was spent sorting out the house and the twins.

Was this what marriage was? Once those early couple-focused years had passed, did it turn into this?

Eight signs that your marriage might be in trouble.

It was just a stupid article. It wasn't personal. She and Sean had been together for twenty years and they were happy enough. True, life felt as if it was nothing but jobs and responsibility, but that was part of being an adult, wasn't it? You didn't get to feel the same carefree joy you did when you were young, and nothing seemed to matter except the moment.

"I know you love your mother. That's why we're in the car on a Friday afternoon," Sean said. "And we'll make it through this current crisis the way we've made it through the others. One step at a time."

But why does life always have to be a crisis?

She almost asked, but Sean had already moved on and was answering a call from a colleague.

Liza only half listened as he dealt with a string of problems. Since the practice had taken off, it wasn't unusual for Sean to be glued to his phone.

"Mmm…" he said as he listened. "But it's about creating a simple crafted space… No, that won't work… Yes, I'll call them."

When he eventually ended the call, she glanced at him. "What if the twins invite Jane over?"

"You can't stop them seeing their friends."

"It's not their friends in general that worry me—just Jane. Did you know she smokes? Sean, are you listening? Stop doing your emails."

"Sorry. But I wasn't expecting to take this afternoon off and I have a lot going on right now." Sean pressed "send" and looked up. "What were you saying? Ah, smoking… Just because Jane is doing it, doesn't mean Caitlin will."

"She's very easily influenced. She badly wants to fit in."

"And that's common at her age. Plenty of other kids are the same. It will do the two of them good to fend for themselves for a weekend."

They wouldn't exactly be fending for themselves. Liza had already filled the fridge with food. She'd removed all the alcohol from the kitchen cupboard, locked it in the garage and removed the key. But she knew that wouldn't stop them buying more if they wanted to.

Her stomach lurched as her mind flew to all the possibilities. "What if they have a wild party?"

"It would make them normal. All teenagers have wild parties."

"I didn't."

"I know. You were unusually well-behaved and innocent." He put his phone away. "Until I met you and changed all that. Remember that day on the beach? You were sixteen. Your mother was away on one of her trips and you went for a walk. A crowd of us were having a party."

"I remember." She'd intended to turn around the moment she saw them, but in the end she'd joined them.

"I put my hand up your dress." He adjusted his seat to give himself more leg room. "I admit it—my technique needed work."

Her first kiss.

She remembered it clearly. The excited fumbling. The forbidden nature of the encounter. Music in the background. The delicious thrill of anticipation.

She'd fallen crazily in love with Sean that summer. She'd known she was out of step with her peers, who'd been dancing their way through different relationships like butterflies seeking nectar. But Liza had never wanted that. She'd never felt the need for romantic adventure. That meant uncertainty, and she'd already had more than enough of that in her life. All she'd wanted was Sean, with his wide shoulders, his easy smile and his calm nature.

She missed the simplicity of that time.

Suddenly she wanted to be young again.

"Are you happy, Sean?" The words escaped before she could stop them.

"What sort of a question is that?" He frowned. "The business is going brilliantly. The girls are getting great marks. Of course I'm happy. Aren't you?"

The business. The girls.

Eight signs that your marriage might be in trouble.

"I feel—a little overwhelmed sometimes, that's all."

She tiptoed cautiously into territory she'd never entered before. In the early days of their marriage they'd shared the load, but as his success had grown Sean had focused more and more on work.

"That's because you take everything so seriously. You worry too much about every small detail. About the twins. About your mother. You need to chill a little."

He smiled to soften his words, but they'd already slid under her skin like a blade, creating a wound that throbbed. She'd used to love the fact that he was so calm, but now it felt like a criticism of her coping skills.

"You're saying I need to 'chill' about the fact my eighty-year-old mother has just been assaulted in her own home?"

"You're taking what I said the wrong way. Obviously that's worrying news, but I was talking generally. You worry about things that haven't happened and you try and control every little thing. Most things turn out fine if you just leave them alone."

"They turn out fine because I anticipate problems before they happen."

And anticipating things was exhausting—like trying to stay afloat when someone had tied weights to her legs.

For a wild moment she wondered what it would be like to be single. To have no one to worry about but herself.

No responsibility. Free time.

She yanked herself back from that thought.

Sean leaned his head back against the seat. "Let's leave this discussion until we're back home. Here we are, spending the weekend together in the countryside. Let's enjoy it."

His ability to focus on the moment was a strength, but also

a flaw that sometimes grated on her. He could live in the moment because *she* took care of all the other stuff.

"It's going to be fine, Liza."

He reached across to squeeze her leg and she thought about a time twenty years ago, when they'd had sex in the car, parking in a quiet country lane and steaming up the windows until neither of them had been able to see through the glass.

What had happened to that part of their lives? What had happened to spontaneity? To joy?

It seemed so long ago she could barely remember it.

These days her life was driven by worry and duty. Duty to her students, duty to her husband, duty to her children, to her mother...

She was being slowly crushed by the ever-increasing weight of responsibility.

"When did we last go away together?" she asked.

"We're going away now."

"This isn't a mini-break, Sean. My mother needed stitches in her head. She has a mild concussion."

She crawled through the heavy London traffic, her head throbbing at the thought of the drive ahead. Friday afternoon was the worst possible time to leave, but they'd had no choice.

When the twins were young they'd traveled at night, dressing them in pajamas and letting them sleep the whole way. They'd arrive at Oakwood Cottage in the early hours of the morning and Sean would carry both children inside and deposit them into the twin beds in the attic room, tucking them under the quilts her mother had brought back from one of her many foreign trips.

"I really don't want to do it, but I think it's time to sell Oakwood Cottage. If she's going into residential care, we can't possibly afford to keep it."

Something tore inside her. Someone else would play hide-and-seek in the overgrown gardens, scramble into the dusty attic and explore the contents of the endless bookshelves. Someone else would sleep in her old bedroom, with its endless views across fields to the sea.

The fact that she couldn't even remember the last time she'd had a relaxing weekend in Cornwall didn't lessen the feelings of loss. If anything it intensified those feelings, because she was now wishing she'd taken greater advantage of the cottage. She'd assumed it would always be there...

Ever since her father had died, visits to Oakwood Cottage had been associated with chores. Clearing the garden. Filling the freezer. Checking that her mother was coping with a house that was far too big for one person, especially when that person was advanced in years and had no interest in home maintenance.

"Honestly? I can't see your mother selling it," Sean said, "and I think it's important not to overreact. This accident wasn't of her own making. She was managing perfectly well before this."

"Was she, though? I don't think she eats properly. Supper is a bowl of cereal. And bacon. She eats too much bacon."

"*Is* there such a thing as too much bacon?" Sean caught her eye and gave a sheepish smile. "Just kidding. You're right. Bacon is bad. Although at your mother's age one has to wonder if it really matters."

"If she gives up bacon maybe she'll live to be ninety."

"But would she enjoy those miserable, bacon-free extra years?"

"Can you be serious?"

"I *am* serious. It's about quality of life, not just quantity. You try and keep every bad thing at bay, but doing that also keeps out the good stuff. Maybe she could stay in the house and we could find some local carers to look in on her."

"She's terrible at taking help from anyone."

Liza hit the brakes as the car in front of her stopped, the seat belt locking hard against her body. Her eyes pricked with tiredness and her head pounded. She hadn't slept well the night before, worrying about Caitlin and her friendship issues.

"Do you think I should have locked our bedroom? And the study?"

"Why? If someone breaks into our house they'll simply kick the doors down if they're locked. Makes more mess."

"I wasn't thinking of burglars. I was thinking about the twins."

"Why would the twins go into our bedroom? Or the study? They have perfectly good rooms of their own."

What did it say about her that she didn't entirely trust her own children? They'd been suitably horrified when they'd discovered that their elderly grandmother had been assaulted, and sweet when Liza had explained that she and Sean were going away for the weekend, but had flat-out resisted her attempts to persuade them to come, too.

"There's nothing to do at Granny's," Alice had said, exchanging looks with her sister.

"Besides, we have work to do." Caitlin had pulled out her laptop and a stack of textbooks. "History exam on Monday. I'll be studying. Probably won't even have time to order in pizza."

It had been a perfectly reasonable response. So why did Liza feel nervous?

She'd call later and check on them. Insist on video-calling, so that she could see what was going on in the background.

The traffic finally cleared and they headed west toward Cornwall.

By the time they turned into the country lane that led to her mother's house it was late afternoon, and the sun sent a rosy glow over the fields and hedges.

She was just allowing herself a rare moment of appreciating the scenery when a bright red sports car sped round the bend, causing her almost to swerve into a ditch.

"For—" She leaned on her horn and caught a brief glimpse of a pair of laughing blue eyes as the car roared past. "Did you see that?"

"Yes. Stunning, isn't it? V8 engine." Sean turned his head, almost drooling, but the car was long gone. "Nought to sixty in—"

"He almost killed us!"

"Well, he didn't. So that's good."

"It was that wretched rock star who moved here last year."

"Ah, yes. That makes sense. I read an article in one of the Sunday papers about his six sports cars."

"I was about to say I don't understand why one man would need six cars, but if he drives like that then I suppose that's the explanation right there. He probably gets through one a day."

Liza turned the wheel and Sean winced as branches scraped the paintwork.

"You're a bit close on my side, Liza."

"It was the hedge or a head-on collision." She was shaken by what had been a close shave, her emotions heightened by the fact that Finn Cool had been laughing. "He laughed—did you see that? He actually smiled as he passed us. Would he have been laughing if he'd had to haul my mangled body out of the twisted wreckage of this car?"

"Relax. He seemed like a pretty skilled driver."

"It wasn't his skill that saved us. It was me driving into the hedge. It isn't safe to drive like that down these roads."

Liza breathed out and drove slowly down the lane, half expecting another irresponsible rock star to come zooming round the corner. Fortunately she reached her mother's house without further mishap, her pulse-rate slowing as she pulled into the drive.

Aubretia clung to the low wall that bordered the property, and lobelia and geraniums tumbled from baskets hung next to the front door. Her mother loved the garden and spent hours in the sunshine, tending her plants.

"This place is a gem. She'd make a fortune if she ever did decide to sell it, leaking roof or not. Do you think she will have made her chocolate cake?" Sean was ever hopeful.

"You mean before or after she was assaulted?"

Liza parked in front of the house. She probably should have baked a cake, but she'd decided that getting on the road as soon as possible was the priority. She had stuffed the contents of the fridge into a bag, along with some basic grocery items and a loaf of bread, because she had no idea what her mother would have in the house.

"Can you call the kids quickly?"

"What for?" Sean uncoiled himself from the front of the car and stretched. "We only left them four hours ago."

"I want to check on them."

He unloaded their luggage. "I'll call if it will make you feel better. But first take a deep breath. I haven't seen you like this before. You're amazing, Liza. A real coper. We'll get through this."

She didn't feel like a coper. She felt like a piece of elastic that was about to snap. She was coping because if she didn't what would happen to them? She knew, even if her family didn't, that they wouldn't be able to manage without her. The twins would die of malnutrition or lie buried under their own mess, because they were incapable of putting away a single thing they owned or cooking anything other than pizza, the laundry would stay unwashed, the cupboards would be bare. Caitlin would yell, *Has anyone seen my blue strap top?* and no one would answer because no one would know.

The front door opened and all thought of the twins left her mind. Because there was her mother, her palm pressed hard against the door frame for support. There was a bandage wrapped around the top of her head, and Liza felt her stomach drop to her feet. She'd always considered her mother to be invincible, and here she was looking frail, tired, and all too human. For all their differences—and there were many—she loved her mother dearly.

"Mum!" She left Sean to handle the luggage and sprinted across the drive. "I've been so worried! How are you feeling? I can't believe this has happened. I'm so sorry."

"Well, what do *you* have to be sorry for? You're not the one who broke into my house."

As always, her mother was brisk and matter-of-fact, treating weakness like an annoying fly to be batted away. She was wearing a long flowing dress in shades of blue and turquoise, with a darker blue wrap around her shoulders. Multiple bangles jangled on her wrists. Her mother's unconventional, eclectic dress style had caused Liza many embarrassing moments as a child, and even now the cheerful colors of Kathleen's outfit seemed to jar with the gravity of the situation. She looked ready to step onto a beach in Corfu.

Despite the lack of encouragement, Liza hugged her mother gently, horrified by how fragile she seemed. "You should have had an alarm, or a mobile phone in your pocket."

Instinctively she checked her mother's head, but there was nothing to be seen except the bandage and the beginnings of a bruise around her eye socket. Even though she'd tried to enliven her appearance with blusher, her skin was waxy and pale.

"Don't fuss." Kathleen eased away from her. "It wouldn't have made a difference. By the time help arrived it would have been over. As it was, I made a phone call from my landline. The old-fashioned way, but it proved perfectly effective."

"But what if he'd knocked you unconscious? You wouldn't have been able to call for help."

"If I'd been unconscious I wouldn't have been able to press a button, either. And the police came quickly. A lovely girl, although she didn't seem much older than the twins, and a kind man. Then an ambulance arrived, and the police took a statement from me. I half expected to be locked up for the night, but nothing so dramatic. Still, it was all rather exciting."

"Exciting?" The remark was typical of her mother. "You could have been killed. He hit you."

"No, he didn't. I hit *him*—with the skillet I'd used for frying bacon earlier."

There was an equal mix of pride and satisfaction in her mother's voice.

"His arm flew up as he fell—reflex, I suppose—and he knocked it back into my head. That part was unfortunate, I admit. But the fortunate part was that the skillet knocked *him* unconscious.

It's funny when you think that bacon may have saved my life. So no more nagging me about my blood pressure and cholesterol."

"Mum—"

"If I'd cooked myself pasta I would have been using a different pan...nowhere near heavy enough. If I'd made a ham sandwich I would have had nothing to tackle him with except a crust of bread. So I'll be filling the fridge with bacon from now on."

"Bacon can be a lifesaver—I said the same thing myself." Sean leaned in and kissed his mother-in-law gently on the cheek. "You're a formidable adversary, Kathleen. Good to see you on your feet."

Liza felt like the only adult in the group. Was she the only one seeing the seriousness of this situation? It was like dealing with the twins.

"How can you possibly joke about it?"

"I'm deadly serious. It's good to know that I can now eat bacon with a clear conscience." Kathleen smiled at her son-in-law. "You really didn't have to come charging down here on a Friday. I'm perfectly fine. You didn't bring the girls?"

"They had work to do. Exams coming up. Teenage stress and drama. You know how it is." Sean hauled their luggage into the house. "Is the kettle on, Kathleen? I could murder a cup of tea."

Did he really have to use the word "murder"? Liza kept picturing a different outcome. One where her mother was the one lying inert on the kitchen floor. She felt lightheaded and a little dizzy—and she wasn't the one who had been hit over the head.

Of course she knew that people had their homes broken into. It was a fact. But knowing it was different from experiencing it.

She glanced uneasily toward the back door, now boarded up.

"A kind man from the village came and did it first thing. You look very pale." Kathleen patted Liza on the shoulder. "You get too stressed about small things. Come in, dear. That drive is murderous...you must be exhausted."

Murderous. Murder.

"Could everyone stop using that word?" Liza exploded, and her mother raised her eyebrows.

"It's a figure of speech, nothing more."

"Well, if we could find a different one I'd appreciate it." She followed her into the hall. "I feel shaken up, and I wasn't even here. How are you feeling, Mum? Honestly? An intruder isn't a small thing."

"True. He was actually large. And the noise his head made when it hit the kitchen floor—awful. It was the first time I've been thankful that your father insisted on those expensive Italian tiles. I've broken so many cups and plates on that damned surface. So unforgiving. But in this case the hard surface worked in my favor. It took me an hour to clean up the blood."

Liza didn't want to picture it. "You should have left that for me to do."

"Nonsense. I've never been much of a housekeeper, but I can mop up blood. And, anyway, I prefer not to eat my lunch in the middle of a crime scene, thank you."

Her mother headed straight for the kitchen. Liza didn't know whether to be relieved or exasperated that she was behaving as if nothing out of the ordinary had happened. If anything, she seemed energized, and perhaps a touch triumphant, as if she'd achieved something of note.

"Where is the man now? What did the police say?"

"The man is in the hospital, recovering from his head injury. The police took a full statement from me, and some photographs, and said they'll keep me updated on his condition—although I won't be sending him a card or flowers, I assure you."

Her mother fussed around the stove, pouring boiling water into the large teapot she'd been using since Liza was a child.

Everything about this room was achingly familiar. With its range cooker, and large pine table, the kitchen had always been her favorite room in the house. Every evening after school Liza had done her homework at this same table, wanting to be close to her mother when she was at home.

Her mother had been one of the pioneers of the TV travel show, her spirited adventures around the world opening people's eyes to the appeal of foreign holidays from the Italian Riviera to the Far East. Every few weeks she would pack a suitcase and disappear on a trip to another faraway destination. Liza's schoolfriends had found it all impossibly glamorous. Liza had found it crushingly lonely. Her earliest memory was of being five years old and holding tight to her mother's scarf to prevent her from leaving, almost throttling her in the process.

To ease the distress of Kathleen's constant departures, her father had glued a large map of the world to Liza's bedroom wall. Each time her mother had left on another trip, Liza and her father would put a pin in the map and research the place. They'd cut out pictures from brochures and make scrapbooks. It had made her feel closer to her mother. And Liza's room would be filled with various eclectic objects. A hand-carved giraffe from Africa. A rug from India.

And then Kathleen would return, her clothes wrinkled and covered in travel dust. And she'd bring with her an energy that had made her seem like a stranger. Those first moments when she and Liza were reunited had always been uncomfortable and forced, but then the work clothes would be replaced by casual clothes, and Kathleen the traveler and TV star would become Kathleen the mother once again. Until the next time, when the map would be consulted and the planning would start.

Liza had once asked her father why her mother always had to go away, and he'd said, *"Your mother needs this."*

Even at a young age Liza had wondered why her mother's needs took precedence over everyone else's, and she'd wondered what it was exactly that her mother *did* need, but she hadn't felt able to ask. She'd noticed that her father drank more and smoked more when Kathleen was away. As a father, he had been practical, but economical in his parenting. He'd make sure that they were safe, but spend long days in the office where he worked, or locked in his study. There had been no games of hide-and-seek in the garden, no puzzles at the kitchen table, no quiet reading or casual conversation.

Liza had never understood her parents' relationship and had never delved for answers.

During school holidays a severe-looking woman called Mrs. Bumble had been enlisted to look after them—an arrangement just barely tolerated by them all.

Liza's younger brother, Matt, had seemed less troubled by the lack of parental involvement, lost in his teenage boy's world of sport. His view of the world and life had always been smaller than hers, his gaze focused on the next game, or the next meal, while Liza had thought about her mother exploring the desert in Tunisia on the back of a camel and wondered why she needed her world to be so large, and why it needed to exclude her family.

Was it those constant absences that had turned Liza into such a home-lover? She'd chosen teaching as a career because the hours and holidays fitted with having a family. When her own children were young she'd stayed home, taking a break from her career. When they'd started school she'd matched her hours to theirs, taking pleasure and pride in the fact that she took them to school and met them at the end of the day. She'd been determined that her children wouldn't have to endure the endless goodbyes that she'd had as a child.

She rarely left them alone—which was another reason she was feeling so uneasy right now.

Sean was chatting to her mother, the pair of them making tea together as if this was a regular visit.

Liza glanced around her, dealing with the dawning realization that clearing out this house would be a monumental task. Over the years her mother had filled it with memorabilia and souvenirs from her travels, from seashells to tribal masks. And maps.

There were maps everywhere—on the walls and piled high in all the rooms. Her mother's diaries and other writing filled two dozen large boxes in the attic, and her photograph albums were crushed onto shelves in Liza's father's study.

When he'd died, five years before, Liza had suggested clearing the room out, but her mother had refused. *"I want it to stay as it is. You know I don't like tidy spaces. A home should be an adventure. You never know what forgotten treasure you might stumble over."*

Stumble over and break an ankle, Liza had thought in despair. It was an interesting way of reframing mess.

Before her mother could sell this place it would need to be cleared, and no doubt Liza would be the one to do it.

When was the right time to broach the subject? Not yet. They'd only just walked through the door. She needed to keep the conversation neutral.

"The garden is looking pretty."

The kitchen's French doors opened onto the patio, where the borders were filled with tumbling flowers. Pots filled with herbs crowded around the back door. Rosemary, with its scented spikes. Variegated sage, which her mother sprinkled over roast pork every Sunday—the only meat she ever produced with enthusiasm. The flagstone path was dappled by sunlight and led to the well-stocked vegetable patch, and beyond that a pond guarded by bulrushes. Beyond the garden were fields, and then the sea.

It was so tranquil and peaceful that for a moment Liza longed for a different life—one that didn't involve rushing around, ticking off items from her endless to-do list.

Her quiet fantasy of one day living in the country was something she'd shared with no one, not even Sean. Probably because she recognized it as a fantasy rather than a reality. Living in the country wasn't practical. For a start, Sean's work was based in London. So was hers. Although teaching was more flexible, of course.

Sean brought the food in from the car and Liza unpacked it into the fridge.

"I had a casserole in the freezer, so I brought that," she said. "And some veg."

"I'm perfectly capable of making food," said her mother.

"Your idea of food is bacon and cereal. You're not eating properly." She filled a bowl with fresh fruit and shot her mother a look. "I assumed you weren't set up for an invasion of people."

"Can two people be an invasion?" Her mother's tone was light, but she gripped the edge of the kitchen table and carefully lowered herself into a chair.

Liza was by her side in a moment. "Maybe I should take a look at your head."

"No one else is touching my head, thank you. It already hurts quite enough. Five stitches. The young doctor who stitched me up warned me that it would leave a scar, and apologized. As if I'm bothered by things like that at my age."

Age.

Was this the moment to mention that it was time to consider a change?

Across the kitchen, Sean was pouring the tea.

Liza paused, nervous about disturbing the atmosphere. She should probably wait until her brother arrived. They could do it together.

"You must have been very frightened," she said.

"I was more worried about Popeye. You know how he dislikes strangers. He must have escaped through the broken window and I haven't seen him since."

"He's always been a bit of a wanderer."

"Yes. That's probably why we get on so well. We understand each other."

Her mother looked wistful and Liza patted her hand. "If he's not back by the morning Matt will search for him. And now I think you should have a lie-down."

"At four in the afternoon? I'm not an invalid, Liza." Kathleen took the tea from Sean with a grateful nod. "Did you just mention Matt?"

"Yes. He's coming tomorrow. On his own, because Gillian is away this weekend on a hen do."

"I didn't realize this was going to be a family gathering." Kathleen put sugar in her tea—another unhealthy habit she refused to abandon. "I don't want a fuss. And I don't think I'm quite up to entertaining this weekend."

"We're not expecting you to entertain us. We're here to look after you, and to—" *To make you see sense.* Liza stopped, reluctant to have a difficult conversation so soon into the visit. She needed to ease into it—maybe after pointing out how much needed to be done in the house.

"And what? Persuade me to wear an emergency buzzer? I'm not doing it, Liza."

"Mum—" She caught Sean's warning glance, but ignored it. Maybe the subject *was* best raised right now, so that they had the whole weekend to discuss details. "This has been a shock for all of us, and it's time to face some difficult truths. Things need to change."

Sean rolled his eyes and turned away with a shake of his head, but her mother was nodding.

"I couldn't agree more. Things *do* have to change. Being hit over the head has brought me to my senses."

Liza felt a rush of relief. Everything was going to be fine. Her mother was going to be reasonable. Sean had been wrong to roll his eyes at her. And she wasn't the only sensible person in the room.

"I'm pleased you feel that way," she said. "I was worried you wouldn't. I have lots of brochures in the car, so all we have to do now is plan. And that can wait. We have all weekend."

"Brochures? You mean travel brochures?"

"For residential homes. We can—"

"Why would you bring those?"

"Because you can't stay here any longer, Mum. You've just admitted things have to change."

"They do. And I'm in the process of formulating a plan which I will certainly share with you when I'm sure of the details. But I won't be going into a residential home. That isn't what I want."

Was her mother saying she wanted to come and live with them in London?

Liza swallowed and forced herself to ask the question. "What is it that you want?"

"Adventure." Kathleen slapped her hand on the table. "I want another adventure. It's summer, and you know how much I love summer. I intend to make the most of it."

"But Mum—" *Oh, this was ridiculous.* "You're going to be eighty-one at the end of this year."

Her mother sat up a little straighter and her eyes gleamed. "All the more reason not to waste another moment."

Don't miss
The Summer Seekers
by USA TODAY *bestselling author Sarah Morgan,*
available May 2021 wherever
Harlequin Books and ebooks are sold.
www.Harlequin.com